PLAYING WITH FIRE

Lawless

and

Impulse

PLAYING WITH FIRE

Lawless

and

Impulse

TWO NOVELS IN ONE

NORA ROBERTS

St. Martin's Paperbacks

Published in the United States by St. Martin's Paperbacks, an imprint of St. Martin's Publishing Group.

PLAYING WITH FIRE: LAWLESS copyright © 1989 by Nora Roberts and IMPULSE copyright © 2005 by Nora Roberts.

All rights reserved.

For information, address St. Martin's Publishing Group, 120 Broadway, New York, NY 10271.

www.stmartins.com

ISBN: 978-1-250-37101-0

Our books may be purchased in bulk for promotional, educational, or business use. Please contact your local bookseller or the Macmillan Corporate and Premium Sales Department at 1-800-221-7945, ext. 5442, or by email at MacmillanSpecialMarkets@macmillan.com.

Printed in the United States of America

St. Martin's Paperbacks edition / February 2025

10 9 8 7 6 5 4 3 2 1

Lawless

To Ruth, Marianne and Jan,
for taking me to Silverado

CHAPTER 1

He wanted a drink. Whiskey, cheap and warm. After six weeks on the trail, he wanted the same kind of woman. Some men usually managed to get what they wanted. He was one of them. Still, the woman could wait, Jake decided as he leaned against the bar. The whiskey couldn't.

He had another ninety long, dusty miles to go before he got home. If anybody could call a frying pan like Lone Bluff home. Some did, Jake thought as he signaled for a bottle and took his first gut-clenching gulp. Some had to.

For himself, home was usually the six feet of space where his shadow fell. But for the past few months Lone Bluff had been as good a place as any. He could get a room there, a bath and a willing woman, all at a reasonable price. It was a town where a man could avoid trouble—or find it, depending on his mood.

For now, with the dust of the trail still scratchy in his throat and his stomach empty except for a shot of whiskey, Jake was just too tired for trouble. He'd have another drink, and whatever passed for a meal in this two-bit town blown up from the desert, then he'd be on his way.

Sunlight poured in over the swinging doors at the saloon's entrance. Someone had tacked a picture of a woman in red feathers to the wall, but that was the extent of the female company. Places like this didn't run to providing women for their clientele. Just to liquor and cards.

Even towns like this one had a saloon or two. A man could depend upon it, the way he could depend on little else. It wasn't yet noon, and half the tables were occupied. The air was thick with the smoke from the cigars the bartender sold, two for a penny. The whiskey went for a couple of bits and burned a line of fire straight from the throat to the gut. If the owner had added a real woman in red feathers, he could have charged double that and not heard a single complaint.

The place stank of whiskey, sweat and smoke. But Jake figured he didn't smell too pretty himself. He'd ridden hard from New Mexico, and he would have ridden straight through to Lone Bluff except he'd wanted to rest his horse and fill his own stomach with something other than the jerky in his saddlebags.

Saloons always looked better at night, and this one was no exception. Its bar was grimy from hundreds of hands and elbows, dulled by spilled drinks, scarred by match tips. The floor was nothing but hard-packed dirt that had absorbed its share of whiskey and blood. He'd been in worse, Jake reflected, wondering if he should allow himself the luxury of rolling a cigarette now or wait until after a meal.

He could buy more tobacco if he had a yearning for another. There was a month's pay in his pocket. And he'd be damned if he'd ever ride cattle again. That was a life for the young and stupid—or maybe just the stupid.

When his money ran low he could always take a job riding shotgun on the stage through Indian country. The line was always looking for a man who was handy with a gun, and it was better than riding at the back end of a steer. It was the middle of 1875 and the easterners were still coming—looking for gold and land, following dreams. Some of them stopped in the Arizona Territory on their way to California because they ran out of money or energy or time.

Their hard luck, Jake thought as he downed his second whiskey. He'd been born here, and he still didn't figure it was the most hospitable place on the map. It was hot and hard and stingy. It suited him just fine.

"Redman?"

Jake lifted his eyes to the dingy glass behind the bar. He saw the man behind him. Young, wiry and edgy. His brown hat was tipped down low over his eyes, and sweat glistened on his neck. Jake nearly sighed. He knew the type too well. The kind that went out of his way looking for trouble. The kind that didn't know that if you hung around long enough it found you, anyway.

"Yeah?"

"Jake Redman?"

"So?"

"I'm Barlow, Tom Barlow." He wiped his palms on his thighs. "They call me Slim."

The way he said it, Jake was sure the kid expected the name to be recognized . . . shuddered over. He decided the whiskey wasn't good enough for a third drink. He dropped some money on the bar, making sure his hands were well clear of his guns.

"There a place where a man can get a steak in this town?" Jake asked the bartender.

"Down to Grody's." The man moved cautiously out of range. "We don't want any trouble in here."

Jake gave him a long, cool look. "I'm not giving you any."

"I'm talking to you, Redman." Barlow spread his legs and let his hand hover over the butt of his gun. A mean-looking scar ran across the back of his hand from his index finger to his wrist. He wore his holster high, a single rig with the leather worn smooth at the buckle. It paid to notice details.

Easy, moving no more than was necessary, Jake met his eyes. "Something you want to say?"

"You got a reputation for being fast. Heard you took out Freemont in Tombstone."

Jake turned fully. As he moved, the swinging door flew back. At least one of the saloon's customers had decided to move to safer ground. The kid was packing a .44 Colt, its black rubber grip well tended. Jake didn't doubt there were notches in it. Barlow looked like the type who would take pride in killing.

"You heard right."

Barlow's fingers curled and uncurled. Two men playing poker in the corner let their hands lie to watch and made a companionable bet on the higher-stakes game in front of them. "I'm faster. Faster than Freemont. Faster than you. I run this town."

Jake glanced around the saloon, then back into Barlow's dark, edgy eyes. "Congratulations." He would have walked away, but Barlow shifted to block him. The move had Jake narrowing his eyes. The look came into them, the hard, flat look that made a smart man give way. "Cut your teeth on somebody else. I want a steak and a bed."

"Not in my town."

Patience wasn't Jake's long suit, but he wasn't in the

mood to waste time on a gunman looking to sharpen his reputation. "You want to die over a piece of meat?"

Jake watched the grin spread over Barlow's face. He didn't think he was going to die, Jake thought wearily. His kind never did.

"Why don't you come find me in about five years?" Jake told him. "I'll be happy to put a bullet in you."

"I found you now. After I kill you, there won't be a man west of the Mississippi who won't know Slim Barlow."

For some—for many—no other reason was needed to draw and fire. "Make it easy on both of us." Jake started for the doors again. "Just tell them you killed me."

"I hear your mother was a squaw." Barlow grinned when Jake stopped and turned again. "Guess that's where you got that streak of yellow."

Jake was used to rage. It could fill a man from stomach to brain and take over. When he felt it rising up, he clamped down on it. If he was going to fight—and it seemed inevitable—he preferred to fight cold.

"My grandmother was Apache."

Barlow grinned again, then wiped his mouth with the back of his left hand. "We don't want no Indians around here. Guess I'll have to clean up the town a little."

He went for his gun. Jake saw the move, not in Barlow's hands but in his eyes. Cold and fast and without regret, Jake drew his own. There were those who saw him who said it was like lightning and thunder. There was a flash of steel, then the roar of the bullet. He hardly moved from where he stood, shooting from the hip, trusting instinct and experience. In a smooth, almost careless movement, he replaced his gun. Tom they-call-me-Slim Barlow was sprawled on the barroom floor.

Jake passed through the swinging doors and walked to his horse. He didn't know whether he'd killed his man or not, and he didn't care. The whole damn mess had ruined his appetite.

Sarah was mortally afraid she was going to lose the miserable lunch she'd managed to bolt down at the last stop. How anyone—*anyone*—survived under these appalling conditions, she'd never know. The West, as far as she could see, was only fit for snakes and outlaws.

She closed her eyes, patted the sweat from her neck with her handkerchief and prayed that she'd make it through the next few hours. At least she could thank God she wouldn't have to spend another night in one of those horrible stage depots. She'd been afraid she would be murdered in her bed. If one could call that miserable sheetless rope cot a bed. And privacy? Well, there simply hadn't been any.

It didn't matter now, she told herself. She was nearly there. After twelve long years, she was going to see her father again and take care of him in the beautiful house he'd built outside Lone Bluff.

When she'd been almost six, he'd left her in the care of the good sisters and gone off to make his fortune. There had been nights, many nights, when Sarah had cried herself to sleep from missing him. Then, as the years had passed, she'd had to take out the faded daguerreotype to remember his face. But he'd always written to her. His penmanship had been strained and childish, but there had been so much love in his letters. And so much hope.

Once a month she'd received word from her father from whatever point he'd stopped at on his journey west. After eighteen months, and eighteen letters, he'd written from the Arizona Territory, where he'd settled, and where he would build his fortune.

He'd convinced her that he'd been right to leave her in Philadelphia, in the convent school, where she could be raised and educated as a proper young lady should be. Until, Sarah remembered, she was old enough to travel across the country to live with him. Now she was nearly eighteen, and she was going to join him. Undoubtedly the house he'd built, however grand, required a woman's touch.

Since he'd never married again, Sarah imagined her father a crusty bachelor, never quite certain where his clean collars were or what the cook was serving for dinner. She'd soon fix all that.

A man in his position needed to entertain, and to entertain he needed a hostess. Sarah Conway knew exactly how to give an elegant dinner party and a formal ball.

True, what she'd read of the Arizona Territory was distressing, to say the least. Stories of ruthless gunmen and wild Indians. But, after all, this was 1875. Sarah had no doubt that even so distant a place as Arizona was under control by this time. The reports she'd read had obviously been exaggerated to sell newspapers and penny dreadfuls.

They hadn't exaggerated about the climate.

She shifted for a better position. The bulk of the woman beside her, and her own corset, gave her little room for relief. And the smell. No matter how often Sarah sprinkled lavender water on her handkerchief, there was no escaping it. There were seven passengers, crammed all but elbow-to-knee inside the rattling stagecoach. It was airless, and that accentuated the stench of sweat and foul breath and whatever liquor it was that the man across from her continued to drink. Right from the bottle. At first, his pockmarked face and grimy neckcloth had fascinated her. But when he'd offered her a drink, she had fallen back on a woman's best defense. Her dignity.

It was difficult to look dignified when her clothes were sticking to her and her hair was drooping beneath her bonnet. It was all but impossible to maintain her decorum when the plump woman beside her began to gnaw on what appeared to be a chicken leg. But when Sarah was determined, she invariably prevailed.

The good sisters had never been able to pray or punish or lecture her stubbornness out of her. Now, with her chin slightly lifted and her body braced against the bouncing sway of the coach, she kept her eyes firmly shut and ignored her fellow passengers.

She'd seen enough of the Arizona landscape, if one could call it that. As far as she could see, the entire territory was nothing but miles of sunbaked desert. True, the first cacti she'd seen had been fascinating. She'd even considered sketching a few of them. Some were as big as a man, with arms that stretched up to the sky. Others were short and squat and covered with hundreds of dangerous-looking needles. Still, after she'd seen several dozen of them, and little else, they'd lost their novelty.

The rocks were interesting, she supposed. The buttes and flat-topped mesas growing out of the sand had a certain rugged charm, particularly when they rose up into the deep, endless blue of the sky. But she preferred the tidy streets of Philadelphia, with their shops and tearooms.

Being with her father would make all the difference. She could live anywhere, as long as she was with him again. He'd be proud of her. She needed him to be proud of her. All these years she'd worked and learned and practiced so that she could become the proper, well-educated young lady he wanted his daughter to be.

She wondered if he'd recognize her. She'd sent him a small, framed self-portrait just last Christmas, but she wasn't certain it had been a truly good likeness. She'd always thought it was too bad she wasn't pretty, in the soft, round way of her dear friend Lucilla. Still, her complexion was good, and Sarah comforted herself with that. Unlike Lucilla, she never required any help from the little pots of rouge the sisters so disapproved of. In fact, there were times she thought her complexion just a bit too healthy. Her mouth was full and wide when she would have preferred a delicate Cupid's bow, and her eyes were an unremarkable brown rather than the blue that would have suited her blond hair so much better. Still, she was trim and neat—or she had been neat before she'd begun this miserable journey.

It would all be worthwhile soon. When she greeted her father and they settled into the lovely house he'd built. Four bedrooms. Imagine. And a parlor with windows facing west. Delightful. Undoubtedly, she'd have to do some redecorating. Men never thought about such niceties as curtains and throw rugs. She'd enjoy it. Once she had the glass shining and fresh flowers in the vases, he would see how much he needed her. Then all the years in between would have been worthwhile.

Sarah felt a line of sweat trickle down her back. The first thing she wanted was a bath—a nice, cool bath laced with the fragrant lilac salts Lucilla had given her as a parting gift. She sighed. She could almost feel it, her body free of the tight corset and hot clothes, the water sliding over her skin. Scented. Delicious. Almost sinful.

When the coach jolted, Sarah was thrown against the fat woman to her left. Before she could right herself, a spray of rotgut whiskey soaked her skirts.

"Sir!" But before she could lecture him she heard the shot, and the screams.

"Indians!" The chicken leg went flying, and the fat woman clutched Sarah to her bosom like a shield. "We're all going to be murdered."

"Don't be absurd." Sarah struggled to free herself, not certain if she was more annoyed by the sudden dangerous speed of the coach or the spot of chicken grease on her new skirt. She leaned toward the window to call to the driver. As she did, the face of the shotgun rider slid into view, inches from hers. He hung there, upside down, for seconds only. But that was long enough for Sarah to see the blood trickling from his mouth, and the arrow in his heart. Even as the woman beside her screamed again, his body thudded to the ground.

"God have mercy!" she shouted.

"Apaches," the man with the whiskey said as he finished off the bottle. "Must've got the driver, too. We're on a runaway." So saying, he drew his gun, made his way to the opposite window and began firing methodically.

Dazed, Sarah continued to stare out the window. She could hear screams and whoops and the thunder of horses' hooves. Like devils, she thought dully. They sounded like devils. That was impossible. Ridiculous. The United States was nearly a century old. Ulysses S. Grant was president. Steamships crossed the Atlantic in less than two weeks. Devils simply didn't exist in this day and age.

Then she saw one, bare chested, hair flying, on a tough paint pony. Sarah looked straight into his eyes.

She could see the fever in them, just as she could see the bright streaks of paint on his face and the layer of dust that covered his gleaming skin. He raised his bow. She could have counted the feathers in the arrow. Then, suddenly, he flew off the back of his horse.

It was like a play, she thought, and she had to pinch herself viciously to keep from swooning.

Another horseman came into view, riding low, with pistols in both hands. He wore a gray hat over dark hair, and his skin was nearly as dark as that of the Apache she'd seen. In his eyes, as they met hers, she saw not fever, but ice.

He didn't shoot her, as she'd been almost certain he would, but fired over his shoulder, using his right hand, then his left, even as an arrow whizzed by his head.

Amazing, she thought as a thudding excitement began to race with her terror. He was magnificent— sweat and grime on his face, ice in his eyes, his lean, tense body glued to the racing horse. Then the fat lady grabbed her again and began to wail.

Jake fired behind him, clinging to the horse with his knees as easily as any Apache brave. He'd caught a glimpse of the passengers, in particular a pale, dark-eyed girl in a dark blue bonnet. His Apache cousins would've enjoyed that one, he thought dispassionately as he holstered his guns.

He could see the driver, an arrow piercing one shoulder, struggling to regain control of the horses. He was doing his best, despite the pain, but he wasn't strong enough to shove the brake down. Swearing, Jake pushed his horse on until he was close enough to the racing coach to gain a handhold.

For one endless second he hung by his fingers alone. Sarah caught a glimpse of a dusty shirt and

one powerful forearm, a long, leather-clad leg and a
scarred boot. Then he was up, scrambling over the top
of the coach. The woman beside her screamed again,
then fainted dead away when they stopped. Too terrified to sit, Sarah pushed open the door of the coach
and climbed out.

The man in the gray hat was already getting down.
"Ma'am," he said as he moved past her.

She pressed a hand to her drumming heart. No hero
had ever been so heroic. "You saved our lives," she
managed, but he didn't even glance her way.

"Redman." The passenger who'd drunk the whiskey
stepped out. "Glad you stopped by."

"Lucius." Jake picked up the reins of his horse and
proceeded to calm him. "There were only six of them."

"They're getting away," Sarah blurted out. "Are you
just going to let them get away?"

Jake looked at the cloud of dust from the retreating horses, then back at Sarah. He had time now for a
longer, more interested study. She was tiny, with *East*
stamped all over her pretty face. Her hair, the color
of honeycombs, was tumbling down from her bonnet.
She looked as if she'd just stepped out of the school-
room, and she smelled like a cheap saloon. He had to
grin.

"Yep."

"But you can't." Her idea of a hero was rapidly
crumbling. "They killed a man."

"He knew the chance he was taking. Riding the line
pays good."

"They murdered him," Sarah said again, as if she
were speaking to a very dull pupil. "He's lying back
there with an arrow through his heart." When Jake said
nothing, just walked his horse to the back of the coach,
Sarah followed him. "At least you can go back and

pick up that poor man's body. We can't just leave him there."

"Dead's dead."

"That's a hideous thing to say." Because she felt ill, Sarah dragged off her bonnet and used it to fan hot air around her face. "The man deserves a decent burial. I couldn't possibly— What are you doing?"

Jake spared her a glance. Mighty pretty, he decided. Even prettier without the bonnet hiding her hair. "Hitching my horse."

She dropped her arm to her side. She no longer felt ill. She was certainly no longer impressed. She was furious. "Sir, you appear to care more about that horse than you do about the man."

He stooped under the reins. For a moment they stood face-to-face, with the sun beating down and the smell of blood and dust all around them. "That's right, seeing as the man's dead and my horse isn't. I'd get back inside, ma'am. It'd be a shame if you were still standing here when the Apaches decide to come back."

That made her stop and look around uneasily. The desert was still, but for the cry of a bird she didn't recognize as a vulture. "I'll go back and get him myself," she said between her teeth.

"Suit yourself." Jake walked to the front of the coach. "Get that stupid woman inside," he told Lucius. "And don't give her any more to drink."

Sarah's mouth fell open. Before she could retaliate, Lucius had her by the arm. "Now, don't mind Jake, miss. He just says whatever he damn pleases. He's right, though. Those Apaches might turn back this way. We sure don't want to be sitting here if they do."

With what little dignity she had left, Sarah stepped back into the coach. The fat woman was still sobbing, leaning heavily against a tight-lipped man in a bowler. Sarah wedged herself into her corner as the stage jumped forward again. Securing her bonnet, she frowned at Lucius.

"Who is that horrible man?"

"Jake?" Lucius settled back. There was nothing he liked better than a good fight, particularly when he stayed alive to enjoy it. "That's Jake Redman, miss. I don't mind saying we was lucky he passed this way. Jake hits what he aims at."

"Indeed." She wanted to be aloof, but she remembered the murderous look in the Apache's eyes when he'd ridden beside the window. "I suppose we do owe him our gratitude, but he seemed cold-blooded about it."

"More'n one says he's got ice in his veins. Along with some Apache blood."

"You mean he's . . . Indian?"

"On his grandmother's side, I hear." Because his bottle was empty, Lucius settled for a plug of tobacco. He tucked it comfortably in his cheek. "Wouldn't want to cross him. No, ma'am, I sure wouldn't. Mighty comforting to know he's on your side when things heat up."

What kind of man killed his own kind? With a shiver, Sarah fell silent again. She didn't want to think about it.

On top of the stage, Jake kept the team to a steady pace. He preferred the freedom and mobility of having a single horse under him. The driver held a hand to his wounded shoulder and refused the dubious comfort of the coach.

"We could use you back on the line," he told Jake.

"Thinking about it." But he was really thinking about the little lady with the big brown eyes and the honey-colored hair. "Who's the girl? The young one in blue?"

"Conway. From Philadelphia." The driver breathed slow and easy against the pain. "Says she's Matt Conway's daughter."

"That so?" Miss Philadelphia Conway sure as hell didn't take after her old man. But Jake remembered that Matt bragged about his daughter back east from time to time. Especially after he started a bottle. "Come to visit her father?"

"Says she's come to stay."

Jake gave a quick, mirthless laugh. "Won't last a week. Women like that don't."

"She's planning on it." With a jerk of his thumb, the driver indicated the trunks strapped to the coach. "Most of that's hers."

With a snort, Jake adjusted his hat. "Figures."

Sarah caught her first glimpse of Lone Bluff from the stagecoach window. It spread like a jumble of rock at the base of the mountains. Hard, cold-looking mountains, she thought with a shudder, fooled—as the inexperienced always were—into thinking they were much closer than they actually were.

She'd forgotten herself enough to crane her head out. But she couldn't get another look at Jake Redman unless she pushed half her body through the opening. She really wasn't interested anyway, she assured herself. Unless it was purely for entertainment purposes. When she wrote back to Lucilla and the sisters, she wanted to be able to describe all the local oddities.

The man was certainly odd. He'd ridden like a warrior one moment, undoubtedly risking his life for a coach full of strangers. Then, the next minute, he'd dismissed his Christian duty and left a poor soul beside a lonely desert road. And he'd called her stupid.

Never in her life had anyone ever accused Sarah Conway of being stupid. In fact, both her intelligence and her breeding were widely admired. She was well-read, fluent in French and more than passably accomplished on the pianoforte.

Taking the time to retie her bonnet, Sarah reminded herself that she hardly needed approval from a man like Jake Redman. After she was reunited with her father and took her place in the local society, it was doubtful she'd ever see him again.

She'd thank him properly, of course. Sarah drew a fresh handkerchief from her reticule and blotted her temples. Just because he had no manners was no excuse to forget her own. She supposed she might even ask her father to offer him some monetary reward.

Pleased with the idea, Sarah looked out the window again. And blinked. Surely this wasn't Lone Bluff. Her father would never have settled in this grimy excuse for a town. It was no more than a huddle of buildings and a wide patch of dust that served as a road. They passed two saloons side by side, a dry goods store and what appeared to be a rooming house. Slack-legged horses were hitched to posts, their tails switching lazily at huge black flies. A handful of young boys with dirty faces began to race alongside the coach, shouting and firing wooden pistols. Sarah saw two women in faded gingham walking arm in arm on some wooden planks that served as a sidewalk.

When the coach stopped, she heard Jake call for a doctor. Passengers were already streaming out through the doors on both sides. Resigned, Sarah stepped down and shook out her skirts.

"Mr. Redman." The brim of her bonnet provided inadequate shade. She was forced to lift her hand over her eyes. "Why have we stopped here?"

"End of the line, ma'am." A couple of men were already lifting the driver down, so he swung himself around to unstrap the cases on top of the coach.

"End of the line? But where are we?"

He paused long enough to glance down at her. She saw then that his eyes were darker than she'd imagined. A smoky slate gray. "Welcome to Lone Bluff."

Letting out a long, slow breath, she turned. Sunlight treated the town cruelly. It showed all the dirt, all the wear, and it heightened the pungent smell of horses.

Dear God, so this was it. The end of the line. The end of her line. It didn't matter, she told herself. She wouldn't be living in town. And surely before long the gold in her father's mine would bring more people and progress. No, it didn't matter at all. Sarah squared her shoulders. The only thing that mattered was seeing her father again.

She turned around in time to see Jake toss one of her trunks down to Lucius.

"Mr. Redman, please take care of my belongings."

Jake hefted the next case and tossed it to a grinning Lucius. "Yes, ma'am."

Biting down on her temper, she waited until he jumped down beside her. "Notwithstanding my earlier sentiments, I'm very grateful to you, Mr. Redman, for coming to our aid. You proved yourself to be quite valiant. I'm sure my father will want to repay you for seeing that I arrived safely."

Jake didn't think he'd ever heard anyone talk quite so fine since he'd spent a week in St. Louis. Tipping back his hat, he looked at her, long enough to make Sarah flush. "Forget it."

Forget it? Sarah thought as he turned his back and walked away. If that was the way the man accepted gratitude, she certainly would. With a sweep of her skirts she moved to the side of the road to wait for her father.

Jake strode into the rooming house with his saddle-bags slung over his shoulder. It was never particularly clean, and it always smelled of onions and strong coffee. There were a couple of bullet holes in the wall. He'd put one of them there personally. Since the door was propped open, flies buzzed merrily in and out of the cramped entrance.

"Maggie." Jake tipped his hat to the woman who stood at the base of the stairs. "Got a room?"

Maggie O'Rourke was as tough as one of her fried steaks. She had iron-gray hair pinned back from a face that should have been too skinny for wrinkles. But wrinkles there were, a maze of them. Her tiny blue eyes seemed to peek out of the folds of a worn blanket. She ran her business with an iron fist, a Winchester repeater and an eye for a dollar.

She took one look at Jake and successfully hid her pleasure at seeing him. "Well, look what the cat dragged in," she said, the musical brogue of her native country still evident in her thin voice. "Got the law on your tail, Jake, or a woman?"

"Neither." He kicked the door shut with his boot, wondering why he always came back here. The old woman never gave him a moment's peace, and her cooking could kill a man. "You got a room, Maggie? And some hot water?"

"You got a dollar?" She held out her thin hand. When Jake dropped a coin into it, she tested it with the few good teeth she had left. It wasn't that she didn't trust Jake. She did. She just didn't trust the United States government. "Might as well take the one you had before. No one's in it."

"Fine." He started up the steps.

"Ain't had too much excitement since you left. Couple drifters shot each other over at the Bird Cage. Worthless pair, the both of them. Only one dead, though. Sheriff sent the other on his way after the doc patched him up. Young Mary Sue Brody got herself in trouble with that Mitchell boy. Always said she was a fast thing, that Mary Sue. Had a right proper wedding, though. Just last month."

Jake kept walking, but that didn't stop Maggie. One of the privileges in running a rooming house was giving and receiving gossip.

"What a shame about old Matt Conway."

That stopped him. He turned. Maggie was still at the base of the steps, using the edge of her apron to swipe halfheartedly at the dust on the banister. "What about Matt Conway?"

"Got himself killed in that worthless mine of his. A cave-in. Buried him the day before yesterday."

CHAPTER 2

The heat was murderous. A plume of thin yellow dust rose each time a rider passed, then hung there to clog the still air. Sarah longed for a long, cool drink and a seat in the shade. From the looks of things, there wasn't a place in town where a lady could go to find such amenities. Even if there were, she was afraid to leave her trunks on the side of the road and risk missing her father.

She'd been so sure he would be waiting for her. But then, a man in his position could have been held up by a million things. Work at the mine, a problem with an employee, perhaps last-minute preparations for her arrival.

She'd waited twelve years, she reminded herself, resisting the urge to loosen her collar. She could wait a little longer.

A buckboard passed, spewing up more dust, so that she was forced to lift a handkerchief to her mouth. Her dark blue traveling skirt and her neat matching jacket with its fancy black braid were covered with dust. With a sigh, she glanced down at her blouse, which was drooping hopelessly and now seemed more yellow than white. It wasn't really vanity. The sisters had never given her a chance to develop any. She was concerned that her father would see her for the first time when she was travel-stained and close to exhaustion. She'd wanted to look her best for him at this first meeting. All she could do now was retie the bow at her chin, then brush hopelessly at her skirts.

She looked a fright. But she'd make it up to him. She would wear her brand-new white muslin gown for dinner tonight, the one with the charming rosebuds embroidered all over the skirt. Her kid slippers were dyed pink to match. He'd be proud of her.

If only he'd come, she thought, and take her away from here.

Jake crossed the street after losing the battle he'd waged with himself. It wasn't his business, and it wasn't his place to tell her. But for the past ten minutes he'd been watching her standing at the side of the road, waiting. He'd been able to see, too clearly, the look of hope that sprang into her eyes each time a horse or wagon approached. Somebody had to tell the woman that her father wasn't going to meet her.

Sarah saw him coming. He walked easily, despite the guns at his sides. As if they had always been there. As if they always would be. They rode low on his hips, shifting with his movements. And he kept his eyes on her in a way that she was certain a man shouldn't keep his eyes on a woman—unless she was his own. When she felt her heart flutter, she automatically stiffened her backbone.

It was Lucilla who was always talking about fluttering hearts. It was Lucilla who painted romantic pictures of lawless men and lawless places. Sarah preferred a bit more reality in her dreams.

"Ma'am." He was surprised that she hadn't already swooned under the power of the afternoon sun. Maybe she was tougher than she looked, but he doubted it.

"Mr. Redman." Determined to be gracious, she allowed her lips to curve ever so slightly at the corners.

He tucked his thumbs into the pockets of his pants. "I got some news about your father."

She smiled fully, beautifully, so that her whole face lit up with it. Her eyes turned to gold in the sunlight. Jake felt the punch, like a bullet in the chest.

"Oh, did he leave word for me? Thank you for letting me know. I might have waited here for hours."

"Ma'am—"

"Is there a note?"

"No." He wanted to get this done, and done quickly. "Matt's dead. There was an accident at his mine." He was braced for weeping, for wild wailing, but her eyes filled with fury, not tears.

"How dare you? How dare you lie to me about something like that?" She would have brushed past him, but Jake clamped a hand over her arm. Sarah's first reaction was simple indignation at being manhandled. Then she looked up at him, really looked, and said nothing.

"He was buried two days ago." He felt her recoil, then go still. The fury drained from her eyes, even as the color drained from her cheeks. "Don't go fainting on me."

It was true. She could see the truth on his face as clearly as she could see his distaste at being the one to tell her. "An accident?" she managed.

"A cave-in." He was relieved that she wasn't going to faint, but he didn't care for the glassy look in her eyes. "You'll want to talk to the sheriff."

"The sheriff?" she repeated dully.

"His office is across the street."

She just shook her head and stared at him. Her eyes *were* gold, Jake decided. The color of the brandy he sometimes drank at the Silver Star. Right now they were huge and full of hurt. He watched her bite down on her bottom lip in a gesture he knew meant she was fighting not to let go of the emotions he saw so clearly in her eyes.

If she'd fainted, he'd happily have left her on the road in the care of whatever woman happened to pass by. But she was hanging on, and it moved something in him.

Swearing, Jake shifted his grip from her arm to her elbow and guided her across the street. He was damned if he could figure out how he'd elected himself responsible.

Sheriff Barker was at his desk, bent over some paperwork and a cup of sweetened coffee. He was balding rapidly. Every morning he took the time to comb what hair he had left over the spreading bare spot on top of his head. He had the beginnings of a paunch brought on by his love of his wife's baking. He kept the law in Lone Bluff, but he didn't worry overmuch about the order. It wasn't that he was corrupt, just lazy.

He glanced up as Jake entered. Then he sighed and sent tobacco juice streaming into the spittoon in the corner. When Jake Redman was around, there was usually work to be done.

"So you're back." The wad of tobacco gave Barker a permanently swollen jaw. "Thought you might take a fancy to New Mexico." His brows lifted when Jake ushered Sarah inside. There was enough gentleman left in him to bring him to his feet. "Ma'am."

"This is Matt Conway's daughter."

"Well, I'll be damned. Begging your pardon, ma'am. I was just fixing to send you a letter."

"Sheriff." She had to pause a moment to find her balance. She would not fall apart, not here, in front of strangers.

"Barker, ma'am." He came around the desk to offer her a chair.

"Sheriff Barker." Sarah sat, praying she'd be able to stand again. "Mr. Redman has just told me that my father . . ." She couldn't say it. No matter how weak or cowardly it might be, she just couldn't say the words.

"Yes, ma'am. I'm mighty sorry. Couple of kids wandered on up by the mine playing games and found him. Appears he was working the mine when some of the beams gave way." When she said nothing, Barker cleared his throat and opened the top drawer of his desk. "He had this watch on him, and his tobacco." He'd had his pipe, as well, but since it had been broken—like most of Conway's bones—Barker hadn't thought anyone would want it. "We figured he'd want to be buried with his wedding ring on."

"Thank you." As if in a trance, she took the watch and the tobacco pouch from him. She remembered the watch. The tears almost won when she remembered how he'd taken it out to check the time before he'd left her in Mother Superior's lemony-smelling office. "I want to see where he's buried. My trunks will need to be taken out to his house."

"Miss Conway, if you don't mind me offering some advice, you don't want to stay way out there. It's no place for a young lady like you, all alone and all. My wife'll be happy to have you stay with us for a few days. Until the stage heads east again."

"It's kind of you to offer." She braced a hand on the

chair and managed to stand again. "But I'd prefer to spend the night in my father's house." She swallowed and discovered that her throat was hurtfully dry. "Is there . . . Do I owe you anything for the burial?"

"No, ma'am. We take care of our own around here."

"Thank you." She needed air. With the watch clutched in her hand, she pushed through the door. Leaning against a post, she tried to catch her breath.

"You ought to take the sheriff up on his offer."

She turned her head to give Jake an even look. She could only be grateful that he made her angry enough to help her hold off her grief. He hadn't offered a word of sympathy. Not one. Well, she was glad of it.

"I'm going to stay in my father's house. Will you take me?"

He rubbed a hand over his chin. He hadn't shaved in a week. "I've got things to do."

"I'll pay you," she said quickly when he started to walk away.

He stopped and looked back at her. She was determined, all right. He wanted to see how determined. "How much?"

"Two dollars." When he only continued to look at her, she said between her teeth, "Five."

"You got five?"

Disgusted, Sarah dug in her reticule. "There."

Jake looked at the bill in her hand. "What's that?"

"It's five dollars."

"Not around here it ain't. Around here it's paper."

Sarah pushed the bill back into her reticule and pulled out a coin. "Will this do?"

Jake took the coin and turned it over in his hand, then stuck it in his pocket. "That'll do fine. I'll get a wagon."

Miserable man, she thought as he strode away.

She hated him. And hated even more the fact that she needed him.

During the long, hot ride in the open wagon, she said nothing. She no longer cared about the desolation of the landscape, the heat or the cold-bloodedness of the man beside her. Her emotions seemed to have shriveled up inside her. Every mile they'd gone was just another mile behind her.

Jake Redman didn't seem to need conversation. He drove in silence, armed with a rifle across his lap, as well as the pistols he carried. There hadn't been trouble out here in quite some time, but the Indian attack had warned him that that could change.

He'd recognized Strong Wolf in the party that had attacked the stage. If the Apache brave had decided to raid in the area, he would hit the Conway place sooner or later.

They passed no one. They saw only sand and rock and a hawk out hunting.

When he reined the horses in, Sarah saw nothing but a small adobe house and a few battered sheds on a patch of thirsty land.

"Why are we stopping here?"

Jake jumped down from the wagon. "This is Matt Conway's place."

"Don't be ridiculous." Because it didn't appear that he was going to come around and assist her, Sarah struggled down herself. "Mr. Redman, I paid you to take me to my father's home and I expect you to keep the bargain."

Before she could stop him, he dumped one of her trunks on the ground. "What do you think you're doing?"

"Delivering your luggage."

"Don't you take another piece off that wagon."

Surprising them both, Sarah grabbed his shirt and pulled him around to face her. "I insist you take me to my father's house immediately."

She wasn't just stupid, Jake thought. She was irritating. "Fine." He clipped her around the waist and hauled her over his shoulder.

At first she was too shocked to move. No man had ever touched her before. Now this, this *ruffian* had his hands all over her. And they were alone. Totally alone. Sarah began to struggle as he pushed open the door of the hut. Before she could draw the breath to scream, he was dropping her to her feet again.

"That good enough for you?"

She stared at him, visions of a hundred calamities that could befall a defenseless woman dancing in her brain. She stepped back, breathing hard, and prayed she could reason with him. "Mr. Redman, I have very little money of my own—hardly enough worth stealing."

Something came into his eyes that had her breath stopping altogether. He looked more than dangerous now. He looked fatal. "I don't steal." The light coming through the low doorway arched around him. She moistened her lips.

"Are you going to kill me?"

He nearly laughed. Instead, he leaned against the wall. Something about her was eating at him. He didn't know what or why, but he didn't like it. Not one damn bit.

"Probably not. You want to take a look around?" She just shook her head. "They told me he was buried around back, near the entrance of the mine. I'll go check on Matt's horses and water the team."

When he left, she continued to stare at the empty doorway. This was madness. Did the man expect her to believe her father had lived here, like this? She had letters, dozens of them, telling her about the house he'd been building, the house he'd finished, the house that would be waiting for her when she was old enough to join him.

The mine. If the mine was near, perhaps she could find someone there she could speak with. Taking a cautious look out the doorway, Sarah hurried out and rounded the house.

She passed what might have been the beginnings of a small vegetable garden, withered now in the sun. There was a shed that served as a stable and an empty paddock made of a few rickety pieces of wood. She walked beyond it to where the ground began to rise with the slope of the mountain.

The entrance to the mine was easily found, though it was hardly more than a hole in the rock wall. Above it was a crudely etched plank of wood.

SARAH'S PRIDE

She felt the tears then. They came in a rush that she had to work hard to hold back. There were no workmen here, no carts shuttling along filled with rock, no picks hacking out gold. She saw it for what it was, the dream of a man who had had little else. Her father had never been a successful prospector or an important landowner. He'd been a man digging in rock and hoping for the big strike.

She saw the grave then. They had buried him only a few yards from the entrance. Someone had been kind enough to fashion a cross and carve his name on it. She knelt and ran her palm along the rubble that covered him.

He'd lied. For twelve years he'd lied to her, telling her stories about rich veins and the mother lode. He'd spun fantasies about a big house with a parlor and fine wooden floors. Had he needed to believe it? When he'd left her he'd made her a promise.

"You'll have everything your heart desires, my sweet, sweet Sarah. Everything your mother would have wanted for you."

He had kept his promise—except for one thing. One vital thing. He hadn't given her himself. All those years, all she'd really wanted had been her father.

He'd lived like this, she thought, in a mud house in the middle of nowhere, so that she could have pretty dresses and new stockings. So that she could learn how to serve tea and waltz. It must have taken nearly everything he'd managed to dig out of the rock to keep her in school back east.

Now he was dead. She could barely remember his face, and he was dead. Lost to her.

"Oh, Papa, didn't you know how little it mattered?" Lying across the grave, she let the tears come until she'd wept her heart clean.

She'd been gone a long time. Too long, Jake thought. He was just about to go after her when he saw her coming over the rise from the direction of the old mine. She paused there, looking down at the house her father had lived in for more than a decade. She'd taken off her bonnet, and she was holding it by the ribbons. For a moment she stood like a statue in the airless afternoon, her face marble-pale, her body slim and elegant. Her hair was pinned up, but a few tendrils had escaped to curl around her face. The sun slanted over it so that it glowed richly, reminding him of the hide of a young deer.

Jake blew out the last of the smoke from the cigarette he'd rolled. She was a hell of a sight, silhouetted against the bluff. She made him ache in places he didn't care to think about. Then she saw him. He could almost see her chin come up as she started down over the rough ground. Yeah, she was a hell of a sight.

"Mr. Redman." The grief was there in her red-rimmed eyes and her pale cheeks, but her voice was strong. "I apologize for the scene I caused earlier."

That tied his tongue for a moment. The way she said it, they might have been talking over tea in some cozy parlor. "Forget it. You ready to go back?"

"I beg your pardon?"

He jerked his thumb toward the wagon. Sarah noted that all her trunks were neatly stacked on it again. "I said, are you ready to go back?"

She glanced down at her hands. Because the palms of her gloves were grimy, she tugged them off. They'd never be the same, she mused. Nothing would. She drew a long, steadying breath.

"I thought you understood me. I'm staying in my father's house."

"Don't be a fool. A woman like you's got no business out here."

"Really?" Her eyes hardened. "Be that as it may, I'm not leaving. I'd appreciate it if you'd move my trunks inside." She breezed by him.

"You won't last a day."

She stopped to look over her shoulder. Jake was forced to admit that he'd faced men over the barrel of a gun who'd had less determination in their eyes. "Is that your opinion, Mr. Redman?"

"That's a fact."

"Would you care to wager on it?"

"Look, Duchess, this is hard country even if you're born to it. Heat, snakes, mountain lions—not to mention Apaches."

"I appreciate you pointing all that out, Mr. Redman. Now my luggage."

"Damn fool woman," he muttered as he strode over to the wagon. "You want to stay out here, hell, it don't matter to me." He hefted a trunk into the house while Sarah stood a few feet back with her hands folded.

"Your language, Mr. Redman, is quite unnecessary."

He only swore with more skill as he carried in the second trunk. "Nobody's going to be around when it gets dark and you change your mind."

"I won't change my mind, but thank you so much for your concern."

"No concern of mine," he muttered, ignoring her sarcasm. He scooped up the rest of her boxes and dumped them inside the doorway. "Hope you got provisions in there, as well as fancy dresses."

"I assure you I'll be fine." She walked to the doorway herself and turned to him. "Perhaps you could tell me where I might get water."

"There's a stream half a mile due east."

Half a mile? she thought, trying not to show her dismay. "I see." Shading her eyes, she looked out. Jake mumbled another oath, took her by the shoulders and pointed in the opposite direction. "That way's east, Duchess."

"Of course." She stepped back. "Thank you again, Mr. Redman, for all your help. And good day," she added before she closed the door in his face.

She could hear him swearing at her as he unhitched the horses. If she hadn't been so weary, she might have been amused. She was certainly too exhausted to be shocked by the words he used. If she was going to stay, she was going to have to become somewhat accustomed

to rough manners. She peeled off her jacket. And she
was going to stay.

If this was all she had left, she was going to make
the best of it. Somehow.

She moved to the rounded opening beside the door
that served as a window. From there she watched Jake
ride away. He'd left her the wagon and stabled the
rented horses with her father's two. For all the good it
did her, Sarah thought with a sigh. She hadn't the vagu-
est idea of how to hitch a team, much less how to drive
one.

She continued to watch Jake until he was nothing
but a cloud of dust fading in the distance. She was
alone. Truly alone. She had no one, and little more than
nothing.

No one but herself, she thought. And if she had only
that and a mud hut, she'd find a way to make the best
of it. Nobody—and certainly not Jake Redman—was
going to frighten her away.

Turning, she unbuttoned her cuffs and rolled up her
sleeves. The good sisters had always claimed that simple hard work eased the mind and cleansed the soul.
She was about to put that claim to the test.

She found the letters an hour later. When she came
across them in the makeshift loft that served as a bedroom, she wiped her grimy hands as best as she could
on the embroidered apron she'd dug out of one of her
trunks.

He'd kept them. From the first to the last she'd written, her father had kept her letters to him. The tears
threatened again, but she willed them back. Tears
would do neither of them any good now. But, oh, it
helped more than she could ever have explained that
he'd kept her letters. To know now, when she would

never see him again, that he had thought of her as she
had thought of him.

He must have received the last, the letter telling him
she was coming to be with him, shortly before his death.
Sarah hadn't mailed it until she'd been about to board
the train. She'd told herself it was because she wanted
to surprise him, but she'd also wanted to be certain he
wouldn't have time to forbid her to come.

Would you have, Papa? she wondered. *Or would
you finally have been willing to share the truth with
me?* Had he thought her too weak, too fragile, to share
the life he'd chosen? Was she?

Sighing, she looked around. Four bedrooms, and
a parlor with the windows facing west, she thought with
a quiet laugh. Well, according to Jake Redman, the window did indeed face west. The house itself was hardly
bigger than the room she'd shared with Lucilla at school.
It was too small, certainly, for all she'd brought with
her from Philadelphia, but she'd managed to drag the
trunks into one corner. To please herself, she'd taken
out a few of her favorite things—one of her wildflower
sketches, a delicate blue glass perfume bottle, a pretty
petit-point pillow and the china-faced doll her father
had sent her for her twelfth birthday.

They didn't make it home, not yet. But they helped.

Setting the letters back in the tin box beside the bed,
she rose. She had practical matters to think about now.
The first was money. After paying the five dollars, she
had only twenty dollars left. She hadn't a clue as to
how long that would keep her, but she doubted it would
be very long. Then there was food. That was of more
immediate concern. She'd found some flour, a few cans
of beans, some lard and a bottle of whiskey. Pressing a
hand to her stomach, Sarah decided she'd have to make

do with the beans. All she had to do now was to figure
out how to start a fire in the battered-looking stove.

She found a few twigs in the wood box, and a box
of matches. It took her half an hour, a lot of frustration
and a few words the sisters would never have approved
of before she was forced to admit she was a failure.

Jake Redman. Disgusted, she scowled at the handful of charred twigs. The least the man could have done
was to offer to start a cook fire for her and fetch some
water. She'd already made the trip down to the stream
and back once, managing to scrounge out half a bucket
from its stingy trickle.

She'd eat the beans cold. She'd prove to Jake Redman that she could do very well for herself, by herself.

Sarah unsheathed her father's bowie knife, shuddered once at the sight of the vicious blade, then
plunged it into the lid of the can until she'd made an
opening. Too hungry to care, she sat beside the small
stone hearth and devoured the beans.

She'd think of it as an adventure, she told herself.
One she could write about to her friends in Philadelphia. A better one, she decided as she looked around
the tiny, clean cabin, than those in the penny dreadfuls
Lucilla had gotten from the library and hidden in their
room.

In those, the heroine had usually been helpless, a
victim waiting for the hero to rescue her in any of a
dozen dashing manners. Sarah scooped out more beans.
Well, she wasn't helpless, and as far as she could tell,
there wasn't a hero within a thousand miles.

No one would have called Jake Redman heroic—
though he'd certainly looked it when he'd ridden beside
the coach. He was insulting and ill-mannered. He had
cold eyes and a hot temper. Hardly Sarah's idea of a
hero. If she had to be rescued—and she certainly

didn't—she'd prefer someone smoother, a cavalry officer, perhaps. A man who carried a saber, a gentleman's weapon.

When she'd finished the beans, she hiccuped, wiped her mouth with the back of her hand and leaned back against the hearth, only to lose her balance when a stone gave way. Nursing a bruised elbow, she shifted. She would have replaced the stone, but something caught her eye. Crouching again, she reached into the small opening that was now exposed and slowly pulled out a bag.

With her lips caught tight between her teeth, she poured gold coins into her lap. Two hundred and thirty dollars. Sarah pressed both hands to her mouth, swallowed, then counted again. There was no mistake. She hadn't known until that moment how much money could mean. She could buy decent food, fuel, whatever she needed to make her way.

She poured the coins back into the bag and dug into the hole again. This time she found the deed to Sarah's Pride.

What an odd man he must have been, she thought. To hide his possessions beneath a stone.

The last and most precious item she discovered in the hiding place was her father's journal. It delighted her. The small brown book filled with her father's cramped handwriting meant more to Sarah than all the gold coins in Arizona. She hugged it to her as she'd wanted to hug her father. Before she rose with it, she replaced the gold and the deed under the stone.

She would read about one of his days each evening. It would be like a gift, something that each day would bring her a little closer to this man she'd never really known. For now she would go back to the stream, wash as best she could and gather water for the morning.

Jake watched her come out of the cabin with a pail in one hand and a lantern in the other. He'd made himself as comfortable as he needed to be among the rocks. There had been enough jerky and hardtack in his saddlebag to make a passable supper. Not what he'd planned on, exactly, but passable.

He'd be damned if he could figure out why he'd decided to keep an eye on her. The lady wasn't his problem. But even as he'd been cursing her and steering his horse toward town, he'd known he couldn't just ride off and leave her there alone.

Maybe it was because he knew what it was to lose everything. Or because he'd been alone himself for more years than he cared to remember. Or maybe, damn her, it had something to do with the way she'd looked coming down that bluff with her bonnet trailing by the ribbons and tears still drying on her face.

He hadn't thought he had a weak spot. Certainly not where women were concerned. He shoved himself to his feet. He just didn't have anything better to do.

He stayed well behind her. He knew how to move silently, over rock, through brush, in sunlight or in the dark of the moon. That was both a matter of survival and a matter of blood. In his youth he'd spent some years with his grandmother's people, and he'd learned more than any white man could have learned in a lifetime about tracking without leaving a mark, about hunting without making a sound.

As for the woman, she was still wearing that fancy skirt with the bustle and shoes that were made for city sidewalks rather than rough ground. Twice Jake had to stop and wait, or even at a crawl he'd have caught up with her.

Probably break an ankle before she was through, he thought. That might be the best thing that could happen to her. Then he'd just cart her on back to town. Couldn't say he'd mind too much picking her up again. She felt good—maybe too good. He had to grin when she shrieked and landed on her fancy bustle because a rabbit darted across her path.

Nope, the pretty little duchess from Philadelphia wasn't going to last a day.

With a hand to her heart, Sarah struggled to her feet. She'd never seen a rabbit that large in her life. With a little sound of distress, she noted that she'd torn the hem of her skirt. How did the women out here manage? she wondered as she began to walk again. In this heat, a corset felt like iron and a fashionable skirt prevented anything but the most delicate walking.

When she reached the stream, she dropped down on a rock and went to work with her buttonhook. It was heaven, absolute heaven, to remove her shoes. There was a blister starting on her heel, but she'd worry about that later. Right now all she could think about was splashing some cool water on her skin.

She glanced around cautiously. There couldn't be anyone there. The sensation of being watched was a natural one, she supposed, when a woman was alone in the wilderness and the sun was going down. She unpinned the cameo at her throat and placed it carefully in her skirt pocket. It was the one thing she had that had belonged to her mother.

Humming to keep herself company, she unbuttoned her blouse and folded it over a rock. With the greatest relief, she unfastened her corset and dropped it on top of the blouse. She could breathe, really breathe, for the first time all day. Hurrying now, she stripped down to her chemise, then unhooked her stockings.

Glorious. She closed her eyes and let out a low sound of pleasure when she stepped into the narrow, ankle-deep stream. The water, trickling down from the mountains, was cold and clear as ice.

What the hell did she think she was doing? Jake let out a low oath and averted his eyes. He didn't need this aggravation. Who would have thought the woman would strip down and play in the water with the night coming on? He glanced back to see her bend down to splash her face. There was nothing between the two of them but shadows and sunlight.

Water dampened the cotton she wore so that it clung here and there. When she bent to scoop up more water, the ruffles at the bodice sagged to tease him. Crouching behind the rock, he began to curse himself instead of her.

His own fault. Didn't he know minding your own business, and only your own, was the best way to get by? He'd just had to be riding along when the Apaches had hit the stage. He'd just had to be the one to tell her about her father. He'd just had to feel obliged to drive her out here. And then to stay.

What he should have been doing was getting good and drunk at Carlotta's and spending the night in a feather bed wrestling with a woman. The kind of woman who knew what a man needed and didn't ask a bunch of fool questions. The kind of woman, Jake thought viciously, who didn't expect you to come to tea on Sunday.

He glanced back to see that one of the straps of Sarah's chemise had fallen down her arm and that her legs were gleaming and wet. Her shoulders were pale and smooth and bare.

Too long on the trail, Jake told himself. Too damn long, when a man started to hanker after skinny city women who didn't know east from west.

Sarah filled the pail as best she could, then stepped

out of the stream. It was getting dark much more quickly than she'd expected. But she felt almost human again. Even the thought of the corset made her ribs ache, so she ignored it. After slipping on her blouse, she debated donning her shoes and stockings again. There was no one to see or disapprove. Instead, she hitched on her skirt and made a bundle of the rest. With the water sloshing in the pail, she made her way gingerly along the path.

She had to fight the urge to hurry. With sunset, the air was cooling rapidly. And there were sounds. Sounds she didn't recognize or appreciate. Hoots and howls and rustles. Stones dug into her bare feet, and the lantern spread more shadow than light. The half mile back seemed much, much longer than it had before.

Again she had the uncomfortable sensation that someone was watching her. Apaches? Mountain lions? Damn Jake Redman. The little adobe dwelling looked like a haven to her now. Half running, she went through the door and bolted it behind her.

The first coyote sent up a howl to the rising moon.

Sarah shut her eyes. If she lived through the night, she'd swallow her pride and go back to town.

In the rocks not far away, Jake bedded down.

CHAPTER 3

Soon after sunrise, Sarah awoke, stiff and sore and hungry. She rolled over, wanting to cling to sleep until Lucilla's maid brought the morning chocolate. She'd had the most awful dream about some gray-eyed man carrying her off to a hot, desolate place. He'd been handsome, the way men in dreams were supposed to be, but in a rugged, almost uncivilized way. His skin had been like bronze, taut over his face. He'd had high cheekbones, and the dark shadow of a beard. His hair had been untidy and as black as coal—but thick, quite thick, as it had swept down past his collar. She'd wondered, even in the dream, what it would be like to run her hands through it.

There had been something familiar about him, almost as if she'd known him. In fact, when he'd forced her to kiss him, a name had run through her mind. Then he hadn't had to force her any longer.

Drowsy, Sarah smiled. She would have to tell Lucilla about the dream. They would both laugh about it before they dressed for the day. Lazily she opened her eyes.

This wasn't the rose-and-white room she used whenever she visited Lucilla and her family. Nor was it the familiar bedroom she had had for years at school.

Her father's house, she thought, as everything came back to her. This was her father's house, but her father was dead. She was alone. With an effort, she resisted the urge to bury her face in the pillow and weep again. She had to decide what to do, and in order to decide she had to think clearly.

For some time last night she'd been certain the best thing would be for her to return to town and use the money she had found to book passage east again. At best, Lucilla's family would welcome her. At worst, she could return to the convent. But that had been before she'd begun reading her father's journal. It had taken only the first two pages, the only two she'd allowed herself, to make her doubt.

He'd begun the journal on the day he'd left her to come west. The love and the hope he'd felt had been in every word. And the sadness. He'd still been raw with grief over the death of Sarah's mother.

For the first time she fully understood how devastated he had been by the loss of the woman they'd both shared so briefly. And how inadequate he'd felt at finding himself alone with a little girl. He'd made a promise to his wife on her deathbed that he would see that their daughter was well cared for.

She remembered the words her father had written on the yellowed paper.

She was leaving me. There was nothing I could do to stop it. Toward the end there was so much pain I prayed for God to take her quickly. My Ellen, my tiny, delicate Ellen. Her thoughts were all for me, and our sweet Sarah. I promised her.

The only comfort I could give was my promise.
Our daughter would have everything Ellen wanted
for her. Proper schooling and church on Sunday.
She would be raised the way my Ellen would have
raised her. Like a lady. One day she'd have a fine
house and a father she could be proud of.

He'd come here to try, Sarah thought as she tossed
back the thin blanket. And she supposed he'd done
as well as he could. Now she had to figure what was
best. And if she was going to think, first she needed
to eat.

After she'd dressed in her oldest skirt and blouse,
she took stock of the cupboard again. She could not,
under any circumstances, face another meal of cold
beans. Perhaps he had a storage cellar somewhere, a
smokehouse, anything. Sarah pushed open the door
and blinked in the blinding sunlight.

At first she thought it was a mirage. But mirages
didn't carry a scent, did they? This one smelled of meat
roasting and coffee brewing. And what she saw was
Jake Redman sitting cross-legged by a fire ringed with
stones. Gathering up her skirt, she forgot her hunger
long enough to stride over to him.

"What are you doing here?"

He glanced up and gave her the briefest of nods. He
poured coffee from a small pot into a dented tin cup.
"Having breakfast."

"You rode all the way out here to have breakfast?"
She didn't know what it was he was turning on the spit,
but her stomach was ready for just about anything.

"Nope." He tested the meat and judged it done.
"Never left." He jerked his head in the direction of the
rocks. "Bedded down over there."

"There?" Sarah eyed the rocks with some amazement. "Whatever for?"

He looked up again. The look in his eyes made her hands flutter nervously. It made her feel, though it was foolish, that he knew how she looked stripped down to her chemise. "Let's say it was a long ride back to town."

"I hardly expect you to watch over me, Mr. Redman. I explained that I could take . . . What is that?"

Jake was eating with his fingers and with obvious enjoyment. "Rabbit."

"Rabbit?" Sarah wrinkled her nose at the idea, but her stomach betrayed her. "I suppose you trapped it on my property."

So it was her property already. "Might've."

"If that's the case, the least you could do is offer to share."

Jake obligingly pulled off a hunk of meat. "Help yourself."

"Don't you have any . . . Never mind." When in Rome, Sarah decided. Taking the meat and the coffee he offered, she sat down on a rock.

"Get yourself some supper last night?"

"Yes, thank you." Never, never in her life, had she tasted anything better than this roast rabbit in the already-sweltering morning. "You're an excellent cook, Mr. Redman."

"I get by." He offered her another hunk. This time she didn't hesitate.

"No, really." She caught herself talking with her mouth full, and she didn't care. "This is delightful." Because she doubted that his saddlebags held any linens, she licked her fingers.

"Better than a can of cold beans, anyway."

She glanced up sharply, but he wasn't even look-ing at her. "I suppose." She'd never had breakfast with a man before, and she decided it would be proper to engage in light conversation. "Tell me, Mr. Redman, what is your profession?"

"Never gave it much thought."

"But surely you must have some line of work."

"Nope." He leaned back against a rock and, taking out his pouch of tobacco, proceeded to roll a cigarette. She looked as fresh and neat as a daisy, he thought. You'd have thought she'd spent the night in some high-priced hotel instead of a mud hut.

Apparently making conversation over a breakfast of roasted rabbit took some skill. Patiently she smoothed her skirts and tried again. "Have you lived in Arizona long?"

"Why?"

"I—" The cool, flat look he sent her had her fum-bling. "Simple curiosity."

"I don't know about back in Philadelphia." Jake took out a match, scraped it on the rock and lit the twisted end of his cigarette, studying her all the while. "But around here people don't take kindly to questions."

"I see." Her back had stiffened. She'd never encoun-tered anyone to whom rudeness came so easily. "In a civilized society, a casual question is merely a way to begin a conversation."

"Around here it's a way to start a fight." He drew on the cigarette. "You want to fight with me, Duchess?"

"I'll thank you to stop referring to me by that name."

He grinned at her, but lazily, the brim of his hat shadowing his eyes. "You look like one, especially when you're riled."

Her chin came up. She couldn't help it. But she an-swered him in calm, even tones. "I assure you, I'm not at all riled. Although you have, on several occasions already, been rude and difficult and annoying. Where I come from, Mr. Redman, a woman is entitled to a bit more charm and gallantry from a man."

"That so?" Her mouth dropped open when he slowly drew out his gun. "Don't move."

Move? She couldn't even breathe. She'd only called him rude and, sweet Mary, he was going to shoot her. "Mr. Redman, I don't—"

The bullet exploded against the rock a few inches away from her. With a shriek, she tumbled into the dirt. When she found the courage to look up, Jake was standing and lifting something dead and hideous from the rock.

"Rattler," he said easily. When she moaned and started to cover her eyes, he reached down and hauled her to her feet. "I'd take a good look," he suggested, still holding the snake in front of her. "If you stay around here, you're going to see plenty more."

It was the disdain in his voice that had her fighting off the swoon. With what little voice she had left, she asked, "Would you kindly dispose of that?"

With a muttered curse, he tossed it aside, then began to smother the fire. Sarah felt her breakfast rising uneasily and waited for it to settle. "It appears you saved my life."

"Yeah, well, don't let it get around."

"I won't, I assure you." She drew herself up straight, hiding her trembling hands in the folds of her skirts. "I appreciate the meal, Mr. Redman. Now, if you'll excuse me, I have a number of things to do."

"You can start by getting yourself into the wagon. I'll drive you back to town."

"I appreciate the offer. As a matter of fact, I would be grateful. I need some supplies."

"Look, there's got to be enough sense in that head of yours for you to see you don't belong out here. It's a two-hour drive into town. There's nothing out here but rattlers and coyotes."

She was afraid he was right. The night she'd spent in the cabin had been the loneliest and most miserable of her life. But somewhere between the rabbit and the snake, she'd made up her mind. Matt Conway's daughter wasn't going to let all his efforts and his dreams turn to dust. She was staying, Lord help her.

"My father lived here. This place was obviously important to him. I intend to stay." She doubted Jake Redman had enough heart to understand her reasons. "Now, if you'd be good enough to hitch up the wagon, I'll go change."

"Change what?"

"Why, my dress, of course. I can hardly go into town like this."

He cast a glance over her. She already looked dolled up enough for a church social in her crisp white blouse and gingham skirt. He'd never known gingham to look quite so good on a woman before.

"Lone Bluff ain't Philadelphia. It ain't anyplace. You want the wagon hitched, I'll oblige you, but you'd better watch how it's done, because there's not going to be anyone around to do it for you next time." With that, he slung his saddlebags over his shoulder and walked away.

Very well, she thought after one last deep breath. He was quite right. It was time she learned how to do things for herself. The sooner she learned, the sooner she'd have no more need of him.

With her head held high, she followed him. She watched him guide the team out. It seemed easy enough. You simply hooked this and tied that and the deed was done. Men, she thought with a little smile. They always exaggerated the most basic chores.

"Thank you, Mr. Redman. If you'll wait just a moment, I'll be ready to go."

Didn't the woman know anything? Jake tipped his hat forward. He'd driven her out of town yesterday. If he drove her back this morning her reputation would be ruined. Even Lone Bluff had its standards. Since she'd decided to stay, at least temporarily, she'd need all the support she could get from the town women.

"I got business of my own, ma'am."

"But—" He was already moving off to saddle his own horse. Setting her teeth, Sarah stamped inside. She added another twenty dollars to what she carried in her reticule. As an afterthought she took down the rifle her father had left on the wall. She hadn't the least idea how to use it, was certain she wouldn't be able to in even the most dire circumstances, but she felt better having it.

Jake was mounted and waiting when she came out. "The road will lead you straight into town," he told her as she fastened her bonnet. "If you give Lucius a dollar he'll drive back out with you, then take the wagon and team back to the livery. Matt's got two horses of his own in the stables. Someone from town's been keeping an eye on them."

"A dollar." As if it were spun glass, she set the rifle in the wagon. "You charged me five."

He grinned at her. "I'm not Lucius." With a tip of his hat, he rode off.

It didn't take her long to climb up into the wagon. But she had to gather her courage before she touched the reins. Though she considered herself an excellent horsewoman, she'd never driven a team before. *You've ridden behind them,* she reminded herself as she picked up the reins. *How difficult can it be?*

She took the horses—or they took her—in a circle three times before she managed to head them toward the road.

Jake sat on his horse and watched her from a ridge. It was the best laugh he'd had in months.

B y the time she reached Lone Bluff, Sarah was sweating profusely, her hands felt raw and cramped and her lower back was on fire. In front of the dry goods store she climbed down on legs that felt like water. After smoothing her skirts and patting her forehead dry, she spotted a young boy whittling a stick.

"Young man, do you know a man named Lucius?"

"Everybody knows old Lucius."

Satisfied, Sarah drew a coin out of her bag. "If you can find Lucius and tell him Miss Sarah Conway wishes to see him, you can have this penny."

The boy eyed it, thinking of peppermint sticks. "Yes, ma'am." He was off at a run.

At least children seemed about the same, east or west.

Sarah entered the store. There were several customers milling around, looking over the stock and gossiping. They all stopped to stare at Sarah before going back to their business. The young woman behind the counter came around to greet her.

"Good morning. May I help you?"

"Yes, I'm Sarah Conway."

"I know." When the pretty brunette smiled, dimples flashed in her cheeks. She was already envying Sarah her bonnet. "You arrived on the stage yesterday. I'm very sorry about your father. Everyone liked Matt."

"Thank you." Sarah found herself smiling back. "I'm going to need a number of supplies."

"Are you really going to stay out there, at Matt's place? Alone?"

"Yes. At least for now."

"I'd be scared to death." The brunette gave her an appraising look, then offered a hand. "I'm Liza Cody. No relation."

"I beg your pardon?"

"To Buffalo Bill. Most people ask. Welcome to Lone Bluff."

"Thank you."

With Liza's help, Sarah began to gather supplies and introductions. Within twenty minutes she'd nodded to half the women in Lone Bluff, been given a recipe for biscuits and been asked her opinion of the calico fabric just arrived from St. Joe.

Her spirits rose dramatically. Perhaps the women dressed less fashionably than their counterparts in the East, but they made her feel welcome.

"Ma'am."

Sarah turned to see Lucius, hat in hand. Beside him, the young boy was nearly dancing in anticipation of the penny. The moment it was in his hand, he raced to the jars of hard candy and began to negotiate.

"Mr. . . ."

"Just Lucius, ma'am."

"Lucius, I was told you might be willing to drive my supplies back for me, then return the wagon and team to the livery."

He pushed his chaw into his cheek and considered. "Well, now, maybe I would."

"I'd be willing to give you a dollar for your trouble."

He grinned, showing a few yellowed—and several missing—teeth. "Glad to help, Miss Conway."

"Perhaps you'd begin by loading my supplies."

Leaving him to it, Sarah turned back to Liza. "Miss Cody."

"Liza, please."

"Liza, I wonder if you might have any tea, and I would dearly love some fresh eggs."

"Don't get much call for tea, but we've got some in the back." Liza opened the door to the rear storeroom. Three fat-bellied puppies ran out. "John Cody, you little monster. I told you to keep these pups outside."

Laughing, Sarah crouched down to greet them. "Oh, they're adorable."

"One's adorable, maybe," Liza muttered. As usual, her young brother was nowhere in sight when she needed him. "Three's unmanageable. Just last night they chewed through a sack of meal. Pop finds out, he'll take a strap to Johnny."

A brown mutt with a black circle around his left eye jumped into Sarah's lap. And captured her heart. "You're a charmer, aren't you?" She laughed as he bathed her face.

"A nuisance is more like it."

"Will you sell one?"

"Sell?" Liza stretched to reach the tea on a high shelf. "My pop'd pay you to take one."

"Really?" With the brown pup cradled in her arms, Sarah stood again. "I'd love to have one. I could use the company."

Liza added the tea and eggs to Sarah's total. "You want that one, you take it right along." She grinned when the pup licked Sarah's face again. "He certainly seems taken with you."

"I'll take very good care of him." Balancing the dog, she took out the money to pay her bill. "Thank you for everything."

Liza counted out the coins before she placed them in the cash drawer and took out Sarah's change. Pop would be pleased, she thought. Not only because of the pup, but because Miss Conway was a cash customer. Liza was pleased because Sarah was young and pretty and would surely know everything there was to know about the latest fashions.

"It's been nice meeting you, Miss Conway."

"Sarah."

Liza smiled again and walked with Sarah to the door. "Maybe I'll ride out and see you, if you don't mind."

"I'd love it. Anytime at all."

Abruptly Liza lifted a hand to pat her hair. "Good morning, Mr. Carlson."

"Liza, you're looking pretty as ever." She blushed and fluttered, though Carlson's eyes were on Sarah.

"Samuel Carlson, this is Sarah Conway."

"Delighted." Carlson's smile made his pale, handsome face even more attractive. It deepened the already-brilliant blue of his eyes. When he lifted Sarah's hand to his lips in a smooth, cavalier gesture, she was doubly glad she'd come into town.

Apparently Lone Bluff had some gentlemen after all. Samuel Carlson was slim and well dressed in a beautiful black riding coat and a spotless white shirt. His trim mustache was the same rich brown as his well-groomed hair. He had, as a gentleman should, swept off his hat at the introduction. It was a particularly fine hat, Sarah thought, black like his coat, with a silver chain for a band.

"My deepest sympathies for your loss, Miss Conway. Your father was a fine man and a good friend."

"Thank you. It's been comforting for me to learn he was well thought of."

The daughter was certainly a pretty addition to a dust hole like Lone Bluff, he thought. "Word around town is that you'll be staying with us for a while." He reached over to scratch the puppy's ears and was rewarded with a low growl.

"Hush, now." Sarah smiled an apology. "Yes, I've decided to stay. At least for the time being."

"I hope you'll let me know if there's anything I can do to help." He smiled again. "Undoubtedly life here isn't what you're used to."

The way he said it made it clear that it was a compliment. Mr. Carlson was obviously a man of the world, and of some means. "Thank you." She handed the puppy to Lucius and was gratified when Carlson assisted her into the wagon. "It was a pleasure to meet you, Mr. Carlson."

"The pleasure was mine, Miss Conway."

"Goodbye, Liza. I hope you'll come and visit soon." Sarah settled the puppy on her lap. She considered it just her bad luck that she glanced across the street at that moment. Jake was there, one hand hooked in his pocket, leaning against a post, watching. With an icy nod, she acknowledged him, then stared straight ahead as Lucius clucked to the horses.

When the wagon pulled away, the men studied each other. There was no nod of acknowledgment. They simply watched, cool and cautious, across the dusty road.

S arah felt positively triumphant. As she stored her supplies, the puppy circled her legs, apparently every bit as pleased as she with the arrangement. Her nights wouldn't be nearly so lonely now, with the dog for company. She'd met people, was perhaps even on the way to making friends. Her cupboard was full, and Lucius had been kind enough to show her how to fire up the old cookstove.

Tonight, after supper, she was going to write to Lucilla and Mother Superior. She would read another page or two from her father's journal before she curled up under the freshly aired blanket.

Jake Redman be damned, she thought as she bent to tickle the pup's belly. She was making it.

With a glass of whiskey at his fingertips, Jake watched Carlotta work the room. She sure was something. Her hair was the color of gold nuggets plucked from a riverbed, and her lips were as red as the velvet drapes that hung in her private room.

She was wearing red tonight, something tight that glittered as it covered her long, curvy body and clung to her smooth white breasts. Her shoulders were bare. Jake had always thought that a woman's shoulders were enough to drive a man to distraction.

He thought of Sarah, standing ankle-deep in a stream with water glistening on her skin.

He took another gulp of whiskey.

Carlotta's girls were dressed to kill, as well. The men in the Silver Star were getting their money's worth. The piano rang out, and the whiskey and the laughter poured.

The way he figured it, Carlotta ran one of the best houses in Arizona. Maybe one of the best west of the Mississippi. The whiskey wasn't watered much, and the girls weren't bad. A man could almost believe they enjoyed their work. As for Carlotta, Jake figured she enjoyed it just fine.

Money came first with her. He knew, because she'd once had enough to drink to tell him that she took a healthy cut of all her girls' pay. If the man one of her girls was with decided to slip her a little extra, that was just fine with Carlotta. She took a cut of that, as well.

She had dreams of moving her business to San Francisco and buying a place with crystal chandeliers, gilt mirrors and red carpets. Carlotta favored red. But for now, like the rest of them, Carlotta was stuck in Lone Bluff.

Tipping back more whiskey, Jake watched her. She moved like a queen, her full red lips always smiling, her cool blue eyes always watching. She was making sure her girls were persuading the men to buy them plenty of drinks. What the bartender served the working girls was hardly more than colored water, but the men paid, and paid happily, before they moved along to one of the narrow rooms upstairs.

Hell of a business, Jake thought as he helped himself to one of the cigars Carlotta provided for her paying customers. She had them shipped all the way from Cuba, and they had a fine, rich taste. Jake had no doubt she added to the price of her whiskey and her girls to pay for them. Business was business.

One of the girls sidled over to light the cigar for him. He just shook his head at the invitation. She was warm and ripe and smelled like a bouquet of roses. For the life of him he couldn't figure out why he wasn't interested.

"You're going to hurt the girls' feelings." Perfume trailing behind her, Carlotta joined Jake at the table. "Don't you see anything you like?"

He tipped his chair back against the wall. "See plenty I like."

She laughed and lifted a hand in a subtle signal.

"You going to buy me a drink, Jake?" Before he could answer, one of the girls was bringing over a new bottle and a glass. No watered-down liquor for Carlotta. "Haven't seen you around in a while."

"Haven't been around."

Carlotta took a drink and let it sweep through her system. She'd take liquor over a man any day. "Going to stay around?"

"Might."

"Heard there was a little trouble on the stage yesterday. It's not like you to do good deeds, Jake." She drank again and smiled at him. In a movement as smooth as the liquor she drank, she dropped a hand to his thigh. "That's what I like about you."

"Just happened to be there."

"Also heard Matt Conway's daughter's in town." Smiling, she took the cigar from him and took a puff. "You working for her?"

"Why?"

"Word around is that you drove her on out to his place." She slowly blew out a stream of smoke from between her painted lips. "Can't see you digging in rock for gold, Jake, when it's easier just to take it."

"Far as I remember, there was never enough gold in that rock to dig for." He took the cigar back and clamped it between his teeth. "You know different?"

"I only know what I hear, and I don't hear much about Conway." She poured a second drink and downed it. She didn't want to talk about Matt Conway's mine or about what she knew. Something in the air tonight, she decided. Made her restless. Maybe she needed more than whiskey after all. "Glad you're back, Jake. Things have been too quiet around here."

Two men hankering after the same girl started to scuffle. Carlotta's tall Black servant tossed them both out. She just smiled and poured a third drink. "If you're not interested in any of my girls, we could make other arrangements." She lifted the small glass in a salute before she knocked it back. "For old times' sake."

Jake looked at her. Her eyes glittered against her white skin. Her lips were parted. Above the flaming red of her dress, her breasts rose and fell invitingly. He knew what she could do to a man, with a man, when the mood was on her. It baffled and infuriated him that she didn't stir him in the least.

"Maybe some other time." He rose and, after dropping a few coins on the table, strolled out.

Carlotta's eyes hardened as she watched him. She only offered herself to a privileged few. And she didn't like to be rejected.

With the puppy snoozing at her feet, Sarah closed her father's journal. He'd written about an Apache attack on the wagon train and his own narrow escape. In simple, often stark terms, he'd written of the slaughter, the terror and the waste. Yet even after that he'd gone on, because he'd wanted to make something of himself. For her.

Shivering a bit despite her shawl, she rose to replace the book beneath the stone. If she had read those words while still in Philadelphia, she would have thought them an exaggeration. She was coming to know better.

With a half sigh, she looked down at her hands. They were smooth and well tended. They were, she was afraid, woefully inadequate to the task of carving out a life here.

It was only the night that made her feel that way, Sarah told herself as she moved to check the bolt on the door. She'd done all she could that day, and it had been enough. She'd driven to town alone, stocked the cabin and replanted the vegetable garden. Her back ached enough to tell her she'd put in a full day. Tomorrow she'd start again.

The lonely howl of a coyote made her heart thud. Gathering the puppy to her breast, she climbed up for bed.

She was in her night shift when the dog started to bark and growl. Exasperated, she managed to grab him before he could leap from the loft.

"You'll break your neck." When he strained against her hold and continued to yelp, she took him in her arms. "All right, all right. If you have to go out, I'll let you out, but you might have let me know before I went to bed." Nuzzling him, she climbed down from the loft again. She saw the fire through the window and ran to the door. "Oh, my God."

The moment she yanked it open the puppy ran out, barking furiously. With her hands to her cheeks, Sarah watched the fire rise up and eat at the old, dry wood of the shed. A scream, eerily like a woman's, pierced the night.

Her father's horses. Following instinct alone, she ran.

The horses were already wild-eyed, stamping and screaming in their stalls. Muttering a prayer, Sarah dragged the first one out and slapped its flank. The fire was moving fast, racing up the walls and onto the roof. The hay had already caught and was burning wildly.

Eyes stinging from the smoke, she groped her way to the second stall. Coughing, swearing, she fought the terrified horse as it reared and shoved against her. Then she screamed herself when a flaming plank fell behind her. Fire licked closer and closer to the hem of her shift.

Whipping off her shawl, she tossed it over the horse's eyes and dragged them both out of the shed.

Blinded by smoke, she crawled to safety. Behind her she could hear the walls collapse, could hear the roar of flames consuming wood. Gone. It was gone. She wanted to beat her fists in the dirt and weep.

It could spread. The terror of that had her pushing up onto her hands and knees. Somehow she had to prevent the fire from spreading. She caught the sound of a horse running hard and had nearly gained her feet when something slammed into her.

CHAPTER 4

The night was clear, with a sharp-edged half-moon and white pinpoint stars. Jake rode easily, arguing with himself.

It was stupid, just plain stupid, for him to be heading out when he could be snuggled up against Carlotta right this minute. Except Carlotta didn't snuggle. What she did was more like devouring. With her, sex was fast and hot and uncomplicated. After all, business was business.

At least he knew what Carlotta was and what to expect from her. She used men like poker chips. That was fine with Jake. Carlotta wouldn't expect posies or boxes of chocolates or Sunday calls.

Sarah Conway was a whole different matter. A woman like that wanted a man to come courting wearing a stiff collar. And probably a tie. He snorted and kicked his mount into a trot. You'd have to see that your boots were shined so you could sit around making fancy talk. With her, sex would be . . . He swore viciously, and the mustang pricked up his ears. You didn't have sex with a woman like that. You didn't even think about it. And even if you did . . .

Well, he just wasn't interested.

So what the hell was he doing riding out to her place in the middle of the night?

"Stupid," he muttered to his horse.

Overhead, a nighthawk dived and killed with hardly a sound. Life was survival, and survival meant ruthlessness. Jake understood that, accepted it. But Sarah . . . He shook his head. Survival to her was making sure her ribbons matched her dress.

The best thing he could do was to turn around now and head back to town. Maybe ride right on through town and go down to Tombstone for a spell. He could pick up a job there if he had a mind to. Better yet, he could travel up to the mountains, where the air was cool and smelled of pine. There wasn't anything or anyone holding him in Lone Bluff. He was a free man and that was the way he intended to stay.

But he didn't turn his horse around.

When he got back from the mountains, he mused—if he got back—Miss Sarah Conway, with her big brown eyes and her white shoulders, would be long gone. Just plain stubbornness was keeping her here now, anyway. Even stubbornness had to give way sometime. If she was gone, maybe he'd stop having this feeling that he was about to make a big mistake.

As far as he could see, the biggest mistakes men made were over three things—money, whiskey and women. None of the three had ever meant enough to him to worry or fight over. He didn't plan on changing that.

Even if this woman *was* different. Somehow. That was what bothered him the most. He'd always been able to figure people. It had helped keep him alive all these years. He couldn't figure Sarah Conway, or what it was about her that made him want to see that she was safe. Maybe he was getting soft, but he didn't like to think so.

He couldn't help feeling for her some, traveling all this way just to find out her father was dead. And he had to admire the way she was sticking it out, staying at the old mine. It was stupid, he mused, but he had to admire it.

With a shrug, he kept riding. He was nearly to the Conway place, anyway. He might as well take a look and make sure she hadn't shot her foot off with her daddy's rifle.

He smelled the fire before he saw it. His head came up, like a wolf's when it scents an enemy. In a similar move, the mustang reared and showed the whites of his eyes. When he caught the first flicker of flame, he kicked the horse into a run. What had the damn fool woman done now?

There had only been a few times in his life when he had experienced true fear. He didn't care for the taste of it. And he tasted it now, as his mind conjured up the image of Sarah trapped inside the burning house, the oil she'd undoubtedly spilled spreading the fire hot and fast.

Another image came back to him, an old one, an image of fire and weeping and gunplay. He'd known fear then, too. Fear and hate, and an anguish he'd sworn he'd never feel again.

There was some small relief when he saw that it was the shed burning and not the house. The heat from it roared out as the last of the roof collapsed. He slowed his horse when he spotted two riders heading up into the rocks. His gun was already drawn, his blood already cold, before he saw Sarah lying on the ground. His horse was still moving when he slid from the saddle and ran to her.

Her face was as pale as the moon, and she smelled of smoke. As he knelt beside her, a small brown dog began to snarl at him. Jake brushed it aside when it nipped him.

"If you were going to do any guarding, you're too late."

His mouth set in a grim line, he pressed a hand to her heart. Something moved in him when he felt its slow beat. Gently he lifted her head. And felt the blood, warm on his fingers. He looked up at the rocks again, his eyes narrowed and icy. As carefully as he could, he picked her up and carried her inside.

There was no place to lay her comfortably but the cot. The puppy began to whine and jump at the ladder after Jake carried her up. Jake shushed him again and, grateful that Sarah had at least had the sense to bring in fresh water, prepared to dress her wound.

Dazed and aching, Sarah felt something cool on her head. For a moment she thought it was Sister Angelina, the soft-voiced nun who had nursed her through a fever when she had been twelve. Though she hurt, hurt all over, it was comforting to be there, safe in her own bed, knowing that someone was there to take care of her and make things right again. Sister would sometimes sing to her and would always, when she needed it, hold her hand.

Moaning a little, Sarah groped for Sister Angelina's hand. The one that closed over hers was as hard as iron. Confused, fooled for a minute into thinking her father had come back for her, Sarah opened her eyes.

At first everything was vague and wavering, as though she were looking through water. Slowly she focused on a face. She remembered the face, with its sharp lines and its taut, bronzed skin. A lawless face. She'd dreamed of it, hadn't she? Unsure, she lifted a hand to it. It was rough, unshaven and warm. Gray eyes, she thought dizzily. Gray eyes and a gray hat. Yes, she'd dreamed of him.

She managed a whisper. "Don't. Don't kiss me."

The face smiled. It was such a quick, flashing and appealing smile that she almost wanted to return it. "I guess I can control myself. Drink this."

He lifted the cup to her lips, and she took a first greedy sip. Whiskey shot through her system. "That's horrible. I don't want it."

"Put some color back in your cheeks." But he set the cup aside.

"I just want to . . ." But the whiskey had shocked her brain enough to clear it. Jake had to hold her down to keep her from scrambling out of bed. Her shift tangled around her knees and drooped over one shoulder.

"Hold on. You stand up now, you're going to fall on that pretty face of yours."

"Fire." She coughed, gasping from the pain in her throat. To balance herself, she grabbed him, then dropped her head weakly on his chest. "There's a fire."

"I know." Relief and pleasure surged through him as he stroked her hair. Her cheek was nestled against his heart as if it belonged there. "It's pretty well done now."

"It might spread. I've got to stop it."

"It's not going to spread." He eased her back with a gentleness that would have surprised her if she'd been aware of it. "Nothing to feed it, no wind to carry it. You lost the shed, that's all."

"I got the horses out," she murmured. Her head was whirling and throbbing. But his voice—his voice and the stroke of his hands soothed her everywhere. Comforted, she let her eyes close. "I wasn't sure I could."

"You did fine." Because he wanted to say more and didn't know how, he passed the cloth over her face. "You'd better rest now."

"Don't go." She reached for his hand again and brought it to her cheek. "Please don't go."

"I'm not going anywhere." He brushed the hair away from her face while he fought his own demons. "Go on to sleep." He needed her to. If she opened her eyes and looked at him again, if she touched him again, he was going to lose.

"The puppy was barking. I thought he needed to go out, so I—" She came to herself abruptly. He could see it in the way her eyes flew open. "Mr. Redman! What are you doing here? Here," she repeated, scandalized, as she glanced around the loft. "I'm not dressed."

He dropped the cloth back in the bowl. "It's been a trial not to notice." She was coming back, all right, he thought as he watched her eyes fire up. It was a pleasure to watch it. With some regret, he picked up the blanket and tossed it over her. "Feel better?"

"Mr. Redman." Her voice was stiff with embarrassment. "I don't entertain gentlemen in my private quarters."

He picked up the cup of whiskey and took a drink himself. Now that she seemed back to normal, it hit him how scared he'd been. Bone-scared. "Ain't much entertaining about dressing a head wound."

Sarah pushed herself up on her elbows, and the room reeled. With a moan, she lifted her fingers to the back of her neck. "I must have hit my head."

"Must have." He thought of the riders, but said nothing. "Since I picked you up off the ground and carted you all the way up here, don't you figure I'm entitled to know what happened tonight?"

"I don't really know." With a long sigh, she leaned back against the pillow she'd purchased only that morning. He was entitled to the story, she supposed. In any case, she wanted to tell someone. "I'd already retired for the night when the puppy began to bark. He seemed determined to get out, so I climbed down. I saw the fire. I don't know how it could have started. It was still light when I fed the stock, so I never even had a lamp over there."

Jake had his own ideas, but he bided his time. Sarah lifted a hand to her throbbing head and allowed herself the luxury of closing her eyes. "I ran over to get the horses out. The place was going up so fast. I've never seen anything like it. The roof was coming down, and the horses were terrified. They wouldn't come out. I'd read somewhere that horses are so frightened by fire they just panic and burn alive. I couldn't have stood that."

"So you went in after them."

"They were screaming." Her brows drew together as she remembered. "It sounded like women screaming. It was horrible."

"Yeah, I know." He remembered another barn, another fire, when the horses hadn't been so lucky.

"I remember falling when I got out the last time. I think I was choking on the smoke. I started to get up. I don't know what I was going to do. Then something hit me, I guess. One of the horses, perhaps. Or perhaps I simply fell again." She opened her eyes and studied him. He was sitting on her bed, his hair disheveled and his eyes dark and intense. Beautiful, she thought. Then she wondered if she was delirious. "Then you were here. Why are you here?"

"Riding by this way. Saw the fire." He looked into the cup of whiskey. If he was going to sit here much longer, watching what the lamplight did to her skin, he was going to need more than a cupful. "I also saw two riders heading away."

"Away?" Righteous indignation had her sitting up again, despite the headache. "You mean someone was here and didn't try to help?"

Jake gave her a long, even look. She looked so fragile, like something you put behind glass in a parlor. Fragile or not, she had to know what she was up against. "I figure they weren't here to help." He watched as the realization seeped in. There was a flicker of fear. That was what he'd expected. What he hadn't counted on and was forced to admire was the passion in her eyes.

"They came on my land? Burned down my shed? Why?"

She'd forgotten that she was wearing no more than a shift, forgotten that it was past midnight and that she was alone with a man. She leaned forward, and the blanket dropped to pool at her waist. Her small, round breasts rose and fell with her temper. Her hair was loose. He'd never seen it that way before. Until that moment he hadn't taken the time or the trouble to really look. A man's hands could get lost in hair like that. The thought ran through his mind and was immediately banished. It glowed warm in the lamplight, sliding over her right shoulder and streaming down her back. Anger had brought the color back to her face and the golden glow back to her eyes.

He finished off the whiskey, reminding himself that he'd do well to keep his mind on the business at hand. "Seems logical to figure they wanted to give you some trouble, maybe make you think twice about keeping this place."

"That doesn't make any sense." She leaned forward. Jake shifted uncomfortably when her thin lawn gown gapped at the throat. "Why should anyone care about an adobe house and a few sagging sheds?"

Jake set the cup down again. "You forgot the mine. Some people'll do a lot more than set a fire for gold."

With a sound of disgust, Sarah propped her elbows on her knees. "Gold? Do you think my father would have lived like this if there'd been any significant amount of gold?"

"If you believe that, why are you staying?"

The brooding look left her eyes as she glanced back at him. "I don't expect you to understand. This is all I have. All I have left of my father is this place and a gold watch." She took the watch from the tilting table beside the bed and closed her hand around it. "I intend to keep what's mine. If someone's played a nasty joke—"

Jake interrupted her. "Might've been a joke. It's more likely somebody thinks this place is worth more than you say. Trying to burn horses alive and hitting women isn't considered much of a joke. Even out here."

She lifted a hand to the wound on her head. He was saying someone had struck her. And he was right, she acknowledged with a quick shudder. He was undoubtedly right. "No one's going to scare me off my land. Tomorrow I'll report this incident to the sheriff, and I'll find a way to protect my property."

"Just what way is that?"

"I don't know." She tightened her grip on the watch. The look in her eyes said everything. "But I'll find it."

Maybe she would, he thought. And maybe, since he didn't care much for people setting fires, he'd help her. "Someone might be offering to buy this place from you," Jake murmured, thinking ahead.

"I'm not selling. And I'm not running. If and when I return to Philadelphia, it will be because I've decided that's what I want to do, not because I've been frightened away."

That was an attitude he could respect. "Fair enough. Since it appears you're going to have your hands full tomorrow, you'd best get some sleep."

"Yes." Sleep? How could she possibly close her eyes? What if they came back?

"If it's all the same to you, I'll bunk down outside."

Her eyes lifted to his and held them. The quiet understanding in them made her want to rest her head on his shoulder. He'd take care of her. She had only to ask. But she couldn't ask.

"Of course, you're welcome to. Mr. Redman . . ." She remembered belatedly to drag the blanket up to her shoulders. "I'm in your debt again. It seems you've come to my aid a number of times in a very short acquaintance."

"I didn't have to go out of my way much." He started to rise, then thought better of it. "I got a question for you."

Because she was feeling awkward again, she offered him a small, polite smile. "Yes?"

"Why'd you ask me not to kiss you?"

Her fingers tightened on the blanket. "I beg your pardon?"

"When you were coming to, you took a good, long look at me, and then you told me not to kiss me."

She could feel the heat rising to her cheeks. Dignity, she told herself. Even under circumstances like these, a woman must keep her dignity. "Apparently I wasn't in my right senses."

He thought that through and then unnerved her by smiling. For his own satisfaction, he reached out to touch the ends of her hair. "A man could take that two ways."

She sputtered. The lamplight shifted across his face.

Light, then shadow. It made him look mysterious, exciting. Forbidden. Sarah found it almost as difficult to breathe as she did when her stays were too tight. "Mr. Redman, I assure you—"

"It made me think." He was close now, so close that she could feel his breath flutter over her lips. They parted, seemingly of their own volition. He took the time—a heartbeat, two—to flick his gaze down to them. "Maybe you've been wondering about me kissing you."

"Certainly not." But her denial lacked the ring of truth. They both knew it.

"I'll have to give it some thought myself." The trouble was, he'd been giving it too much thought already. The way she looked right now, with her hair loose around her shoulders and her eyes dark, just a little scared, made him not want to think at all. He knew that if he touched her, head wound or not, he'd climb right in the bed with her and take whatever he wanted.

He was going to kiss her. Her head swam with the idea. He had only to lean closer and his mouth would be on hers. Hard. Somehow she knew it would be hard, firm, masterful. He could take her in his arms right now and there would be nothing she could do about it. Maybe there was nothing she wanted to do about it.

Then he was standing. For the first time she noticed that he had to stoop so that his head didn't brush the roof. His body blocked the light. Her heart was thudding so hard that she was certain he must hear it. For the life of her, she couldn't be sure if it was fear or excitement. Slowly he leaned over and blew out the lamp.

In the dark, he moved down from the loft and out into the night.

Shivering, Sarah huddled under the blanket. The man was— She didn't have words to describe him. The only thing she was certain of was that she wouldn't sleep a wink.

She went out like a light.

When Sarah woke, her head felt as though it had been split open and filled with a drum-and-bugle corps. Moaning, she sat on the edge of the cot and cradled her aching head in her hands. She wished she could believe it had all been a nightmare, but the pounding at the base of her skull, and the rust-colored water in the bowl, said differently.

Gingerly she began to dress. The best she could do for herself at the moment was to see how bad the damage was and pray the horses came back. She doubted she could afford two more on her meager budget. In deference to her throbbing head, she tied her hair back loosely with a ribbon. Even the thought of hairpins made her grimace.

The power of the sun had her gasping. Small red dots danced in front of her eyes, and her vision wavered and dimmed. She leaned against the door, gathering her strength, before she stepped out.

The shed was gone. In its place was rubble, a mass of black, charred wood. Determined, Sarah crossed over to it. She could still smell the smoke. If she closed her eyes she could hear the terrifying sound of fire crackling over dry wood. And the heat. She'd never forget the heat—the intensity of it, the meanness of it.

It hadn't been much of a structure, but it had been hers. In a civilized society a vandal was made to pay for the destruction of property. Arizona Territory or Philadelphia, she meant to see that justice was done here. But for now she was alone.

Alone. She stood in the yard and listened. Never

before had she heard such quiet. There was a trace of wind, hot and silent. It lacked the strength to rustle the scrub that pushed its way through the rocks. The only sound she heard was the quick breathing of the puppy, who was sitting on the ground at her feet.

The horses had run off. So, Sarah thought as she turned in a circle, had Jake Redman. It was better that way, she decided—because she remembered, all too clearly, the way she had felt when he had sat on the cot in the shadowy lamplight and touched her hair. Foolish. It was hateful to admit it, but she'd felt foolish and weak and, worst of all, willing.

There was no use being ashamed of it, but she considered herself too smart to allow it to happen again. A man like Jake Redman wasn't the type a woman could flirt with harmlessly. Perhaps she didn't have a wide and worldly experience with men, but she recognized a dangerous one when she saw him.

There were some, she had no doubt, who would be drawn to his kind. A man who killed without remorse or regret, who came and went as he pleased. But not her. When she decided to give her heart to a man, it would be to one she understood and respected.

With a sigh, she bent down to soothe the puppy, who was whimpering at her feet. There was a comfort in the way he nuzzled his face against hers. When she fell in love and married, Sarah thought, it would be to a man of dignity and breeding, a man who would cherish her, who would protect her, not with guns and fists but with honor. They would be devoted to each other, and to the family they made between them. He would be educated and strong, respected in the community.

Those were the qualities she'd been taught a woman looked for in a husband. Sarah stroked the puppy's head and wished she could conquer this strange feeling that what she'd been taught wasn't necessarily true.

What did it matter now? As things stood, she had too much to do to think about romance. She had to find a way to rebuild the shed. Then she'd have to bargain for a new wagon and team. She stirred some of the charred wood with the toe of her shoe. She was about to give in to the urge to kick it when she heard horses approaching.

Panic came first and had her spinning around, a cry for help on her lips. The sunbaked dirt and empty rocks mocked her. The Lord helped those who help themselves, she remembered, and raced into the house with the puppy scrambling behind her.

When she came out again her knees were trembling, but she was carrying her father's rifle in both hands.

Jake took one look at her, framed in the doorway, her eyes mirroring fear and fury. It came to him with a kind of dull, painful surprise that she was the kind of woman a man would die for. He slid from his horse.

"I'd be obliged, ma'am, if you'd point that someplace else."

"Oh." She nearly sagged with relief. "Mr. Redman. I thought you'd gone." He merely inclined his head and took another meaningful look at the rifle. "Oh," she said again, and lowered it. She felt foolish, not because of the gun but because when she'd looked out and seen him, all her thoughts about what she wanted and didn't want had shifted ground. There he was, looking dark and reckless, with guns gleaming at his hips. And there she was, fighting back a driving instinct to run into his arms.

"You . . . found the horses."

He took his time tying the team to a post before he approached her. "They hadn't gone far." He took the rifle from her and leaned it against the house. The stock was damp from her nervous hands. But he'd seen more than nerves in her eyes. And he wondered.

"I'm very grateful." Because she felt awkward, she leaned down to gather the yapping puppy in her arms. Jake still hadn't shaved, and she remembered how his face had felt against the palm of her hand. Fighting a blush, she curled her fingers. "I'm afraid I don't know what to do with them until I have shelter again."

What was going on in that mind of hers? Jake wondered. "A lean-to would do well enough for the time being. Just need to rig one over a corner of the paddock."

"A lean-to, yes." It was a relief to deal with something practical. Her mind went to work quickly. "Mr. Redman, have you had breakfast?"

He tipped his hat back on his head. "Not to speak of."

"If you could fashion a temporary shelter for the horses, I'd be more than glad to fix you a meal."

He'd meant to do it anyway, but if she wanted to bargain, he'd bargain. "Can you cook?"

"Naturally. Preparing meals was a very important part of my education."

He wanted to touch her hair again. And more. Instead, he hooked his thumb in his pocket. "I ain't worried about you preparing a meal. Can you cook?"

She tried not to sigh. "Yes."

"All right, then."

When he walked away and didn't remount his horse, Sarah supposed a deal had been struck. "Mr. Redman?" He stopped to look over his shoulder. "How do you prefer your eggs?"

"Hot," he told her, then continued on his way.

She'd give him hot, Sarah decided, rattling pans. She'd give him the best damn breakfast he'd ever eaten. She took a long breath and forced herself to be calm. His way of talking was beginning to rub off on her. That would never do.

Biscuits. Delighted that she'd been given a brand-new recipe only the day before, she went to work.

Thirty minutes later, Jake came in to stand in the doorway. The scents amazed him. He'd expected to find the frying pan smoking with burned eggs. Instead, he saw a bowl of fresh, golden-topped biscuits wrapped in a clean bandanna. Sarah was busy at the stove, humming to herself. The pup was nosing into corners, looking for trouble.

Jake had never thought much about a home for himself, but if he had, it would have been like this. A woman in a pretty dress humming by the stove, the smells of good cooking rising in the air. A man could do almost anything if the right woman was waiting for him.

Then she turned. One look at her face, the elegance of it, was a reminder that a man like him didn't have a woman like her waiting for him.

"Just in time." She smiled, pleased with herself. Conquering the cookstove was her biggest accomplishment to date. "There's fresh water in the bowl, so you can wash up." She began to scoop eggs onto an ironstone plate. "I'm afraid I don't have a great deal to offer. I'm thinking of getting some chickens of my own. We had them at school, so I know a bit about them. Fresh eggs are such a comfort, don't you think?"

He lifted his head from the bowl, and water dripped down from his face. Her cheeks were flushed from cooking, and her sleeves were rolled up past her elbows, revealing slender, milk-white arms. Comfort was the last thing on his mind. Without speaking, he took his seat.

Sarah wasn't sure when he made her more nervous,

when he spoke to her or when he lapsed into those long silences and just looked. Gamely she tried again. "Mrs. Cobb gave me the recipe for these biscuits yesterday. I hope they're as good as she claimed."

Jake broke one, and the steam and fragrance poured out. Watching her, he bit into it. "They're fine."

"Please, Mr. Redman, all this flattery will turn my head." She scooped up a forkful of eggs. "I was introduced to several ladies yesterday while I was buying supplies. They seem very hospitable."

"I don't know much about the ladies in town." At least not the kind Sarah was speaking of.

"I see." She took a bite of biscuit herself. It was more than fine, she thought with a pout. It was delicious. "Liza Cody—her family runs the dry goods store. I found her very amiable. She was kind enough to let me have one of their puppies."

Jake looked down at the dog, who was sniffing at his boot and thumping his tail. "That where you got this thing?"

"Yes. I wanted the company."

Jake broke off a bite of biscuit and dropped it to the dog, ignoring Sarah's muttered admonition about feeding animals from the table. "Scrawny now, but he's going to be a big one."

"Really?" Intrigued, she leaned over to look. "How can you tell?"

"His paws. He's clumsy now because they're too big for him. He'll grow into them."

"I fancy it's to my advantage to own a large dog."

"Didn't do you much good last night," he pointed out, but pleased both the pup and Sarah by scratching between the dog's floppy ears. "You give him a name yet?"

"Lafitte."

Jake paused with his fork halfway to his lips. "What the hell kind of name is that for a dog?"

"After the pirate. He had that black marking around his eye, like a patch."

"Pretty fancy name for a mutt," Jake said over a mouthful of eggs. "Bandit's better."

Sarah lifted a brow. "I'd certainly never give him a name like that."

"A pirate's a bandit, isn't he?" Jake dived into another biscuit.

"Be that as it may, the name stands."

Chewing, Jake looked down at the puppy who was groveling a bit, obviously hoping for another handout. "Bet it makes you feel pretty stupid, doesn't it, fella?"

"Would you care for more coffee, Mr. Redman?" Frustrated, Sarah rose and, wrapping a cloth around the handle, took the pot from the stove. Without waiting for an answer, she stood beside Jake and poured.

She smelled good, he thought. Soft. Kind of subtle, like a field of wildflowers in early spring. At the ends of her rolled sleeves, her hands were delicate. He remembered the feel of them on his cheek.

"They taught you good," he muttered.

"I beg your pardon?" She looked down at him. There was something in his eyes, a hint of what she'd seen in them the night before. It didn't make her nervous, as she'd been certain it would. It made her yearn.

"The cooking." Jake put a hand over hers to straighten the pot and keep the coffee from overflowing the cup. Then he kept it there, feeling the smooth texture of her skin and the surprisingly rapid beating of her pulse. She didn't back away, or blush, or snatch her hand from his. Instead, she simply looked back at him. The question in her eyes was one he wanted badly to answer.

She moistened her lips but kept her eyes steady. "Thank you. I'm glad you enjoyed it."

"You take too many chances, Sarah." Slowly, when he was certain she understood his meaning, he removed his hand.

With her chin up, she returned the pot to the stove. How dare he make her feel like that, then toss it back in her face? "You don't frighten me, Mr. Redman. If you were going to hurt me, you would have done so by now."

"Maybe, maybe not. Your kind wears a man down."

"My kind?" She turned, the light of challenge in her eyes. "Just what kind would that be?"

"The soft kind. The soft, stubborn kind who's right on the edge of stepping into a man's arms."

"You couldn't be more mistaken." Her voice was icy now in defense against the blood that had heated at his words. "I haven't any interest in being in your arms, or any man's. My only interest at the moment is protecting my property."

"Could be I'm wrong." He rocked back in his chair. She was a puzzle, all right, and he'd never known how pleasurable it could be to get a woman's dander up. "We'll both find out sooner or later. Meanwhile, just how do you plan to go about protecting this place?"

Not much caring whether he was finished or not, she began to stack the plates. "I'm going to alert the sheriff, of course."

"That's not going to hurt, but it's not going to help much, either, if you get more trouble out here. The sheriff's ten miles away."

"Just what do you suggest?"

He'd already given it some thought, and he had an answer. "If I were you, I'd hire somebody to help out around here. Somebody who can give you a hand with the place, and who knows how to use a gun."

A thrill sprinted through her. She managed, just barely, to keep her voice disinterested. "Yourself, I suppose."

He grinned at her. "No, Duchess, I ain't looking for that kind of job. I was thinking of Lucius."

Frowning, she began to scrub out the frying pan. "He drinks."

"Who doesn't? Give him a couple of meals and a place to bunk down and he'll do all right for you. A woman staying out here all alone's just asking for trouble. Those men who burned your shed last night might've done more to you than give you a headache."

His meaning was clear enough, clearer still because she'd thought of that possibility herself. She'd prefer him—though only because she knew he was capable, she assured herself. But she did need someone. "Perhaps you're right."

"No perhaps about it. Someone as green as you doesn't have the sense to do more than die out here."

"I don't see why you have to insult me."

"The plain truth's the plain truth, Duchess."

Teeth clenched, she banged dishes. "I told you not to—"

"I got a question for you," he said, interrupting her easily. "What would you have done this morning if it hadn't been me bringing back the horses?"

"I would have defended myself."

"You ever shot a Henry before?"

She gave him a scandalized look. "Why in the world would I have shot anyone named Henry?"

With a long sigh, he rose. "A Henry rifle, Duchess. That's what you were pointing at my belt buckle before you fixed my eggs."

Sarah wiped the pan clean, then set it aside. "No, I

haven't actually fired one, but I can't imagine it's that complicated. In any case, I never intended to shoot it."

"What did you have in mind? Dancing with it?"

She snatched up a plate. "Mr. Redman, I'm growing weary of being an amusement to you. I realize that someone like you thinks nothing of shooting a man dead and walking away. I, however, have been taught—rightfully—that killing is a sin."

"You're wrong." Something in his voice had her turning toward him again. "Surviving's never a sin. It's all there is."

"If you believe that, I'm sorry for you."

He didn't want her pity. But he did want her to stay alive. Moving over, he took the plates out of her hands. "If you see a snake, are you going to kill it or stand there and let it bite you?"

"That's entirely different."

"You might not think it's so different if you stay out here much longer. Where's the cartridges for the rifle?"

Wiping her hands on her apron, Sarah glanced at the shelf behind her. Jake took the cartridges down, checked them, then gripped her arm. "Come on. I'll give you a lesson."

"I haven't finished cleaning the dishes."

"They'll keep."

"I never said I wanted lessons," she told him as he pulled her outside.

"If you're going to pick up a gun, you ought to know how to use it." He hefted the rifle and smiled at her. "Unless you're afraid you can't learn."

Sarah untied her apron and laid it over the rail. "I'm not afraid of anything."

CHAPTER 5

He'd figured a challenge would be the best way to get her cooperation. Sarah marched along beside him, chin up, eyes forward. He didn't think she knew it, but when she'd held the rifle that morning she'd been prepared to pull the trigger. He wanted to make sure that when she did she hit what she aimed at.

From the rubble of the burned shed, Jake selected a few pieces of charred wood and balanced three of them against a pile of rocks.

"First thing you do is learn how to load it without shooting off your foot." Jake emptied the rifle's chamber, then slowly reloaded. "You've got to have respect for a weapon, and not go around holding it like you were going to sweep the porch with it."

To prove his point, he brought the rifle up, sighted in and fired three shots. The three pieces of scrap wood flew backward in unison. "Bullets can do powerful damage to a man," he told her as he lowered the gun again.

She had to swallow. The sound of gunfire still

echoed. "I'm aware of that, Mr. Redman. I have no intention of shooting anyone."

"Most people don't wake up in the morning figuring on it." He went to the rocks again. This time he set up the largest piece of wood. "Unless you're planning on heading back to Philadelphia real soon, you'd better learn how to use this."

"I'm not going anywhere."

With a nod, Jake emptied the rifle and handed her the ammo. "Load it."

She didn't like the feel of the bullets in her hands. They were cold and smooth. Holding them, she wondered how anyone could use them against another. Metal against flesh. No, it was inconceivable.

"You going to play with them or put them in the gun?"

Because he was watching her, Sarah kept her face impassive and did as he told her.

He pushed the barrel away from his midsection. "You're a quick study."

It shouldn't have pleased her, but she felt the corners of her mouth turn up nonetheless. "So I've been told."

Unable to resist, he brushed the hair out of her eyes. "Don't get cocky." Stepping behind her, he laid the gun in her hands, then adjusted her arms. "Balance it and get a good grip on it."

"I am," she muttered, wishing he wouldn't stand quite so close. He smelled of leather and sweat, a combination that, for reasons beyond her comprehension, aroused her. One hand was firm on her arm, the other on her shoulder. Hardly a lover's touch, and yet she felt her system respond as it had never responded to the gentle, flirtatious hand-holding she'd experienced in

Philadelphia. She had only to lean back the slightest bit
to be pressed close against him.

Not that she wanted to be. She shifted, then grumbled under her breath when he pushed her into place
again.

"Hold still. Not stiff, woman, still," he told her when
her body went rigid at his touch.

"There's no need to snap at me."

"You stand like that when you fire, you're going to
get a broken shoulder. Loosen up. You see the sight?"

"That little thing sticking up there?"

He closed his eyes for a moment. "Yeah, that little
thing sticking up there. Use it to sight in the target. Bring
the stock up some." He leaned over. Sarah pressed her
lips together when his cheek brushed hers. "Steady," he
murmured, resisting the urge to turn his face into her
hair. "Wrap your finger around the trigger. Don't jerk
it, just pull it back, slow and smooth."

She shut her eyes and obeyed. The rifle exploded in
her hands and would have knocked her flat on her back
if he hadn't been there to steady her. She screamed,
afraid she'd shot herself.

"Missed."

Breathing hard, Sarah whirled around. Always a
cautious man, Jake took the rifle from her. "You might
have warned me." She brought her hand up to nurse
her bruised shoulder. "It felt like someone hit me with
a rock."

"It's always better to find things out firsthand. Try
it again."

With her teeth clenched, Sarah took the rifle and
managed to get back into position.

"This time use your arm instead of your shoulder
to balance it. Lean in a bit."

"My ears are ringing."

"You'll get used to it." He put a steadying hand on her waist. "It helps if you keep your eyes open. Sight low. Good. Now pull the trigger."

This time she was braced for the kick and just staggered a little. Jake kept a hand at her waist and looked over her head. "You caught a corner of it."

"I did?" She looked for herself. "I did!" Laughing, she looked over her shoulder at him. "I want to do it again." She lifted the rifle and didn't complain when Jake pushed the barrel three inches to the right. She kept her eyes wide open this time as she pressed her finger down on the trigger. She let out a whoop when the wood flew off the rocks. "I hit it."

"Looks like."

"I really hit it. Imagine." When he took the gun from her, she shook her hair back and laughed. "My arm's tingling."

"It'll pass." He was surprised he could speak. The way she looked when she laughed made his throat slam shut. He wasn't a man for pretty words, not for saying them or for thinking them. But just now it ran through his head that she looked like an angel in the sunlight, with her hair the color of wet wheat and her eyes like gold dust.

And he wanted her, as he'd wanted few things in his life. Slowly, wanting to give himself time to regain control, he walked over to the rocks to pick up the target. She had indeed hit it. The hole was nearly at the top, and far to the right of center, but she'd hit it. He walked back to drop the wood in Sarah's hands and watched her grin about it.

"Trouble is, most things you shoot at don't sit nice and still like a block of wood."

He was determined to spoil it for her, Sarah thought, studying his cool, unreadable eyes. The man was impossible to understand. One moment he was going to the trouble to teach her how to shoot the rifle, and the next he couldn't even manage the smallest of compliments because she'd learned well. The devil with him.

"Mr. Redman, it's very apparent that nothing I do pleases you." She tossed the block of wood aside. "Isn't it fortunate for both of us that it doesn't matter in the least?" With that she gathered up her skirts and began to stamp back toward the house. She managed no more than a startled gasp as he spun her around.

She knew that look, she thought dazedly as she stared at him. It was the same one she'd first seen on his face, when he'd ridden beside the stage, firing his pistol over his shoulder. She hadn't a clue as to how to deal with him now, so she took the only option that came to mind.

"Take your hands off me."

"I warned you, you took too many chances." His grip only tightened when she tried to shrug him off. "It's not smart to turn your back on a man who's holding a loaded gun."

"Did you intend to shoot me in the back, Mr. Redman?" It was an unfair remark, and she knew it. But she wanted to get away from him, quickly, until that look faded from his eyes. "I wouldn't put that, or anything else, past you. You're the rudest, most ill-mannered, most ungentlemanly man I've ever met. I'll thank you to get back on your horse and ride off my land."

He'd resisted challenges before, but he'd be damned if he'd resist this one. From the first time he'd seen her she'd started an itch in him. It was time he scratched it.

"Seems to me you need another lesson, Duchess."

"I neither need nor want anything from you. And I won't be called by that ridiculous name." Her breath

came out in a whoosh when he dragged her against him.
He saw her eyes go wide with shock.

"Then I won't call you anything." He was still holding the rifle. With his eyes on hers, he slid his hand up
her back to gather up her hair. "I don't much like talking, anyway."

She fought him. At least she needed to believe she
did. Despite her efforts, his mouth closed over hers.
In that instant the sun was blocked out and she was
plunged, breathless, into the deepest, darkest night.

His body was like iron. His arm bonded her against
him so that she had no choice, really no choice, but to
absorb the feel of him. He made her think of the rifle,
slim and hard and deadly. Through the shock, the panic
and the excitement she felt the fast, uneven beating of
his heart against hers.

Her blood had turned into some hot, foreign liquid
that made her pulse leap and her heart thud. The rough
stubble of his beard scraped her face, and she moaned.
From the pain, she assured herself. It couldn't be from
pleasure.

And yet . . . Her hands were on his shoulders, holding on now rather than pushing away.

He wondered if she knew she packed a bigger kick
than her father's rifle. He'd never known that anything
so sweet could be so potent. That anything so delicate
could be so strong. She had him by the throat and didn't
even know it. And he wanted more. In a move too desperate to be gentle, he dragged her head back by the hair.

She gasped in the instant he allowed her to breathe,
dragging in air, unaware that she'd been stunned into
holding her breath. Then his mouth was on hers again,
his tongue invading, arousing in a way she hadn't
known she could be aroused, weakening in a way she
hadn't believed she could be weakened.

She moaned again, but this time there was no denying the pleasure. Tentatively, then boldly, she answered
the new demand. Savoring the hot, salty taste of his lips,
she ran her hands along the planes of his face and into
his hair. Glorious. No one had ever warned her that a
kiss could make the body burn and tremble and yearn.
A sound of stunned delight caught in her throat.

The sound lit fires in him that he knew could never
be allowed to burn free. She was innocent. Any fool
could see that. And he . . . he hadn't been innocent
since he'd drawn his first breath. There were lines he
crossed, laws he broke. But this one had to be respected.
He struggled to clear his mind, but she filled it. Her
arms were around his neck, pulling him closer, pulling
him in. And her mouth . . . Sweet Lord, her mouth. His
heart was hammering in his head, in his loins . . . all
from the taste of her. Honeyed whiskey. A man could
drown in it.

Afraid he would, and even more afraid he'd want
to, he pushed her away. Her eyes were dark and
unfocused—the way they'd been last night, when she'd
started to come to. It gave him some satisfaction to see
it, because he felt as though he'd been knocked cold
himself.

"Like I said, you learn fast, Sarah." His hand was
shaking. Infuriated, he curled it into a fist. He had
a flash, an almost painful one, of what it would be
like to drag her to the ground and take everything
from her. Before he could act, one way or the other,
he heard the sound of an approaching wagon. "You
got company coming." He handed her the rifle and
walked away.

What had he done to her? Sarah put a hand to her
spinning head. He'd . . . he'd forced himself on her.
Forced her until . . . until he hadn't had to force her any

longer. Until it had felt right to want him. Until wanting him had been all there was.

Just like the dream. But this wasn't a dream, Sarah told herself, straightening her shoulders. It was more than real, and now he was walking away from her as if it hadn't mattered to him in the least. Pride was every bit as dangerous an emotion as anger.

"Mr. Redman."

When he turned, he saw her standing there with the rifle. If the look in her eyes meant anything, she'd have dearly loved to use it.

"Apparently you take chances, too." She tilted her head. There was challenge in the gesture, as well as a touch of fury and a stab of hurt. "This rifle's still loaded."

"That's right." He touched the brim of his hat in a salute. "It's a hell of a lot harder to pull the trigger when you're aiming at flesh and blood, but go ahead. It'd be hard to miss at this range."

She wished she could. She wished she had the skill to put a bullet between his feet and watch him jump. Lifting her chin, she walked toward the house. "The difference between you and me, Mr. Redman, is that I still have morals."

"There's some truth in that." He strode easily beside her. "Seeing as you fixed me breakfast and all, why don't you call me Jake?" He swung up into the saddle as a buggy rumbled into the yard.

"Sarah?" With her hands still on the reins, Liza cast an uncertain glance at her new friend, then at the man in the saddle. She knew she wasn't supposed to approve of men like Jake Redman. But she found it difficult not to when he looked so attractive and exciting. "I hope you don't mind us coming out." A young boy jumped out of the buggy and began to chase the puppy, who was running in circles.

"Not at all. I'm delighted." Sarah shaded her eyes with her hand so that she could see Jake clearly. "Mr. Redman was just on his way."

"Those sure are some pretty guns you got there, mister." Young John Cody put a hand on the neck of Jake's gray mustang and peered up at the smooth wooden grip of one of the Colt .45s he carried. He knew who Jake Redman was—he'd heard all the stories—but he'd never managed to get this close before.

"Think so?" Ignoring the two women, Jake shifted in his saddle to get a better look at the boy. No more than ten, he figured, with awe in his eyes and a smudge of dirt on his cheek.

"Yessiree. I think that when you slap leather you're just about the fastest there is, maybe in the whole world."

"John Cody." Liza stayed in the buggy, wringing her hands. "You oughtn't to bother Mr. Redman."

Jake shot her a quick, amused look. Did she think he'd shoot the kid for talking to him? "No bother, ma'am." He glanced down at Johnny again. "You can't believe everything you hear."

But Johnny figured he knew what was what. "My ma says that since you saved that stage there's probably some good in you somewhere."

This time Liza called her brother's name in a strained, desperate whisper. Jake had to grin. He shifted his attention to Sarah long enough to see that she was standing as stiff as a rod, with one eyebrow arched.

"That's right kind of her. I'll tell the sheriff about your trouble . . . Miss Conway. I reckon he'll be out to see you."

"Thank you, Mr. Redman. Good day."

He tipped his hat to her, then to Liza. "See you around, Johnny." He turned his horse in a half circle and rode away.

"Yessir," Johnny shouted after him. "Yessiree."

"John Cody." Liza collected herself enough to climb out of the buggy. Johnny just grinned and raced off after the puppy again, firing an imaginary Peacemaker. "That's my brother."

"Yes, I imagined it was."

Liza gave Johnny one last look of sisterly disgust before going to Sarah. "Ma's tending the store today. She wanted you to have this. It's a loaf of her cinnamon bread."

"Oh, how kind of her." One whiff brought memories of home. "Can you stay?"

Liza gave Sarah the bread and a quick, dimpled smile. "I was hoping I could."

"Come in, please. I'll fix us some tea."

While Sarah busied herself at the stove, Liza looked around the tiny cabin. It was scrubbed clean as a whistle. "It's not as bad as I thought it would be." Instantly she lifted a hand to her mouth. "I'm sorry. Ma always says I talk too much for my own good."

"That's all right." Sarah got out two tin cups and tried not to wish they were china. "I was taken by surprise myself."

At ease again, Liza sat at the table. "I didn't expect to run into Jake Redman out here."

Sarah brought the knife down into the bread with a *thwack*. "Neither did I."

"He said you had trouble."

Unconsciously Sarah lifted a finger to her lips. They were still warm from his, and they tingled as her arms had from the kick of the Henry. She had trouble, all right. Since she couldn't explain the kiss to herself, she could hardly explain it to Liza. "Someone set fire to my shed last night."

"Oh, Sarah, no! Who? Why?"

"I don't know." She brought the two cups to the table. "Fortunately, Mr. Redman happened to be riding by this way."

"Do you think he might have done it?"

Sarah's brow rose as she considered the possibility. She remembered the way he'd bathed her face and tended her hurts. "No, I'm quite certain he didn't. I believe Mr. Redman takes a more direct approach."

"I guess you're right about that. I can't say he's started any trouble here in Lone Bluff, but he's finished some."

"What do you know about him?"

"I don't think anyone knows much. He rode into town about six months ago. Of course, everybody's heard of Jake Redman. Some say he's killed more than twenty men in gunfights."

"Killed?" Stunned, Sarah could only stare. "But why?"

"I don't know if there always is a why. I did hear that some rancher up north hired him on. There'd been trouble . . . rustling, barn-burning."

"Hired him on," Sarah murmured. "To kill."

"That's what it comes down to, I suppose. I do know that plenty of people were nervous when he rode in and took a room at Maggie O'Rourke's." Liza broke off a corner of the slice of bread Sarah had served her. "But he didn't seem to be looking for trouble. About two weeks later he found it, anyway."

A hired killer, Sarah thought, her stomach churning. And she'd kissed him, kissed him in a way no lady kissed a man who wasn't her husband. "What happened?"

"Jim Carlson was in the Bird Cage. That's one of the saloons in town."

"Carlson?"

"Yes, he's Samuel Carlson's brother. You wouldn't know it," Liza continued, pursing her lips. "Jim's nothing like Samuel. Full of spit, that one. Likes to brag and swagger and bully. Cheats at cards, but nobody had the nerve to call him on it. Until Jake." Liza drank more tea and listened with half an ear to her brother's war whoops in the yard. "The way I heard it, there were some words over the card table. Jim was drunk and a little careless with his dealing. Once Jake called him on it, some of the other men joined in. Word is, Jim drew. Everybody figured Jake would put a bullet in him there and then, but he just knocked him down."

"He didn't shoot him?" She felt a wave of relief. Perhaps he wasn't what people said he was.

"No. At least, the way I heard it, Jake just knocked him silly and gave Jim's gun to the bartender. Somebody had already hightailed it for the sheriff. By the time he got there, Jake was standing at the bar having himself a drink and Jim was picking himself up off the floor. I think Barker was going to put Jim in a cell for the night until he sobered up. But when he took hold of him, Jim pulled the gun from the sheriff's holster. Instead of getting a bullet in the back, Jake put one in Jim Carlson, then turned around and finished his drink."

Dead's dead. "Did he kill him?"

"No, though there's some in town wished he had. The Carlsons are pretty powerful around here, but there were enough witnesses, the sheriff included, to call it self-defense."

"I see." But she didn't understand the kind of justice that had to be meted out with guns and bullets. "I'm surprised Jake—Mr. Redman—hasn't moved on."

"He must like it around here. What about you? Doesn't it scare you to stay out here alone?"

Sarah thought of her first night, shivering under the blanket and praying for morning. "A little."

"After living back east." Liza gave a sigh. To her, Philadelphia sounded as glamorous and foreign as Paris or London. "All the places you've seen, the pretty clothes you must have worn."

Sarah struggled with a quick pang of homesickness. "Have you ever been east?"

"No, but I've seen pictures." Liza eyed Sarah's trunks with longing. "The women wear beautiful clothes."

"Would you like to see some of mine?"

Liza's face lit up. "I'd love to."

For the next twenty minutes Liza oohed and aahed over ruffles and lace. Her reaction caused Sarah to appreciate what she had always taken for granted. Crouched on the cabin floor, they discussed important matters such as ribbons and sashes and the proper tilt of a bonnet while Johnny was kept occupied with a hunk of bread and the puppy.

"Oh, look at this one." Delighted, Liza rose, sweeping a dress in front of her. "I wish you had a looking glass."

It was the white muslin with the rosebuds on the skirt. The dress she'd planned to wear for her first dinner with her father. He'd never see it now. She glanced at the trunks. Or any of the other lovely things he'd made certain she had in her life.

"What's wrong?" With the dress still crushed against her, Liza stepped forward. "You look so sad."

"I was thinking of my father, of how hard he worked for me."

Liza's fascination with the clothes was immediately outweighed by her sympathy. "He loved you. Often when he came in the store he'd talk about you, about what you'd written in one of your letters. I remember how he brought in this picture of you, a drawing in a little frame. He wanted everyone to see how pretty you were. He was so proud of you, Sarah."

"I miss him." With a shake of her head, Sarah blinked back tears. "It's strange, all those years we were separated. Sometimes I could barely remember him. But since I've been here I seem to know him better, and miss him more."

Gently Liza laid a hand on her shoulder. "My pa sure riles me sometimes, but I guess I'd about die if anything happened to him."

"Well, at least I have this." She looked around the small cabin. "I feel closer to him here. I like to think about him sitting at that table and writing to me." After a long breath she managed to smile. "I'm glad I came."

Liza held out a hand. "So am I."

Rising, Sarah fluffed out the sleeves of the dress Liza was holding. "Now, let me be your looking glass. You're taller and curvier than I . . ." With her lips pursed, she walked in a circle around Liza. "The neckline would flatter you, but I think I'd do away with some of the ruffles in the bodice. A nice pink would be your color. It would show off your hair and eyes."

"Can you imagine me wearing a dress like that?" Closing her eyes, Liza turned in slow circles. "It would have to be at a dance. I'd have my hair curled over my shoulder and wear a velvet ribbon around my throat. Will Metcalf's eyes would fall right out."

"Who's Will Metcalf?"

Liza opened her eyes and giggled. "Just a man. He's a deputy in town. He'd like to be my beau." Mischief flashed across her face. "I might decide to let him."

"Liza loves Will," Johnny sang through the window.

"You hush up, John Cody." Rushing to the window,

Liza leaned out. "If you don't, I'll tell Ma who broke Grandma's china plate."

"Liza loves Will," he repeated, unconcerned, then raced off with the puppy.

"Nothing more irritating than little brothers," she muttered. With a sigh of regret, she replaced the dress in the trunk.

Tapping a finger on her lips, Sarah came to a quick decision. She should have thought of it before, she reflected. Or perhaps it had been milling around in her mind all along. "Liza, would you like a dress like that . . . in pink, like that pretty muslin I saw in your store yesterday?"

"I guess I'd think I'd gone to heaven."

"What if I made it for you?"

"Made it for me?" Wide-eyed, Liza looked at the trunk, then back at Sarah. "Could you?"

"I'm very handy with a needle." Caught up in the idea, Sarah pushed through her trunks to find her measuring tape. "If you can get the material, I'll make the dress. If you like it, you can tell the other women who come in your store."

"Of course." Obediently Liza lifted her arms so that Sarah could measure her. "I'll tell everyone."

"Then some of those women might want new dresses, fashionable new dresses." Looking up, she caught the gleam of understanding in Liza's eyes.

"You bet they would."

"You get me that material and I'll make you a dress that will have Will Metcalf standing on his head."

Two hours later Sarah was pouring water over her vegetable garden. In the heat of the afternoon, with her back smarting from the chores and sun baking the dirt almost as fast as she could dampen it, she wondered if it was worth it. A garden out here would require little less than a miracle. And she would much prefer flowers.

You couldn't eat flowers, she reminded herself, and poured the last of the water out. Now she would have to walk back to the stream and fill the pail again to have water for cooking and washing.

A bath, she thought as she wiped the back of her hand over her brow. What she wouldn't give for a long bath in a real tub.

She heard the horses. It pleased her to realize that she was becoming accustomed to the sound—or lack of sound—that surrounded her new home. With her hand shading her eyes, she watched two riders come into view. It wasn't until she recognized one as Lucius that she realized she'd been holding her breath.

"Lafitte!" she called, but the dog continued to race around the yard, barking.

"Miss Conway." Sheriff Barker tipped his hat and chuckled at the snarling pup. "Got yourself a fierce-looking guard dog there."

"Makes a ruckus, anyhow," Lucius said, swinging down from his horse. Lafitte sprang at him, gripping the bottom of his pant leg with sharp puppy teeth. Bending, Lucius snatched him up by the cuff of the neck. "You mind your manners, young fella." The second he was on the ground again, Lafitte ran to hide behind Sarah's skirts.

"Heard you had some trouble out here." Barker nodded toward the remains of the shed. "This happen last night?"

"That's right. If you'd like to come inside, I was just about to get some water. I'm sure you'd like some coffee after your ride."

"I'll fetch you some water, miss," Lucius said, taking the pail from her. "Hey, boy." He grinned down at the pup. "Why don't you come along with me? I'll keep you out of trouble." After a moment's hesitation, Lafitte trotted along after him.

"Are you thinking about hiring him on?"

With her lip caught between her teeth, Sarah watched Lucius stroll off. "I was considering it."

"You'd be smart to do it." Barker took out a bandanna and wiped his neck. "Lucius has a powerful affection for the bottle, but it doesn't seem to bother him. He's honest. Did some soldiering a while back. He's amiable enough, drunk or sober."

Sarah managed a smile. "I'll take that as a recommendation, Sheriff Barker."

"Well, now." The sheriff looked back at the shed. "Why don't you tell me what happened here?"

As clearly as she could, Sarah told him everything she knew. He listened, grunting and nodding occasionally. Everything she said jibed with the story Jake had given him. But she didn't add, because she didn't know, that Jake had followed the trail of two riders into the rocks, where he'd discovered the ashes of a campfire.

"Any reason you can think of why somebody'd want to do this?"

"None at all. There's nothing here that could mean anything to anyone other than myself. Did my father have any enemies?"

Barker spit tobacco juice in the dirt. "I wouldn't think so right off. I got to tell you, Miss Conway, there ain't much I can do. I'll ask some questions and poke around some. Could be some drifters passed through and wanted to raise some hell. Begging your pardon." But he didn't think so.

"I'd wondered the same myself."

"You'll feel safer having old Lucius around."

She glanced over to see him coming back with the pail and the puppy. "I suppose you're right." But he didn't look like her idea of a protector. It was unfortunate for her that her idea of one had taken the form of Jake Redman. "I'm sure we'll do nicely," she said with more confidence than she felt.

"I'll ride out now and again and see how you're getting on." Barker pulled himself onto his horse. "You know, Miss Conway, Matt tried to grow something in that patch of dirt for as long as I can recollect." He spit again. "Never had any luck."

"Perhaps I'll have better. Good afternoon, Sheriff."

"Good day, ma'am." He lifted a hand to Lucius as he turned for home.

CHAPTER 6

Within a week Sarah had orders for six dresses. It took all her creativity and skill to fashion them, using her wardrobe and her imagination instead of patterns. She set aside three hours each day and three each evening for sewing. Each night when she climbed up to bed her eyes and fingers ached. Once or twice, when the exhaustion overwhelmed her, she wept herself to sleep. The grief for her father was still too raw, the country surrounding her still too rugged.

But there were other times, and they were becoming more common, when she fell asleep with a sense of satisfaction. In addition to the dresses, she'd made pretty yellow curtains for the windows and a matching cloth for the table. It was her dream, when she'd saved enough from her sewing, to buy planks for a real floor. In the meantime, she made do with what she had and was more grateful than she'd ever imagined she could be for Lucius.

He'd finished building a new shed and he was busy repairing the other outbuildings. Though he'd muttered about it, he'd agreed to build Sarah the chicken coop she wanted. At night he was content to sleep with the horses.

Sometimes he watched, tickling Lafitte's belly, as she took her daily rifle practice.

She hadn't seen Jake Redman since the day he'd given her a shooting lesson. Just as well, Sarah told herself as she pulled on her gloves. There was no one she wanted to see less. If she thought about him at all—and she hated to admit she had—it was with disdain.

A hired gun. A man with no loyalty or morals. A drifter, moving from place to place, always ready to draw his weapon and kill. To think she'd almost begun to believe there was something special about him, something good and admirable. He'd helped her, there was no denying that. But he'd probably done so out of sheer boredom. Or perhaps, she thought, remembering the kiss, because he wanted something from her. Something, she was ashamed to admit, she had nearly been willing to give.

How? Sarah picked up her hand mirror and studied her face, not out of vanity but because she hoped to see some answers there. How had he managed to make her feel that way in just a few short days, with just one embrace? Now, time after time, in the deepest part of the night, she brought herself awake because she was dreaming of him. Remembering, she thought, experiencing once again that stunning moment in the sun when his mouth had been on hers and there had been no doubt in her mind that she belonged there.

A momentary madness, she told herself, placing the mirror facedown on the table. Sunstroke, perhaps. She would never, could never, be attracted to a man who lived his life the way Jake Redman lived his.

It was time to forget him. Perhaps he had already moved on and she would never see him again. Well, it didn't matter one way or the other. She had her own life to see to now, and with a little help from Liza it appeared she had her own business. Picking up the three bundles wrapped in brown paper, Sarah went outside.

"You real sure you don't want me to drive you to town, Miss Conway?"

Sarah put the wrapped dresses in the back of the wagon while Lucius stood at the horses' heads. "No, thank you, Lucius."

She was well aware that her driving skills were poor at best, but she'd bartered for the wagon with the owner of the livery stable. He had two daughters whom she'd designed gingham frocks for, and she intended to deliver them herself. For Lucius she had a big, sunny smile.

"I was hoping you'd start on the chicken coop today. I'm going to see if Mrs. Miller will sell me a dozen young chicks."

"Yes'm." Lucius shuffled his feet and cleared his throat. "Going to be a hot, dry day."

"Yes." What day wasn't? "I have a canteen, thank you."

He waited until Sarah had gained the seat and smoothed out her skirts. "There's just one thing, Miss Conway."

Anxious to be on her way, Sarah took the reins. "Yes, Lucius, what is it?"

"I'm plumb out of whiskey."

Her brow rose, all but disappearing under the wispy bangs she wore. "And?"

"Well, seeing as you're going into town and all, I thought you could pick some up for me."

"I? You can hardly expect me to purchase whiskey."

He'd figured on her saying something of the kind. "Maybe you could get somebody to buy a bottle for you." He gave her a gap-toothed smile and was careful not to spit. "I'd be obliged."

She opened her mouth, ready to lecture him on the evils of drink. With a sigh, she shut it again. The man worked very hard for very little. It wasn't her place to deny him his comforts, whatever they might be.

"I'll see what can be done."

His grizzled face brightened immediately. "That's right kind of you, miss. And I sure will get started on that coop." Relieved, he spit in the dirt. "You look real pretty today, miss. Just like a picture."

Her lips curved. If anyone had told her a week ago that she would grow fond of a smelly, whiskey-drinking creature like Lucius, she'd have thought them mad. "Thank you. There's chicken and fresh bread in the cabin." She held her breath and snapped the reins.

Sarah had dressed very carefully for town. If she was going to interest the ladies in ordering fashionable clothes from her, then it was wise to advertise. Her dress was a particularly flattering shade of moss green with a high neckline she'd graced with her cameo. The trim of rose-colored ribbon and the rows of flounces at the skirt made it a bit flirtatious. She'd added a matching bonnet, tilted low as much for dash as for added shade. She felt doubly pleased with her choice when her two young customers came running out of the livery and goggled at it.

Sarah left them to race home and try on their new dresses while she completed her errands.

"Sarah." Liza danced around the counter of the dry goods store to take both of her hands. "Oh, what a wonderful dress. Every woman in town's going to want one like it."

"I was hoping to tempt them." Laughing, Sarah turned in a circle. "It's one of my favorites."

"I can see why. Is everything all right with you? I haven't been able to get away for days."

"Everything's fine. There's been no more trouble." She wandered over to take a look at the bolts of fabric. "I'm certain it was just an isolated incident. As the sheriff said, it must have been drifters." Glancing over, she smiled. "Hello, Mrs. Cody," she said as Liza's mother came in from the stockroom.

"Sarah, it's nice to see you, and looking so pretty, too."

"Thank you. I've brought your dress."

"Well, that was quick work." Anne Cody took the package in her wide, capable hands and went immediately to the cash drawer.

"Oh, I don't want you to pay for it until you look and make sure it's what you wanted."

Anne smiled, showing dimples like her daughter's. "That's good business. My Ed would say you've got a head on your shoulders. Let's just take a look, then." As she unwrapped the package, two of her customers moved closer to watch.

"Why, Sarah, it's lovely." Clearly pleased, Anne held it up. The dress was dove gray, simple enough to wear for work behind the counter, yet flatteringly feminine, with touches of lace at the throat and sleeves. "My goodness, honey, you've a fine hand with a needle." Deliberately she moved from behind the counter so that the rest of her customers could get the full effect. "Look at this work, Mrs. Miller. I'll swear you won't see better."

Grinning, Liza leaned over to whisper in Sarah's ear. "She'll have a dozen orders for you in no time. Pa always says Ma could sell a legless man new boots."

"Here you are, Sarah." Anne passed her the money. "It's more than worth every penny."

"Young lady." Mrs. Miller peered through her spectacles at the stitches in Anne's new dress. "I'm going to visit my sister in Kansas City next month. I think a traveling suit of this same fabric would be flattering to me."

"Oh, yes, ma'am." Sarah beamed, ignoring the fact that very little would be flattering to Mrs. Miller's bulky figure. "You have a good eye for color. This fabric trimmed in purple would be stunning on you."

By the time she was finished, Sarah had three more orders and an armful of fabric. With one hand muffling her giggles, Liza walked out with her. "Imagine you talking that old fuddy-duddy Mrs. Miller into two dresses."

"She wants to outshine her sister. I'll have to make sure she does."

"It won't be easy, considering what you have to work with. And she's overcharging you for those chicks."

"That's all right." Sarah turned with a grin. "I'm going to overcharge her for the dresses. Do you have time to walk with me? I'd like to go down and see if this blue-and-white stripe takes Mrs. O'Rourke's fancy."

They started down the walkway. After only a few steps, Liza stopped and swept her skirts aside. Sarah watched the statuesque woman approach. In all her life she'd never seen hair that color. It gleamed like the brass knob on Mother Superior's office door. The vivid blue silk dress she wore was too snug at the bodice and entirely too low for day wear. Smooth white breasts rose out of it, the left one adorned with a small beauty mark that matched another at the corner of her red lips. She carried an unfurled parasol and strolled, her hips swaying shamelessly.

As she came shoulder-to-shoulder with Sarah, the

woman stopped and looked her up and down. The tiny smile she wore became a smirk as she walked on, rolling her hips.

"My goodness." Sarah could think of little else to say as she rubbed her nose. The woman's perfume remained stubbornly behind.

"That was Carlotta. She runs the Silver Star."

"She looks . . . extraordinary."

"Well, she's a—you know."

"A what?"

"A woman of ill repute," Liza said in a whisper.

"Oh." Sarah's eyes grew huge. She'd heard, of course. Even in Philadelphia one heard of such women. But to actually pass one on the street . . . "Oh, my. I wonder why she looked at me that way."

"Probably because Jake Redman's been out your way a couple times. Jake's a real favorite with Carlotta." She shut her mouth tight. If her mother heard her talking that way she'd be skinned alive.

"I should have known." With a toss of her head Sarah started to walk again. For the life of her she didn't know why she felt so much like crying.

Mrs. O'Rourke greeted her with pleasure. Not only had it been a year since she'd had a new dress, she was determined to know all there was to know about the woman who was keeping Jake so churned up.

"I thought you might like this striped material, Mrs. O'Rourke."

"It's right nice." Maggie fingered the cotton with a large, reddened hand. "No doubt it'll make up pretty. Michael . . . my first husband was Michael Bailey, he was partial to a pretty dress. Died young, did Michael. Got a little drunk and took the wrong horse. Hung him for a horse thief before he sobered up."

Not certain what response was proper, Sarah

murmured something inaudible. "I'm sure the colors would flatter you."

Maggie let out a bray of laughter. "Girl, I'm past the age where I care about being flattered. Buried me two husbands. Mr. O'Rourke, rest his soul, was hit by lightning back in '63. The good Lord doesn't always protect fools and drunkards, you know. Save me, I'm not in the market for another one. The only reason a woman decks herself out is to catch a man or keep one." She ran her shrewd eyes over Sarah. "Now you've got a rig on this day, you do."

Deciding to take the remark as a compliment, Sarah offered a small smile. "Thank you. If you'd prefer something else, I could—"

"I wasn't saying I didn't like the goods."

"Sarah can make you a very serviceable dress, Mrs. O'Rourke," Liza put in. "My ma's real pleased with hers. Mrs. Miller's having her make up two for her trip to Kansas City."

"That so?" Maggie knew what a pinchpenny the Miller woman was. "I reckon I could do with a new dress. Nothing fancy, mind. I don't want any of my boarders getting ideas in their heads." She let out a cackle.

"If a man got ideas about you, Maggie, he'd lose them quick enough after a bowl of your stew."

Sarah's fingers curled into her palms when she heard Jake's voice. Slowly, her body braced, she turned to face him. He was halfway down the stairs.

"Some men want something more from a woman than a bowl of stew," Maggie told him, and cackled again. "You ladies want to be wary of a man who smiles like that," she added, pointing a finger at Jake. "I ought to know, since I married two of them." As she spoke, she watched the way Jake and Sarah looked at

each other. Someone had lit a fire there, she decided.
She wouldn't mind fanning it a bit. "Liza, all this talk
about cooking reminds me. I need another ten pounds
of flour. Run on up and fetch it for me. Have your ma
put it on my account."

"Yes, ma'am."

Anxious to be off, Sarah picked up the bolt of material again. "I'll get started on this right away, Mrs.
O'Rourke."

"Hold on a minute. I've got a dress upstairs you
can use for measuring. Needs some mending, too. I'm
no hand with a needle. Liza, I can use two pounds of
coffee." She motioned at the girl with the back of her
hand. "Go on, off with you."

"I'll just be a minute," Liza promised as she walked
out the door. Pleased with her maneuvering, Maggie
started up the stairs.

"You're about as subtle as a load of buckshot," Jake
murmured to her.

With the material still in her hands, Sarah watched
Jake approach her. Though she was standing in the
center of the room, she had the oddest sensation that
her back was against the wall. He was staring at her
in that way he had that made her stomach flutter
and her knees shake. She promised herself that if he
touched her, if he even looked as though he might
touch her, she would slap him hard enough to knock
his hat off.

He had images of touching her. Of tasting her. Of
rolling around on the ground and filling himself with
her. Seeing her now, looking like some flower that had
sprung up out of the sand, he had to remind himself that
they could only be images.

He figured that was no reason he couldn't needle her
a bit.

"Morning, Duchess. You come by to see me?"

"Certainly not."

He couldn't help but enjoy the way her eyes fired up. Casually he brushed a finger over the fabric she held and felt her jolt. "Mighty pretty, but I like the dress you've got on better."

"It isn't for me." There was no reason in the world she should feel flattered, Sarah reminded herself. No reason at all. "Mrs. O'Rourke expressed interest in having a dress made."

"So you sew, too." His gaze traveled over her face, lingering on her mouth too long for comfort. "You're full of surprises."

"It's an honest way to make a living." Deliberately she looked down at the gun on his hip. "It's a pity not everyone can say the same."

It was difficult to say what the cool, disapproving tone made him feel. Rage, familiar and bitter-tasting. Futility, with its cold, hollow ring. Both emotions and flickers of others showed in his eyes as he stared down at her.

"So you heard about me," he said before she could follow her first impulse and lay a soothing hand on his arm. "I'm a dangerous man, Sarah." He took her chin in his hand so that her eyes stayed on his. "I draw my gun and leave women widows and children orphans. The smell of gunsmoke and death follows me wherever I go. I got Apache blood in my veins, so I don't look on killing the way a white man might. I put a bullet in a man the same way a wolf rips out throats. Because it's what I was made for. A woman like you had best keep her distance."

She heard the fury licking at his words. More, she heard frustration, a deep, raw frustration. Before he could reach the door, she was calling after him.

"Mr. Redman. Mr. Redman, please." Gathering up her skirts, she hurried after him. "Jake."

He stopped and turned as she came through the doorway. They were outside only a step, but that was enough to have the heat and dust rising around them.

"You'd do better to stay inside until Maggie comes down for you."

"Please, wait." She laid a hand on his arm. "I don't understand what you do, or who you are, but I do know you've taken the trouble to be a help to me. Don't tell me to forget it," she said quickly. "Because I won't."

"You've got a talent for tying a man up in knots," he murmured.

"I don't mean—"

"No, I don't reckon you do. Anything else you want to say?"

"Actually, I—" She broke off when she heard a burst of wild laughter from the next building. As she looked, a man was propelled headfirst through a pair of swinging doors. He landed in a heap in the dust of the road. Even as Sarah started forward, Jake shifted to block her.

"What do you think you're doing?"

"That man might be hurt."

"He's too drunk to be hurt."

Her eyes wide, Sarah looked past Jake's shoulder and saw the drunk struggle to his feet and stagger back inside. "But it's the middle of the day."

"Just as easy to get drunk in the daylight as it is when the sun's down."

She pursed her lips. "It's just as disgraceful." Whiskey might be the work of the devil, Sarah thought, but she had promised Lucius. "I wonder if I might ask you another favor?"

"You can ask."

"I need a bottle of whiskey."

Jake took off his hat and smoothed back his hair, then replaced the hat. "I thought you didn't care for it much."

"It's not for me. It's for Lucius." She was certain she heard the sound of breaking glass from the neighboring saloon as she reached for her reticule. "I'm afraid I don't know the price."

"Lucius is good for it. Go back inside," he told her, then passed through the swinging doors.

"Quite a man, isn't he?"

Sarah lifted a hand to her heart. "Mrs. O'Rourke, you startled me."

Grinning, Maggie stepped outside. "Your mind was elsewhere." She handed Sarah a bundle. "Good-looking, Jake is. Strong back, good hands. A woman can hardly ask for more." Maggie glanced over as the din from the saloon grew louder. "You don't have a fella back east, do you?"

"A what?" Distracted, Sarah inched closer to the saloon. She hated to admit it, but she was dying to see inside. "Oh, no. At least there was no one I cared for enough to marry."

"A smart woman knows how to bring a man around to marriage and make him think it was his idea all along. You take Jake—" Maggie broke off when Sarah squealed. Two men burst through the swinging doors and rolled into the street, fists flying.

"My goodness." Her mouth hanging open, Sarah watched the two men kick and claw and pummel each other.

"I thought I told you to go inside." Jake strolled out, carrying a bottle of whiskey by the neck.

"I was just— Oh!" She saw blood fly as a fist connected with a nose. "This is dreadful. You have to stop them."

"Like hell I do. Where's your wagon?"

"But you must," Sarah insisted. "You can't simply stand here and watch two men beat each other like this."

"Duchess, if I try to break that up, both of them are going to start swinging at me." He passed her the bottle of whiskey. "I don't feel much like killing anybody today."

With a huff, Sarah thrust the bottle back into his hands and followed it with the fabric and Maggie's bundle. "Then I'll stop them myself."

"It's going to be a shame when you lose some of those pretty teeth."

Taking time only to glare at him, Sarah bent down and scooped up the spittoon Maggie kept beside her doorway. Her skirts in one hand, weapon in the other, she marched toward the middle of the melee.

"That's some woman," Maggie said with a grin. Jake merely grunted. "Got grit."

"Go water down your stew."

Maggie just laughed. "She's got you, too. Hope I'm around when she figures it out."

A little breathless, Sarah dodged the rolling bodies. The men were groaning and hissing as they struggled to land punches. The smell of stale whiskey and sweat rose from both of them. She had to scramble a bit for aim before she brought the brass down with a thunk on one head and then the other. A roar of laughter, then a few cheers, poured out the doorway of the saloon. Ignoring the sound, Sarah looked down at the two men, who were frowning at her and rubbing their heads.

"You should be ashamed of yourselves," she told them, in a tone that would have made Mother Superior proud. "Fighting in the street like a couple of schoolboys. You've done nothing but bloody your faces and make a spectacle of yourselves. Now stand up." Both men reached for their hats and struggled to their feet. "I'm sure whatever disagreement you have can be better solved by talking it out." Satisfied, Sarah nodded politely, then glided back across the street to where Jake and Maggie stood.

"There." She handed Maggie the spittoon. Her self-satisfied smirk was for Jake alone. "It was only a matter of getting their attention, then applying reason."

He glanced over her head to where the two men were wrestling in the dirt again. "Yes, ma'am." Taking her arm, he started up the street before she could get it in her head to do something else. "Did you learn to swing like that in your fancy school?"

"I had occasion to observe the nuns' techniques for handling disagreements."

"Ever get knocked on the head with a spittoon?"

She tilted her head, her eyes laughing under the cover of her lashes. "No, but I know what a wooden ruler feels like." Sarah glanced in the dry goods store as she stopped by her wagon. Inside, she could see Liza flirting with a thin, gangly man with straw-colored hair and shiny brown boots.

"Is that Will Metcalf?"

Jake stowed the rest of her things in the back of the wagon. "Yeah."

"I think Liza's quite taken with him." She bit back a sigh. Romance was as far away from her right now as the beautiful house her father had built for her in his mind. Turning, she bumped into Jake's chest. His hands came up to steady her and stayed on her arms. *Not so far away,* she thought again. *It wasn't far away at all when it could reach out and touch you.*

"You got to watch where you're going."

"I usually do, I used to." He was going to kiss her again, right there in the center of town. She could feel it. She could almost taste it.

He wanted to. He wanted five minutes alone with her, though he knew there was no use, it was no good. "Sarah—"

"Good morning, Jake." Twirling her parasol, Carlotta sauntered up to the wagon. Smiling slightly she ignored the warning look he sent her and turned her attention to Sarah. She'd already decided to hate her, for what she was, for what she had. Her smile still in place, she skimmed her gaze up and down Sarah. Pure and proper and dull, she decided. Jake would be tired of her in a week. But in the meantime it would give her pleasure to make the little priss uncomfortable.

"Aren't you going to introduce me to your friend?"

Jake ignored her and kept a hand on Sarah's arm to steer her to the front of the wagon.

Sarah didn't recognize the basic female urge, the primal urge, to face the enemy down. She only knew she wouldn't have the woman smirking at her back. "I'm Sarah Conway." She didn't offer her hand, she simply nodded. It was as much of an insult as Carlotta's sneering scrutiny.

"I know who you are." Carlotta smiled, fully, even as her eyes turned to blue ice. "I knew your pa. I knew him real well."

The blow hit home. Carlotta was delighted to see it. But when her eyes skimmed up to meet Jake's, most of the pleasure she felt died. She'd seen him look at men that way when they'd pushed him too far. With a toss of her head, she turned away. He'd come around, she told herself. Men always did.

His mouth grim, Jake reached for Sarah's arm again to help her into the wagon. The moment his fingers brushed her, she jerked away.

"Don't touch me." She had to turn, to grip the edge of the wagon, until she caught the breath Carlotta had knocked out of her. All of her illusions were shattered now. The idea of her father, her own father, with a woman like that was more than she could take.

He'd have preferred to walk away. Just turn and keep going. Infuriated, he dug his hands into his pockets. "Let me help you into the damn wagon, Sarah."

"I don't want your help." She whirled back to face him. "I don't want anything from you. Do you understand?"

"No, but then I don't figure I'm supposed to."

"Do you kiss her the same way you kissed me? Did you think of me the same way you think of her and women like her?"

His hand shot out to stop her before she could scramble into the wagon. "I wasn't thinking at all when I kissed you, and that was my mistake."

"Miss Conway." Samuel Carlson stopped his horse at the head of the wagon. His eyes stayed on Jake's as he dismounted. "Is there a problem?"

"No." Instinctively she stepped between the men. Carlson's gun had a handle of polished ivory, and it looked deadly and beautiful below his silver brocade vest. It no longer shocked her to realize that even a man as obviously cultured and educated as he wouldn't hesitate to use a weapon. "Mr. Redman's been an invaluable help to me since I arrived."

"I heard you'd had some trouble."

Sarah discovered she was digging her nails into her

palms. Slowly, stiffly, she uncurled her fingers, but she could do nothing about the tension that was pounding at the base of her throat. It sprang, she knew, from the men, who stood on either side of her, watching each other, ready, almost eager.

"Yes. Fortunately, the damage wasn't extensive."

"I'm glad to hear that." At last Carlson shifted his gaze to Sarah. She heard her own sigh of relief. "Did you ride into town alone, Miss Conway?"

"Yes, I did. As a matter of fact, I'd better be on my way."

"I'd be obliged if you'd allow me to drive you back. It's a long ride for a woman alone."

"That's kind of you, Mr. Carlson. I couldn't impose."

"No imposition at all." Taking her arm, he helped her into the seat. "I've been meaning to ride out, pay my respects. I'd consider it a favor if you'd allow me to drive you."

She was about to refuse again when she looked at Jake. There was ice in his eyes. She imagined there would be a different look in them altogether when he looked at Carlotta.

"I'd love the company," she heard herself say, and she waited while Carlson tied his horse to the rear of the wagon. "Good day, Mr. Redman." Folding her hands in her lap, she let Carlson guide her team out of town.

They talked of nothing important for most of the drive. The weather, music, the theater. It was a pleasure, Sarah told herself, to spend an hour or two in the company of a man who understood art and appreciated beauty.

"I hope you won't take offense if I offer some advice, Miss Conway."

"Advice is always welcome." She smiled at him. "Even if it's not taken."

"I hope you'll take mine. Jake Redman is a dangerous man, the kind who brings trouble to everyone around him. Stay away from him, Miss Conway, for your own good."

She said nothing for a moment, surprised by the strength of the anger that rose up in her. Carlson had said nothing but the truth, and nothing she hadn't already told herself. "I appreciate your concern."

His voice was calm and quiet and laced with regret. "But you won't take my advice."

"I don't think it will be necessary. It's unlikely I'll be seeing Mr. Redman now that I've settled in."

Carlson shook his head and smiled. "I have offended you."

"Not at all. I understand your feelings for Jake—" She corrected herself carefully. "Mr. Redman. I'm sure the trouble between him and your brother was very distressing for you."

Carlson's mouth thinned. "It pains me to say that Jim brought that incident on himself. He's young and a bit wild yet. Redman's a different matter. He lives by his gun and his reputation with it."

"That sounds like no life at all."

"Now I've stirred your sympathies. That certainly wasn't my intention." He touched a hand lightly to hers. "You're a beautiful, sensitive woman. I wouldn't want to see you hurt."

She hadn't been called beautiful in what felt like a very long time. Since a waltz, she remembered, at a ball at Lucilla's big house. "Thank you, but I assure you I'm learning very quickly to take care of myself."

As they drove into the yard, the puppy bounded up, racing around the wagon and barking. "He's grown some," Carlson commented as Lafitte snapped at his ankles.

"Hush, now." Lafitte snarled when Carlson lifted Sarah from the wagon. "He has the makings of an excellent guard dog, I think. And, thank heaven, he gets along well with Lucius. May I offer you some coffee?"

"I'd like that." Once inside, Carlson took a long look. "I've had some difficulty picturing you here. A drawing room with flowered wallpaper and blue draperies would suit you."

She laughed a little as she put the coffee on. "I think it will be some time yet before I put up wallpaper and draperies. I'd like a real floor first. Please sit down."

From the tin on the shelf she took a few of the sugar cookies she'd baked earlier in the week. It pleased her to be able to offer him a napkin she'd sewed out of scrap material.

"It must be a lonely life for you."

"I haven't had time to be lonely, though I admit it's not what I'd hoped for."

"It's a pity your father never made the mine pay."

"It gave him hope." She thought of the journal she was reading. "He was a man who needed hope more than food."

"You're right about that." Carlson sipped at the coffee she served him. "You know, I offered to buy this place from him some time back."

"You did?" Sarah took the seat across from him. "Whatever for?"

"Sentiment." Carlson sent her an embarrassed smile. "Foolish, really. My grandfather once owned this land. He lost it in a poker game when I was a boy. It always infuriated him." He smiled again and sampled a cookie. "Of course, he had the ranch. Twelve hundred acres, with the best water that can be had in these parts.

But he grumbled about losing that old mine until the day he died."

"There must be something about it that holds a man. It certainly held my father."

"Matt bought it from the gambler and dived right in. He always believed he'd find the mother lode, though I don't think there is one. After the old man died and I took over, I thought it might be fitting somehow for me to bring it back into the family. A tribute. But Matt, he wouldn't part with it."

"He had a dream," Sarah murmured. "It killed him, eventually."

"I'm sorry. I've upset you. I didn't mean to."

"It's nothing. I still miss him. I suppose I always will."

"It might not be healthy for you to stay here, so close to where he died."

"It's all I have."

Carlson reached over to pat her hand. "As I said, you're a sensitive woman. I was willing to buy this place from Matt. I'd be willing to buy it from you if you feel you'd like to sell."

"Sell?" Surprised, she looked over. The sun was streaming through the yellow curtains at the window. It made a stream of gold on the floor. Before long, the strength of it would fade the material. "That's very generous of you, Mr. Carlson."

"I'd be flattered if you'd call me Samuel."

"It's very generous, and very kind, Samuel." Rising, she walked to the window. Yes, the sun would bleach it out, the same way it bleached the land. She touched a hand to the wall. The adobe stayed cool. It was a kind of miracle, she thought. Like the endurance that kept men in this place. "I don't think I'm ready to give up here."

"You don't have to decide what you want now." He rose, as well, and moved over to lay a gentle hand on her shoulder. She smiled at the gesture. It was comforting to have friends who cared.

"It's been difficult, adjusting here. Yet I feel as though I can't leave, that in leaving I'd be deserting my father."

"I know what it is to lose family. It takes time to think straight again." He turned her to face him. "I can say that I feel I knew Matt enough to be sure he'd want the best for you. If you decide you want to let it go, all you have to do is tell me. We'll leave it an open offer."

"Thank you." She found herself flustered when he lifted both her hands to his lips.

"I want to help you, Sarah. I hope you'll let me."

"Miss Conway."

She jolted, then sighed when she saw Lucius in the doorway. "Yes?"

He eyed Carlson, then turned his head to spit. "You want me to put this team away?"

"Please."

Lucius stayed where he was. "How about the extra horse?"

"I'll be riding out. Thank you for the company, Sarah."

"It was a pleasure."

As they stepped outside, Carlson replaced his hat. "I hope you'll let me call again."

"Of course." Sarah was forced to snatch up the dog when he came toward her guest, snarling and snapping. "Goodbye, Samuel."

She waited until he'd started out before she put the puppy down and walked over to Lucius.

"Lucius." She leaned over to speak to him as he unhitched the horses. "You were quite rude just now."

"If you say so, miss."

"Well, I do." Frustrated, she ducked under the horses to join him. "Mr. Carlson was considerate enough to drive me back from town. You looked at him as though you wanted to shoot him in the head."

"Maybe."

"For heaven's sake. Why?"

"Some snakes don't rattle."

Casting her eyes to the sky, she gave up. Instead, she snatched the bottle of whiskey from the wagon and watched his eyes light up. "If you want this, take off your shirt."

His mouth dropped as if she'd hit him with a board. "Beg pardon, ma'am?"

"The pants, too. I want you to strip right down to the skin."

He groped at his neckcloth. "Mind if I ask why you'd be wanting me to do that, Miss Conway?"

"I'm going to wash your clothes. I've tolerated the smell of them—and you—quite long enough. While I'm washing them, you can take that extra cake of soap I bought and do the same with yourself."

"Now, miss, I—"

"If, and only if, you're clean, I'll give you this bottle. You get a pail of water and the soap and go into that shed. Toss your clothes out."

Not sure he cared for the arrangement, Lucius shifted his feet. "And if I don't?"

"Then I'll pour every drop of this into the dirt."

Lucius laid a hand on his heart as she stamped off. He was mortally afraid she'd do it.

CHAPTER 7

Sarah rolled up the sleeves of her oldest shirtwaist, hitched up her serviceable black skirt and went to work.

They'd be better off burned, she thought as she dunked Lucius's stiff denim pants into the stream. The water turned a mud brown instantly. With a sound of disgust, she dunked them again. It would take some doing to make them even marginally acceptable, but she was determined.

Cleanliness was next to godliness.

That had been one of the proverbs cross-stitched on Mother Superior's office wall. Well, she was going to get Lucius as close to God as was humanly possible. Whether he liked it or not.

Leaving the pants to soak, she picked up his faded blue shirt by the tips of her fingers. Deplorable, she decided as she dampened and scrubbed and soaked. Absolutely deplorable. She doubted the clothes had seen clean water in a year. Which meant Lucius's skin had been just as much in need of washing. That would soon be fixed.

She began to smile as she worked. The expression on his face when she'd threatened to empty out the whiskey had been something to see. Poor Lucius. He might look tough and crusty, but underneath he was just a sweet, misguided man who needed a woman to show him the way.

Most men did. At least that was what Lucilla had always said. As she beat Lucius's weathered shirt against the rocks, Sarah wondered what her friend would think of Jake Redman. There was certainly nothing sweet about him, no matter how deep down a woman might dig. Though he could be kind. It baffled her that time and time again he had shown her that streak of good-heartedness. Always briefly, she added, her lips thinning. Always right before he did something inexcusable.

Like kissing the breath out of her. Kissing her until her blood was hot and her mind was empty and she wanted something she didn't even understand. He'd had no right to do it, and still less to walk away afterward, leaving her trembling and confused.

She should have slapped him. With that thought in mind, Sarah slapped the shirt on the water and gave a satisfied nod at the sound. She should have knocked the arrogance right out of him, and then it should have been she who walked away.

The next time . . . There would be no next time, she assured herself. If Jake Redman ever touched her again, she'd . . . she'd . . . melt like butter, she admitted. Oh, she hated him for making her wish he would touch her again.

When he looked at her, something happened, something frantic, something she'd never experienced before. Her heart beat just a little too fast, and dampness sprang out on the palms of her hands. A look was all that was necessary. His eyes were so dark, so penetrating. When he looked at her it was as if he could see everything she was, or could be, or wanted to be.

It was absurd. He was a man who lived by the gun, who took what he wanted without regret or compunction. All her life she'd been taught that the line between right and wrong was clear and wide and wasn't to be crossed.

To kill was the greatest sin, the most unforgivable. Yet he had killed, and would surely kill again. Knowing it, she couldn't care for him. But care she did. And want she did. And need.

Her hands were wrist-deep in water when she brought herself back. She had no business even thinking this way. Thinking about him. If she had to think of a man, she'd do better to think of Samuel Carlson. He was well-mannered, polished. He would know the proper way to treat a lady. There would be no wild, groping kisses from a man like him. A woman would be safe, cherished, cared for.

But she wished Jake had offered to drive her home.

This was nonsense. Sarah wrung out the shirt and rubbed her nose with the back of her damp hand. She'd had enough nonsense for the time being. She would wash thoughts of Jake away just as she washed the grime and grit and the good Lord knew what from Lucius's shirt.

She wanted her life to be tidy. Perhaps it wouldn't be as grand as she'd once imagined, but it would be tidy. Even here. Sitting back on her heels, she looked around. The sun was heading toward the buttes in the west. Slowly, like a big golden ball in a sky the color of Indian paintbrush. The rocks towered, their odd, somewhat mystical shapes rising up and up, some slender as needles, others rough and thick.

There was a light smell of juniper here, and the occasional rustle that didn't alarm her as it once would have. She watched an eagle soar, its wings spread wide. King of the sky. Below, the stream gurgled, making its lazy way over the rocks.

Why, it was beautiful. She lifted a hand to her throat, surprised to discover that it was aching. She hadn't seen it before, or hadn't wanted to. There was a wild, desolate, marvelous beauty here that man hadn't been able to touch. Or hadn't dared. If the land was lawless, perhaps it deserved to be.

For the first time since she had arrived, she felt a sense of kinship, of belonging. Of peace. She'd been right to stay, because this was home. Hers. At long last, hers.

When she rose to spread the shirt over a rock, she was smiling. Then she saw the shadow, and she looked up quickly.

There were five of them. Their black hair was loose past their bare shoulders. All but one sat on a horse. It was he who stepped toward her, silent in knee-length moccasins. There was a scar, white and puckered, that ran from his temple, catching the corner of his eye, then curving like a sickle down his cheek. She saw that, and the blade of the knife he carried. Then she began to scream.

Lucius heard the rider coming and strapped his gunbelt on over his long underwear. With soap still lathered all over his face, he stepped out of the shed. Jake pulled up his mount and took a long, lazy look.

"Don't tell me it's spring already."

"Damn women." Lucius spit expertly.

"Ain't that the truth?" After easing off his horse,

Jake tossed the reins over the rail. Lafitte immediately leaped up to rest his paws on his thigh. In the way dogs have, he grinned and his tongue lolled. "Going to a dance or something?"

"No, I ain't going anywhere." Lucius cast a vicious look toward the house. "She threatened me. Yes, sir, there's no two ways about it, it was a threat. Said less'n I took myself a bath and let her wash my clothes she'd pour out every last drop of whiskey in the bottle she brought."

With a grin of his own, Jake leaned against the rail and rolled a cigarette. "Maybe she's not as stupid as she looks."

"She looks okay," Lucius muttered. "Got a streak of stubborn in her, though." He wiped a soapy hand on the thigh of his long underwear. "What are you doing out here?"

"Came out to talk to you."

"Like hell. I got eyes. She ain't in there," he said when Jake continued to stare at the house.

"I said I came to talk to you." Annoyed, Jake flicked a match and lit his cigarette. "Have you done any checking in the mine?"

"I've taken a look. She don't give a body much free time." He picked up a rock and tossed it so that the puppy would have something to chase. "Always wanting something built or fixed up. Cooks right good, though." He patted his belly. "Can't complain about that."

"See anything?"

"I saw where Matt was working some, right enough. And the cave-in." He spit again. "Can't say I felt real good about digging my way past it. Now, maybe if you told me what it was I was supposed to be looking for."

"You'll know if you find it." He looked back at the

house. She'd put curtains on the windows. "Does she ever go up there?"

"Goes up, not in. Sits by his grave sometimes. Breaks your heart."

"Sounds like you're going soft on her, old man." He reached down to give Lafitte a scratch on the head.

"Wouldn't talk if I was you." He only laughed when Jake looked at him. There weren't many men who would have dared. "Don't go icing up on me, boy. I've known you too long. Might interest you to know that Samuel Carlson paid a call."

Jake blew out smoke with a shrug. "I know." He waited, took another drag, then swore under his breath. "Did he stay long?"

"Long enough to make up to her. Kissing her hands, he was. Both of them."

"Is that so?" The fury burned low in his gut and spread rapidly. Eyes narrowed, he flicked the cigarette away, half finished, and watched it smolder. "Where is she?"

"Down to the stream, I imagine."

Lucius smothered a laugh and bent down to pick up Lafitte before the puppy could scramble after Jake. "I wouldn't, if'n I was you, young fella. There's going to be fireworks fit for Independence Day."

Jake wasn't sure what he was going to do, but he didn't think Sarah was going to like it. He hoped she didn't. She needed a short rein, he decided. And he was going to see to it himself. Letting Carlson paw all over her. Just the thought of it made small, jagged claws of jealousy slice through him.

When he heard her scream, both guns were out of their holsters and in his hands in a heartbeat. He took the last quarter of a mile at a run, her screams and the sound of running horses echoing in his head.

When he reached the stream he saw the dust the ponies had kicked up. Even at a distance he recognized
Little Bear's profile. There was a different kind of
fire in him now. It burned ice-cold as he holstered his
weapons. Lafitte came tearing down the path, snarling.

"You're too late again," Jake told the dog as he sniffed
the ground and whined. He turned as Lucius came running in nothing more than his gunbelt and long johns.

"What happened?" Jake said nothing. Hunkering
down, Lucius studied the marks left by the struggle.
"'Paches." He saw his shirt, freshly washed and drying
in the sun. "Damn it all to hell." Still swearing, he raced
down the path toward Jake. "Let me get on my spare
shirt and my boots. They don't have much of a lead."

"I'm going alone."

"There was four of them, maybe more."

"Five." Jake strode back into the clearing. "I ride
alone."

"Listen, boy, even if it was Little Bear, that don't
give you no guarantees. You weren't no more than kids
last time, and you chose different ways."

"It was Little Bear, and I'm not looking for guarantees." He swung into the saddle. "I'm going to get her
back."

Lucius put a hand on the saddle horn. "See that you
do."

"If I'm not back tomorrow sundown, go get Barker.
I'll leave a trail even he can follow." He kicked his horse
into a gallop and headed north.

S he hadn't fainted, but she wasn't so sure that was a
blessing. She'd been tossed roughly onto the back
of a horse, and she was forced to grip its mane to keep
from tumbling off. The Indian with the scar rode be-

hind her, calling out to his companions occasionally and gesturing with a new government-issue Winchester. He'd dragged her by her hair to get her astride the horse, and he still seemed fascinated by it. When she felt him push his nose into it, she closed her eyes, shuddered and prayed.

They rode fast, their ponies apparently tireless and obviously sure-footed, as they left the flats for the rocks and the hills. The sun was merciless here. She felt it beating down on her head as she struggled not to weep. She didn't want to die weeping. They would undoubtedly kill her. But what frightened her more than whatever death was in store for her was what they would do to her first.

She'd heard stories, horrible, barbaric stories, about what was done to captive white women. Once, she'd thought them all foolishness, like the stories of bogeymen conjured up to frighten small children. Now she feared that the stories were pale reflections of reality.

They climbed higher, to where the air cooled and the mountains burst to life with pine and fast-running streams. When the horses slowed, she slumped forward, her thighs screaming from the effort of the ride. They talked among themselves in words that meant nothing to her. Time had lost all meaning, as well. It had been hours. She was only sure of that because the sun was low and just beginning to turn the western sky red. Bloodred.

They stopped, and for one wild moment she thought about kicking the horse and trying to ride free. Then she was being dragged to the ground. With the breath knocked from her, she tried to get her bearings.

Three of the men were filling waterskins at the stream. One seemed hardly more than a boy, but she doubted age mattered. They watered their mounts and paid no attention to her.

Pushing herself up on her elbows, she saw the scar-faced Apache arguing with one she now took to be the leader. He had a starkly beautiful face, lean and chiseled and cold. There was an eagle feather in his hair, and around his neck was a string of what looked like small bleached bones. He studied her dispassionately, then signaled to the other man.

She began to pray again, silently, desperately, as the scar-faced brave advanced on her. He dragged her to her feet and began to toy with her hair. The leader barked out an order that the brave just snarled at. He reached for her throat. Sarah held her breath as he ripped the cameo from her shirtwaist. Apparently satisfied for the moment, he pushed her toward the stream and let her drink.

She did, greedily. Perhaps death wasn't as close as she'd feared. Perhaps somehow, somehow, she could evade it. She wouldn't despair, she told herself as she soothed her burning skin with the icy water. Someone would come after her. Someone.

Jake.

She nearly cried out his name when she was dragged to her feet again. Her captor had fastened her brooch to his buckskin vest. Like a trophy, she thought. Her mother's cameo wouldn't be a trophy for anyone. Furious, she reached for it, and was slapped to the ground. She felt the shirtwaist rip away from her shoulder as she was pulled up by it. Instinctively she began to fight, using teeth and nails. She heard a cry of pain, then rolling masculine laughter. As she kicked and squirmed, her hands were bound together with a leather strap. She was sobbing now, but with rage. Tossed astride the pony again, she felt her ankles bound tight under its belly.

There was the taste of blood in her mouth, and tears in her eyes. They continued to climb.

She dozed somehow. When the pain in her arms and legs grew unbearable, it seemed the best escape. The height was dizzying. They rode along the edge of a narrow canyon that seemed to drop forever. Into hell, she thought as her eyes drooped again. Straight into hell.

Wherever they were taking her, it was a different world, one of forests and rivers and sheer cliffs. It didn't matter. She would die or she would escape. There was nothing else.

Survival. That's all there is.

She hadn't understood what Jake had meant when he'd said that to her. Now she did. There were times when there was nothing but life or death. If she could escape, and had to kill to do so, then she would kill. If she could not escape, and they were planning what she feared they were, she would find a way to kill herself.

They climbed. Endlessly, it seemed to Sarah, they rode up a winding trail and into the twilight. Around her she could hear the call of night birds, high and musical, accented by the hollow hooting of an owl. The trees glowed gold and red, and as the wind rose it sounded through them. The air chilled, working through the torn shirtwaist. Only her pride remained as she shivered in silence.

Exhaustion had her dreaming. She was riding through the forest with Lucilla, chatting about the new bonnet they had seen that morning. They were laughing and talking about the men they would fall in love with and marry. They would be tall and strong and devastatingly handsome.

She dreamed of Jake—of a dream kiss, and a real one. She dreamed of him riding to her, sweeping her up on his big gray mount and taking her away. Holding her, warming her, keeping her safe.

Then the horses stopped.

Her heart was too weary even for prayer as her ankle bonds were cut. She was pulled unresisting from the horse, then sprawled on the ground when her legs buckled under her. There was no energy left in her for weeping, so she lay still, counting each breath. She must have slept, because when she came to again, she heard the crackling of a fire and the quiet murmuring of men at a meal.

Biting back a moan, she tried to push herself up. Before she could, a hand was on her shoulder, rolling her onto her back.

Her captor leaned over her, his dark eyes gleaming in the firelight. He spoke, but the words meant nothing to her. She would fight him, she promised herself. Even knowing she would lose, she would fight. He touched her hair, running his fingers through it, lifting it and letting it fall. It must have pleased him, for he grinned at her before he took out his knife.

She thought, almost hoped, that he would slit her throat and be done with it. Instead, he began to cut her skirt away. She kicked, as viciously as she could, but he only parried the blows, then locked her legs with his own. Hearing her skirt rip, she struck out blindly with her bound hands. As he raised his own to strike her, there was a call from the campfire. Her kidnappers rose, bows and rifles at the ready.

She saw the rider come out of the gloom and into the flickering light. Another dream, she thought with a little sob. Then he looked at her. Strength poured back into her body, and she scrambled to her feet.

"Jake!"

She would have run to him, but she was yanked ruthlessly back. He gave no sign, barely glanced her way as he walked his horse toward the group of Apaches. He spoke, but the words were strange, incomprehensible to her.

"Much time has passed, Little Bear."

"I felt breath on my back today." Little Bear lowered his rifle and waited. "I thought never to see you again, Gray Eyes."

Slowly, ignoring the rage bubbling inside him, Jake dismounted. "Our paths have run apart. Now they come together again." He looked steadily into eyes he knew as well as he knew his own. There was between them a love few men would have understood. "I remember a promise made between boys. We swore in blood that one would never lift a hand against the other."

"The promise sworn in blood has not been forgotten." Little Bear held out his hand. They gripped firm, hand to elbow. "Will you eat?"

With a nod, Jake sat by the fire to share the venison. Out of the corner of his eye, he saw Sarah huddled on the ground, watching. Her face was pale with fear and exhaustion. He could see bruises of fatigue under eyes that were glazed with it. Her clothes were torn, and he knew, as he ate and drank, that she must be cold. But if he wanted her alive, there were traditions to be observed.

"Where is the rest of our tribe?"

"Dead. Lost. Running." Little Bear stared broodingly into the fire. "The long swords have cut us down like deer. Those who are left are few and hide in the mountains. Still they come."

"Crooked Arm? Straw Basket?"

"They live. North, where the winters are long and the game is scarce." He turned his head again, and Jake saw a cold, depthless anger—one he understood. "The children do not laugh, Gray Eyes, nor do the women sing."

They talked, as the fire blazed, of shared memories, of people both had loved. Their bond was as strong as it had been when Jake had lived and learned and felt like an Apache. But they both knew that time had passed.

When the meal was over, Jake rose from the fire. "You have taken my woman, Little Bear. I have come to take her back."

Little Bear held up a hand before the scarred man beside him could speak. "She is not my prisoner, but Black Hawk's. It is not for me to return her to you."

"Then the promise can be kept between us." He turned to Black Hawk. "You have taken my woman."

"I have not finished with her." He put a hand on the hilt of his knife. "I will keep her."

He could have bargained with him. A rifle was worth more than a woman. But bargaining would have cost him face. He had claimed Sarah as his, and there was only one way to take her back.

"The one who lives will keep her." He unstrapped his guns, handing them to Little Bear. There were few men he would have trusted with his weapons. "I will speak with her." He moved to Sarah as Black Hawk began to chant in preparation for the fight.

"I hope you enjoyed your meal," she said, sniffing. "I actually thought you might have come to rescue me."

"I'm working on it."

"Yes, I could see that. Sitting by the fire, eating, telling stories. My hero."

His grin flashed as he hauled her against him for a

long, hard kiss. "You're a hell of a woman, Sarah. Just sit tight and let me see what I can do."

"Take me home." Pride abandoned, she gripped the front of his shirt. "Please, just take me home."

"I will." He squeezed her hands as he removed them from his shirt. Then he rose, and he, too, began to chant. If there was magic, he wanted his share.

They stood side by side in the glow of the fire as the youngest warrior bound their left wrists together. The glitter of knives had Sarah pushing herself to her feet. Little Bear closed a hand over her arm.

"You cannot stop it," he said in calm, precise English.

"No!" She struggled as she watched the blades rise. "Oh, God, no!" They came down, whistling.

"I will spill your white blood, Gray Eyes," Black Hawk murmured as their blades scraped, edge to edge.

Locked wrist to wrist, they hacked, dodged, advanced. Jake fought in grim silence. If he lost, even as his blood poured out, Black Hawk would celebrate his victory by raping Sarah. The thought of it, the fury of it, broke his concentration, and Black Hawk pushed past his guard and sliced down his shoulder. Blood ran warm down his arm. Concentrating on the scent of it, he blocked Sarah from his mind and fought to survive.

In the frigid night air, their faces gleamed with sweat. The birds had flown away at the sound of blades and the smell of blood. The only sound now was the harsh breathing of the two men locked in combat, intent on the kill. The other men formed a loose circle around them, watching, the inevitability of death accepted.

Sarah stood with her bound hands at her mouth, holding back the need to scream and scream until she had no air left. At the first sight of Jake's blood she had closed her eyes tight. But fear had had them wide again in an instant.

Little Bear still held her arm, his grip light but inescapable. She already understood that she was to be a kind of prize for the survivor. As Jake narrowly deflected Black Hawk's blade, she turned to the man beside her.

"Please, if you stop it, let him live, I'll go with you willingly. I won't fight or try to escape."

For a moment, Little Bear took his eyes away from the combat. Gray Eyes had chosen his woman well. "Only death stops it now."

As she watched, both men tumbled to the ground. She saw Black Hawk's knife plunge into the dirt an inch from Jake's face. Even as he drew it out, Jake's knife was ripping into his flesh. They rolled toward the fire.

Jake didn't feel the heat, only an ice-cold rage. The fire seared the skin on his arm before he yanked free. The hilt of his knife was slick with his own sweat but the blade dripped red with his opponent's blood.

The horses whinnied and shied when the men rolled too close. Then they were in the shadows. Sarah could see only a dark blur and the sporadic gleam of a knife. But she could hear desperate grunts and the scrape of metal. Then she heard nothing but the sound of a man breathing hard. One man. With her heart in her throat, she waited to see who would come back into the light.

Bruised, bloodied, Jake walked to her. Saying nothing, he cut through her bonds with the blade of the stained knife. Still silent, he pushed it into his boot and took his guns back from Little Bear.

"He was a brave warrior," Little Bear said.

With pain and triumph singing through him, Jake strapped on his gunbelt. "He died a warrior's death." He offered his hand again. "May the spirits ride with you, brother."

"And with you, Gray Eyes."

Jake held out a hand for Sarah. When he saw that she was swaying on her feet, he picked her up and carried her to his horse. "Hold on," he told her, swinging up into the saddle behind her. He rode out of camp without looking back, knowing he would never see Little Bear again.

She didn't want to cry, but she couldn't stop. Her only comfort was that her tears were silent and he couldn't hear them. Or so she thought. They'd ridden no more than ten minutes at a slow walk when he turned her around in the saddle to cradle her against him.

"You've had a bad time, Duchess. Go on and cry for a while."

So she wept shamelessly, her cheek pressed against his chest, the movement of the horse lulling her. "I was so afraid." Her voice hitching, she clung to him. "He was going to—"

"I know. You don't want to think about it." He didn't. If he did, he'd lose the already-slippery grip he had on his control. "It's all over now."

"Will they come after us?"

"No."

"How can you be sure?" As the tears passed, the fear doubled back.

"It wouldn't be honorable."

"Honorable?" She lifted her head to look at him. In the moonlight his face looked hard as rock. "But they're Apache."

"That's right. They'll stand by their honor a lot longer than any white man."

"But—" She had forgotten for a moment the Apache in him. "You seemed to know them."

"I lived with them five years. Little Bear, the one with the eagle feather, is my cousin." He stopped and dismounted. "You're cold. I'll build a fire and you can rest awhile." He pulled a blanket out of his saddlebag and tossed it over her shoulders. Too tired to argue, Sarah wrapped it tight around herself and sat on the ground.

He had a fire burning quickly and started making coffee. Without hesitation, Sarah bit into the jerky he gave her and warmed her hands over the flames.

"The one you . . . fought with. Did you know him?"

"Yeah."

He'd killed for her, she thought, and had to struggle not to weep again. Perhaps it had been a member of his own family, an old friend. "I'm sorry," she managed.

"For what?" He poured coffee into a cup, then pushed it into her trembling hands.

"For all of it. They were just there, all at once. There was nothing I could do." She drank, needing the warmth badly. "When I was in school, we would read the papers, hear stories. I never really believed it. I was certain that the army had everything under control."

"You read about massacres," he said with a dull fury in his voice that had her looking up again. "About settlers slaughtered and wagon trains attacked. You read about savages scalping children. It's true enough. But did you read any about soldiers riding into camps and butchering, raping women, putting bullets in babies long after treaties were signed and promises made? Did you hear stories about poisoned food and contaminated blankets sent to the reservations?"

"But that can't be."

"The white man wants the land, and the land isn't his—or wasn't." He took out his knife and cleaned it in the dirt. "He'll take it, one way or the other."

She didn't want to believe it, but she could see the truth in his eyes. "I never knew."

"It won't go on much longer. Little Bear and men like him are nearly done."

"How did you choose? Between one life and the other?"

He moved his shoulders. "There wasn't much choice. There's not enough Apache in me to have been accepted as a warrior. And I was raised white, mostly. Red man. That's what they called my father when he was coming up outside an army post down around Tucson. He kept it. Maybe it was pride, maybe it wasn't."

He stopped, annoyed with himself. He'd never told anyone so much.

"You up to riding?"

She wanted him to go on, to tell her everything there was to tell about himself. Instinct held her back. If she pushed, she might never learn. "I can try." Smiling, she reached out to touch his arm. "I want to— Oh, you're bleeding."

He glanced down. "Here and there."

"Let me see. I should have tended these already." She was up on her knees, pulling away the rent material of his sleeve.

"Nothing a man likes better than to have his clothes ripped off by a pretty woman."

"I'll thank you to behave yourself," she told him, but she couldn't muffle a chuckle.

It was good to hear her laugh, even if only a little. Most of the horror had faded from her eyes. But he wanted it gone, all of it. "Heard you made Lucius strip down to the skin. He claimed you threatened him."

This time her laughter was warmer. "The man needed to be threatened. I wish you'd seen his face when I told him to take off his pants."

"I don't suppose you'd like me to do the same."

"Just the shirt should do. This arm certainly needs to be bandaged." She rose and, modesty prevailing, turned her back before she lifted the hem of her skirt to rip her petticoat.

"I'm obliged." He eased painfully out of his shirt. "I've been wondering, Duchess, just how many of those petticoats do you wear?"

"That's certainly not a subject for discussion. But it's fortunate that I . . ." She turned back to him, and the words slipped quietly down her throat. She'd never seen a man's chest before, had certainly never thought a man could be so beautiful. But he was firm and lean, with the dark skin taut over his rib cage and gleaming in the firelight. She felt the heat flash inside her, pressing and throbbing in her center and then spreading through her like a drug.

An owl hooted behind her and made her jolt. "I'll need some water." She was forced to clear her throat. "Those wounds should be cleaned."

With his eyes still on hers, he lifted the canteen. Saying nothing, she knelt beside him again to tend the cut that ran from his shoulder to his elbow.

"This is deep. You'll want a doctor to look at it."

"Yes, ma'am."

Her eyes flicked up to his, then quickly away. "It's likely to scar."

"I've got others."

Yes, she could see that. His was the body of a hero, scarred, disciplined and magnificent. "I've caused you a great deal of trouble."

"More than I figured on," he murmured as her fingers glided gently over his skin.

She tied the first bandage, then gave her attention

to the slice in his side. "This one doesn't look as serious, but it must be painful."

Her voice had thickened. He could feel the flutter of her breath on his skin. He winced as she cleaned the wound, but it was the firelight on her hair that was making him ache. He held his breath when she reached around him to secure the bandage.

"There are some nicks," she murmured. Fascinated, she touched her palm to his chest. "You'll need some salve."

He knew what he needed. His hand closed over her wrist. Her pulse jumped, but she only stared, as if she were mesmerized by the contrast of his skin against hers. Dazed, she watched her own fingers spread and smooth over the hard line of his chest.

The fire had warmed it, warmed her. Slowly she lifted her head and looked at him. His eyes were dark, darker than she'd ever seen them. Storm clouds, she thought. Or gunsmoke. She thought she could hear her heart pounding in her head. Then there was no sound. No sound at all.

He reached for her face, just to rub his palm over her cheek. Nothing in his life had ever seemed so soft or looked so beautiful. The fire was in her eyes, glowing, heating. There was passion there. He knew enough of women to recognize it. Her cheeks, drained of color by fatigue, were as delicate as glass.

He leaned toward her, his eyes open, ready for her to shy away.

She leaned toward him, her pulse pounding, waiting for him to take.

An inch apart, they hesitated, his breath merging with hers. Softly, more softly than either of them would have thought he could, he brushed his lips over hers. And heard her sigh. Gently, with hands more used to molding the grips of guns, he drew her to him. And felt her give. Her lips parted, as they would only for him.

Boldly, as she had never known she could, she ran her hands up his chest. Was he trembling? She murmured to him, lost in the wonder of it. His body was rigid with tension, even as he took the kiss deeper, gloriously deeper. She tasted the hot flavor of desire on his lips as they moved, restless and hungry, over hers.

Eager for more, she pressed against him, letting her arms link tight behind him, and her mouth tell him everything.

He felt the need burst through him like wildfire, searing his mind and loins and heart. Her name tore out of him as he twisted her in his arms and plundered her mouth. The flames beside them leaped, caught by the wind, and sent sparks shooting into the air. He felt her body strain against his, seeking more. Desperate, he tugged at the torn neck of her blouse.

She could only gasp when he covered her breast with his hand. His palm was rough with calluses, and the sensation made her arch and ache. Then his mouth was on her, hot and wet and greedy as it trailed down. Helpless, she dragged her hands through his hair.

She had faced death. This was life. This was love.

His lips raced over her until she was a mass of nerves and need. Recklessly she dragged his mouth back to hers and drove them both toward delirium. His hands were everywhere, pressing, bruising, exciting. With her breath hammering in and out of her lungs, she began to tremble.

His mouth was buried at her throat. The taste of her had seeped into him, and now it was all he knew, all he wanted to know. She was shuddering. Over and over, beneath his own, her body shook. Jake dug his fingers into the dirt as he fought to drag himself back. He'd forgotten what he was. What she was. Hadn't he proven that by nearly taking her on the ground? He heard her soft, breathless moan as he rolled away from her.

She was dizzy, dazed, desperate. With her eyes half closed, she reached out. The moment she touched him, he was moving away, standing.

"Jake."

He felt as though he'd been shot, low in the gut, and would bleed for the rest of his life. In silence, he smothered the fire and began to break camp.

Sarah suddenly felt the cold, and she wrapped her arms around herself. "What's wrong?"

"We've got to ride."

"But . . ." Her skin still tingled where his hands had scraped over it. "I thought . . . that is, it seemed as though . . ."

"Damn it, woman, I said we've got to ride." He yanked a duster out of his saddlebag and tossed it to her. "Put that on."

She held it against her as she watched him secure his saddlebags again. She wouldn't cry. Biting her lip hard to make sure, she vowed she would never cry over him. He didn't want her. It had just been a whim. He preferred another kind of woman. After dragging the duster around her shoulders, she walked to the horse.

"I can mount," she said coldly when he took her arm.

With a nod, he stepped back, then vaulted into the saddle behind her.

CHAPTER 8

The crack of the rifle echoed over the rock and sent a lone hawk wheeling. Sarah gritted her teeth, cocked the lever and squeezed again. The empty whiskey bottle exploded. She was improving, she decided as she mopped her brow and reloaded. And she was determined to get better still.

Lucius wandered over, Lafitte dancing at his heels. "You got a good eye there, Miss Sarah."

"Thank you." She lowered the rifle to give the pup a scratch. Jake was right. He was going to be a big one. "I believe I do."

No one was going to have to rescue her again, not from a rattlesnake, not from Apache marauders, not from the wrath of God himself. In the two weeks since Jake had dropped her, without a word and apparently without a thought, on her doorstep, she'd increased her daily rifle practice. Her aim had sharpened a great deal since she'd taken to imagining that the empty bottles and cans were Jake's grinning face.

"I told you, Lucius, there's no need for you to watch

my every move. What happened before wasn't your fault."

"I can't help feeling it was. You hired me on to keep a lookout around here. Then the first time my pants're down—so to speak, Miss Sarah—you're in trouble."

"I'm back now, and unharmed."

"And I'm mighty grateful for it. If Jake hadn't just ridden up . . . I'd have tried to get you back, Miss Sarah, but he was the man for it."

She bit back the unkind remark that sprang to mind. He had saved her, had risked his life to do so. Whatever had happened afterward couldn't diminish that.

"I'm very grateful to Mr. Redman, Lucius."

"Jake just done what he had to."

She remembered the knife fight with a shudder. "I sincerely hope he won't be required to do anything like it again."

"That's why I'm going to keep a better eye on you. I tell you the God's truth now, Miss Sarah, worrying after a woman's a troublesome thing. I ain't had to bother since my wife died."

"Why, Lucius, I never knew you'd been married."

"Some years back. Quiet Water was her name. She was mighty dear to me."

"You had an Apache wife?" Wanting to hear more, Sarah sat down on a rock, spreading her skirts.

He didn't talk about it often, at least not when he was sober. But he found he was making himself comfortable and telling his tale. "Yes, ma'am. She was Apache, one of Little Bear's tribe. Fact is, she'd've been some kind of aunt to him. I met her when I'd come out here to do some soldiering. Fought Cheyenne, mostly. That would have been back in '62. Didn't mind the fighting, but I sure got tired of the marching. I headed south some to do a little prospecting. Anyways, I met up with John Redman. That was Jake's pa."

"You knew Jake's father?"

"Knew him right well. Partnered up for a while. He and his missus had hit some hard times. Lot of people didn't care much for the idea of him being half-Apache." With a little laugh, he shrugged. "He told me once that some of his tribe didn't care much for the idea of him being half-white. So there you go."

"What kind of man was he?"

"Hardheaded, but real quiet. Didn't say much less'n you said something first. Could be funny. Sometimes it wouldn't occur to you for a minute or two that he'd made a joke. He was good for a laugh. Guess he was the best friend I ever had." He took out his bottle and was relieved when Sarah said nothing. "John had in mind to do some ranching, so I lent a hand here and there. That's how I came to meet Quiet Water."

Casually Sarah pleated her skirt. "I suppose you knew Jake as a boy."

"I'll say I did." Lucius let go a whistling laugh. "Tough little cuss. Could look a hole right through you. Ain't changed much. He was spending some time with his grandma's people. Would've thought he was one of them then, 'cept for the eyes. Course, he wasn't. They knew it and he knew it. Like John said, it's hard not being one or the other. I used to wonder what would've happened if Quiet Water and me had had kids."

"What happened to her, Lucius?"

"I had gone off looking for gold." His eyes narrowed as he stared off into the sun. "Seems a regiment rode through early one morning. Some settler claimed his stock was stolen, and that the Apaches had done it. So the soldiers came in, looking for trouble, hating

Apache. Killed most everybody but those who made it up into the rocks."

"Oh, Lucius. Lucius, I'm so sorry." Unable to find words, she took both his hands in hers.

"When I come back, it was done. I was half-crazy, I guess. Rode around for days, not going anywhere. I guess I was hoping somebody'd come along and shoot me. Then I headed to the Redman place. They'd been burned out."

"Oh, dear God."

"Nothing left but charred wood and ashes."

"How horrible." She tightened her grip on his hands. "Oh, Lucius, it wasn't the soldiers?"

"No. Leastwise they weren't wearing uniforms. Seemed like some men from town got liquored up and decided they didn't want no breed that close by. John and his missus had had trouble before, like I said, but this went past hard words and threats. They started out to burn the barn, raise hell. One of them started shooting. Maybe they'd meant to all along, there's no saying. When it was over, they'd burned them out and left the family for dead."

Horror made her eyes dark and huge. "Jake. He would have been just a boy."

"Thirteen, fourteen, I reckon. But he was past being a boy. I found him where he'd buried his folks. He was just sitting there, between the two fresh graves. Had his pa's hunting knife in his hands. Still carries it."

She knew the knife. She'd seen it stained with blood, for her. But now all she could think of was the boy. "Oh, the poor child. He must have been so frightened."

"No, ma'am. I don't believe frightened's the word. He was chanting, like in a trance the Apache sometimes use. War chant, it was. He figured on going into town and finding the men who killed his folks."

"But you said he was only thirteen."

"I said he was past being a boy. Best I could do was talk him out of it for a time, till he learned to handle a gun better. He learned mighty fast. I ain't never seen a man do with a gun what Jake can do."

Though it was hot out, she rubbed the chill from her arms. "Did he . . . go back for them?"

"I don't rightly know. I never asked. I thought it best we move on until he had some years on him, so we headed south. Didn't know what to do for him. Bought him a horse, and we rode together awhile. I always figured he'd hook up with the wrong kind, but Jake was never much for hooking up with anybody. He'd've been about sixteen when we parted ways. Heard about him off and on. Then he rode into Lone Bluff a few months back."

"To lose everything that way." A tear ran down her cheek. "It's a wonder he's not filled with hate."

"He's got it in him, but it's cold. Me, I use the bottle, wash it away now and then. Jake uses something in here." He tapped his temple. "That boy holds more inside than anybody should have to. He ever lets it out, people better stand back."

She understood what he meant. Hadn't she seen it, that flat, dangerous look that came into his eyes? That expressionless stare that was more passionate than fury, more deadly than rage.

"You care for him."

"He's all I got that you might call family. Yeah, I got an affection for the boy." Lucius squinted over at her. "I figure you do, too."

"I don't know what I feel for him." That was a lie. She knew very well what she felt, how she felt. She was even coming to understand why she felt. He wasn't the man she had once imagined she would love, but he was the only man she ever would. "It doesn't matter what I feel," she said, "if he doesn't feel it back."

"Maybe he does. It might be hard for him to say it right out, but I always figure a woman's got a sense about those things."

"Not always." With a little sigh, she rose. "There's work to be done, Lucius."

"Yes'm."

"There is one question. What have you been doing in the mine?"

"The mine, Miss Sarah?"

"You said yourself I have a good eye. I know you've been going in there. I'd like to know why."

"Well, now." Fabricating wasn't Lucius's strong suit. He coughed and shifted his feet and peered off at nothing. "Just having a look around."

"For gold?"

"Could be."

"Do you think you'll find any?"

"Matt always figured there was a rich vein in that rock, and when Jake—" He broke off.

"When Jake what? Asked you to look?"

"Maybe he might have suggested it sometime."

"I see." Sarah looked up to the top of the ridge. She had always wondered what Jake wanted, she thought, her heart shattering. Perhaps she knew now. Gold seemed to pull at the men she loved. "I have no objection to you working the mine, Lucius. In fact, I think it's an excellent idea. You must let me know if you require any tools." When she looked back at him, her eyes were as cool and hard as any man's. "The next time you ride into town, you might mention to Jake that Sarah's Pride is mine."

"Yes, ma'am, if you'd like."

"I insist." She looked toward the road. "There's a buggy coming."

Lucius spit and hoped it wasn't Carlson. As far as he was concerned, the man had been too free with his visits to Sarah in the past few weeks.

It wasn't Carlson. As the buggy drew closer, Sarah saw it was a woman holding the reins. Not Liza, she realized with a pang of disappointment. The woman was dark and delicate and a stranger to her.

"Good morning." Sarah set the rifle against the wall of the house.

"Good morning, ma'am." The young woman sat in the buggy and sent Sarah a nervous smile. "You sure live a ways out."

"Yes." Since her visitor didn't seem in a hurry to alight, Sarah walked to the buggy. "I'm Sarah Conway."

"Yes, ma'am, I know. I'm Alice. Alice Johnson." She gave the puppy a bright, cheerful smile, then looked at Sarah again. "Pleased to meet you."

"It's nice to meet you, too, Miss Johnson. Would you like to come in for some tea?"

"Oh, no, ma'am, I couldn't."

Baffled by Alice's horrified expression, Sarah tried again. "Perhaps you're lost?"

"No, I've come to talk with you, but I couldn't come in. It wouldn't be fitting."

"Oh? Why?"

"Well, you see, Miss Conway, I'm one of Carlotta's girls."

Carlotta? Wide-eyed, Sarah looked her visitor over again. She was hardly more than a girl, a year or more younger than Sarah herself. Her face was scrubbed clean, and her dress was certainly modest. As Sarah stared, thick lashes lowered over her dark eyes and a blush rushed into her cheeks.

"Do you mean you work at the Silver Star?"

"Yes, ma'am, for nearly three months now."

"But—" Sarah swallowed the words when she saw Alice bite her lip. "Miss Johnson, if you've come to see me, I suggest we talk inside. It's much too hot to stand in the sun."

"I couldn't. Really, it wouldn't be fitting, Miss Conway."

"Fitting or not, I don't wish sunstroke on either of us. Please, come in." Leaving the decision in the hands of her visitor, Sarah walked inside.

Alice hesitated. It didn't feel right, not when Miss Conway was a real lady. But if she went back and couldn't tell Carlotta that she'd done what she'd been sent for, she'd get slapped around for sure. Carlotta always knew when you lied. And you always paid for it.

Sarah heard the timid footsteps as she put water on to boil. Before she could turn and offer Alice a seat, the girl was bubbling.

"Oh, my, isn't this pretty? You've got a real nice place here, Miss Conway. Curtains and all."

"Thank you." Her smile was full and genuine. It was the first time she'd had company who had thought so. "I'm more and more at home here. Please, sit down, Miss Johnson. I'm making tea."

"It's real kind of you, but I don't feel right, you giving me tea. It ain't proper."

"This is my house, and you're my guest. Of course it's proper. I hope you'll enjoy these cookies. I made them only yesterday."

With her fingers plucking nervously at her skirt, Alice sat. "Thank you, ma'am. And don't worry. I won't tell a soul I came in and sat at your table."

Intrigued, Sarah poured the tea. "Why don't you tell me what brought you out to see me?"

"Carlotta. She's been looking at all the dresses you've been making for the ladies in town. They're real pretty, Miss Conway."

"Thank you."

"Just the other day, after Jake left—"

"Jake?"

"Yes'm." Hoping she was holding the cup properly, Alice drank. "He comes into the Silver Star pretty regular. Carlotta's real fond of him. She don't work much herself, you know. Unless it's somebody like Jake."

"Yes, I see." She waited for what was left of her heart to break. Instead, it swelled with fury. "I suppose she might find a man like him appealing."

"She surely does. All the girls got a fondness for Jake."

"I'm sure," she murmured.

"Well, like I was saying, Carlotta got it into her head one day after he left that we should have us some new clothes. Something classy, like ladies would wear. She told me Jake said you could sew some up for us."

"Did he?"

"Yes, ma'am. She said she thought Jake had a real fine idea there, and she sent me on out to see about it. I got me all the measurements."

"I'm sorry, Miss Johnson, I really couldn't. Be sure to tell Carlotta that I appreciate the offer."

"There's eight of us girls, miss, and Carlotta said she'd pay you in advance. I got the money."

"That's generous, but I can't do it. Would you like more tea?"

"I don't—" Confused, Alice looked at her cup. She didn't know anyone who'd ever said no to Carlotta. "If it's not too much trouble." She wanted to stretch out her visit, though she knew that, and the message she'd be taking back, would make Carlotta box her ears.

"Miss Johnson—"

"You can call me Alice, Miss Conway. Everybody does."

"Alice, then. Would you mind telling me how it was you came to work for Carlotta? You're very young to be . . . on your own."

"My daddy sold me off."

"*Sold* you?"

"There was ten of us at home, and another on the way. Every time he got drunk he whipped one of us or made another. He got drunk a lot. Few months back, a man passed through and Daddy sold me for twenty dollars. I ran off as soon as I could. When I got to Lone Bluff I went to work for Carlotta. I know it ain't right and proper, but it's better than what I had. I get my meals and a bed to myself when I'm finished work." She gave a quick, uncomfortable shrug. "Most of the men are all right."

"Your father had no right to sell you, Alice."

"Sometimes there's right and there's what's done."

"If you wanted to leave Carlotta, I'm sure there would be other work for you in town. Proper work."

"Begging your pardon, Miss Conway, but that ain't true. None of the town ladies would hire me for anything. And they shouldn't. Why, how would they know if I'd been with one of their husbands?"

It was sound thinking, but Sarah shook her head. "If you decide to leave, I'll find work for you."

Alice stared at her, wide-eyed. "That's kind of you. I knew you were a real lady, Miss Conway, and I'm obliged. I'd better be heading back."

"If you'd like to visit again, I'd be happy to see you," Sarah told her as she walked her out.

"No, ma'am, that wouldn't be proper. Thank you for the tea, Miss Conway."

Sarah thought a great deal about Alice's visit. That night, as she read her father's journal by lamplight, she tried to imagine what it had been like. To be sold, she thought with an inward shudder. By her own father, like a horse or a steer. It was true that she, too, had spent years of her life without a real family, but she had always known her father loved her. What he had done, he had done with her best interests at heart.

Once, she would have condemned Alice's choice out of hand. But now she thought she understood. It was all the girl knew. The cycle had begun with her father's callousness, and the girl was caught in it, helplessly moving in the same circle, selling herself time after time because she knew nothing else.

Had it been the same for Jake? Had the cruelty he'd lived through as a child forced him into a life of restlessness and violence? The scars he carried must run deep. And the hate. Sarah looked into the soft glow of the lamp. As Lucius had said, the hate ran cold.

She should have hated him. She wanted to, she wished the strong, destructive emotion would come, filling all the cracks in her feelings, blocking out everything else. With hate, a coolheaded, sharply honed hate, she would have felt in control again. She needed badly to feel in control again. But she didn't hate him. She couldn't.

Even though she knew he had spent the night with another woman, kissing another woman's lips, touching another woman's skin, she couldn't hate him. But she could grieve for her loss, for the death of a beauty that had never had a chance to bloom fully.

She had come to understand what they might have had together. She had almost come to accept that they belonged together, whatever their differences, whatever the risks. He would always live by his gun and by his own set of rules, but with her, briefly, perhaps reluctantly, he had shown such kindness, such tenderness.

There was a place for her in his heart. Sarah knew it. Beneath the rough-hewn exterior was a man who believed in justice, who was capable of small, endearing kindnesses. He'd allowed her to see that part of him, a part she knew he'd shared with few others.

Then why, the moment she had begun to soften toward him, to accept him for what and who he was, had he turned to another woman? A woman whose love could be bought with a handful of coins?

What did it matter? With a sigh, she closed her father's journal and prepared for bed. She had only fooled herself into believing he could care for her. Whatever kindness Jake had shown her would always war with his lawless nature and his restless heart. She wanted a home, a man by her side and children at her feet. As long as she loved Jake, she would go on wanting and never having.

Somehow, no matter how hard it was, no matter how painful, she would stop loving him.

Jake hated himself for doing it, but he rode toward Sarah's place, a dozen excuses forming in his head. He wanted to talk to Lucius and check on the progress in the mine. He wanted to make sure she hadn't been bitten by a snake. He'd wanted a ride, and her place was as good as any.

They were all lies.

He just wanted to see her. He just wanted to look

at her, hear her talk, smell her hair. He'd stayed away from her for two weeks, hadn't he? He had a right. . . . He had no rights, he told himself as he rode into the yard. He had no rights, and no business thinking about her the way he was thinking about her, wanting her the way he wanted her.

She deserved a man who could make her promises and keep them, who could give her the kind of life she'd been born to live.

He wasn't going to touch her again. That was a promise he'd made himself when he'd ridden away from her the last time. If he touched her, he wouldn't pull back. That would only cause them both more misery.

He'd hurt her. He had seen that plain enough when he'd left her. But that was nothing compared to what he would have done if he'd stayed.

It was quiet. Jake pulled up his mount and took a long, cautious look around, his hand hovering over the butt of his gun. The dog wasn't yapping, nor was there any smoke rising from the chimney. The saddle creaked as he dismounted.

He didn't knock, but pushed open the door and listened. There wasn't a sound from inside. He could see, as his eyes scanned from one corner to the next, that the cabin was empty and as tidy as a church. The curtains she'd sewed had already begun to fade, but they moved prettily in the hot wind. His shoulders relaxed.

She'd done something here. That was something else he had to admire about her. She'd taken less than nothing and made it a home. There were pictures on the walls. One was a watercolor of wildflowers in soft, dreamy hues. It looked like her, he thought as he took a closer study. All dewy and fresh and delicate. Flowers like that would wither fast if they weren't tended.

He moved to the next, his brows drawing together

as he scanned it. It was a pencil drawing—a sketch, he figured she'd call it. He recognized the scene, the high, arrogant buttes, the sun-bleached rock. If you looked west from the stream you'd see it. It wasn't an empty place. The Apache knew the spirits that lived there. But oddly, as he studied the lines and shadows, he thought Sarah might know them, too. He would never have imagined her taking the time to draw something so stark and strong, much less hang it on the wall so that she would see it every time she turned around.

Somehow—he couldn't quite figure out the why of it—it suited her every bit as much as the wildflowers.

Annoyed with himself, he turned away. She knew something about magic, he figured. Didn't the cabin smell of her, so that his stomach kept tying itself in knots? He'd be better off out in the air—fifty miles away.

A book caught his eye as he started out. Without giving a thought to her privacy, he opened it. Apparently she'd started a diary. Unable to resist, he scanned the first page.

She'd described her arrival in Lone Bluff. He had to grin as he read over her recounting of the Apache raid and his timely arrival. She'd made him sound pretty impressive, even if she'd noted what she called his "infuriating and unchristian behavior."

There was a long passage about her father, and her feelings about him. He passed it by. Grief was to be respected, unless it needed to be shared. He chuckled out loud as she described her first night, the cold can of beans and the sounds that had kept her awake and trembling until morning. There were bits and pieces he found entertaining enough about the townspeople and her impressions of life in the West. Then he caught his name again.

"Jake Redman is an enigma." He puzzled over the word, sure he'd never heard it before. It sounded a little too fancy to be applied to him.

I don't know if one might call him a diamond in the rough, though rough he certainly is. Honesty forces me to admit that he has been of some help to me and shown glimmers of kindness. I can't resolve my true feelings about him, and I wonder why I find it necessary to try. He is a law unto himself and a man wholly lacking in manners and courtesy. His reputation is distressing, to say the least. He is what is referred to as a gunslinger, and he wears his weapons as smoothly as a gentleman wears a watch fob. Yet I believe if one dug deeply enough one might discover a great deal of goodness there. Fortunately, I have neither the time nor the inclination to do the digging.

Despite his manner and his style of living, there is a certain, even a strong, attractiveness about him. He has fine eyes of clear gray, a mouth that some women might call poetic, particularly when he smiles, and truly beautiful hands.

He stopped there to frown down at his hands. They'd been called a lot of things, but beautiful wasn't one of them. He wasn't sure he cared for it. Still, she sure did have a way with words.

He turned the page and would have read on, but the slightest of sounds at his back had him whirling, his guns gripped firmly in his hands.

Lucius swore long and skillfully as he lowered his

own pistol. "I ain't lived this long to have you blow holes in me."

Jake slipped his guns home. "You'd better be careful how you come up on a man. Didn't you see my horse?"

"Yeah, I saw it. Just making sure. Didn't expect to find you poking around in here." He glanced down at the book. Without a word, Jake shut it.

"I didn't expect to find the place deserted."

"I've been up to the mine." Lucius pulled a small bottle of whiskey from his pocket.

"And?"

"It's interesting." He took a long pull, then wiped his mouth with the back of his hand. "I can't figure how Matt got himself caught in that cave-in. He was pretty sharp, and I recollect them beams being secure enough. Looks to me like someone worked pretty hard to bring them down."

With a nod, Jake glanced at the watercolor on the wall. "Have you said anything to her yet?"

"Nope." He didn't think it was the best time to tell Jake that Sarah had found him out. "There's something else I haven't mentioned." His face split into a grin as Jake looked at him. "There's gold in there, boy. Just like Matt always claimed. He'd found the mother lode." Lucius took a swig from the bottle, then corked it. "You figured on that?"

"Just a hunch."

"Want me to keep it under my hat?"

"For the time being."

"I don't care much for playing tricks on Miss Sarah, but I reckon you've got your reasons."

"I've got them."

"I won't ask you what they are. I won't ask you

neither what reasons you got for not coming around lately. Miss Sarah, she's been looking a mite peaked since you brought her back from the hills."

"She's sick?" he asked, too quickly.

Lucius rubbed a hand over his mouth to hide a grin. "I figure she's got a fever, all right. Heart fever."

"She'll get over it," Jake muttered as he walked outside.

"You're looking peaked yourself." When Jake didn't answer, he tried again. "Sure is some woman. Looks soft, but that streak of stubborn keeps her going. See there?" He pointed to the vegetable patch. "She's got something growing there. Never thought I'd see a speck of green, but there you go. She waters that thing every day. Stubborn. A stubborn woman's just bound to make things happen."

"Where is she?"

Lucius had been hoping he'd ask. "Gone off driving with Carlson. He's been coming around here near every day. Drinks tea." He spit. "Kisses her fingers and calls her right out by her first name." It warmed his heart to see Jake's eyes harden. "Said something about taking her to see his ranch. Been gone better than an hour now."

I don't know when I've spent a more pleasant day." Sarah rose from the glossy mahogany table in Carlson's dining room. "Or had a more delightful meal."

"The pleasure has been mine." Carlson took her hand. "All mine."

Sarah smiled and gently took her hand away. "You have such a beautiful home. I never expected to see anything like it out here."

"My grandfather loved beautiful things." He took

her elbow. "I inherited that love from him. Most of the furniture was shipped in from Europe. We had to make some concessions to the land." He patted a thick adobe wall. "But there's no reason to sacrifice all our comforts. This painting—" He guided her to a portrait of a pale, elegant woman in blue silk. "My mother. She was my grandfather's pride and joy. His wife died before this house was completed. Everything he did from that day on was for his daughter."

"She's lovely."

"She was. Even my grandfather's love and devotion couldn't keep her alive. The women in my family have always been delicate. This land is hard, too hard for the fragile. It baked the life out of her. I suppose that's why I worry about you."

"I'm not as delicate as you might think." She thought of the ride into the mountains with her hands and feet bound.

"You're strong-willed. I find that very attractive."

He took her hand again. Before she could decide how to respond, a man strode into the house. He was shorter and leaner than Carlson, but there was enough of a resemblance around the mouth and eyes for her to recognize him. His hat was pushed back so that it hung around his neck by its strap. Yellow dust coated his clothes. He hooked his thumbs in the pockets of his pants and looked at her in a way that made her blood chill.

"Well, now, what have we got here?"

"Miss Conway." There was a warning, mild but definite, in Carlson's voice. "My brother, Jim. You'll have to excuse him. He's been working the cattle."

"Sam handles the money, I handle the rest. You didn't tell me we were having company." He swaggered closer. He carried the scents of leather and tobacco, but she found nothing appealing about it. "Such nice-looking company."

"I invited Miss Conway to lunch."

"And it was lovely, but I really should be getting back." And away, she thought, from Jim Carlson.

"You don't want to rush off the minute I get in." Grinning, Jim laid a dirty hand on the polished surface of a small table. "We don't get enough company here, at least not your kind. You're just as pretty as a picture." He glanced at his brother with a laugh Sarah didn't understand. "Just as pretty as a picture."

"You'd better wash up." Though his voice was mild, Carlson sent him a hard look. "We have some business to discuss when I get back."

"It's all business with Sam." Jim winked at Sarah. "Now, me, I got time for other things."

Sarah swallowed a sigh of relief when Carlson took her elbow again. "Good day, Mr. Carlson."

Jim watched her retreating back. "Yeah, good day to you. A real good day."

"You'll have to excuse him." Carlson helped Sarah into the waiting buggy. "Jim's a bit rough around the edges. I hope he didn't upset you."

"No, not at all," she said, struggling to keep a polite smile. With her hands folded in her lap, she began to chat about whatever came to mind.

"You seem to be adjusting well to your new life," Carlson commented.

"Actually, I'm enjoying it."

"For selfish reasons, I'm glad to hear it. I was afraid you'd lose heart and leave." He let the horses prance as he turned to smile at her. "I'm very glad you're staying." He pulled up so that they could have a last look at the ranch from the rise. The house spread out, rising two stories, glowing pink in the sunlight, its small glass windows glimmering. Neat paddocks and out-buildings dotted the land, which was cut through by a blue stream and ringed by hills.

"It's lovely, Samuel. You must be very proud of it."

"Pride isn't always enough. A place like this needs to be shared. I've regretted not having a family of my own to fill it. Until now I'd nearly given up hoping I'd find a woman to share it with me." He took her hand and brought it to his lips. "Sarah, nothing would make me happier than if that woman were you."

She wasn't sure she could speak, though she could hardly claim to be surprised. He'd made no secret about the fact that he was courting her. She studied his face in silence. He was everything she had dreamed of. Handsome, dashing, dependable, successful. Now he was offering her everything she had dreamed of. A home, a family, a full and happy life.

She wanted to say yes, to lift a hand to his cheek and smile. But she couldn't. She looked away, struggling to find the right words.

She saw him then. He was hardly more than a silhouette on the horizon. An anonymous man on horseback. But she knew without seeing his face, without hearing his voice, that it was Jake. That knowledge alone made her pulse beat fast and her body yearn.

Deliberately she turned away. "Samuel, I can't begin to tell you how flattered I am by your offer."

He sensed refusal, and though anger tightened within him, he only smiled. "Please, don't give me an answer now. I'd like you to think about it. Believe me, Sarah, I realize we've known each other only a short time and your feelings might not be as strong as mine. Give me a chance to change that."

"Thank you." She didn't object when he kissed her hand again. "I will think about it." That she promised herself. "I'm very grateful you're patient. There's so much on my mind right now. I've nearly got my life under control again, and now that I'm going to open the mine—"

"The mine?" His hand tightened on hers. "You're going to open the mine?"

"Yes." She gave him a puzzled look. "Is something wrong?"

"No, no, it's only that it's dangerous." It was a measure of his ambition that he was able to bring himself under control so quickly. "And I'm afraid doing so might distress you more than you realize. After all, the mine killed your father."

"I know. But it also gave him life. I feel strongly that he would have wanted me to continue there."

"Will you do something for me?"

"I'll try."

"Think about it carefully. You're too important to me. I would hate to have you waste yourself on an empty dream." With another smile, he clucked to the horses. "And if you marry me, I'll see that the mine is worked without causing you any heartache."

"I will think about it." But her mind was crowded with other thoughts as she looked over her shoulder at the lone rider on the hill.

CHAPTER 9

Sarah had never been more excited about a dance in her life. Nor had she ever worked harder. The moment the plans had been announced for a town dance to celebrate Independence Day, the orders for dresses began to pour in. She left all the chores to Lucius and sewed night and day.

Her fingers were cramped and her eyes burned, but she had earned enough to put through an order for the wood floor she wanted so badly.

After the floor, Sarah thought, she would order glass for the windows and a proper set of dishes. Then, when time and money allowed, she was going to have Lucius build her a real bedroom. With a little laugh, she closed her eyes and imagined it. If the mine came through, she would have that house with four bedrooms and a parlor, but for now she'd settle for a real floor beneath her feet.

Soon, she thought. But before floors and windows came the dance.

She might have made every frock as pretty and as fashionable as her skill allowed, but she wasn't about to be outdone. On the afternoon of the dance she took out her best silk dress. It was a pale lavender blue, the color of moonbeams in a forest. White lace flirted at the square-cut bodice that accented the line of her throat and a hint of shoulder. There were pert bows of a deeper lavender at the edge of each poufed sleeve.

She laced her stays so tightly that her ribs hurt, telling herself it would be worth it. With her hand mirror, she struggled to see different parts of herself and put them together in her mind for a complete image. The flounced skirt with the bows was flattering, she decided, and the matching velvet ribbon at her throat was a nice touch. She would have pinned her cameo to it, but that, like so much else, had been lost.

She wouldn't think about that tonight, she told herself as she patted her hair. She'd swept it up, and its weight had caused her to use every hairpin she could find. But, she thought with a nod, it looked effortless, curling ever so slightly at her ears and temples.

It was important that she look her best. Very important, she added, pulling on her long white gloves. If Jake was there, she wanted him to see just what he'd tossed aside. She swept on her white lace shawl, checked the contents of her reticule, then stepped outside.

"Glory be." Lucius stood by the wagon with his hat in his hand. He'd cleaned up without her having to remind him, and had even taken a razor to his chin. When she smiled at him, he decided that if he'd been ten years younger he'd have given Jake a run for his money.

"Lucius, how handsome you look."

"Hell, Miss Sarah. I mean—" He cleared his throat. "You sure look a sight."

Recognizing that as a compliment, Sarah smiled and held out a hand. With as much style as he could muster, Lucius helped her into the wagon.

"You're going to set them on their ears."

"I hope so." At least she hoped she set one person on his ear. "You're going to save a dance for me, aren't you, Lucius?"

"I'd be pleased to. If I do say so, I dance right well, drunk or sober."

"Perhaps you'll try it sober tonight."

Jake saw them ride into town. He was sitting at his window, smoking and watching some of the cowboys racing in the streets, waving their hats, shooting off guns and howling.

Independence Day, he thought, blowing smoke at the sky. Most of them figured they had a right to freedom and the land they'd claimed. He'd come to accept that they, and others like them, would take the Arizona Territory and the rest of the West. Black Hawk, and others like him, would never stop the rush.

And he was neither invader nor invaded.

Maybe that was why he had never tried to put his mark on the land. Not since he'd lost what his father had tried to build. It was better to keep whatever you owned light, light enough that it fit on your horse.

The town was full of noise and people. Most of the cowhands were going to get three-quarters drunk, and they were liable to end up shooting themselves instead of the targets Cody had set up for the marksmanship contest. He didn't much care. He just sat at the window and watched.

Then he saw her. It hurt. Unconsciously he rubbed a hand over his heart, where the ache centered. She laughed. He could hear the sound float right up to him and shimmer like water over his skin. The wanting, the pure strength of it, made him drag his eyes away. For survival.

But he looked back, unable to stop himself. She stepped out of the wagon and laughed again as Liza Cody ran out of her father's store. She twirled in a circle for Liza, and he saw all of her, the white skin of her throat, the hint of high, round breasts, the tiny waist, the glow in her eyes. The cigarette burned down to his fingers, and he cursed. But he didn't stop looking.

"You going to sit in the window all day or take me down like you promised?" Maggie came farther into the room, her hands on her hips. The boy hadn't heard a word. She tugged on his shoulder, ignored the name he called her and repeated herself.

"I never promised to do anything."

"You promised, all right, the night I poured you into that bed when you came in so drunk you couldn't stand."

He remembered the night clearly enough. It had been a week after he'd brought Sarah back from the mountains. A week since he'd been going to the Silver Star, trying to work up enough interest to take Carlotta or any other woman to bed. Drinking had been simpler, but getting blind drunk was something he'd never done before and didn't intend to do again.

"I could have gotten myself into bed well enough."

"You couldn't even crawl up the stairs. If there's one thing I know, it's a man who's too drunk to think. Now, are you going to take me down or are you going to back down?"

He grumbled but pushed himself away from the window. "Nothing worse than a nagging woman."

She only grinned and handed him his hat.

They had no more than stepped outside when John Cody came racing up. "Mr. Redman. Mr. Redman. I've been waiting for you."

"Yeah?" He pulled the boy's hat over his face. "Why's that?"

Delighted with the attention, Johnny grinned. "The contest. My pa's having a contest. Best shooting gets a brand-new saddle blanket. A red one. You're going to win, ain't you?"

"I wasn't figuring on it."

"How come? Nobody shoots better'n you. It's a real nice blanket, too."

"Go on, Jake." Maggie gave him a slap on the arm. "The boy's counting on you."

"I don't shoot for sport." He meant to walk on, but he saw Johnny's face fall. "A red blanket?"

The boy's eyes lit instantly. "Yessiree, about the prettiest one I ever seen."

"I guess we could look." Before the sentence was complete, Johnny had him by the hand and was pulling him across the street.

At the back of the store Cody had set up empty bottles and cans of varying sizes. Each contestant stood behind a line drawn in the dirt and took his best six shots. Broken glass littered the ground already.

"It costs two bits to enter," Johnny told him. "I got a short bit if you need it."

Jake looked at the dime the boy offered. The gesture touched him in a way that only those who had been offered very little through life would have understood. "Thanks, but I think I got two bits."

"You can shoot better than Jim Carlson. He's winning now." Johnny glanced over to where Jim was showing off a fancy railman's spin with his shiny new Smith & Wesson .44. "Can you do that?"

"Why? It doesn't help you shoot any better." He flipped a quarter to Johnny. "Why don't you go put my name down?"

"Yessir. Yessiree." He took time out to have a friendly shoving match with another boy, then raced away.

"Going to shoot for the blanket?" Lucius asked from behind him.

"Thinking about it." But he was watching Jim Carlson. He remembered that Jim rode a big white gelding. Jake had seen the gleam of a white horse riding away the night Sarah's shed had burned.

Lucius tipped his hat to Maggie. "Ma'am."

"That you, Lucius? I don't believe I've ever seen you with that beard shaved."

He colored up and stepped away. "I guess a man can shave now and then without a body gawking at him."

"I forgot you had a face under there," Jake commented as he watched Will Metcalf hit four out of six bottles. "You looking for a new red blanket, too?"

"Nope. Just thought I'd come around and tell you Burt Donley rode into town."

Only his eyes changed. "Is that so? I thought he was in Laramie."

"Not anymore. He came this way while you were in New Mexico. Started working for Carlson."

In an easy move, Jake turned and scanned the area behind him. "Donley doesn't punch cattle."

"Hasn't been known to. Could be Carlson hired him to do something else."

"Could be," Jake murmured, watching Donley walk toward the crowd.

He was a big man, burly at the shoulders, thick at the waist. He wore his graying hair long, so long it merged with his beard. And he was fast. Jake had good reason to know just how fast. If the law hadn't stepped in two years before, one of them would be dead now.

"Heard you had some trouble a while back."

"Some." Through the crowd, Jake's eyes met Donley's. They didn't need words. There was unfinished business between them.

As she stood beside Liza, Sarah watched Jake. And shivered. Something had come into his eyes. Something cold and deadly and inevitable. Then the crowd roared when the next contestant shattered all six bottles.

"Oh, look." Liza gave Sarah a quick shake. "Jake's going to shoot. I know it's wrong, but I've always wanted to see how he does it. You hear such stories. There was one—" Her mouth fell open when he drew with his right hand and fired. "I didn't even see him take it out," she whispered. "It was just in his hand, quick as a blink."

"He hit them all." Sarah wrapped her shawl tighter around her. He had hardly moved. His gun was still smoking when he slid it back in place.

Donley strode over, flipped a quarter and waited until more targets were set. Sarah watched his big hand curl over the butt of his gun. Then he drew and fired.

"Goodness. He hit all of them, too. That leaves Dave Jeffrey, Jim Carlson, Jake and Burt Donley."

"Who is he?" Sarah asked, wondering why Jake looked like he wanted to kill him. "The big man in the leather vest."

"Donley? He works for Samuel Carlson. I've heard talk about him, too. The same kind of talk as you hear about Jake. Only . . ."

"Only?"

"Well, you know how I told you Johnny's been tagging after Jake, pestering him and talking his ear off? I can't say it worries me any. But if he got within ten feet of Burt Donley I'd skin him alive."

The crowd shifted as Cody brought the line back five feet. When the first man aimed and fired, missing two bottles, Sarah saw Johnny tug on Jake's arm and whisper something. To her surprise, Jake grinned and ruffled the boy's hair. There it was again, she thought. That goodness. That basic kindness. Yet she remembered the look that had come into his eyes only moments before.

Who are you? she wanted to ask.

As if he'd heard her, Jake turned his head. Their eyes met and held. She felt a flood of emotions rise up uncontrollably and again wished she could hate him for that alone.

"You keep looking at her like that," Maggie murmured at his side, "you're going to have to marry her or ride fast in the other direction."

"Shut up, Maggie."

She smiled as sweetly as if he'd kissed her cheek. "Just thought you'd like to know that Sam Carlson ain't too pleased by the way you two are carrying on."

Jake's gaze shifted and met Carlson's. He had come up to stand behind Sarah and lay a proprietary hand on her shoulder. Jake considered allowing himself the pleasure of shooting him for that alone. "He's got no claim."

"Not for lack of trying. Better move fast, boyo."

The onlookers cheered again as Jim Carlson nipped five out of six targets.

Taking his time, Jake reloaded his pistol, then moved to the line. The six shots sounded almost like one. When he lowered his Colt, six bottles had been shattered.

Donley took his place. Six shots, six hits.

The line was moved farther back.

"They can't do it from here," Liza whispered to Sarah. "No one could."

Sarah just shook her head. It wasn't a game anymore. There was something between the two men, something much deeper, much darker, than a simple contest of skill. Others sensed it, too. She could hear the murmur of the crowd and see the uneasy looks.

Jake moved behind the line. He scanned the targets, judging the distance, taking mental aim. Then he did what he did best. He drew and fired on instinct. Bottles exploded, one by one. There was nothing left but a single jagged base. Without pausing, he drew his other gun and shattered even that.

There was silence as Donley stepped forward. He drew, and the gun kicked in his hand with each shot. When he was done, a single bottle remained unbroken.

"Congratulations, Redman." Cody brought the blanket over, hoping to dispel some of the tension. Relief made him let out his breath audibly when Sheriff Barker strolled over.

"That was some shooting, boys." He gave each man a casual nod. Will Metcalf stood at his shoulder as directed. "Good to get it out of your system with a few bottles. Either one of you catches a bullet tonight, there's sure no way I can doubt who put it there."

The warning was given with a smile that was friendly enough. Behind Sarah, Carlson gave a quick shake of his head. Without speaking, Donley made his way through the crowd, which parted for him.

"I ain't never seen nobody shoot like that." Johnny looked up at Jake with awe and wonder in his eyes.

Jake tossed the blanket to him. "There you go."

His eyes widened even farther. "I can have it?"

"You got a horse, don't you?"

"Yes, sir, I got me a bay pony."

"Red ought to look real nice on a bay. Why don't you go see?"

With a whoop, Johnny raced off, only to be caught by his mother. After a minor scuffle, he turned back, grinning. "Thanks, Mr. Redman. Thanks a lot."

"You sure did please that boy pink," Barker commented.

"I don't need a blanket."

Barker only shook his head. "You're a puzzle, Jake. I can't help but have a liking for you."

"That's a puzzle to me, Sheriff. Most lawmen got other feelings."

"Maybe so. Either way, I'd be obliged if you'd keep those guns holstered tonight. You wouldn't want to tell me what there is between you and Donley?"

Jake sent him an even look. "No."

"Didn't figure you would." He spit out tobacco juice. "Well, I'm going to have me some chicken and dance with my wife."

There were a dozen tables lined up along one side of the big canvas tent. Even before the music started, more than half of the food was gone. Women, young and old, were flirting, pleased to be shown off in their best dresses. When the fiddle started, couples swarmed onto the floor. Liza, in her pink muslin, grabbed Will's hand and pulled him with her. Lucius, dashing in his light brown suit and string tie, bowed to Sarah.

"I'd be honored if you'd step out with me, Sarah."

With a little laugh, she gave him a formal curtsy. "I'd be delighted."

The music was fast and cheerful. Despite the heat, the dancing followed suit. At the front of the tent the musicians fiddled and plucked and strummed tirelessly, and the caller wet his whistle with free beer. Couples swung and sashayed and kicked up their heels in a reel. It was different from the dances Sarah had attended in Philadelphia. Wonderfully different, she thought as she twirled in Lucius's arms. Hoots and hollers accompanied the music, as well as hand-clapping, foot-stamping and whistles.

"You were right, Lucius." Laughing, she laid a hand on her speeding heart when the music stopped.

"I was?"

"Yes, indeed. You're a fine dancer. And this is the best party I've ever been to." She leaned over impulsively and kissed his cheek.

"Well, now." His face turned beet red with embarrassed pleasure. "Why don't I fetch you a cup of that punch?"

"That would be lovely."

"Sarah!" Liza's face was nearly as pink as Lucius's when she rushed over and grabbed Sarah's arm.

"My goodness, what's wrong?"

"Nothing. Nothing in the world is wrong." Impatient, Liza dragged Sarah to a corner of the tent. "I just got to tell somebody or bust."

"Then tell me. I'd hate to see you rip the seams of that dress."

"I was just outside, taking a little air." She looked quickly right, then left. "Will came out after me. He kissed me."

"He did?"

"Twice. I guess my heart just about stopped."

One brow lifted, Sarah struggled with a smile. "I suppose that means you've decided to let him be your beau."

"We're getting married," Liza blurted out.

"Oh, Liza, really? That's wonderful." Delighted, Sarah threw her arms around her friend. "I'm so happy for you. When?"

"Well, he's got to talk to Pa first." Liza chewed her lip as she glanced toward her father. "But I know it's going to be all right. Pa likes Will."

"Of course he does. Liza, I can't tell you how happy I am for you."

"I know." When her eyes filled, Liza blinked and sniffled. "Oh, Lordy, I don't want to cry now."

"No, don't, or I'll start."

Laughing, Liza hugged her again. "I can't wait. I just can't wait. It'll be your turn before long. The way Samuel Carlson can't take his eyes off you. I have to admit, I used to have a crush on him." She gave a quick, wicked smile. "Mostly, I thought about using him to make Will jealous."

"I'm not going to marry Samuel. I don't think I'm ever going to get married."

"Oh, nonsense. If not Samuel, there's bound to be a man around here who'll catch your eye."

The musicians began to play again. A waltz. Half smiling, Sarah listened. "The trouble is," she heard herself saying, "one has, but he isn't the kind who thinks about marriage."

"But who—" Liza broke off when she saw Sarah's eyes go dark. "Oh, my," she said under her breath as she watched Jake come into the tent and cross the room.

There might have been no one else there. No one at all. The moment he'd walked in, everything had faded but the music, and him. She didn't see Carlson start toward her to claim the waltz. Nor did she see his jaw clench when he noted where her attention was focused. She only saw Jake coming toward her.

He didn't speak. He just stopped in front of her and held out a hand. Sarah flowed like water into his arms.

She thought it must be a dream. He was holding her, spinning her around and around the room while the music swelled in her head. His eyes never left hers. Without thinking, she lifted her hand from his shoulder to touch his face. And watched his eyes darken like storm clouds.

Flustered by her own behavior, she dropped her hand again. "I didn't imagine you would dance."

"My mother liked to."

"You haven't—" She broke off. It was shameless. The devil with it. "You haven't been by to see me."

"No."

He was never any help, Sarah thought. "Why?"

"You know why." He was crazy to be doing even this. Holding her, torturing himself. She had lowered her eyes at his words, but she raised them again now. The look was clear and challenging.

"Are you afraid to see me?"

"No." That was a lie, and he didn't lie often. "But you should be."

"You don't frighten me, Jake."

"You haven't got the sense to be scared, Sarah." When the music stopped, he held her a moment longer. "If you did, you'd run like hell any time I got close."

"You're the one doing the running." She drew out of his arms and walked away.

It was difficult to hold on to her composure, difficult not to fume and stamp and scream as she would have liked. With her teeth gritted, she stood up for the next dance with the first man who asked her. When she looked again, Jake was gone.

"Sarah." Carlson appeared at her side with a cup of lemonade.

"Thank you." Her small silk fan was hardly adequate for the July heat. "It's a lovely party, isn't it?"

"Yes. More so for me because you're here."

She sipped, using the drink as an excuse not to respond.

"I don't want to spoil your evening, Sarah, but I feel I must speak my mind."

"Of course. What is it?"

"You're stepping on very dangerous ground with Jake Redman."

"Oh." Her dander rose, and she fought it down again. "How is that, Samuel?"

"You must know him for what he is, my dear. A killer, a hired gun. A man like that will treat you with no more respect than he would a woman who was . . . less of a lady."

"Whatever you think of him, Samuel, Mr. Redman has come to my aid a number of times. If nothing else, I consider him a friend."

"He's no one's friend. Stay away from him, Sarah, for your own sake."

Her spine shot ramrod-straight. "That doesn't sound like advice any longer, but like a demand."

Recognizing the anger in her eyes, he shifted ground. "Consider it a request." He took her hand. "I like to think we have an understanding, Sarah."

"I'm sorry." Gently she took her hand from his. "We don't. I haven't agreed to marry you, Samuel. Until I do I feel no obligation to honor a request. Now, if you'll excuse me, I'd like some air. Alone."

Knowing she had been unnecessarily short with him, she hurried out of the tent.

The moon was up now, and nearly full. Taking the deep, long breaths Sister Madeleine had always claimed would calm an unhealthy temper, she studied it. Surely the moon had been just as big and white in the East. But it had never seemed so. Just as the sky had never seemed so vast or so crowded with stars. Or the men as impossible.

The breathing wasn't going to work, she discovered.

She'd walk off her anger instead. She'd taken no more than five steps when the shadow of a man brought her up short. She watched Jake flick away a cigarette.

"It's a hot night for walking."

"Thank you for pointing that out," she said stiffly, and continued on her way.

"There's a lot of drinking going on tonight. A lot of men in town who don't get much chance to see pretty women, much less hold on to one. Walking alone's not smart."

"Your advice is noted." She stormed away, only to have her arm gripped.

"Do you have to be so ornery?"

"Yes." She yanked her arm free. "Now, if that's all you have to say, I'd like to be alone."

"I got more to say." He bit off the words, then dug into his pocket. "This belongs to you."

"Oh." She took the cameo, closing her fingers around it. "I thought it was gone. The Apache with the scar. He'd taken it. He was wearing it when—" *When you killed him*, she thought.

"I took it back. I've been meaning to give it to you, but it slipped my mind." That was another lie. He'd kept it because he'd wanted to have something of her, even for a little while.

"Thank you." She opened her bag and slipped the cameo inside. "It means a great deal to me." The sound of high, wild feminine laughter tightened her lips. Apparently there was a party at the Silver Star tonight, as well. She wouldn't soften toward him, not now, not ever again. "I'm surprised you're still here. I'd think a dance would be a bit tame for your tastes. Don't let me keep you."

"Damn it, I said I don't want you walking around alone."

Sarah looked down at the hand that had returned
to her arm. "I don't believe I'm obliged to take orders
from you. Now let go of me."

"Go back inside."

"I'll go where I want, when I want." She jerked free
a second time. "And with whom I want."

"If you're talking about Carlson, I'm going to tell
you now to stay away from him."

"Are you?" The temper that had bubbled inside her
when one man had warned her boiled over at the nerve
of this one. "You can tell me whatever you choose, but
I don't choose to listen. I'll see Samuel when it pleases
me to see him."

"So he can kiss your hand?" The anger he was keeping on a short rein strained for freedom. "So you can
have the town talking about you spending the day at his
place?"

"You have quite a nerve," she whispered. "You, who
spends your time with—that woman. Paying her for attention. How dare you insinuate that there's anything
improper in my behavior?" She stepped closer to stab a
finger at his chest. "If I allow Samuel to kiss my hand,
that's my affair. He's asked me to marry him."

The last thing she expected was to be hauled off her
feet so that her slippers dangled several inches from the
ground. "What did you say?"

"I said he asked me to marry him. Put me down."

He gave her a shake that sent hairpins flying. "I warn
you, Duchess, you think long and hard about marrying
him, because the same day you're his wife, you're his
widow. That's a promise."

She had to swallow her heart, which was lodged in
her throat. "Is a gun your answer for everything?"

Slowly, his eyes on hers, he set her down. "Stay
here."

"I don't—"

He shook her again. "By God, you'll stay here. Right here, or I'll tie you to a rail like a bad-tempered horse."

Scowling after him, she rubbed the circulation back into her arms. Of all the rude, high-handed— Then her eyes grew wide. Oh, dear Lord, she thought. He's going to kill someone. Flinging a hand to her throat, she started to run. He caught her on his way back, when she was still two feet from the tent.

"Don't you ever listen?"

"I thought— I was afraid—"

"That I was going to put a bullet in Carlson's heart?" His mouth thinned. So she cared that much, to come running to save him. "There's time for that yet." Taking a firmer grip on her arm, he pulled her with him.

"What are you doing?"

"Taking you home."

"You are not." She tried and failed to dig in her heels. "I'm not going with you, and I'm not ready to go home."

"Too bad." Impatient with her struggles, he swooped her up.

"Stop this at once and put me down. I'll scream."

"Go right ahead." He dumped her on the wagon seat. She scrambled for the reins, but he was faster.

"Lucius will take me home when I choose to go home."

"Lucius is staying in town." Jake cracked the reins.

"Now why don't you sit back and enjoy the ride? And keep quiet," he added when she opened her mouth. "Or I swear I'll gag you."

CHAPTER 10

Dignity. Despite the circumstances . . . No, Sarah thought, correcting herself, *because* of the circumstances, she would maintain her dignity. It might be difficult at the speed Jake was driving, and given the state of her own temper, but she would never, never forget she was a lady.

She wished she were a man so she could knock him flat.

Control. Jake kept his eyes focused over the horses' heads as they galloped steadily and wished it was as easy to control himself. It wasn't easy, but he'd used his control as effectively as he had his Colts for most of his life. He wasn't about to lose it now and do something he'd regret.

He thought it was a shame that a man couldn't slug a woman.

In stony silence, they drove under the fat, full moon. Some might consider it a night for romance, Sarah thought with a sniff. Not her. She was certain she'd never see another full moon without becoming furious. Dragging her off in the middle of a party, she fumed, trying to give her orders on her personal affairs. Threatening to tie her up like—like a horse, she remembered. Of all the high-handed, arrogant, ill-mannered— Taking a long, cautious breath, she blocked her thoughts.

She'd lose more than her dignity if she allowed herself to dwell on Jake Redman.

The dog sent up a fast, frantic barking as they drove into the yard. He scented Sarah and the tall man who always scratched him between the ears. Tongue lolling, he jumped at the side of the wagon, clearly pleased to have his mistress home. One look had him subsiding and slinking off again. She'd worn that same look when he'd tried to sharpen his teeth on one of her kid slippers.

The moment Jake had pulled the horses up in front of the house, Sarah gathered her skirts to step down. Haste and temper made her careless, and she caught the hem. Before she could remind herself about her dignity, she was tugging it free. She heard the silk rip.

"Now see what you've done."

Just as angry, but without the encumbrances, Jake climbed down from the opposite side. "If you'd have held on a minute, I'd have given you a hand."

"Oh, really?" With her chin lifted, she marched around the front of the wagon. "You've never done a gentlemanly thing in your life. You eat with your hat on, swear and ride in and out of here without so much as a good day or a goodbye."

He decided she looked much more likely to bite than her scrawny dog. "Those are powerful faults."

"Faults?" She lifted a brow and stepped closer. "I haven't begun to touch on your faults. If I began, I'd be a year older before I could finish. How dare you toss me in the wagon like a sack of meal and bring me back here against my wishes?"

She was stunning in the moonlight, her cheeks flushed with anger, her eyes glowing with it. "I got my reasons."

"Do you? I'd be fascinated to hear them."

So would he. He wasn't sure what had come over him, unless it was blind jealousy. That wasn't a thought he wanted to entertain. "Go to bed, Duchess."

"I have no intention of going anywhere." She grabbed his arm before he could lead the horses away. "And neither will you until you explain yourself. You accosted me, manhandled me and threatened to kill Samuel Carlson."

"It wasn't a threat." He took her hand by the wrist and dragged it away from his arm. "The next time he touches you, I'll kill him."

He meant it, Sarah realized. She stood rooted to the spot. The ways of the West might still be new to her, but she recognized murder when she saw it in a man's eyes. With her shawl flying behind her, she raced after him.

"Are you mad?"

"Maybe."

"What concern is my relationship with Samuel Carlson to you? I assure you that if I didn't wish Samuel, or any man, to touch me, I would not be touched."

"So you like it?" The horses shied nervously when he spun around to her. "You like having him hold you, put his hands over you, kiss you."

She would have suffered the tortures of hell rather than admit that Carlson had done no more than kiss her fingers. And that the only man who had done more was standing before her now. She stepped forward until she was toe-to-toe with him.

"I'll risk repeating myself and say that it's none of your business."

The way she lifted that chin, he thought, she was just asking to have it punched. "I figure it is." He dragged the horses inside the shed to unharness them.

"You figure incorrectly." Sarah followed him inside. Dignified or not, she was going to have her say. "What I do is my business, and mine alone. I've done nothing I'm ashamed of, and certainly nothing I feel requires justification to you. If I allow Samuel to court me, you have no say in the matter whatsoever."

"Is that what you call it?" He dragged the first horse into its stall. "Courting?"

She went icily still. "Have you another name for it?"

"Maybe I've been wrong about you." He took the second horse by the bridle as he studied Sarah. "I thought you were a bit choosier. Then again, you didn't pull back when I put my hands on you." He grabbed her wrist before she could have the satisfaction of slapping his face.

"How dare you?" Her breath heaved through her lips. "How dare you speak to me that way?" When she jerked free, her shawl fell to the ground unnoticed. "No, I didn't object when you touched me. By God, I wish I had. You make me feel—" The words backed up in her throat. Sarah dug her fingers into her palms until she could choke them free. "You made me feel things I still don't understand. You made me trust you, and those feelings, when it was all a lie. You made me want you when you didn't want me back. After you'd done that, you turned away as though it had meant nothing."

Pain clawed through his gut. What she was saying was true. The hurt shining from her eyes was real. "You're better off," he said quietly as he led the horse into a stall.

"I couldn't agree more." She wanted to weep. "But

if you think that gives you any right to interfere in my
life, you're wrong. Very wrong."

"You jumped mighty fast from my arms to his." Bit-
terness hardened the words even as he cursed himself
for saying them.

"I?" It was too much—much more than she could
bear. Driven by fury, she grabbed his shirt with both
hands. "It wasn't I who jumped, it was you. You left
me here without a word, then rode straight to the Silver
Star. You kissed me, then rubbed my taste from your
mouth so that you could kiss her."

"Who?" He caught her by the shoulder before she
could rush back outside. "Who?"

"I have nothing more to say to you."

"You started it. Now finish it. Whose bed do you
have me jumping in, Sarah?"

"Carlotta's." She threw the name at him with all the
hurt and fury that was bottled up inside of her. "You
left me to go to her. If that wasn't enough hurt and humiliation, you told her to hire me."

"Hire you?" Shock had his fingers tightening, bruising her flesh. "What the hell are you talking about?"

"You know very well you told her she should hire
me to sew dresses for her and her—the others."

"Sew?" He didn't know if he should laugh or curse.
Slowly he released his grip and let his hands fall to his
sides. "Whatever else you think about me, you should
know I'm not stupid."

"I don't know what I think about you." She was
fighting back tears now, and it infuriated her.

It was the gleam of those tears that had him explaining when he would have preferred to keep silent. "I
never told Carlotta to hire you, for anything. And I
haven't been with—" He broke off, swearing. Before
he could stride out, she snatched his arm again. She'd

conquered her tears, but she couldn't stop her heart from pounding.

"Are you telling me that you haven't been to the Silver Star?"

"No. I'm not telling you that."

"I see." With a bitter little laugh, she rubbed her temple. "So you've simply found, and bought, another woman who suits you. Poor Carlotta. She must be devastated."

"It would take a hell of a lot more than that. And I haven't bought anything in the Silver Star but whiskey since you—since I got back to town."

"Why?" She had to force even a whisper through her lips.

"That's my business." Cursing himself, he started out again, only to have her rush to stop him.

"I asked you a question."

"I gave you my answer." He scooped up her shawl and pushed it into her hands. "Now go to bed."

She tossed the filmy lace on the ground again. "I'm not going anywhere, and neither are you until you tell me why you haven't been with her, or anyone."

"Because I can't stop thinking about you." Enraged, he shoved her back against the wall with a force that had pins scattering and her hair tumbling wild and free to her waist. He wanted to frighten her, frighten her half as much as she frightened him. "You're not safe with me, Duchess." He leaned close to her, dragging a hand roughly through her hair. "Remember that."

She pressed her damp hands against the wall. It wasn't fear she felt. The emotion was strong and driving, but it wasn't fear. "You don't want me."

"Wanting you's eating holes in me." His free hand slid up to circle her neck. "I'd rather be shot than feel the way you make me feel."

"How do I make you feel?" she murmured.

"Reckless." It was true, but it wasn't everything. "And that's not smart, not for either of us. I'll hurt you." He squeezed lightly, trying to prove it to them both. "And I won't give a damn. So you better run while I still have a mind to let you."

"I'm not running." Even if she had wanted to, it would have been impossible. Her legs were weak and trembling. She was already out of breath. "But you are." Knowing exactly what she was doing, what she was risking, she raised her chin. "Threats come easily to you. If you were the kind of man you say you are, and you wanted me, you'd take me. Right here, right now."

His eyes darkened. They were almost black as they bored into hers. She didn't wince as his fingers tightened painfully in her hair. Instead, she kept her chin up and dared him.

"Damn you." He brought his mouth down hard on hers. To scare her, he told himself as he pressed her back against the wall and took his fill. To make her see once and for all what he was. Ruthless, knowing she would bruise, he dragged his hands over her. He touched her the way he would have touched a girl at the Silver Star. Boldly, carelessly. He wanted to bring her to tears, to make her sob and tremble and beg him to leave her alone.

Maybe then he would be able to.

He heard her muffled cry against his mouth and tried to pull back. Her arms circled him, drawing him in.

She gave herself totally, unrestrainedly, to the embrace. He was trying to hurt her, she knew. But he couldn't. She would make him see that being in his arms would never cause her pain. She gasped, forced to grip him tighter to keep her balance, when his mouth roamed down her throat, spreading luxuriant heat. The scraping of his teeth against her skin had her moaning. Too aroused to be shocked by her own actions, she tugged at his shirt. She wanted to touch his skin again, wanted to feel the warmth of it.

He was losing himself in her. No, he was already lost. Her scent, the fragility of it, had his senses spinning. Her mouth, the hunger of it, clawed at his control. Then she said his name—it was a sigh, a prayer—and broke the last bonds.

He pulled her down into the hay, desperate for her. The silk of her dress rustled against his hands as he dragged it from her shoulders. A wildness was on him, peeling away right and wrong as he tore the silk away to find her.

Terror rose up to grab her by the throat. But it wasn't terror of him. It was terror of the need that had taken possession of her. It ruled her, drove her beyond what could and could not be. As ruthless as he, she ripped at his shirt.

He was yanking at her laces, cursing them, cursing himself. Impatient with encumbrances, he shrugged out of his shirt, then sucked in his breath when her fingers dug into his flesh to pull him closer.

Hot, quick kisses raced over her face. She couldn't catch her breath, not even when he tore her laces loose. They rolled over on the hay as they fought to free themselves, and each other, of the civilized barrier of clothing. She arched when he filled his hands with her breasts, too steeped in pleasure to be ashamed of her nakedness. Her pulse hammered at dozens of points, making her thoughts spin and whirl and center only on him.

She was willow-slim, soft as the silk he'd torn, delicate as glass. For all her fragility, he couldn't fight her power over him. He could smell the hay, the horses, the night. He could see her eyes, her hair, her skin, as the moonlight pushed through the chinks in the shed to shimmer over them. Once more, just once more, he tried to bring himself to sanity. For her sake. For his own.

Then she lifted her arms to him and took him back.

He was lean and firm and strong. Sarah tossed her common sense aside and gave herself to the need, to the love. His eyes were dark, dangerously dark. His skin gleamed like copper in the shadowed light. She saw the scar that ran down his arm. As his mouth came bruisingly back to hers, she ran a gentle finger over it.

There was no turning back for either of them. The horses scraped the ground restlessly in their stalls. In the hills, a coyote sent up a wailing, lonesome song. They didn't hear. She heard her name as he whispered it. But that was all.

The hay scratched her bare skin as he covered her body with his own. She only sighed. He felt the yielding, gloried in it. He tasted the heat and the honey as he drew her breast into his mouth. A breathless moan escaped her at this new intimacy. Then his tongue began to stroke, to tease.

The pleasure built, painful, beautiful, tugging at her center as his teeth tugged at her nipples. It was unbearable. It was glorious. She wanted to tell him, wanted to explain somehow, but she could only say his name over and over.

He felt her thigh tremble when he stroked a hand along it. Then he heard her gasp of surprise, her moan of desire, when he touched what no man had ever dared to touch.

His. He took her as gently as his grinding need would allow toward her first peak. She was his. She cried out, her body curving like a bow as she crested. The breath burned in his lungs as he crushed his mouth to hers and took her flying again.

She held on, rocked, dazed and desperate. So this was love. This was what a man and woman brought to each other in the privacy of the night. It was more, so much more, than she had ever dreamed. Tears streamed from her eyes to mix with the sweat that slicked her body and his.

"Please," she murmured against his mouth, unsure of what she was asking. "Please."

He didn't want to hurt her. With that part of his mind that still functioned, he prayed he could take her painlessly. His breathing harsh and ragged, he entered her slowly, trying to soothe her with his mouth and his hands.

Lights exploded behind her eyes, brilliant white lights that flashed into every color she'd ever seen or imagined. The heat built and built until she was gasping from it, unaware that her nails had scraped down his back and dug in.

Then she was running, racing, speeding, toward something unknown, something urgently desired. Like life. Like breath. Like love. Instinct had her hips moving. Joy had her arms embracing.

She lost her innocence in a wild burst of pleasure that echoed endlessly.

The moonlight slanted across her face as she slept. He watched her. Though his body craved sleep, his mind couldn't rest. She looked almost too beautiful to be real, curled into the hay, her hair spread out, her skin glowing, covered by nothing more than the thin velvet ribbon around her neck.

He'd recognized the passion in her from the beginning. He had suppressed his own for too long not to
recognize it when it was suppressed in another. She'd
come to him openly, honestly, innocently. And of all the
sins he'd ever committed, the greatest had been taking
that innocence from her.

He'd had no right. He pressed his fingers against his
eyes. He'd had no choice. The kind of need he'd felt for
her—still felt, he realized—left no choice.

He was in love with her. He nearly laughed out
loud. That kind of thinking was dangerous. Dangerous
to Sarah. The things he loved always seemed to end
up dead, destroyed. His gaze shifted. Her dress was
bundled in a heap near her feet. On the pale silk lay
his gunbelt.

That said it all, Jake decided. He and Sarah didn't
belong together any more than his Colts and her silk
dress did. He didn't belong with anyone.

He shifted, started to rise, but Sarah stirred and
reached for his hand. "Jake."

"Yeah." Just the way she said his name made desire
quicken in him.

Slowly, a smile curving her lips, she opened her
eyes. She hadn't been dreaming, she thought. He was
here, with her. She could smell the hay, feel it. She could
see the glint of his eyes in the shadowed light. Her smile
faded.

"What's wrong?"

"Nothing's wrong." Turning away, he reached for
his pants.

"Why are you angry?"

"I'm not angry." He yanked his pants over his hips
as he rose. "Why the hell should I be angry?"

"I don't know." She was determined to be calm.
Nothing as beautiful as what had happened between

them was going to be spoiled by harsh words. She found
her chemise, noted that one shoulder strap was torn and
slipped it on. "Are you going somewhere?"

He picked up his gunbelt because it troubled him
to see it with her things. "I don't think I'd care to walk
back to town, and Lucius has my horse."

"I see. Is that the only reason you're staying?"

He turned, ready to swear at her. She was standing
very straight, her hair drifting like clouds around her
face and shoulders. Her chemise skimmed her thighs
and dipped erotically low at one breast. Because his
mouth had gone dry, he could only shake his head.

She smiled then, and held out a hand. "Come to the
house with me. Stay with me."

It seemed he still had no choice. He closed his hand
over hers.

S arah awoke with Lafitte licking her face. "Go away,"
she muttered, and turned over.

"You asked me to stay." Jake hooked an arm around
her waist. He watched her eyes fly open, saw the shock,
the remembering and the pleasure.

"I was talking to the dog." She snuggled closer.
Surely there was no more wonderful way to wake up
than in the arms of the man you loved. "He figured out
how to climb up, but he hasn't figured out how to get
down."

Jake leaned over to pat Lafitte's head. "Jump," he
said, then rolled Sarah on top of him.

"Is it morning?"

"Nope." He slid a hand up to cup her breast as he
kissed her.

"But the sun's up— Oh . . ." It dimmed as his hands
moved over her.

Day. Night. Summer. Winter. What did time matter? He was here, with her, taking her back to all those wonderful places he had shown her. She went willingly at dawn, as she had on the blanket of hay and then again and again on the narrow cot as the moon had set.

He taught her everything a woman could know about the pleasures of love, about needs stirred and needs met. He showed her what it was like to love like lightning and thunder. And he showed her what it was to love like soft rain. She learned that desire could be a pain, burning hot through the blood. She learned it could be a joy, rushing sweet under the skin.

But, though she was still unaware of it, she taught him much more, taught him that there could be beauty, and comfort, and hope.

They came together with the sun rising higher and the heat of the day chasing behind it.

Later, when she was alone in the cabin, Sarah cooled and bathed her skin. This was how it could be, she thought dreamily. Early every morning she would heat the coffee while he fed the stock and fetched fresh water from the stream. She would cook for him and tend the house. Together they would make something out of the land, out of their lives. Something good and fine.

They would start a family. She pressed a hand lightly against her stomach and wondered if one had already begun. What a beautiful way to make a child, she thought, running her fingers over her damp skin. What a perfect way.

She caught herself blushing and patted her skin dry. It wasn't right to think that way, not when they weren't married. Not when he hadn't even asked her. Would he? Sarah slipped on her shirtwaist and buttoned it quickly.

Hadn't she herself said he wasn't the kind of man who thought of marriage?

And yet . . . Could he love her the way he had loved her and not want to spend his life with her?

What had Mrs. O'Rourke said? Sarah thought back as she finished dressing. It had been something about a smart woman bringing a man around to marriage and making him think it had been his idea all along. With a light laugh, she turned toward the stove. She considered herself a very smart woman.

"Something funny?"

She glanced around as Jake walked in. "No, not really. I guess I'm just happy."

He set a basket of eggs on the table. "I haven't gathered eggs since my mother—for a long time."

As casually as she could, she took the eggs and started preparations for breakfast. "Did your mother have chickens when you were a boy?"

"Yeah. Is that coffee hot?"

"Sit down. I'll pour you some."

He didn't want to talk about his past, she decided. Perhaps the time wasn't right. Yet.

"I was able to get a slab of bacon from Mr. Cobb." She sliced it competently while the pan heated. "I've thought about getting a few pigs. Lucius is going to grumble when I ask him to build a sty, but I don't think he'd complain about eating ham. I don't suppose you know anything about raising pigs?"

Would you listen to her? Jake thought as he tilted back in her chair. *The duchess from Philadelphia talking about raising pigs.* "You deserve better," he heard himself say.

The bacon sizzled as she poured the coffee. "Better than what?"

"Than this place. Why don't you go back east, Sarah, and live like you were meant to?"

She brought the cup to him. "Is that what you want, Jake? You want me to go?"

"It's not a matter of what I want."

She stood beside him, looking down. "I'd like to hear what you want."

Their eyes held. He'd had some time to think, and think clearly. But nothing seemed clear enough when he looked at her. "Coffee," he said, taking the cup.

"Your wants are admirably simple. Take your hat off at my table." She snatched it off his head and set it aside.

He just grinned, running a hand through his hair. "Yes, ma'am. Good coffee, Duchess."

"It's nice to know I do something that pleases you." She let out a yelp when he grabbed her from behind and spun her around.

"You do a lot that pleases me." He kissed her, hard and long. "A whole lot."

"Really?" She tried to keep her tone aloof, but her arms had already wound around his neck. "A pity I can't say the same."

"I guess that was some other woman who had her hands all over me last night." Her laugh was muffled against his lips. "I brought your things over from the shed. Dress is a little worse for wear. Four petticoats." He nipped her earlobe. "I hope you don't pile that many on every day around here."

"I don't intend to discuss—"

"And that contraption you lace yourself into. Lucky you don't pass out. Can't figure you need it. Your waist's no bigger around than my two hands. I ought to know." He proved it by spanning her. "Why do you want to strap yourself into that thing?"

"I have no intention of discussing my undergarments with you."

"I took them off you. Seems I should be able to talk about them."

Blushing to the roots of her hair, she struggled away. "The bacon's burning."

He took his seat again and picked up his coffee. "How many of those petticoats do you have on now?"

After rescuing the bacon, she sent him a quick, flirtatious look over her shoulder. "You'll just have to find out for yourself." Pleased at the way his brows shot up, she went back to her cooking.

He was no longer certain how to handle her. With breakfast on the table, the scents wafting cozily in the air and Sarah sitting across from him, Jake searched his mind for something to say.

"I saw your pictures on the wall. You draw real nice."

"Thank you. I've always enjoyed it. If I'd known that my father was living here—that is, if I'd known how a few sketches would brighten the house up—I would have sent him some. I did send a small watercolor." She frowned a little. "It was a self-portrait from last Christmas. I thought he might like to know what I looked like since I'd grown up. It's strange. He had all the letters I'd written to him in that little tin box in the loft, but the sketch is nowhere to be found. I've been meaning to ask the sheriff if he might have forgotten to give it to me."

"If Barker had it, he'd have seen you got it back." He didn't care for the direction his thoughts were taking. "You sure it got this far? Mail gets lost."

"Oh, yes. He wrote me after he received it. Liza also mentioned that my father had been rather taken with it and had brought it into the store to show around."

"Might turn up."

"I suppose." She shrugged. "I've given this place a thorough cleaning, but I might not have come across it. I'll look again when Lucius puts in the floor."

"What floor?"

"The wooden floor. I've ordered boards." She broke off a bite of biscuit. "Actually, I ordered extra. I have my heart set on a real bedroom. Out the west wall, I think. My sewing money's coming in very handy."

"Sarah, last night you said something about Carlotta telling you I'd given her some idea about having you sew for her." He watched her stiffen up immediately. "When did you talk to her?"

"I didn't. I have no intention of talking to that woman."

He rolled his tongue into his cheek. He doubted Sarah would be pleased to know that her tone amused him. "Where did you hear that from?"

"Alice Johnson. She works in . . . that place. Apparently Carlotta had her drive out here to negotiate for my services."

"Alice?" He cast his mind back, juggling faces with names. "She's the little one—dark hair, big eyes?"

Sarah drew in a quiet, indignant breath. "That's an accurate description. You seem to know the staff of the Silver Star very well."

"I don't know as I'd call them staff, but yeah, I know one from the other."

Rising, she snatched up his empty plate. "And I'm sure they know you quite well." When he just grinned, she had to fight back the urge to knock the look off his face with the cast-iron skillet. "I'll thank you to stop smirking at me."

"Yes, ma'am." But he went right on. "You sure are pretty when you get fired up."

"If that's a compliment," she said, wishing it didn't make her want to smile, "you're wasting your breath."

"I ain't much on compliments. But you're pretty, and that's a fact. I guess you're about the prettiest thing I've ever seen. Especially when you're riled."

"Is that why you continue to go out of your way to annoy me?"

"I expect. Come here."

She smoothed down her skirt. "I will not."

He rose slowly. "You're ornery, too. Can't figure why it appeals to me." He dragged her to him. After a moment's feigned struggle, she laughed up at him.

"I'll have to remember to stay ornery and annoyed, then."

He said nothing. The way she'd looked up at him had knocked the breath out of his body. He pulled her closer, holding on, wishing. Content, Sarah nuzzled his shoulder. Before he could draw her back, she framed his face with her hands and brushed her lips over his.

"You're still tying me up in knots," he muttered.

"That's good. I don't intend to stop."

He stepped back, then gripped her hands with his. "Which one did he kiss?"

"I don't know what you mean."

"Carlson." She gave a surprised gasp when his fingers tightened on hers. "Which hand did he kiss?"

Sarah kept her eyes on his. "Both."

She watched the fury come then, and was amazed at how quickly, how completely, he masked it. But it was still there. She could feel it rippling through him. "Jake—"

He shook his head. Then, in a gesture that left her limp, he brought her hands to his lips. Then he dropped them, obviously uncomfortable, and dug his own hands into his pockets.

"I don't want you to let him do it again."

"I won't."

Her response should have relaxed him, but his tension doubled. "Just like that?"

"Yes, just like that."

He turned away and began to pace. Her brow lifted. She realized she'd never before seen him make an unnecessary movement. If he took a step, it was to go toward or away.

"I've got no right." There was fury in his voice. The same kind she'd heard outside the tent the night before. In contrast, hers was soft and soothing.

"You have every right. The only right. I'm in love with you."

Now he didn't move at all. He froze as a man might when he heard a trigger cocked at the back of his head. She simply waited, her hands folded at her waist, her eyes calm and clear.

"You don't know what you're saying," he managed at last.

"Of course I do, and so do you." With her eyes on his, she walked to him. "Do you think I could have been with you as I was last night, this morning, if I didn't love you?"

He stepped back before she could touch him. It had been so long since he'd been loved that he'd forgotten what it could feel like. It filled him like a river, and its currents were strong.

"I've got nothing for you, Sarah. Nothing."

"Yourself." She reached a hand to his cheek. "I'm not asking for anything."

"You're mixing up what happened last night with—"

"With what?" she challenged. "Do you think because you were the first man that I don't know the difference between love and . . . lust? Can you tell me it's been like that for you before, with anyone? Can you?"

No, he couldn't. And he couldn't tell her it would never be that way with anyone but her. "Lucius will be back soon," he said instead. "I'll go down and get the water you wanted before I leave."

And that was all? she thought. Damn him for turning his back on her again. He didn't believe her, she thought. He thought she was just being foolish and romantic. . . . But no, no, that wasn't right, she realized. That wasn't it at all.

It came to her abruptly and with crystalline clarity. He did believe her, and that was why he had turned away. He was as frightened and confused by her love as she had been by the land. It was just as foreign to him. Just as difficult to understand and accept.

She could change that. Taking a long, cleansing breath, she turned to her dishes. She could change that in the same way she had changed herself. She embraced the land now, called it her own. One day he would do the same with her.

She heard the door open again, and she turned, smiling.

"Jake—"

But it was Burt Donley who filled the doorway.

CHAPTER 11

"Where's Redman?"

Panic came first, and it showed in her wide, wild eyes. She was still holding the skillet, and she had one mad thought of heaving it at his head. But his hand was curled over the butt of his gun. She saw in his eyes what she had never seen in Jake's, what she realized she'd never seen in any man's, not even in those of the Apache who had kidnapped her. A desire, even an eagerness, to kill.

He stepped inside, and through the thickness of his beard she saw that he was smiling. "I asked you, where's Redman?"

"He's not here." It surprised her how calm a voice could sound even when a heart was pounding. She had a man to protect. The man she loved. "I don't believe I asked you in."

His smile widened into a grin. "You ain't going to tell me he brought you all the way out here last night and then left a pretty thing like you all alone?"

She was terrified Jake would come back. And terrified he wouldn't. She had no choice but to hold her ground. "I'm not telling you anything. But as you can see, I'm alone."

"I can see that, real plain. Funny, 'cause his horse is in town and he ain't." He picked up a biscuit from the bowl on the table with his wide, blunt-edged fingers, studied it, then bit in. "Word is he spends time out here."

"Mr. Redman occasionally visits. I'll be sure to tell him you were looking for him, if and when I see him."

"You do that. You be sure and do that." He took another bite, chewing slowly, watching her.

"Good day, then."

But he didn't leave. He only walked closer. "You're prettier than I recollect."

She moistened her lips, knowing they were trembling. "I don't believe we've met."

"No, but I've seen you." She strained backward when he put a hand to her hair. "You don't favor your pa none."

"You'll have to excuse me." She tried to step to the side, but he blocked her.

"He sure did set some store by you. A man can see why." He pushed the rest of the biscuit into his mouth, chewing as he reached down to toy with the small bow at her collar. "Too bad he got himself killed over that mine and left you orphaned. Smart man would've kept himself alive. Smart man would've seen the sense in that."

She shifted again, and was again blocked. "He could hardly be blamed for an accident."

"Maybe we'll talk about that later." Enjoying her trembling, he tugged the little bow loose. "You look smarter than your pa was."

Lafitte burst in, snarling. Donley had his hand on the butt of his gun when Sarah grabbed his arm. "No, please. He's hardly more than a puppy." Moving quickly, she gathered the growling dog up. "There's no need for you to hurt him. He's harmless."

"Donley likes killing harmless things." Jake spoke from the doorway. The men stood ten feet apart, Jake backed by sun, Donley by shadow. "There was a man in Laramie—more of a boy, really. Daniel Little Deer was harmless, wasn't he, Donley?"

"He was a breed." Donley's teeth gleamed through his beard. "I don't think no more of killing a breed than a sick horse."

"And it's easier when it's back-shooting."

"I ain't shooting at your back, Redman."

"Move aside, Sarah."

"Jake, please—"

"Move aside." He was over the sick fear he'd felt when he'd seen Donley's horse outside the house. He was cold, killing-cold. His guns hung low on his hips, and his hands were limber and ready.

Donley shifted, settling his weight evenly. "I've waited a long time for this."

"Some of us get lucky," Jake murmured, "and wait a long time to die."

"When I've killed you, I'm going to have the woman, and the gold." His hand slapped the butt of his gun. The .44 was aimed heart-high. He was fast.

The sound of a gunshot exploded, ripping through the still morning air. Sarah watched in horror as Donley stumbled, forward, then back. A red stain spread across his shirt and his leather vest before he fell by the stone hearth and lay still.

Jake stood in the doorway, his face expressionless, his mind calm and cold. He'd never once felt the rush some men spoke of that came from killing. To him it was neither power nor curse. It was survival.

"Oh, God." Pressed back against the wall, Sarah

stared. Lafitte leaped out of her limp arms to crouch, growling, by Donley's gun hand. Her vision grayed, wavered, then snapped back when Jake gripped her arms.

"Did he hurt you?"

"No, I—"

"Get outside."

Hysteria bubbled up in her throat. A man was dead, lying dead on her floor, and the one holding her looked like a stranger. "Jake—"

"Get outside," he repeated, doing his best to shield her from the man he'd killed. "Go on into the shed or down to the stream." When she only continued to stare, he pulled her to the door and shoved her out. "Do what I tell you."

"What—what are you going to do?"

"I'm going to take him into town."

Giving in to weakness, she leaned on the rail, dragging in gulps of the hot, dusty air as though it were water. "What will they do to you? You killed him."

"Barker'll take me at my word. Or he'll hang me."

"No, but—" Nausea was churning now, coating her skin with a thin, clammy sweat. "He wanted to kill you. He came looking for you."

"That's right." He took both her arms again because he wanted her to look at him, really look. "And tomorrow, next week, next month, there'll be someone else who comes looking for me. I got fast hands, Sarah, and somebody's always going to want to prove they got faster. One day they'll be right."

"You can change. It can change. It has to." She struggled out of his hold, only to throw her arms around him. "You can't want to live this way."

"What I want and what is have always been two different things." He pushed her away. "I care about you."

It was easy to mean it, hard to say it. "That's why I'm telling you to walk away."

He'd just killed a man in front of her eyes. And killed him coldly. Even through her horror she'd seen that. But it hadn't left him untouched. What she saw now was the frustration and anger of a man caught in a trap. He needed someone to offer him a way out, or at least the hope of one. If she could do nothing else, she could give him hope.

"No." She stepped forward to frame his face with her hands. "I can't. I won't."

Her hands were trembling. Cold and trembling, he thought as he reached for them. "You're a damn fool."

"Yes. I'm quite sure you're right. But I love you."

He couldn't have begun to tell her what it did to him inside when she said that. When he looked into her eyes and saw that she meant it. He pulled her against him for a rough, hungry kiss. "Go away from the house. I don't want you here when I bring him out."

She nodded, took a long breath and stepped back. The sickness had passed, though the raw feeling inside remained. "Once, I was sure there was only right and wrong, and that to kill another person was the greatest wrong. But there isn't only right and wrong, Jake. What you did, what you had to do, kept you alive. There's nothing more important to me than that." She paused and touched his hand. "Come back."

He watched her, as he had watched her once before, start up the rise to her father's grave. When she was gone, he went back inside.

Two days passed, and Sarah tried to follow her daily routine and not to wonder why Jake hadn't ridden back to her. It seemed everyone else had paid her a visit, but not Jake. Barker had come out and, in his usual take-your-time way, questioned her about Burt Donley. It seemed no more than a token investigation to Sarah. Barker, either because he was lazy or because he was a shrewd judge of character, had taken Jake at his word.

The story had spread quickly. Soon after Barker, Liza and Johnny had driven up to hear the details and eat oatmeal cookies. Before she had left, Liza had chased Johnny outside to pester Lucius so that she could spend an hour talking about Will and her upcoming wedding. She was to have a new dress, and she had already ordered the pink silk and the pattern from Santa Fe.

The following morning, the sound of a rider approaching had Sarah rushing out of the chicken coop, eggs banging dangerously against each other in the basket she carried. She struggled to mask her disappointment when she saw Samuel Carlson.

"Sarah." He dismounted quickly, and would have taken her hand, but she used both to grip the handle of the basket. "I've been worried about you."

"There's no need." She smiled as he tied his horse at the rail.

"I was shocked to learn that Donley and Redman had drawn guns right here in your house. It's a miracle you weren't injured."

"I'm sure I would have been if Jake hadn't come back when he did. Donley was . . . very threatening."

"I feel responsible."

"You?" She stopped in front of the house. "Why?"

"Donley worked for me. I knew what kind of man he was." There was a grimness around his eyes and mouth as he spoke. "I can't say I had any trouble with him until Redman came back to town."

"It was Donley who sought Jake out, Samuel." Her voice sharpened with the need to defend him. "It was he who deliberately provoked a fight. I was there."

"Of course." He laid a soothing hand on her arm. Manners prevented him from stepping inside the house without an invitation. He was shrewd enough to see that something had changed, and that he wouldn't get one. "I detest the fact that you were forced to witness a killing, and in your own home. It must distress you to stay here now."

"No." She glanced over her shoulder. It had been difficult, the first time she had gone inside afterward. There were still traces of dried blood in the dirt, the sight of which had given Johnny ghoulish pleasure. But it was her home. "I'm not as frail as that."

"You're a strong woman, Sarah, but a sensitive one. I'm concerned about you."

"It's kind of you to be. Your friendship is a great comfort to me."

"Sarah." He touched a gentle hand to her cheek. "You must realize that I want to be much more than your friend."

"I know." Regret was in her eyes, in her voice. "It's not possible, Samuel. I'm sorry."

She saw the anger mar his face, and was surprised by the depth of it before he brought it under control again. "It's Redman, isn't it?"

She felt it would be dishonorable, and insulting, to lie to him. "Yes."

"I thought you were more sensible, Sarah. You're an intelligent, gently bred woman. You must understand that Redman is a dangerous man, a man without scruples. He lives by violence. It's part of him."

She smiled a little. "He describes himself the same way. I believe you're both wrong."

"He'll only hurt you."

"Perhaps, but I can't change my feelings. Nor do I wish to." Regret had her reaching out to touch his arm. "I'm sorry, Samuel."

"I have faith that in time you'll get over this infatuation. I can be patient."

"Samuel, I don't—"

"Don't distress yourself." He patted her hand. "Along with patience, I have confidence. You were meant to belong to me, Sarah." He stepped back to untie his horse. Inside, he was boiling with rage. He wanted this woman, and what belonged to her—and he intended to have them, one way or the other.

When he turned to stand beside his mount with his reins in his hands, his face was touched only with affection and concern. "This doesn't change the fact that I worry about you, living out here all alone."

"I'm not alone. I have Lucius."

Carlson cast a slow, meaningful look around the yard.

"He's up in the mine," Sarah explained. "If there was trouble, he'd come down quickly enough."

"The mine." Carlson cast his eyes up at the rock. "At least promise me that you won't go inside. It's a dangerous place."

"Gold doesn't lure me." She smiled again, relieved that they would remain friends.

He swung gracefully into the saddle. "Gold lures everyone."

She watched him ride off. Perhaps he was right, she mused. Gold had a lure. Even though in her heart she didn't believe she'd ever see the mine pay, it was exciting knowing there was always a chance. It kept Lucius in the dark and the dust for hours on end. Her father had died for it.

Even Jake, she thought, wasn't immune. It was he who had asked Lucius to pick up where her father had left off. She had yet to discover why. With death on his mind, Donley's last words had been . . . A glimmer of suspicion broke into her mind.

I'm going to have the woman, and the gold.

Why should a man like Donley speak of gold before he drew his gun? Why would a worthless mine be on his mind at such a time? Or was it worthless?

Her promise to Samuel forgotten, she started toward the rise.

A movement caught her eye and, turning around again, she scanned the road. Someone was coming, on foot. Even as she watched, the figure stumbled and fell. Sarah had her skirts in her hand and was running before the figure struggled to stand again.

"Alice!" Sarah quickened her pace. The girl was obviously hurt, but until Sarah reached her, catching her before she fell again, she couldn't see how badly.

"Oh, dear Lord." Gripping the sobbing girl around the waist, she helped her toward the house. "What happened? Who did this to you?"

"Miss Conway . . ." Alice could hardly speak through her bruised and bloodied lips. Her left eye was blackened and swollen nearly shut. There were ugly scratches, like the rake of fingernails, down her cheek, and every breath she took came out with a hitch of pain.

"All right, don't worry, just lean on me. We're nearly there."

"Didn't know where else to go," Alice managed. "Shouldn't be here."

"Don't try to talk yet. Let me get you inside. Oh, Lucius." Half stumbling herself, Sarah looked up with relief as he came hurrying down the rocks. "Help me get her inside, up to bed. She's badly hurt."

"What in the holy hell—?" Wheezing a bit from the exertion, he picked Alice up in his scrawny arms. "You know who this girl is, Miss Sarah?"

"Yes. Take her up to my bed, Lucius. I'll get some water."

Alice swooned as he struggled to carry her up the ladder to the loft. "She's done passed out."

"That may be a blessing for the moment." Moving quickly, Sarah gathered fresh water and clean cloths. "She must be in dreadful pain. I can't see how she managed to get all the way out here on foot."

"She's taken a mighty beating."

He stepped out of the way as best he could when Sarah climbed the stairs to sit on the edge of the bed. Gently she began to bathe Alice's face. When she loosened the girl's bodice, he cleared his throat and turned his back.

"Oh, my God." With trembling hands, Sarah unfastened the rest of the buttons. "Help me get this dress off of her, Lucius. It looks as though she's been whipped."

His sense of propriety was overcome by the sight of the welts on Alice's back and shoulders. "Yeah, she's been whipped." The cotton of her dress stuck to the raw, open sores. "Whipped worse'n a dog. I'd like to get my hands on the bastard who done this."

Sarah found her own hands were clenched with fury. "There's some salve on the shelf over the stove, Lucius. Fetch it for me." She did her best to bathe and cool the wounds. As Alice's eyes fluttered open and she moaned, Sarah soothed her in a low, calming voice. "Try not to move, Alice. We're going to take

care of you. You're safe now. I promise you you're
safe."

"Hurts."

"I know. Oh, I know." There were tears stinging her
eyes as she took the salve from Lucius and began to
stroke it over the puffy welts.

It was a slow, painful process. Though Sarah's fingers were light and gentle, Alice whimpered each time
she touched her. Her back was striped to the waist with
angry red lines, some of which had broken open and
were bleeding. With sweat trickling down her face,
Sarah tended and bandaged, talking, always talking.

"Would you like another sip of water?"

"Please." With Sarah's hand cradling her head, Alice drank from the cup. "I'm sorry, Miss Conway." She
lay back weakly as Sarah held a cool cloth to her swollen eye. "I know I shouldn't have come here. It ain't
right, but I wasn't thinking straight."

"You did quite right by coming."

"You was—were—so nice to me before. And I was
afraid if I didn't get away . . ."

"You aren't to worry." Sarah applied salve to her facial scratches. "In a few days you'll be feeling much
better. Then we can think about what's to be done. For
now, you'll stay right here."

"I can't—"

"You can and you will." Setting the salve aside,
Sarah took her hand. "Do you feel strong enough to tell
us what happened? Did a man—one of your customers—do this to you?"

"No, ma'am." Alice moistened her swollen lips. "It
was Carlotta."

"Carlotta?" Sarah's eyes narrowed to slits. "Are you
saying that Carlotta beat you like this?"

"I ain't never seen her so mad. Sometimes she gets mean if something don't go her way, or if she's been drinking too much you get a slap or two. She went crazy. I think she might've killed me if the other girls hadn't broke in the door and started screaming."

"Why? Why would she hurt you like this?"

"I can't say for sure. I done something wrong." Her voice slurred, and her eyes dropped shut. "She was mad, powerful mad, after Jake came by. They had words. Nancy, she's one of the other girls, listened outside of Carlotta's office. He said something to set her off, I expect. Nancy said she was yelling. Said something about you, Miss Conway, I don't rightly know what. When he left she went crazy. Started smashing things. I went on up to my room. She came after me, beat me worse'n Pa ever did. Eli, he brought me out."

"Eli's the big Black Carlotta has working for her," Lucius explained.

"He drove me out as far as he could. She finds out, she'll make him sorry. Took a belt to me," she murmured as sleep took her under. "Kept hitting me and hitting me, saying it was my fault Jake don't come around no more."

"Bitch," Lucius said viciously. Then he wiped his mouth. "'Scuse me, Miss Sarah."

"No excuse necessary. I couldn't agree more." There was a rage running through her, hotter and huger than anything she'd ever experienced. She stared at the girl asleep in her bed, her small, pretty face bruised and swollen. She remembered each welt she'd tended. "Hitch up the wagon, Lucius."

"Yes'm. You want me to go somewheres?"

"No, I'm going. I want you to stay with Alice."

"I'll hitch it up, Miss Sarah, but if you're thinking

about talking to the sheriff, it won't do much good. Alice here ain't going to talk to him like she done with you. She'd be too scared."

"I'm not going to the sheriff, Lucius. Just hitch up the wagon."

She pushed the horses hard, pleased that the fury didn't subside as she approached town. She wanted the fury. Since she'd come west she'd learned to accept many things—the grief, the violence, the labor. Perhaps the land was lawless, but there were times and reasons, even here, for justice.

Johnny raced out of the dry goods store as Sarah rode by, then raced back in again to complain to Liza that Sarah hadn't waved at him. She hadn't even seen him. There was only one face in her mind now. She drew up in front of the Silver Star.

Three women lounged in what might have been called a parlor. The late-morning heat had them half dozing in their petticoats and their feathered wraps. The room itself was dim and almost airless. Vivid red drapes hung limp at the windows. Gold leaf glowed dull and dusty on the frames of the mirrors.

As Sarah entered, a heavy-eyed redhead popped up from her sprawled position on a settee. She plopped back again with a howling laugh. "Well, look here, girls, we got ourselves some company. Get out the teacups."

The others looked over. One of them hitched her wrap up around her shoulders. Her hands folded, Sarah stood in the doorway and took it all in.

So this was a bordello. She couldn't say she saw anything remotely exciting. It looked more like a badly furnished parlor in need of a good dusting. There was a heavy floral scent of mixed perfumes that merged, none too appealingly, with plain sweat. Carefully, finger by finger, Sarah drew off her driving gloves.

"I'd like to speak with Carlotta, please. Will someone tell her I'm here?"

No one moved. The women merely exchanged looks. The redhead went back to examining her nails. After a long breath, Sarah tried another tactic.

"I'm here to speak with her about Alice." That caught their attention. Every one of the women looked over at her. "She'll be staying with me until she's well."

Now the redhead rose. Her flowered wrap slid down her shoulders with the movement. "You took Alice in?"

"Yes. She needs care, Miss—"

"I'm Nancy." She took a quick look behind her. "How come somebody like you's going to see to Alice?"

"Because she needs it. I'd be grateful to you if you would tell Carlotta I'd like to speak with her."

"I reckon I could do that." The redhead pulled her wrap up. "You tell Alice we was asking about her."

"I'll be glad to."

While Nancy disappeared up the stairs, Sarah tried to ignore the other women's stares. She had changed to one of her best day dresses. Sarah thought the dove gray very distinguished, particularly with its black trim. Her matching hat had been purchased just before her trip west and was the latest Paris fashion. Apparently it wasn't proper attire for a bordello, she thought as she watched Carlotta descend the stairs.

The owner of the Silver Star was resplendent in her trademark red. The silk slithered down her tall, curvaceous body, clinging, shifting, swaying. Her high white breasts rose like offerings from the scalloped bodice, which was threaded with silver threads. In her hand she carried a matching fan. As she flicked it in front of her face, the heavy scent of roses filled the room.

Despite her feelings, Sarah couldn't deny that the woman was stunning. In another place, another time, she could have been a queen.

"My, my, this is a rare honor, Miss Conway."

She'd been drinking. Sarah caught the scent of whiskey under the perfume. "This is hardly a social call."

"Now you disappoint me." Her painted mouth curved. "I can always use a new girl around here. Isn't that right . . . ladies?"

The other women shifted uncomfortably and remained tactfully silent.

"I thought maybe you'd come in looking for work." Still waving the fan, she strolled around Sarah, sizing her up. "Little scrawny," she said. "But some men like that. Could use some fixing up, right, girls? Little more here." She patted Sarah's unrouged cheek. "Little less there." She flicked a hand at the neckline of Sarah's dress. "You might make a tolerable living."

"I don't believe I'd care to . . . work for you, Carlotta."

"That so?" Her eyes, already hardened by the whiskey, iced over. "Too much of a lady to take pay for it, but not too much of a lady to give it away."

Sarah curled her fingers into a fist, then forced them to relax again. She would not resort to violence, or be driven to it. "No. I wouldn't care to work for anyone who beats their employees. Alice is with me now, Carlotta, and she'll stay with me. If you ever put your hands on her again, I'll see to it that you're thrown in jail."

"Oh, will you?" An angry flush darkened cheeks already bright with rouge. "I'll put my hands on who I please." She stabbed the fan into Sarah's chest. "No prim-faced bitch from back east is going to come into my place and tell me different."

With surprising ease, Sarah reached out and snapped

the fan in two. "I just have." She had only an instant to brace herself for the slap. It knocked her backward. To balance herself she grabbed a table and sent a statuette crashing to the floor.

"Your kind makes me sick." Carlotta's voice was high and brittle as she leaned toward Sarah. Whiskey and anger had taken hold of her and twisted her striking face. "Looking as though they wouldn't let a man touch them. But you'll spread your legs as easy as any. You think because you went to school and lived in a big house that makes you special? You're nothing out here, nothing." She scooped up a fat plaster cherub and sent it crashing into the wall.

"The fact that I went to school and lived in a house isn't all that separates us." Sarah's voice was a sharp contrast to Carlotta's in its calmness. "You don't make me sick, Carlotta. You only make me sorry."

"I don't need pity from you. I made this place. I got something, and nobody handed it to me. Nobody ever gave me money for fine dresses and fancy hats. I earned it." Breasts heaving, she stepped closer. "You think you got Jake dangling on a string, honey, you're wrong. Soon as he's had his fill of you, he'll be back. What he's doing to you on these hot, sweaty nights, he'll be doing to me."

"No." Amazingly, Sarah's voice was still calm. "Even if he comes back and puts your price in your hands, you'll never have what I have with him. You know it," Sarah said quietly. "And that's why you hate me." With her eyes on Carlotta, she began to pull on her gloves again. Her hands would tremble any moment. She knew it, and she wanted to be on her way first. "But the issue here is Alice, not Jake. She is no longer in your employ."

"I'll tell that slut when she's through here."

It happened so quickly, Sarah was hardly aware of it. She had managed to hold her temper during Carlotta's insulting tirade against her own person. But to hear Alice called by that vile name while the girl was lying helpless and hurt was too much. Her ungloved hand shot out and connected hard with the side of Carlotta's face.

The three women, and the one who had come creeping down the stairs to look in on the commotion, let out gasps of surprise in unison. Sarah barely had time to feel the satisfaction of her action when Carlotta had her by the hair. They tumbled to the floor in a flurry of skirts.

Sarah shrieked as Carlotta tried to pull her hair out by the roots. She had handfuls of it, tugging and ripping while she cursed wildly. Fighting the pain, Sarah swung out and connected with soft flesh. She heard Carlotta grunt, and they rolled across the rug. Crockery smashed as they collided with a table, each trying to land a blow or defend against one. Sarah took a fist in the stomach with a gasp, but managed to evade a lethal swipe of Carlotta's red-tipped nails.

There was hate in Carlotta's eyes, a wild, almost mad hate. Sarah grabbed her wrist and twisted, knowing that if the other woman got her hands on her throat she'd squeeze until all her breath was gone.

She had no intention of being strangled, or pummeled. Her own rage had her rolling on top of her opponent and grabbing a handful of dyed hair. When she felt teeth sink into her arm, she cried out and yanked with all her strength, jerking Carlotta's head back and bringing out a howl of rage and pain. Other screams rose up, but Sarah was lost in the battle. She yanked and clawed and tore as viciously as Carlotta. They were equals now, with no barriers of class or background. A lamp shattered in a shower of glass as the two writhing bodies careened into another table.

"What in the hell is going on here?" Barker burst into the parlor. He took one look at the scene on the floor and shut his eyes. He'd rather have faced five armed, drunken cowboys than a pair of scratching women. "Break it up," he ordered as the two of them tumbled across the floor. "Somebody's going to get hurt here." He shook his head and sighed. "Most likely me."

He stepped into the melee just as Jake strode through the parlor doors.

"Let's pull them apart," Barker said heavily. "Take your pick." But Jake was already hauling Sarah up off the floor. She kicked out, her breath hissing as she tried to struggle away.

"Pull in your claws, Duchess." He clamped an arm around her waist as Barker restrained Carlotta.

"Get her out of here." Carlotta shoved away from Barker and stood, her dress ripped at both shoulders, her hair in wild tufts. "I want that bitch out of here and in jail. She came in here and started breaking up my place."

"Now, that don't seem quite logical," Barker mused. "Miss Sarah, you want to tell me what you're doing in a place like this?"

"Business." She tossed her hair out of her eyes. "Personal business."

"Well, looks to me like you've finished with your business here. Why don't you go on along home now?"

Sarah drew on her dignity like a cape over her torn dress. "Thank you, Sheriff." She cast one last look at Carlotta. "I am quite finished here." She glided toward the door to the secret admiration of Carlotta's girls.

"Just one damn minute." Jake took her arm the second she stepped outside. She had time now for embarrassment when she noted the size of the crowd she'd drawn.

"If you'll excuse me," she said stiffly, "I must get home." She reached up to tidy her tousled hair. "My hat."

"I think I saw what was left of it back in there." Jake ran his tongue over his teeth as he looked at her. She had a bruise beginning under her eye. It would make up to be a pretty good shiner by the end of the day. Her fashionable gray dress was ripped down one arm, and her hair looked as though she'd been through a windstorm. Thoughtfully, he tucked his hands in his pockets. Carlotta had looked a hell of a lot worse.

"Duchess, a man wouldn't know it to look at you, but you're a real firebrand."

Grimly she brushed at her rumpled skirts. "I can see that amuses you."

"I have to say it does." He smiled, and her teeth snapped together. "I guess I'm flattered, but you didn't have to get yourself in a catfight over me."

Her mouth dropped open. The man looked positively delighted. She was scratched and bruised and aching and humiliated, and he looked as though his grin might just split his face. Over him? she thought, and made herself return the smile.

"So you think I fought with Carlotta over you, because I was jealous?"

"Can't think of another reason."

"Oh, I'll give you a reason." She brought her fist up and caught him neatly on the jaw. He was holding a hand to his face and staring after her when Barker strolled out.

"She's got what you might call a mean right hook." In the street, people howled and snickered as Sarah climbed into the wagon and drove off. "Son," Barker said with a hand on Jake's shoulder, "you're the fastest hand I ever saw with those Colts of yours. You play a fine game of poker, and you hold your whiskey like a man. But you got a hell of a lot to learn about women."

"Apparently," Jake murmured. He walked across to O'Rourke's and untied his horse.

Sarah seethed as she raced the wagon toward home. She'd made a spectacle of herself. She'd engaged in a crude, despicable sparring match with a woman with no morals. She'd brought half the town out into the street to stare and snicker at her. And then, to top it all off, she'd had to endure Jake Redman's grinning face.

She'd shown him. Sarah tossed her head up and spurred the horses on. Her hand might possibly be broken, but she'd shown him. The colossal conceit of the man, to believe that she would stoop to such a level out of petty jealousy.

She wished she'd torn Carlotta's brass-colored hair out by its black roots.

Not over him, she reminded herself. At least not very much over him.

She heard the rider coming up fast and looked over her shoulder. With a quick gasp of alarm, she cracked the reins. She would not speak to him now. Jake Redman could go to the devil, as far as she was concerned. And he could take his grin with him.

But her sturdy workhorses were no match for his mustang. Nor was her driving skill a match for his riding. Even as she cursed him, he came up beside her. She had a flash, clear as a bell, of how he'd looked when he'd raced beside the stagecoach, firing over his shoulder. He looked just as untamed and dangerous now.

"Stop that damn thing."

Chin up, she cracked the reins again.

One of these days somebody was going to teach her to listen, Jake thought. It might just be today. He judged the timing and rhythm, then leaped from his horse into the wagon. Sure-footed, he stepped over onto the seat, and though she fought him furiously he pulled the horses in.

"What the hell's got into you, woman?" He scrambled for a hold as she shoved him aside and tried to jump out.

"Take your hands off me. I won't be handled this way."

"Handling you is a sight more work than I care for." He snatched his hand out of range before she could bite him. "Haven't you had enough scratching for one day? Sit down before you hurt yourself."

"You want the blasted wagon, take it. I won't ride with you."

"You'll ride with me, all right." Out of patience, he twisted her into his lap and silenced her. She squirmed and pushed and held herself as rigid as iron. Then she melted. He felt the give, slow, easy, inevitable. In her. In himself. As her lips parted for his, he forgot about keeping her quiet and just took what he kept trying to tell himself he couldn't have.

"You pack a punch, Duchess." He drew her away to rub a hand over his chin. "In a lot of ways. You want to tell me what that was for?"

She pulled away, furious that she'd gone soft with just one kiss. "For assuming that I was jealous and would fight over any worthless man."

"So now I'm worthless. Well, that may be, but you seem to like having me around."

She did her best to straighten what was left of her dress. "Perhaps I do."

He needed to know it more than he'd imagined. Jake

took her chin in his hand and turned her to face him. "You change your mind?"

Again she softened, this time because she saw the doubt in his eyes. "No, I haven't changed my mind." She drew a long breath. "Even though you didn't come back and you've been to the Silver Star to see Carlotta."

"You sure do hear things. Can't imagine what you'd know if you lived closer to town. Stay in the wagon." He recognized the look in her eye by now. "Stay in the wagon, Sarah, until I get my horse tied on. I'll just catch you again if you run."

"I won't run." She brought her chin up again and stared straight ahead. When he'd joined her again, she continued her silence. Jake clucked to the horses and started off.

"I like to know why a woman's mad at me. Why don't you tell me how you know I've been to Carlotta's?"

"Alice told me."

"Alice Johnson?"

"That's right. Your friend Carlotta nearly beat her to death."

He brought the horses up short. "What?"

Her fury bounded back and poured over him. "You heard what I said. She beat that poor girl as cruelly as anyone can be beaten. Eli helped Alice get out of town. Then she walked the rest of the way to my place."

"Is she going to be all right?"

"With time and care."

"And you're going to give it to her?"

"Yes." Her eyes dared him. "Do you have any objections?"

"No." He touched her face, gently, in a way that was new to him. Abruptly he snatched his hand back and snapped the reins again. "You went into the Silver Star to have it out with Carlotta over Alice."

"I've never been so furious." Sarah lifted a hand to where Jake had touched her. "Alice is hardly more than a child. No matter what she did, she didn't deserve that kind of treatment."

"Did she tell you why Carlotta did it?"

"She didn't seem to know, only that she must have made some kind of mistake. Alice did say that Carlotta was in a temper after you had been there."

He said nothing for a moment as he put the pieces together. "And she took it out on Alice."

"Why did you go? Why did you go to Carlotta? If there's something you . . ." She hadn't any idea how to phrase it properly. "If I don't know enough about your needs . . . I realize I don't have any experience in these matters, but I—"

She found her mouth crushed again in a kiss that was half hungry, half angry. "There's never been any-one else who's known so much about what I need." He watched her face clear into a smile. "I went to see Car-lotta to tell her I don't care much for having my name used as a reference."

"So she took it out on Alice, because Alice was the one who'd come to talk to me." Sarah shook her head and tried not to let her temper take over again. "Alice only told me what Carlotta wanted her to tell me. It didn't work the way she'd planned, and Alice paid for it."

"That's about the size of it."

Sarah linked her fingers again and set them in her lap. "Is that the only reason you went to Carlotta?"

"No." He waited for the look. The look of passion-ate fury. "I went for that, and to tell her to stay away from you. Of course, I didn't know at the time that you were going to go and bloody her lip."

"Did I?" She tried and failed to bank down the pleasure she felt at the news. "Did I really?"

"And her nose. Guess you were a little too involved to notice."

"I've never struck anyone before in my life." She tried to keep her voice prim, then gave up. "I liked it."

With a laugh, Jake pulled her to his side. "You're a real wildcat, Duchess."

CHAPTER 12

Jake learned something new when he watched Sarah with Alice. He had always assumed that a woman who had been raised in the sheltered, privileged world would ignore, even condemn, one who lived as Alice lived. There were many decent women, as they called themselves, who would have turned Alice away as if she were a rabid dog.

Not Sarah.

And it was more than what he supposed she would have called Christian charity. He'd run into his share of people who liked to consider themselves good Christians. They had charity, all right, unless they came across somebody who looked different, thought different. There had been plenty of Christian women who had swept their skirts aside from his own mother because she'd married a man of mixed blood.

They went into church on Sundays and quoted the Scriptures and professed to love their neighbor. But when their neighbor didn't fit their image of what was right, love turned to hate quickly enough.

With Sarah it wasn't just words. It was compassion,

caring and an understanding he hadn't expected from her. He could hear, as he sat at the table, the simple kindness in her voice as she talked to the girl and tended her wounds.

As for Alice, it was obvious the girl adored Sarah. He'd yet to see her, as Sarah claimed her patient wasn't up to visitors. But he could hear the shyness and the respect in her voice when she answered Sarah's questions.

She'd fought for Alice. He couldn't quite get over that. Most people wouldn't fight for anything unless it was their own, or something they wanted to own. It had taken pride, and maybe what people called valor, for her to walk into a place like the Silver Star and face Carlotta down. And she'd done it. He glanced up toward the loft. She'd more than done it. She'd held her own.

Rising, he walked outside to where Lucius was doing his best to teach an uncooperative Lafitte to shake hands.

"Damn it, boy, did I say jump all over me? No, you flea-brained mongrel, I said shake." Lucius pushed the dog's rump down and grabbed a paw. "Shake. Get it?" Lafitte leaped up again and licked Lucius's face.

"Doesn't appear so," Jake commented.

"Fool dog." But Lucius rubbed the pup's belly when he rolled over. "Grows on you, though." He squinted up at Jake. "Something around here seems to be growing on you, too."

"Somebody had to bring her back."

"Reckon so." He waited until Jake crouched to scratch the puppy's head. "You want to tell me how Miss Sarah came to look like she'd been in a fistfight?"

"She looked like she was in a fistfight because she was in a fistfight."

Lucius snorted and spit. "Like hell."

"With Carlotta."

Lucius's cloudy eyes widened, and then he let out a bark of laughter that had Lafitte racing in circles. "Ain't that a hoot? Are you telling me that our Miss Sarah went in and gave Carlotta what for?"

"She gave her a bloody nose." Jake looked over with a grin. "And pulled out more than a little of her hair."

"Sweet Jesus, I'd've given two pints of whiskey to've seen that. Did you?"

Chuckling, Jake pulled on Lafitte's ears. "The tail end of it. When I walked in, the two of them were rolling over the floor, spitting like cats. I figure Carlotta outweighs Sarah by ten pounds or more, but Sarah was sitting on her, skirts hiked up and blood in her eye. It was one hell of a sight."

"She's got spunk." Lucius pulled out his whiskey and toasted Sarah with a healthy gulp. "I knew she had something in her head when she tore out of here." Feeling generous, he handed the bottle to Jake. "Never would have thought she'd set her mind on poking a fist into Carlotta. But nobody ever deserved it more. You seen Alice?"

"No." Jake let the whiskey spread fire through him. "Sarah's got the idea that it's not fitting for me to talk to the girl until she's covered up or something."

"I carried her in myself, and I don't mind saying I ain't seen no woman's face ever smashed up so bad. Took a belt to her, too, from the looks of it. Her back and shoulders all come up in welts. Jake, you wouldn't whup a dog the way that girl was whupped. That Carlotta must be crazy."

"Mean and crazy's two different things." He handed Lucius the bottle. "Carlotta's just mean."

"Reckon you'd know her pretty well."

Jake watched Lucius take another long sip. "I paid

for her a few times, sometime back. Doesn't mean I know her."

"Sooner plop my ass next to a rattler's." Lucius handed the bottle back to Jake again, then fell into a fit of coughing. "Miss Sarah, I didn't hear you come out."

"So I surmised," she said with a coolness that had Lucius coughing again. "Perhaps you gentlemen have finished drinking whiskey and exchanging crude comments and would like to wash for supper. If not, you're welcome to eat out here in the dirt." With that she turned on her heel, making certain she banged the door shut behind her.

"Ooo-whee." Lucius snatched back the bottle and took another drink. "She's got a mighty sharp tongue for such a sweet face. I tell you, boy, you'll have to mind your step if'n you hitch up with her."

Jake was still staring at the door, thinking how beautiful she'd looked, black eye and all, standing there like a queen addressing her subjects. "I ain't planning on hitching up with anyone."

"Maybe you are and maybe you ain't." Lucius rose and brushed off his pants. A little dirt and she'd have them off him again and in the stream. "But she's got plans, all right. And a woman like that's hard to say no to."

Sarah spoke politely at supper, as if she were entertaining at a formal party. Her hair was swept up and tidied, and she'd changed her dress. She was wearing the green one that set off her hair and eyes. The stew was served in ironstone bowls, but the way she did it, it could have been a restaurant meal on fancy china.

It made him think, as he hadn't in years, of his mother and how she had liked to fuss over Sunday supper.

She said nothing about the encounter in town, and it was clear that she didn't care to have the subject brought up. It was hard to believe she was the same woman he'd dragged off the floor in the Silver Star. But he noticed that she winced now and then. He bit into a hunk of fresh bread and held back a grin. She was hurting, all right, and it was more than her pride, from the look of it. As he ate he entertained thoughts of how he would ease those hurts when the sun went down.

"Would you like some more stew, Lucius?"

"No, ma'am." He patted his belly. "Full as a tick. If it's all the same to you, I'll just go take a walk before I feed the stock and such. Going to be a pretty night." He sent them both what he thought was a bland look. "I'll sleep like a log after a meal like this. Yessir. I don't believe I'll stir till morning." He scraped back his chair and reached for his hat. "Mighty fine meal, Miss Sarah."

"Thank you, Lucius."

Jake tipped back his chair. "I wouldn't mind a walk myself."

Sarah had to smile at the way Lucius began to whistle after he'd closed the door. "You go ahead."

He took her hand as she rose. "I'd like it better if you went with me."

She smiled. He'd never asked her to do something as ordinary, and as romantic, as going for a walk. Thank goodness she hadn't forgotten how to flirt. "Why, that's nice of you, but I have to see to the dishes. And Alice may be waking soon. I think she could eat a bit now."

"I imagine I could occupy myself for an hour or two. We'll take a walk when you're done."

She sent him a look from under lowered lashes. "Maybe." Then she laughed as he sent her spinning into his lap. "Why, Mr. Redman. You are quite a brute."

He ran a finger lightly over the bruise under her eye. "Then you'd best be careful. Kiss me, Sarah."

She smiled when her lips were an inch from his. "And if I don't?"

"But you will." He traced her bottom lip with his tongue. "You will."

She did, sinking into it, into him. Her arms wound around him, slender and eager. Her mouth opened like a flower in sunlight. Her lips softened against him even as they heated. They yielded even as they demanded.

"Don't be long," he murmured. He kissed her again, passion simmering, then set her on her feet. She let out a long, shaky breath when he closed the door behind him.

With Alice settled for the night and the day's work behind her, Sarah stepped out into the quieting light of early evening. It was still too warm to bother with a shawl, but she pushed her sleeves down past her elbows and buttoned the cuffs. There were bruises on her arms that she didn't care to dwell on.

From where she stood she could hear Lucius in the shed, talking to Lafitte. He'd become more his dog than hers, Sarah thought with a laugh. Or perhaps they'd both become something of hers.

As the land had.

She closed her eyes and let the light breeze flutter over her face. She could, if she concentrated hard enough, catch the faintest whiff of sage. And she could, if she used enough imagination, picture what it would be like to sit on the porch she envisioned having, watching the sun go down every evening while Jake rolled a cigarette and listened with her to the music of the night.

Bringing herself back, she looked around. Where was he? She stepped farther out into the yard when she heard the sound of hammer against wood. She saw him, a few yards from the chicken coop, beating an old post into the ground. He'd taken his shirt off, and she could see the light sheen of sweat over his lean torso and the rippling and bunching of his muscles as he swung the heavy hammer down.

Her thoughts flew back to the way his arms had swung her into heat, into passion. The hands that gripped the thick, worn handle of the hammer now had roamed over her, touching, taking whatever they chose.

And she had touched, wantonly, even greedily, that long, limber body, taking it, accepting it as her own.

Her breath shuddered out as she watched him bend and lift and pound. Was it wrong to have such thoughts, such wonderful, exciting visions? How could it be, when she loved so completely? She wanted his heart, but oh, she wanted his body, as well, and she could find no shame in it.

His head came up quickly, as she imagined an animal's might when it caught a scent. And he had. Though she was several yards away, he had sensed her, the trace of lilac, the subtlety of woman. He straightened, and just as she had looked her fill of him, he looked his of her.

She might have stepped from a cool terrace to walk in a garden. The wind played with her skirts and her hair, but gently. The backdrop of the setting sun was like glory behind her. Her eyes, as she walked toward him, were wide and dark and aware.

"You've got a way of moving, Duchess, that makes my mouth water."

"I don't think that's what the good sisters intended when they taught me posture. But I'm glad." She moved naturally to his arms, to his lips. "Very glad."

For the first time in his life he felt awkward with a woman, and he drew her away. "I'm sweaty."

"I know." She pulled a handkerchief from her pocket and dabbed at his face. "What are you doing?"

She made him feel like a boy fumbling over his first dance. "You said you wanted pigs. You need a pen." He picked up his shirt and shrugged it on. "What are you doing?"

"Watching you." She put a hand to his chest, where the shirt lay open. "Remembering. Wondering if you want me as much as you did."

He took her hand before she could tear what was inside of him loose. "No, I don't. I want you more." He picked up his gunbelt, but instead of strapping it on he draped it over his shoulder. "Why don't we go for that walk?"

Content, she slipped her hand into his. "When I first came here I wondered what it was that had kept my father, rooted him here. At first I thought it was only for me, because he wanted so badly to provide what he thought I'd need. That grieved me. I can't tell you how much." She glanced up as they passed the rise that led to his grave. "Later I began to see that even though that was part of it, perhaps the most important part to him, he was also happy here. It eases the loss to know he was happy."

They started down the path to the stream she had come to know so well.

"I didn't figure you'd stick." Her hand felt right, easy and right, tucked in his. "When I brought you out here the first time, you looked as if someone had dropped you on your head."

"It felt as though someone had. Losing him . . . Well, the truth is, I'd lost him years and years ago. To me, he's exactly the same as he was the day he left.

Maybe there's something good about that. I never told you he had spun me a tale." At the stream she settled down on her favorite rock and listened to the water's melody. "He told me of the fine house he'd built after he'd struck the rich vein of gold in Sarah's Pride. He painted me a picture of it with his words. Four bedrooms, a parlor with the windows facing west, a wide porch with big round columns." She smiled a little and watched the sun glow over the buttes. "Maybe he thought I needed that, and maybe I did, to see myself as mistress of a fine, big house with curving stairs and high, cool walls."

He could see it, and her. "It was what you were made for."

"It's you I was made for." Rising, she held out her hands.

"I want you, Sarah. I can't offer you much more than a blanket to spread on the ground."

She glanced over at the small pile of supplies he'd already brought down to the stream. She moved to it and lifted the blanket.

It was twilight when they lowered to it. The air had softened. The wind was only a rustle in the thin brush. Overhead, the sky arched, a deep, ever-darkening blue. Under the wool of the blanket the ground was hard and unforgiving. She lifted her arms to him and they left the rest behind.

It was as it had been the first time, and yet different. The hunger was there, and the impatient pull of desire. With it was a knowledge of the wonder, the magic, they could make between them. A little slower now, a little surer, they moved together.

There was urgency in his kiss. She could feel it. But beneath it was a tenderness she had dreamed of, hoped for. Seduced by that alone, she murmured his name. Beneath her palm, his cheek was rough. Under her fingers, his skin was smooth. His body, like his mind, like his heart, was a contrast that drew her, compelled her to learn more.

A deep, drugging languor filled her as he began to undress her. There was no frantic rush, as there had been before. His fingers were slow and sure as they moved down the small covered buttons. She felt the air whisper against her skin as he parted the material. Then it was his mouth, warmer, sweeter, moving over her. Her sigh was like music.

He wanted to give her something he'd never given another woman. The kind of care she deserved. Tenderness was new to him, but it came easily now as he peeled off layer after layer to find her. He sucked in his breath as her fingers fumbled with the buttons at his waist. Her touch wasn't hesitant, but it was still innocent. It would always be. And her innocence aroused him as skill never could have.

She removed the layers he'd covered himself with. Not layers of cotton or leather, but layers of cynicism and aloofness, the armor he'd used to survive, just as he'd used his pistols. With her he was helpless, more vulnerable than he had been since childhood. With her he felt more of a man than he had ever hoped to be.

She felt the change, an explosion of feelings and needs and desires, as he dragged her up into his arms to crush his mouth against hers. What moved through him poured into her, leaving her breathless, shaken and impossibly strong. Without understanding, without needing to, she answered him with everything in her heart.

Then came the storm, wild, windy, wailing. Rocked by it, she cried out as he drove her up, up, into an airless, rushing cloud of passion. Sensations raced through her—the sound of her own desperate moans, the scrape of his face against her skin as he journeyed down her trembling body, the taste of him that lingered on her lips, on her tongue, as he did mad, unspeakably wonderful things to her. Lost, driven beyond reason, she pressed his head closer to her.

She was like something wild that had just been unchained. He could feel the shocked delight ripple through her when he touched her moist heat with his tongue. He thought her response was like a miracle, though he'd long ago stopped believing in them. There was little he could give her besides the pleasures of her own body. But at least that he would do.

Sliding upward, he covered her mouth with his. And filled her.

Long after her hands had slipped limply from his back, long after their breathing had calmed and leveled, he lay over her, his face buried in her hair. She'd brought him peace, and though he knew it wouldn't last, for now she'd brought him peace of mind, of body, of heart.

He hadn't wanted to love, hadn't dared to risk it. Even now, when it was no longer possible to hide it from himself, he couldn't tell her.

"Lucius was right," she murmured against his ear.

"Mmm?"

"It's a pretty night." She ran her hands up his back. "A very pretty night."

"Am I hurting you?"

"No." She gripped her own wrists so that she could hold him closer. "Don't move yet."

"I'm heavy, and you've got some colorful bruises."

If she'd had the energy, she might have laughed. "I'd forgotten about them."

"I put some on you myself." He lifted his head to look down at her. "I don't know much about going easy."

"I'm not complaining."

"You should." Fascinated, he stroked a finger down her cheek. "You're so beautiful. Like something I made up."

She turned her lips into his palm as her eyes filled. "You've never told me you thought I was beautiful."

"Sure I did." He shifted then, frustrated by his own lack of words. "I should have."

She curled comfortably against his side. "I feel beautiful right now."

They lay in contented silence, looking up at the sky.

"What's an enigma?" he asked her.

"Hmm? Oh, it's a puzzle. Something difficult to understand. Why?"

"I guess I heard it somewhere." He thought of her diary, and her description of him, but couldn't see how it applied. He'd always seen himself as being exactly what he appeared to be. "You're getting cold."

"A little."

Sitting up, he pushed through her discarded undergarments for her chemise. She smiled, lifting her arms over her head. Her lips curved when she saw his gaze slide over her skin. When he pulled the cotton over her, she linked her hands behind his neck.

"I was hoping to stay warm a different way."

With a laugh, he slid a hand down over her hip. "I remember telling you once before that you were a quick study." Experimentally he pushed the strap of her chemise off her shoulder. "You want to do something for me?"

"Yes." She nuzzled his lips. "Very much."

"Go on over and stand in that stream."

Confused, she drew back. "I beg your pardon?"

"Nobody says that better than you, Duchess. I'll swear to that." He kissed her again, in a light, friendly manner that pleased and puzzled her.

"You want to go wading?"

"Not exactly." He toyed with the strap. Women wore the damnedest things. Then they covered them all up anyhow. "I thought you'd go stand in the stream wearing just this little thing. Like you did that first night."

"What first night?" Her puzzled smile faded as he traced his fingertip along the edge of her bodice. "That first— You! You were watching me while I—"

"I was just making sure you didn't get yourself into any trouble."

"That's disgraceful." She tried to pull away, but he held her still.

"I started thinking then and there how much I'd like to get my hands on you. Had some trouble sleeping that night." He lowered his lips to the curve of her throat and began to nibble. "Fact is, I haven't had a good night's sleep since I set eyes on you."

"Stop it." She turned her head, but it only made it easier for him to find her mouth.

"Are you going to go stand in the stream?"

"I am not." She smothered a laugh when he rolled her onto the blanket again. "I'm going to get dressed and go back to the house to check on Alice."

"No need. Lucius is keeping an eye on her."

"Oh, I see. You've already decided that for me."

"I guess you could put it like that. You're not going anywhere but this blanket. And maybe the stream, once I talk you into it."

"You won't talk me into it. I have no intention of sleeping outside."

"I don't figure on sleeping much at all." He stretched out on his back again and gathered her close. "Haven't you ever slept outside before, looked at the sky? Counted stars?"

"No." But, of course, tonight she would. She wanted nothing more. She turned her head to study his profile. "Have you ever counted stars, Jake?"

"When I was a kid." He stroked a hand lazily up and down her arm. "My mother used to say there were pictures. She'd point them out to me sometimes, but I could never find them again."

"I'll show you one." Sarah took his hand and began to draw in the air. "It's a horse. A winged horse. Pegasus," she added. Then she caught her breath. "Look, a shooting star." She watched, his hand held in hers, as it arced across the sky. She closed her eyes quickly, then made a wish. "Will you tell me about your mother?"

For a long moment he said nothing, but continued to stare up at the sky. The arc of light was gone, without a trace. "She was a teacher." Sarah's gaze flicked up quickly to his face. "She'd come out here from St. Louis."

"And met your father?"

"I don't know much about that. He wanted to learn to read and write, and she taught him. She set a lot of store by reading."

"And while she was teaching him, they fell in love."

He smiled a little. It sounded nice the way she said it. "I guess they did. She married him. It wouldn't have been easy, with him being half Apache. They wanted to build something. I remember the way my father used to talk about taking the land and making it work for him. Leaving something behind."

She understood that, because it was what she wanted
for herself. "Were they happy?"

"They laughed a lot. My mother used to sing. He
always talked about buying her a piano one day, so
she could play again like she did in St. Louis. She'd
just laugh and say she wanted lace curtains first. I'd
forgotten that," he murmured. "She wanted lace curtains."

She turned her face into his shoulder because she
felt his pain as her own. "Lucius told me what happened
to them. To you. I'm so sorry."

He hadn't known he needed to talk about it, needed
to tell her. "They came in from town . . . eight, ten
of them, I've never been sure." His voice was quiet
now, his eyes on the sky. He could still see them, as
he hadn't allowed himself to see them for years. "They
lit the barn first. Maybe if my father had stayed in the
house, let them shoot and shout and trample, they'd
have left the rest. But they'd have come back. He knew
it. He took his rifle and went out to protect what was
his. They shot him right outside the door."

Sarah held him tighter, seeing it with him.

"We ran out. They tasted blood now, like wolves,
wild-eyed, teeth bared. She was crying, holding on to
my father and crying. Inside the barn, the horses were
screaming. The sky was lit up so I could see their faces
while they torched the rest."

And he could smell the smoke as he lay there, could
hear the crackle of greedy flames and his mother's piti-
ful weeping.

"I picked up the rifle. That's the first time I ever
wanted to kill. It's like a fever in the blood. Like a hand
has ahold of you, squeezing. She started to scream. I
saw one of the riders take aim at me. I had the rifle in
my hands, but I was slow. Better with a bow or a knife

back then. She threw herself up and in front of me so when he pulled the trigger the bullet went in her."

Sarah tightened her arms around him as tears ran fast and silent down her cheeks.

"One of them hit me with a rifle butt as he rode by. It was morning before I came to. They'd burned everything. The house was still smoking—even when it cooled there was nothing in it worth keeping. The ground was hard there, and I got dizzy a few times, so it took me all day to bury them. I slept there that night, between the two graves. I told myself that if I lived until morning I'd find the men who'd done it and kill them. I was still alive in the morning."

She said nothing, could say nothing. It wasn't necessary to ask what he'd done. He'd learned to use a gun, and use it well. And he had found the men, or some of them.

"When Lucius came, I told him what happened. That was the last time I told anyone."

"Don't." She turned to lay her body across his. "Don't think about it anymore."

He could feel her tears on his chest, the warmth of them. As far as he knew, no one had ever cried for him before. Taking her hand, he kissed it. "Show me that picture in the sky, Sarah."

Turning, keeping her hand in his, she began to trace the stars. The time for tears, for regrets—and, she hoped, for revenge—was done. "The stars aren't as big in the East, or as bright." They lay quietly for a while, wrapped close, listening to the night sounds. "I used to jump every time I heard a coyote. Now I like listening for them. Every night, when I read my father's journal—"

"Matt kept a journal?" He sat up as he asked, dragging her with him.

"Why, yes." There was an intensity in his eyes that made her heart skip erratically. "What is it?"

"Have you read it?"

"Not all of it. I've been reading a few pages each night."

He suddenly realized that he was digging his fingers into her arms. He relaxed them. "Will you let me read it?"

Her heart was steady again, but something cold was inching its way over her skin. "Yes. If you tell me why you want to."

He turned away to reach casually into his saddle-bag for his tobacco pouch and papers. "I just want to read it."

She waited while he rolled a cigarette. "All right. I trust you. When are you going to trust me, Jake?"

He struck a match on a rock. The flame illuminated his face. "What do you mean?"

"Why did you ask Lucius to work in the mine?"

He flicked the match out, then tossed it aside. The scent of tobacco stung the air. "Maybe I thought Matt would have liked it."

Determined, she put a hand to his face and turned it toward hers. "Why?"

"A feeling I had, that's all." Shifting away, he blew out a stream of smoke. "People usually have a reason for setting fires, Sarah. There was only one I could figure when it came to you. Somebody didn't want you there."

"That's ridiculous. I hardly knew anyone at that point. The sheriff said it was drifters." She curled her hands in her lap as she studied his face. "You don't think it was."

"No. Maybe Barker does, and maybe he doesn't.

There's only one thing on this land that anyone could want. That's gold."

Impatient, Sarah sat back on her heels. "But there isn't any gold."

"Yes, there is." Jake drew deep on his cigarette and watched the range of expressions cross her face.

"What are you talking about?"

"Lucius found the mother lode, just the way Matt did." He glanced at the glowing tip of his cigarette. "You're going to be a rich woman, Duchess."

"Wait." She pressed a hand to her temple. It was beginning to throb. "Are you telling me that the mine is really worth something?"

"More than something, according to Lucius."

"I can't believe it." With a quick, confused laugh, she shook her head. "I never thought it was anything but a dream. Just this morning, I'd begun to wonder, but— How long have you known?"

"Awhile."

"Awhile?" she repeated, looking back at him. "And you didn't think it important enough to mention to me?"

"I figured it was important enough not to." He took a last drag before crushing the cigarette out. "I've never known a woman who could keep her mouth shut."

"Is that so?"

"Yes, ma'am."

"I'm perfectly capable of keeping my mouth shut, as you so eloquently put it. But why should I?"

There was no way to tell her but straight out. "Matt found the gold, and then he was dead."

"There was an accident . . ." she began. Suddenly cold, she hugged her elbows. He didn't have to speak for her to see what was in his mind. "You're trying to tell me that my father was murdered. That can't be."

She started to scramble up, but he took her arms and held her still.

"Ten years he worked the mine and scratched a few handfuls of gold from it. Then he hits, hits big. The minute he does, there's a cave-in, and he's dead."

"I don't want to think about it."

"You're going to think about it." He gave her a quick shake. "The mine's yours now, and the gold in it. I'm not going to let what happened to Matt happen to you." His hands gentled and slid up to frame her face. "Not to you."

She closed her eyes. She couldn't take it in, not all at once. Fear, hysteria and fresh grief tangled within her. She lifted her hands to his wrists and held on until she felt herself calming. He was right. She had to think about it. Then she would act. When she opened her eyes, they were clear and steady.

"Tell me what you want me to do."

"Trust me." He touched his lips to hers, then laid her back gently on the blanket. She'd given him peace early in the night. Now, as the night deepened, he would try to do the same for her.

CHAPTER 13

I'm feeling lots better, Miss Conway." Alice took the tin cup and sipped gingerly.

She didn't want to complain about her back, or about the pain that still galloped along it despite the cooling salve. The morning light showed her facial bruises in heart-wrenching detail and caused the girl to look even younger and smaller and more vulnerable. Though the scratches on her cheeks were no longer red and angry, Sarah judged it would be several days before they faded.

"You look better." It wasn't strictly true, and Sarah vowed to keep her patient away from a mirror a bit longer. Though the swelling had eased considerably, she was still worried about Alice's eye and had already decided to drive into town later and talk with the doctor.

"Try a little of this soft-boiled egg. You need your strength."

"Yes, ma'am." Privately Alice thought the glossy wet yolk looked more like a slimy eye than food. But if Sarah had told her to eat a fried scorpion she'd have opened her mouth and swallowed. "Miss Conway?"

"Yes, Alice?" Sarah spooned up more egg.

"I'm beholden to you for taking me in like you did, and I can't— Miss Conway, you gave me your own bed last night. It ain't fitting."

Smiling a little, Sarah set the plate aside. "Alice, I assure you, I was quite comfortable last night."

"But, Miss Conway—"

"Alice, if you keep this up I'm going to think you're ungrateful."

"Oh!" Something close to horror flashed in Alice's eyes. "No, ma'am."

"Well, then." Because the response was exactly what she'd expected, Sarah rose. She remembered that the nuns had nursed with compassion tempered with brisk practicality. "You can show your gratitude by being a good patient and getting some more rest. If you're feeling up to it later, I'll have Lucius bring you down and we can sit and talk awhile."

"I'd like that. Miss Conway, if it hadn't been for you and Eli, I think I'd've died. I was hoping . . . Well, I got some money saved. It ain't much, but I'd like you to have it for all your trouble."

"I don't want your money, Alice."

The girl flushed and looked away. "I know you're probably thinking about where it comes from, but—"

"No." She took Alice's hand firmly in hers. "That has nothing to do with it." Pride, Sarah thought. She had plenty of her own. Alice was entitled to hers. "Alice, did Eli want money for driving you out of town?"

"No, but . . . he's a friend."

"I'd like to be your friend, if you'd let me. You rest now, and we'll talk about all this later." She gave Alice's hand a reassuring squeeze before she picked up the empty dishes and started down the ladder. She barely muffled a squeal when hands closed around her waist.

"Told you you didn't need that corset."

Sarah sent Jake what she hoped was an indignant look over her shoulder. "Is that why I couldn't find it when I dressed this morning?"

"Just doing you a favor." Before she could decide whether to laugh or lecture, he was whirling her around and kissing her.

"Jake, Alice is—"

"Not likely to faint if she figures out what I'm doing." But he set her aside, because he liked the way the sunlight streamed through the curtains and onto her hair. "You're mighty nice to look at, Duchess."

It was foolish to blush, but her color rose. "Why don't you sit down, and you can look at me some more while I fix you breakfast?"

"I'd like to, but I've got some things to see to." He touched her again, just a fingertip to the single wispy curl that had escaped from the neat bun on top of her head. "Sarah, will you let me have Matt's journal?"

Both the grief and the dread showed clearly in her eyes before she lowered them. During the night, after love and before sleep, she had thought of little else but what Jake had told her. Part of her wondered if she would be better off not knowing, not being sure. But another part, the same part that had kept her from turning back and going east again, had already accepted what needed to be done.

"Yes." She walked to the hearth to work the rock loose. "I found this the first night. His journal, what must have been his savings and the deed to Sarah's Pride."

When she held the book out to him, Jake resisted the urge to open it there and then. If he found what he thought he would find, he would have business to take care of before he said anything else to her. "I'll take it along with me, if it's all the same to you."

She opened her mouth to object, wanting the matter settled once and for all. But he'd asked for her trust. Perhaps this was the way to show him he had it. "All right."

"And the deed? Will you let me hold on to it until we have some answers?"

In response, she offered it to him, without hesitation, without question. For a moment they held the deed, and the dream, between them. "Just like that?" he murmured.

"Yes." She smiled and released her hold. "Just like that."

That her trust was so easily given, so total in her eyes, left him groping for words. "Sarah, I want . . ." What? he wondered as he stared down at her. To guard and protect, to love and possess? She was like something cool and sweet that had poured into him and washed away years of bitter thirst. But he didn't have the words, he thought. And he didn't have the right.

"I'll take care of this."

She lifted a brow. There had been something else, something in his eyes. She wanted it back, so that she could see it, understand it. "I thought *we* were going to take care of it."

"No." He cupped her chin in his hand. "You're going to leave this to me. I don't want anything to happen to you."

Her brow was still lifted as her lips curved. "Why?"

"Because I don't. I want you to—" Whatever he might have said was postponed. He moved to the window quickly. "You've got company coming." As he spotted the buggy, his shoulders relaxed. "Looks like Mrs. Cody and her girl."

"Oh." Sarah's hands shot up automatically to straighten her hair. "I must look— Oh, how would I know? I haven't had a chance to so much as glance in the mirror."

"Wouldn't matter much." Without glancing back, he pulled open the door. "Too bad you're so homely."

Muttering, she pulled off her apron and followed him outside. Then memory came flooding back and had her biting her lip. "I imagine they would have heard all about the, ah, incident yesterday."

"I expect." Jake secured the deed and the journal in the saddlebags that he'd tossed over the rail.

"You needn't look so amused." She fiddled nervously with the cameo at her throat, then put on her brightest smile. "Good morning, Mrs. Cody. Liza."

"Good morning, Sarah." Anne Cody brought the horses to a stop. "I hope you don't mind an early call."

"Not at all." But her fingers were busy pleating her skirt. She was afraid there was a lecture coming. The good sisters had given Sarah more than what she considered her share over the past twelve years. "I'm always delighted to see you," she added. "Both of you."

Anne glanced over at the dog, who'd run out to bark at the horses. "My, he's grown some, hasn't he?" She held out a hand. "Mr. Redman?"

Jake stepped over to help her, then Liza, down, remaining silent until he'd slung his saddlebags over his shoulder. "I'd best be on my way." He touched a hand to his hat. "Ladies."

"Mr. Redman." Anne held up a hand in the gesture she used to stop her children from rushing out before their chores were finished. "Might I have a word with you?"

He shifted his bags until their weight fell evenly. "Yes, ma'am."

"My son, John, has been dogging your heels these last weeks. I'm surprised you put up with it."

Jake didn't imagine it pleased her, either, to have the boy spending time with him. "He hasn't made a pest of himself."

Curious, Anne studied his face. "That's a kind thing to say, Mr. Redman, when I'm sure he's done just that."

"Johnny was born a pest," Liza put in, earning a slow, measured look from her mother.

"It appears my children have that in common." With Liza effectively silenced, Anne turned back to Jake. "He's been going through what most boys his age go through, I expect. Fascinated with guns, gunfights. Gunfighters. I don't mind saying it's given me some worry."

"I'll keep my distance," Jake said, and turned to leave.

"Mr. Redman." Anne hadn't raised two willful children without knowing how to add the right tone of authority to her voice. "I'll have my say."

"Ma." Both Liza's cheeks and voice paled when she saw the look in Jake's eyes. Cold, she thought, and moistened her lips. She'd never seen eyes so cold. "Maybe we should let Mr. Redman be on his way."

"Your mother's got something to say," Jake said quietly. "I reckon she ought to say it."

"Thank you." Pleased, Anne drew off her riding gloves. "Johnny was real excited about what happened here between you and Burt Donley."

"Mrs. Cody," Sarah began, only to be silenced by a look from both her and Jake.

"As I was saying," Anne continued, "Johnny hardly talked about anything else for days. He figured having a shoot-out made a man a man and gave him something to strut about. Even started pestering his pa for a Peacemaker." She glanced down at the guns on Jake's hips. "Wooden grip, he said. Nothing fancy, like some

of the glory boys wear. Just a good solid Colt. Mr.
Cody and I had just about run clean out of patience
with the boy. Then, just yesterday, he came home and
told me something." She paused, measuring her words.
"He said that killing somebody in a gunfight or any
other way doesn't make a man grown-up or important.
He said that a smart man doesn't look for trouble. He
walks away from it when he can, and faces it when he
can't."

For the first time, Anne smiled. "I guess I'd been
telling him pretty near the same, but it didn't get through
coming from me or his pa. Made me wonder who got
him thinking that way." She offered her hand again. "I
wanted to tell you I'm obliged."

Jake stared at the hand before taking it. It was the
kind of gesture, one of gratitude, even friendship, that
had rarely been made to him. "He's a smart boy, Mrs.
Cody. He'd have come around to it."

"Sooner or later." Anne stepped toward the door
of the house and then she turned back. "Maggie
O'Rourke thinks a lot of you. I guess I found out why.
I won't keep you any longer, Mr. Redman."

Not quite sure how to respond, he touched his hat
before he started toward the paddock to saddle his
horse.

"That's quite a man, Sarah," Anne commented. "If
I were you, I'd want to go say a proper goodbye."

"Yes, I . . ." She looked at Anne, then back toward
Jake, torn between manners and longings.

"You won't mind if I fix tea, will you?" Anne asked
as she disappeared inside.

"No, please, make yourself at home." Sarah looked
toward Jake again. "I'll only be a minute." Gathering
her skirts, she ran. "Jake!" He turned, the saddle held in
both hands, and enjoyed the flash of legs and petticoats.

"Wait. I—" She stopped, a hand on her heart, when she realized she not only was out of breath but hadn't any idea what she wanted to say to him. "Are you . . . When will you be back?"

The mustang shifted and nickered softly as Jake settled the saddle in place. "Haven't left yet."

She hated feeling foolish, and hated even more the idea that he could swing onto his horse and ride out of her life for days at a time. Perhaps patience would do the job.

"I was hoping you'd come back for supper."

He tossed up a stirrup to tighten the cinch. "You asking me to supper?"

"Unless you've something else you'd rather be doing."

His hand snaked out, fast and smooth, to snag her arm before she could flounce away. "It's not often I get invitations to supper from pretty ladies." His grip firm, he glanced back toward the house. Things were changing, he decided, and changing fast, when he looked at the adobe cabin and thought of home. He still didn't know what the hell to do about it.

"If I'd known you'd need so long to think about it," Sarah said between her teeth, "I wouldn't have bothered. You can just—" But before she could tell him, he swept her off her feet.

"You sure do get fired up easy." He brought his mouth down hard on hers to taste the heat and the honey. "That's one of the things I like about you."

"Put me down." But her arms encircled his neck. "Mrs. Cody might see." Then she laughed and kissed him again as he swung her down. "Well, will you come to supper or not?"

He vaulted into the saddle in one fluid, economical motion. His eyes were shadowed by the brim of his hat when he looked down at her. "Yeah, I'll come to supper."

"It'll be ready at seven," she called after him as he spurred his horse into a gallop. She watched until dust and distance obscured him. Gathering her skirts again, she ran back to the house. The laughter that was bubbling in her throat dried up when she heard Alice's weeping.

Liza stood by the stove, the kettle steaming in her hand. "Sarah, Ma's . . ." But Sarah was already rushing up the ladder, ready to defend the girl.

Anne Cody held the weeping Alice in her arms, rocking her gently. One wide, capable hand was stroking the girl's dark hair.

"There now, honey, you cry it all out," she murmured. "Then it'll be behind you." Wanting quiet, she sent Sarah a warning glance. Her own eyes were damp. Slowly Sarah descended the ladder.

"Alice called for you," Liza explained, still holding the kettle. "Ma went up to see what she needed." Liza set the sputtering kettle aside. Tea was the last thing on her mind. "Sarah, what's going on?"

"I'm not sure I know."

Liza cast another look toward the loft and said in a low voice, "Was she . . . that girl . . . really beaten?"

"Yes." The memory of it had Sarah touching a fingertip to the bruise under her own eye. "Horribly. Liza, I've never known one person was capable of hurting another so viciously." She needed to be busy, Sarah decided. There was too much to think about. Her father, the mine, Jake, Alice. After running a distracted hand over her hair, she began to slice honey cake.

"Did she really work for Carlotta?"

"Yes. Liza, she's just a girl, younger than you and I."

"Really?" Torn between sympathy and fascination, Liza edged closer to Sarah. "But she . . . Well, I mean, at the Silver Star she must have . . ."

"She didn't know anything else." Sarah looked down at her hands. Honey cake and tea. There had been a time when she had thought life was as ordered and simple as that. "Her father sold her. Sold her to a man for twenty dollars."

"But that's—" The curiosity in Liza's eyes heated to fury. "Why, he's the one who should be beat. Her own pa. Somebody ought to—"

"Hush, Liza." Anne slipped quietly down the ladder. "No one deserves to be beat."

"Ma. Sarah says that girl's pa sold her. Sold her off for money, like a horse."

Anne paused in the act of brushing down her skirts. "Is that true, Sarah?"

"Yes. She ran away and ended up at the Silver Star."

Anne's lips tightened as she fought back words that even her husband had never heard her utter. "I'd dearly love that tea now."

"Oh, yes." Sarah hurried back to the stove. "I'm sorry. Please sit down." She set out the napkins she'd made out of blue checked gingham. "I hope you'll enjoy this honey cake. It's a recipe from the cook of a very dear friend of mine in Philadelphia." As she offered the plate, Philadelphia and everyone in it seemed years away.

"Thank you, dear." Anne waited for Sarah to sit down, then said, "Alice is sleeping now. I wasn't sure you'd done the right thing by taking her in here. Truth is, I drove out this morning because I was concerned."

"I had to take her in."

"No, you didn't." When Sarah bristled, Anne laid a hand on hers. "But you did what was right, and I'm proud of you. That girl needs help." With a sigh, she sat back and looked at her own daughter. Pretty Liza, she thought, always so bright and curious. And safe, she reflected, adding a quick prayer of thanksgiving. Her children had always had a full plate and a solid roof over their heads—and a father who loved them. She made up her mind to thank her husband very soon.

"Alice Johnson has had nothing but hard times." Anne took a sip of tea. Her mind was made up. She had only to convince her husband. At that thought her lips curved a little. It was never hard to convince a man whose heart was soft and open. The other ladies in town would be a bit more difficult, but she'd bring them around. The challenge of it made her smile widen and the light of battle glint in her eyes.

"What that girl needs is some proper work and a real home. When she's on her feet again, I think she should come work at the store."

"Oh, Mrs. Cody."

Anne brushed Sarah's stunned gratitude aside. "Once Liza's married to Will I'm going to need new help. She can take Liza's room in the house, as well . . . as part of her wage."

Sarah fumbled for words, then gave up and simply leaned over to wrap her arms around Anne. "It's kind of you," she managed. "So kind. I've spoken with Alice about just that, but she pointed out that the women in town wouldn't accept her after she'd worked at the Silver Star."

"You don't know Ma." Pride shimmered in Liza's voice. "She'll bring the ladies around, every one. Won't you, Ma?"

Anne patted her hair. "You can put money on it." Satisfied, she broke off a corner of the honey cake. "Sarah, now that we've got that settled, I feel I have to talk to you about the . . . visit you paid to the Silver Star yesterday."

"Visit?" Though she knew it was hopeless, Sarah covered the bruise under her eye with her fingers.

"You know, when you tangled with Carlotta," Liza put in. "Everyone in town's talking about how you wrestled with her and even punched Jake Redman. I wish I'd seen it." She caught her mother's eye and grimaced. "Well, I do."

"Oh, Lord." This time Sarah covered her entire face. "Everyone?"

"Mrs. Miller was standing just outside when the sheriff went in." Liza took a healthy bite of cake. "You know how she loves to carry tales."

When Sarah just groaned, Anne shook her head at Liza. "Honey, you eat some more of that cake and keep your mouth busy. Now, Sarah." Anne pried Sarah's hands away from her face. "I have to say I was a mite surprised to hear that you'd gone in that place and had a hair-pulling match with that woman. Truth is, a nice young girl like you shouldn't even know about places and people like that."

"Can't live in Lone Bluff two days and not know about Carlotta," Liza said past a mouthful of cake. "Even Johnny—"

"Liza." Anne held up a single finger. "Chew. Seeing as you're without kin of your own, Sarah, I figured I'd come on out and speak to you about it." She took another sip of tea while Sarah waited to be lectured. "Well, blast it, now that I've seen that girl up there, I wished I'd taken a good yank at Carlotta myself."

"Ma!" Delighted, Liza slapped both hands to her mouth. "You wouldn't."

"No." Anne flushed a little and shifted in her chair.

"But I'd like to. Now, I'm not saying I want to hear about you going back there, Sarah."

"No." Sarah managed a rueful smile. "I think I've finished any business I might have at the Silver Star."

"Popped you a good one, did she?" Anne commented, studying Sarah's eye.

"Yes." Sarah grinned irrepressibly. "But I gave her a bloody nose. It's quite possible that I broke it."

"Really. Oh, I do wish I'd seen that." Ready to be impressed, Liza leaned forward, only to straighten again at a look from Anne. "Well, it's not as if I'd go inside myself."

"Not if you want to keep the hide on your bottom," Anne said calmly. She smoothed her hair, took another sip of tea, then gave up. "Well, darn it, are you going to tell us what it looks like in there or not?"

With a laugh, Sarah propped her elbows on the table and told them.

Scheming came naturally to Carlotta. As she lay in the wide feather bed, she ran through all the wrongs that had been done to her and her plans for making them right. The light was dim, with only two thin cracks appearing past the sides of the drawn shades. It was a large room by the Silver Star's standards. She'd had the walls between two smaller rooms removed to fashion her own private quarters, sacrificing the money one extra girl would have made her for comfort.

For Carlotta, money and comfort were one and the same. She wanted plenty of both.

Though it was barely nine, she poured a glass of whiskey from the bottle that was always at her bedside. The hot, powerful taste filled the craving she awoke with every morning. Sipping and thinking, she cast her eyes around the room.

The walls were papered in a somewhat virulent red-and-silver stripe she found rich and elegant. Thick red drapes, too heavy for the blistering Arizona summers, hung at the windows. They made her think, smugly, of queens and palaces. The carpet echoed the color and was badly in need of cleaning. She rarely noticed the dirt.

On the mirrored vanity, which was decorated with painted cherubs, was a silver brush set with an elaborate *C* worked into the design. It was the only monogram she used. Carlotta had no last name, at least none she cared to remember.

Her mother had always had a man in her bed. Carlotta had gone to sleep most nights on a straw pallet in the corner, her lullaby the grunts and groans of sex. It had made her sick, the way men had pounded themselves into her mother. But that had been nothing compared to the disgust she had felt for her mother's weeping when the men were gone.

Crying and sniveling and begging God's forgiveness, Carlotta thought. Her mother had been the whore of that frigid little town in the Carolina mountains, but she hadn't had the guts to make it work for her.

Always claimed she was doing it to feed her little girl, Carlotta remembered with a sneer. She poured more whiskey into the glass. If that had been so, why had her little girl gone hungry so many nights? In the dim light, Carlotta studied the deep amber liquid. *Because Ma was just as fond of whiskey as I am,* she decided. She drank, and savored the taste.

The difference between you and me, Ma, she thought to herself, *is that I ain't ashamed—not of the whiskey, not of the men. And I made something of myself.*

Did you cry when I left? Carlotta laughed as she thought back to the night she'd left the smelly, window-less shack for the last time. She'd been fifteen and she'd saved nearly thirty dollars she'd made selling herself to trappers. Men paid more for youth. Carlotta had learned quickly. Her mother had never known her daughter was her stiffest competition.

She despised them all. Every man who'd pushed himself into her. She took their money, arched her hips and loathed them. Hate made a potent catalyst for pas-sion. Her customers went away satisfied, and she saved every coin.

One night she'd packed her meager belongings, sto-len another twenty dollars from the can her mother kept hidden in the rafters and headed west.

She'd worked saloons in the early years, enjoying the fancy clothes and bottles of paint. Her affair with whiskey had blossomed and helped her smile and se-duce hungry-eyed cowboys and rough-handed drifters. She'd saved, keeping her mouth firmly shut about the bonuses she wheedled from men.

When she'd turned eighteen she had had enough to open her own place. A far cry from the Silver Star, Carlotta remembered. Her first brothel had been hardly more than a shack in a stinking cattle town in east Texas. But she'd made certain her girls were as young and pretty as she could get.

She'd had a brief affair with a gambler who'd sported brocade vests and string ties. He'd filled her head with talk of crystal chandeliers and red carpets. When she'd moved on, she'd taken his pearl stickpin, two hundred in cash and her own profits.

Then she'd opened the Silver Star.

One day she'd move on again, on to California. But she intended to do it in style. She'd have those crystal chandeliers, she vowed. And a white porcelain tub with gold handles. Gold.

Carlotta felt a pleasure flow through her, a pleasure as fluid as the whiskey. It was gold she needed to bring her dream to full life. And gold she intended to have.

The man beside her was the tool she would use to gain it.

Jim Carlson. Carlotta looked down at his face. It was rough with several days' growth of beard and slack from sleep, sex and whiskey. She knew him for a fool, hot-tempered, small-minded and easily manipulated. Still, he was better-looking than many she had taken into her bed. His body was tough and lean, but she preferred young, limber bodies. Like Jake's.

Scowling, Carlotta took another drink. She'd broken her most important rule with Jake Redman. She'd let herself want him, really want him, in a way she'd never desired another man. Her body had responded to his so that for the first time in her life she hadn't feigned the ecstasy men wanted from a whore. She'd felt it. Now she craved it, as she craved whiskey, and gold, and power.

With Jake, desire was a hot, tight fist in her gut. Not just because he had a style in bed most men who came to her didn't feel obliged to employ. But because Jake Redman held something of himself back, something that she sensed was powerful and exciting. Something she wanted for herself. And had been on her way to getting, she thought, before that pasty-faced bitch had come to town.

She had a lot to pay Miss Sarah Conway back for. Thoughtful, Carlotta touched a hand to her bruised cheek. A whole lot. Pay her back she would, and in doing so she would take Jake and the gold.

Jim Carlson, though he was unaware of it, was going to help her on all counts.

Setting the empty glass aside, Carlotta picked up a hand mirror. The bruises annoyed her, but they would fade. The faint lines fanning out from her eyes and bracketing her mouth would not. They would only deepen. She cursed and pushed the mirror aside. With a pleased smile, she ran both hands down her body. It was long, smooth-skinned and curvaceous.

It was her body men wanted and her body she had used, and would continue to use, to get what life had cheated her of.

She shifted, took Jim in her hand and brought him breathlessly awake.

"God Almighty, Carlotta." Groaning, he tried to roll over and into her.

"In a hurry, Jim?" She evaded him expertly, all the while using her skill to keep him aroused.

"Thought you'd burned the life out of me last night." He shuddered. "Glad to find out it ain't so."

"I want to talk to you, Jim."

"Talk." He filled his hands with her breasts. "Honey, I got better ways to spend my money than talk."

She let him suck and nuzzle, calculating how far she could let him go and keep him in line. Rooting about like a puppy, she thought in disgust while she stroked his hair.

"Your money ran out at dawn, sweetheart."

"I got more." He bit her, hard. Because she knew he expected it, she gave a soft moan of pleasure.

"House rules, Jim. Money first."

He swore at her and considered taking his pleasure as he chose. But if he forced her and managed to avoid getting tossed out by Eli, the doors of the Silver Star would be barred to him. He had money, he thought. And a need that was rock-hard.

When he started to shift, Carlotta trailed a finger

down his arm. "Talk, Jim, and I'll . . ." With a long sigh, she arched back so that he could look his fill. "I'll give you the rest for free."

Sweat beaded on his upper lip as he studied her. "You don't do nothing for free."

Deliberately she ran a hand over her breast and down her rib cage and stroked the soft swell of her belly. "Talk. We're going to talk first." Her lips curved as she watched him swallow. "About gold." When he stiffened, her smile only widened. "Don't worry, Jim. I haven't told anyone, have I? I've never said a word about how you and Donley killed old Matt Conway."

"I was drunk when I told you about that." He wiped a hand over the back of his mouth as fear and desire twined inside him. "A man says all kinds of things when he's drunk."

That made her laugh. She pillowed her head on her folded arms. "Nobody knows that better than a whore or a wife, Jim, honey. Relax. Who was the one who told you old Matt had finally hit? Who was the one who told you his daughter was coming and you had to move fast? Don't try dealing from the bottom with me, sweetheart. It's business, remember. Yours and mine."

After pushing himself up in bed, he reached bad-temperedly for the whiskey bottle. "I told you that once Sam got things worked out you'd get your share."

"And what does Sam have to work out?" She let him take a swallow, two. It never hurt to loosen a man's tongue, but there were some who went from relaxed to mean with whiskey. With Jim the line was all too easily crossed. She took the bottle back.

"We've already been through this," he muttered. He no longer felt like having sex, and he sure as hell didn't want to talk.

"If Sam had some idea about getting that Conway

bitch to the altar to get his hands on the deed, he's had time enough. Everybody in town knows she doesn't have her eye on your brother, but on Jake Redman."

"How about you?" He tapped a finger, none too gently, against her bruised cheekbone. "Who do you have those blue eyes on?"

"The main chance, sweetheart. Always the main chance." She ran her tongue over her lips, grimly pleased with the way Jim's eyes followed the movement. The surest way to lead a man, she knew, was from a point just below his gunbelt. She rose, knowing the shuttered light would be flattering to her skin. Slowly she ran her hands up her body, letting them linger on her breasts.

"You know, Jim," she began, slipping into a thin red negligee that was as transparent as glass, "I've always been drawn to men who take risks, who know what they want and take it." She left the negligee open as she walked back toward the bed. "That night you came in and told me how you and Donley had dragged Matt up to the mine and how you'd killed him because he wouldn't hand over the deed. You told me just how you'd killed him, how you'd hurt him first. Remember that night, Jim? You and me sure had ourselves a good time after we came upstairs."

He wet his lips. Her nipples were dark and just out of reach. "I remember."

"It was exciting. Knowing you'd just come from killing a man. Killing him to get what you wanted. I knew I was with a real man." The negligee fell carelessly off one shoulder. "Trouble is, nothing's happened since. I keep waiting."

"I told you. Sam's going—"

"The hell with Sam." She battled back her temper to smile at him. "He's too slow, too careful. A real man takes action. If he wants the Conway girl, why doesn't

he just take her? Or you could take her for him." She
moved closer, letting the idea take root. "She's all that's
in the way, Jim. You deal with her—and I ain't talking
about firing one of her sheds." The quick wariness in
his eyes pleased her. "Hurt her, Jim. She'll hand over
the deed quick enough. Then kill her." She murmured
the words like a love song. "When she's dead, you
come to me. We can do anything you want." She stood
beside the bed, glorious and gleaming. "Anything.
And it won't cost you a cent."

She didn't cry out when his hand clamped over her
wrist. Their faces were close, each of them aroused in
different ways, for different reasons.

"You'll take care of her?"

"Yes, damn you. Come here."

Carlotta smiled bitterly at the ceiling while Jim collapsed on top of her.

From her window an hour later, Carlotta watched as
Jake rode into town. Her hands clenched into fists—
from anger, yes, but also from a stab of desire. Soon,
she thought, very soon, he'd come back to her.

She turned as Jim pulled up his pants. She was
smiling.

"I think it's a real good time for you to pay Sarah
Conway a visit."

CHAPTER 14

When Jake walked into Maggie's, she set her fisted hands on her hips and looked him up and down with a sniff.

"Fine time to be strolling in, boyo." What she wanted was gossip, and she hoped to annoy it out of him. "Can't figure why a man would be paying good money for a bed and never sleep in it."

"I pay for your chicken and dumplings, too, but I ain't stupid enough to eat them." He started resignedly up the stairs, knowing she would follow.

"You don't seem to be suffering any from lack of food." With the audacity she'd been born with, she poked a finger in his ribs. "Must be getting meals someplace."

"Must be."

"Sarah a good cook, is she?"

Saying nothing, he pushed open the door to his room.

"Don't go pokering up on me, Jake, my boy." Maggie swiped a dustcloth here and there. "It's too late. Every blessed soul in town saw the way you looked at her at the dance. Then there was the way you rode out of town after her when she socked you in the jaw."

The dark, furious glint in his eyes had Maggie cackling. "That's more like it. Always said you could drop a man dead with a look as quick as with those guns of yours. No need to draw on me, though. I figure Sarah Conway's just what you need."

"Do you?" Jake tossed his saddlebags on the bed. He considered starting to strip to get rid of her. But he'd tried that before, and it hadn't budged her an inch. "I reckon you want to tell me why before you leave me the hell alone."

"Like to see the back of me, would you?" She just laughed again and patted his cheek. "More than one man's considered it my best side."

He barely managed to control a grin. He was damned if he knew why the nosy old woman appealed to him. "Why don't you get yourself another husband, Maggie? Then you could nag him."

"You'd miss me."

"I reckon some dogs miss the fleas once they manage to scratch them off." Then he sat by the window, propping his back against one side and his boot against the other.

"Somebody's got to bite at you. Might as well be me. I got something to say about you and Sarah Conway."

Staring out the window, he frowned. "It won't be anything I haven't said to myself. Go away, Maggie."

"Now listen to me, boy," she said in an abruptly serious tone. "There's some who're born to the pretty. They slide out of their mothers and straight into silk and satin. Then there's others who have to fight and claw and scratch for every good thing. We know something about that, you and me."

Still frowning, he looked back at her. With a nod, she continued. "Some go hungry, and some have their bellies full. The sweet Lord himself knows why he set things up that way, and no one else. But he didn't make the one man better than the other. It's men themselves who decide if they're going to be strong or weak—and that's the same as good or bad. Sometimes there's a woman who shoves them one way or the other. You take ahold of Sarah Conway, Jake. She'll shove you right enough."

"Could work the other way around," he murmured. "A woman's easier to shove than a man."

Maggie's brows rose in two amused peaks. "Jake, my boy, you've got a lot to learn about women."

It was the second time in so many days he'd been told that, Jake mused when Maggie clicked the door shut behind her. But it wasn't a woman he had to think about now.

It was gold. And it was murder.

He took Matt Conway's journal and started to read.

Unlike Sarah, Jake didn't bother with the early pages. He scanned a few at the middle, where Matt had written of working the mine and of his hopes for a big strike. There were mentions of Sarah here and there, of Matt's regrets at leaving her behind, of his pride in the letters she wrote him. And always he wrote of his longing to send for her.

He had wanted to build her a home first, a real home, like the one he'd described to her. The mine would do it, or so he had thought. Throughout the pages, his confidence never wavered.

Each time I enter, I feel it. Not just hope, but certainty. Today. Each time I'm sure it will be today. There is gold here, enough to give my Sarah the life of a princess—the life I had wanted so badly to give her mother. How alike they are. The miniature Sarah sent me for Christmas might be my own lost, lovely Ellen. Looking at it each night

before I sleep makes me grieve for the little girl
I left behind and ache for the young woman my
daughter has become.

So there had been a painting, Jake mused. Questions
might be answered once it was found. He skipped on,
toward the end.

In my years of prospecting, I've learned that
success is as elusive as any dream. A man may
have a map and tools, he may have skill and per-
sistence. But there is one factor that cannot be
bought, cannot be learned. Luck. Without it a
man can dig and hammer for years with the vein
he seeks always inches out of reach. As I have
been. Sweet God, as I have been.

Was it the hand of chance that caused my own
to slip, that had me sprawled in the dirt nursing my bruised and bloody fingers and cursing
God as I learned to curse him so eloquently?
And when I stumbled, half-blind with tears of
frustration and pain, was it his hand that led me
deeper into the tunnel, swinging my pick like a
madman?

There it was, under my still-bleeding fingers.
Glinting dull against the dark rock. It ran like
a river, back, back into the dark mouth of the
mine, narrow, then widening. I know it cannot
be, yet to me it seemed to shimmer and pulse
like a living thing. Gold. At long last.

I am not ashamed that I sat on the dusty floor of
the mine, my lamp between my knees, and wept.

He'd found it, Jake thought as he frowned over the words. It was no longer just a hunch, a feeling, but fact. Matt Conway had found his gold, and he'd died. Perhaps there would be an answer to why and how in the remaining pages.

Do men grow more foolish with age? Perhaps. Perhaps. But then, whiskey makes fools of young and old. There need be no excuses. A man finds his heart's desire after years of sweat. To what does he turn? A woman, and a bottle. I found both at the Silver Star.

It had been my intention to keep my discovery to myself for a little longer. Sarah's letter changed that. She's coming. My own little girl is already on her way to join me. There is no way to prepare her for what she will find. Thank God I will soon be able to give her all that I promised.

It wasn't my intent to tell Carlotta of the gold, or of Sarah's arrival. Whiskey and weakness. Undoubtedly I paid for my lack of discretion with a vicious head the next morning. And the visit from Samuel Carlson.

Could it be coincidence that now, after all these years, he wants the mine? His offer was generous. Too generous for me to believe the purchase was to be made from sentiment on his part. Perhaps my suspicions are unfounded. He took my refusal in good temper, leaving the offer open. Yet there was something, something in the way he held his brother and his man Donley to silence—like holding wild dogs on a leash.

Tomorrow I will ride into town and tell Barker about my discovery. It may be wise to hire a few men to help me work the mine. The sooner it is begun, the sooner I can build my Sarah the house she believes is already waiting for her.

It was the last entry. Closing the book, Jake rose. He had his answers.

M iss Sarah, seeing as you're going into town and all . . ."

Sarah sighed as she adjusted her straw bonnet. "Again, Lucius?"

He scratched his grizzled beard. "A man gets powerful thirsty doing all this work."

"Very well." She'd managed to cure him of his abhorrence of water. Easing him away from his passion for whiskey would take a bit more time.

"I'm obliged, Miss Sarah." He grinned at her. In the weeks he'd been working for her he'd discovered she had a soft heart—and a tough mind. "You check on that wood you ordered. I'll be right pleased to put that floor in for you when it gets here."

Easily said, she mused, when the wood was still hundreds of miles away. "You might finish building the pen Jake started. I intend to inquire about buying some piglets while I'm in town."

"Yes'm." He spit. He'd build the cursed pen, but he'd be damned if he'd tend pigs. "Miss Sarah, I'm getting a mite low on tobacco."

Whiskey and tobacco, Sarah thought, rolling her eyes heavenward. What would Mother Superior have said? "I'll see to it. You look in on Alice regularly, Lucius. See that she has a bit of that broth and rests."

She heard him grumble about being a nursemaid and snagged her lip to keep it from curving. "I'll be back by three. I'm going to fix a very special meal tonight." She gave him a final glance. "You'll want to change your shirt." She cracked the reins and headed out before she allowed herself to laugh.

Life was glorious. Life was, she thought as she let the horses prance, magnificent. Perhaps she was rich, as Jake had said, but the gold no longer mattered. So many things that had seemed so important only a short time before really meant nothing at all.

She was in love, beautifully, wildly, in love, and all the gold in the world couldn't buy what she was feeling.

She would make him happy. It would take some time, some care and more than a little patience, but she would make Jake Redman see that together they could have everything two people could want. A home, children, roots, a lifetime.

What they had brought to each other had changed them both. She was not the same woman who had boarded the train in Philadelphia. How far she'd come, Sarah reflected as she scanned the distant buttes. Not just in miles. It was much more than miles. Only weeks before she'd been certain her happiness depended on having a new bonnet. She laughed as the hot wind tugged at the brim of the one she wore now. She had come to Lone Bluff with dreams of fine parties and china dishes. She hadn't found them. But she had found more, much more.

And she had changed him. She could see it in the way he looked at her, in the way he reached for her as he slept, just to hold her, to keep her close. Perhaps the words were difficult for him to say. She could wait.

Now that she had found him, nothing and no one would keep her from being with him.

She saw the rider coming, and for an instant her smile bloomed. But it wasn't Jake. Sarah watched Jim Carlson slow his horse to a trot as he crossed the road in front of her. She intended to ride by with a brief nod of greeting, but he blocked her way.

"Morning, ma'am." He shifted in his saddle to lean toward her. The stink of whiskey colored his words. "All alone?"

"Good morning, Mr. Carlson. I'm on my way to town, and I'm afraid I'm a bit pressed for time."

"That so?" It was going to be easier than he'd thought. He wouldn't have to go through Lucius to get to her. "Now that's a shame, since I was just riding out to see you."

"Oh?" She didn't care for the look in his eyes, and the smell of whiskey on his breath didn't seem harmless, as it did with Lucius. "Is there something I can do for you, Mr. Carlson?"

"There sure is." Slowly, his eyes on hers, he drew his gun. "Step on out of the wagon."

"You must be mad." She'd frozen at the first sight of the barrel, but now, instinctively, her fingers inched toward her rifle.

"I wouldn't touch that rifle, ma'am. It'd be a shame for me to put a hole in that pretty white hand of yours. Now, I said get out of the wagon."

"Jake will kill you if you touch me."

He'd already thought that one through. That was the reason he was altering Carlotta's plan to suit himself. He wasn't going to kill Sarah here and now, unless she did something stupid. "Oh, I got plans for Redman, honey, don't you worry. You just step out of that wagon before I have to put a bullet in your horses."

She didn't doubt he would, or that he would shoot

her in the back should she try to run. Trapped, she stepped down and stood stiffly beside the wagon.

"God Almighty, you got looks, Sarah. That's why Sam took to you." With his gun still in his hand, Jim slid out of the saddle. "You got those fine lady looks like our mama did. You saw her picture at the house. Sam, he's mighty fond of pictures." He grinned again. When he reached out to touch Sarah's face, she hissed and jerked it aside. "But you, you got some fire. Mama was just crazy. Plumb crazy." He stepped forward so that his body pushed hers against the side of the wagon. "Sam told you she was delicate, didn't he? That's the word he uses. Crazy was what she was, so that the old man would lock her up sometimes for days. One day when he opened up the door, he found her hanging dead with a pretty pink silk scarf around her neck."

Horror leaped into her eyes and warred with fear. "Let me go. If Samuel finds out what you've done, he'll—"

"You think I run scared of Sam?" Laughing, Jim forced Sarah's face back to his. "Maybe you figure he's smoother than me, got more brains. But we're blood." His fingers bit into her skin. "Don't forget it. You ever let him get this close, let him do what he wanted? Or did you save yourself for that breed?"

She slapped him with all the force of her fear and rage. Then she was clawing at him, blindly, with some mad hope of getting to his horse. She felt the barrel of the gun press into the soft underside of her jaw and heard the click of the hammer.

"Try that again and I'll leave what's left of you here for the buzzards, gold or no gold. Your pa tried to get away, too." The stunned look in her eyes pleased him, gave him the edge he wanted. "You think on what happened to him and take care." He was breathing quickly, his finger trembling on the trigger. He'd lied when he'd said he wasn't scared of his brother. If it hadn't been for the rage Sam would heap on him, Jim would have sent a bullet into her. "Now you're going to do just like I say, and you'll stay alive awhile longer."

Interesting reading." Barker squinted down at Matt's journal while he fanned the hot, still air around his face with his hat. "Matt had a fine way of putting words on paper."

"Fine or not, it's plain enough." Jake fidgeted at the window, annoyed with himself for coming to the law with something he could, and should, have handled himself. Sarah's doing, he thought. He hadn't even felt the shove.

"It's plain that Matt thought he'd found gold."

"He'd found it. Lucius dug through to where Matt was working. It's there, just the way Matt wrote."

Thoughtful, Barker closed the book and leaned back in his chair. "Poor old Matt. Finally makes the big strike, then gets caught in a cave-in."

"He was dead before those beams gave way."

Taking his time, Barker pushed a cozy plug of tobacco in his cheek. "Well, now, maybe you think so, and maybe I'm doing some pondering on it, but this here journal isn't proof. It's not going to be easy to ride out to the Carlson ranch and talk to Sam about murder with no more than a book in my hand. Now hold on," he added when Jake snatched the book from the desk. "I didn't say I wasn't going out, I just said it wasn't going to be easy." Still fanning himself with his hat, he sat back in his chair. He wanted to think it through, and think it through carefully. The Carlson family had a long reach. He was more concerned about that than about the quick temper and gun of young Jim.

"Got a question for you, Jake. Why'd you bring me that journal instead of riding on out and putting a hole in the Carlson brothers?"

Jake skimmed his eyes over Barker's comfortable paunch. "My deep and abiding respect for the law."

After a bark of laughter, the sheriff spit a stream of tobacco juice into the spittoon. "I once knew a woman—before Mrs. Barker—who lied as smooth as that. Couldn't help but admire her." With a sigh, he perched his hat on his head. "Whatever your reason, you brought it, so I'm duty-bound to do something about it. Got to tell you, nothing's more tiring than duty." He reached unenthusiastically for his gunbelt as the door burst open.

"Sheriff." Nancy stood, darting glances over her shoulder and tugging restlessly at the shoulder of her hastily donned dress. "I got to talk to you."

"You'll just have to hold on to it till I get back. One of them cowboys got a little too enthusiastic over at the Silver Star, I ain't getting worked up about it."

"You'd better listen." Nancy stood firm in front of the door. "I'm only doing this 'cause of Alice." She glanced at Jake then. "Carlotta'd strip my skin if she found out I come, but I figured Miss Conway done right by Alice, I ought to do right by her."

"Quit babbling. If you're hell-bent on talking, say it."

"It's Carlotta." Nancy kept her voice low, as if it might carry back to the Silver Star. "She's been feeling real mean since yesterday."

"Carlotta was born feeling mean," Barker muttered. Then he waved to Nancy to continue. "All right, finish it out."

"Last night she took Jim Carlson up. She don't usually let men stay overnight in her room, but he was still there this morning. My room's next to hers, and I heard them talking."

Jake took her arm to draw her farther into the room. "Why don't you tell me what you heard?"

"She was talking about how Jim and Donley killed Matt Conway, and how he was supposed to take care of Matt's girl." She yelped when Jake's fingers bit into her arm. "I didn't have no part in it. I'm telling you what I heard 'cause she took Alice in after Carlotta near killed her."

"Looks like I'd better have a talk with Carlotta," Barker mused, straightening his hat.

"No, you can't." Fear for her own skin had her yanking free of Jake. "She'll kill me. That's the God's truth. Anyways, it's too late for that."

"Why?" Jake caught her again before she could dash out the door.

She'd gone this far, Nancy thought, dragging the back of her hand over her mouth. She might as well finish. "Carlotta said Jim was to scare Miss Conway good, hurt her. Then, when he had the deed to the mine, he was to kill her. He rode out an hour ago, and I couldn't get away till now."

Jake was already through the door and halfway to his horse when Barker caught up with him. "Will and me'll be right behind you."

There had been times when killing had come easily to Jake, so easily that after it was done he'd felt nothing. This time would be different. He knew it, felt it, as he sped down the road toward Sarah's house. If Jim Carlson was ahead of him and he got within range, he would kill him without question. It would be easy. And it would be a pleasure.

He heard the horses behind him, but he didn't look back.

His own mount seemed to sense the urgency and lengthened his strides until his powerful legs were a blur and the dust was a yellow wall behind them.

When Jake saw the wagon, the cold rage dropped into his gut and turned into a hot, bubbling fear. He vaulted from the saddle beside the two horses, which stood slack-hipped and drowsy.

Surprisingly agile, Barker slipped down beside him. "Take it easy." He began to place a hand on Jake's shoulder, but then he thought better of it. "If he took her off somewhere, we'll track him." He held up a hand before any of the men with him could speak. Along with Will were three men from town, including Ed Cody, who still wore his store apron. "We take care of our own here, Jake. We'll get her back."

In silence, Jake bent down to pick up the cameo lying facedown in the road. Its slender pin was snapped. There were a few pale blue threads clinging to the broken point. The signs told him she'd struggled, and the picture of her frightened and fighting clawed at him. The signs also told him where she was being taken. With the brooch in his pocket, he jumped into the saddle and rode hard for the Carlson ranch.

Her hands were bound together and tied to the saddle horn. If it had been possible, she would have jumped to the ground. Though there was nowhere to run, at least she would have had the satisfaction of making him sweat.

Everything Jake had said was true—about the gold, about her father's death. Sarah had no doubt that the man responsible for it all was sitting behind her.

At first she thought he was taking her into the hills, or to the desert, where he could kill her and leave her body hidden. But she saw, with some confusion, the graceful lines of the Carlson ranch house in the shallow valley below.

It was a peaceful scene, lovely despite the waves of radiant heat rising up from the ground. She heard a dog bark. As they approached, Samuel burst out of the house, hatless and pale, to stare at his brother.

"What in God's name have you done?"

Jim loosened the rope around the saddle horn, then lifted Sarah to the ground. "Brought you a present."

"Sarah, my dear." His mouth grim, Carlson tugged at her bonds. "I'm speechless. There's no way I could ever . . ." He let his words trail off and began to massage the raw skin of her wrists. "He must be drunk. Stable that horse, damn you," he shouted at Jim. "Then come inside. You've a great deal to answer for."

It stunned her, left her limp, when Jim merely shrugged and led his horse away. It must be a joke, a bizarre joke, she thought, bringing her trembling hands to her lips. But it wasn't. She knew it was much too deadly to be a joke.

"Samuel—"

"My dear, I don't know what to say." He slipped a supporting arm around her waist. "I can't begin to apologize for my brother's outrageous behavior. Are you hurt? Dear Lord, your dress is torn." He had her by the shoulders then, and the look in his eyes froze her blood. "Did he touch you, molest you?"

She managed to shake her head, once, then twice. Then the words came. "Samuel, he killed my father. It was for the gold. There's gold in the mine. He must have found out and he—he murdered my father."

She was breathless now, her hands clinging to his

trim black vest. He only stared at her, stared until she wanted to scream. "Samuel, you must believe me."

"You're overwrought," he said stiffly. "And no wonder. Come in out of the heat."

"But he—"

"You needn't worry about Jim." He led her inside the thick adobe walls. "He won't bother you again. You have my word. I want you to wait in my office." His voice was quiet, soothing, as he led her past his mother's portrait and into a room. "Try to relax. I'll take care of everything."

"Samuel, please be careful. He might— He could hurt you."

"No." He patted her hand as he eased her into a chair. "He'll do exactly what I tell him."

When the door shut, she covered her face with her hands. For a moment she let the hysteria she'd fought off take control. He'd intended to kill her. She was certain of it, from the way he'd looked at her, the way he'd smiled at her. Why in God's name had he brought her here, where she would be protected by Samuel?

Protected. After letting out a shaky breath, she waited until her heartbeat leveled and the need to scream passed. She was safe now. But it wasn't over. She closed her eyes briefly. It was far from over.

It was madness. Jim Carlson was as mad as his poor mother had been, but instead of killing himself he had killed her father. She wanted to weep, to let the new, aching grief come. But she couldn't. She couldn't weep, and she couldn't sit.

Rising, she began to pace. The room was small but beautifully furnished. There were delicate porcelain figurines and a painting in fragile pastels. It reflected Samuel's elegant taste and eye for beauty. How unlike the brothers were, she thought.

Cain and Abel.

With a hand on her heart, she rushed to the door. She could never have borne the guilt if one brother killed the other over her.

But the door was locked. For a moment she thought it was only her nerves making her fumble. After a deep breath she tried the knob again. It resisted.

Whirling around, she stared at the room. Locked in? But why? For her own protection? Samuel must have thought she would be safer behind a locked door until he came back for her.

And if it was Jim who came back with the key? Her heart thudding in her throat, she began a frantic search for a weapon.

She pulled out desk drawers, pushing ruthlessly through papers. If not a pistol, she thought, then a knife, even a letter opener. She would not be defenseless. Not again. She tugged open the middle drawer, and the brass pulls knocked against the glossy mahogany. Her hand froze when she saw the miniature. Her miniature.

Like a sleepwalker, she reached for it, staring blindly.

It was the self-portrait that she had painted the year before, the one she had shipped to her father for Christmas. The one, Sarah realized as her fingers closed over it, that he had shown with pride to his friends in town. The one that had been missing from his possessions. Missing because it had been taken by his murderer.

When the key turned in the lock, she didn't bother to close the drawer or to hide what she held in her hand. Instead, she rose and faced him.

"It was you," she murmured as Samuel Carlson closed and locked the door behind him. "You killed my father."

CHAPTER 15

Carlson crossed the room until only the desk was between them. "Sarah." His voice was almost a sigh, a sigh touched with patience. In his hand he carried a delicate cup filled with fragrant tea. But she noted that he had strapped on his gun. "I realize how upset you must be after Jim's inexcusable behavior. Now, why don't you sit down, compose yourself?"

"You killed my father," she repeated. It was rage she felt now, waves of it.

"That's ridiculous." The words were said gently. "I haven't killed anyone. Here, my dear. I've brought you some tea. It should help calm you."

The quiet sincerity in his eyes caused her to falter. He must have sensed it, because he smiled and stepped forward. Instantly she backed away. "Why was this in your desk?"

Carlson looked at the miniature in her hand. "A woman should never intrude on a man's personal belongings." His voice became indulgent as he set the cup on the desk. "But since you have, I'll confess. I can be faulted for being overly romantic, I suppose. The moment I saw it, I fell in love with you. The moment I saw your face, I wanted you." He held out a hand, palm up, as if he were asking for a dance. "Come, Sarah, you can't condemn me for that."

Confused, she shook her head. "Tell me how this came to be in your drawer when it belonged to my father."

Impatience clouded his face, and he dropped his hand to his side. "Isn't baring my soul enough for you? You knew, right from the beginning, you knew the way I felt about you. You deceived me." There was more than impatience in his face now. Something else was building in him. Something that had the bright, hot taste of fear clogging her throat.

"I don't know what you're talking about, Samuel." She spaced her words carefully and kept her eyes on his. "But you're right. I'm upset, and I'm not myself. I'd prefer to go home now and discuss all of this later." With the miniature still clutched in her hand, she stepped around the desk and toward the door. The violence with which he grabbed her and shoved her back against the wall had her head reeling.

"It's too late. Jim's interference has changed everything. His interference, and your prying. I was patient with you, Sarah. Now it's too late."

His face was close to hers—close enough for her to see clearly what was in his eyes. She wondered, as the blood drained slowly from her face, how it was that she'd never seen it before. The madness was bright and deadly. She tried to speak and found she had to swallow first.

"Samuel, you're hurting me."

"I would have made you a queen." He took one hand and brought it up to stroke her face. She cringed, but his eyes warned her not to move. "I would have given you everything a woman could want. Silk." He traced a finger over her cheekbone. "Diamonds." Then he ran it lightly down her throat. "Gold." His hand tightened abruptly around her windpipe. Before she could begin to struggle, it was loosened again. "Gold, Sarah. It belonged to me, truly to me. My grandfather had no right to lose that part of my heritage. And your father . . . he had no right to deny me what was already mine."

"He did it for me." Perhaps she could calm him, if only she could remain calm herself, before it was too late. "He only wanted to see that I was taken care of."

"Of course." He nodded, as if he were pleased that she understood. "Of course he did. As I do. It would have been yours as much as mine. I would never have let you suffer because I had taken it back. As my wife, you would have had every luxury. We would have gone back east together. That was always my plan. I was going to follow you back east and court you. But you stayed. You should never have stayed, Sarah. This isn't the place for you. I knew it the moment I saw your picture. It was there, in that miserable little cabin, beside the cot. I found it while I was looking for the deed to the mine."

His face changed again. He looked petulant now, like a boy who had been denied an extra piece of pie. "I was very annoyed that my brother and Donley killed Matt. Clumsy. They were only to . . . convince him to turn over the deed. Then, of course, it was up to me to think of causing the cave-in to cover up what they'd done. I never found the deed. But I found your picture."

She didn't think he was aware of how viciously his fingers were digging into her arms. She was almost certain he was no longer aware of how much he was telling her. She remained silent and still, knowing her only hope now was time.

"Delicate," he murmured. "Such a delicate face. The innocence shining in the eyes, the soft curve of the mouth. It was a lie, wasn't it, Sarah?" The violence sprang back into his face, and she could only shake her head and wait. "There was no delicacy, no innocence. You toyed with me, offering me smiles, only smiles, while you gave yourself to Redman like a whore. He should be dead for touching what belonged to me. You should both be dead."

She prepared to scream. She prepared to fight for what she knew was her life.

"Sam!" The banging on the door brought with it a mixture of fear and relief.

Swearing, Carlson dragged Sarah to the door to unlock it. "Goddamn it, I told you to go back and get rid of the wagon and team."

"Riders coming in." The sweat on Jim's face attested to the fact that he had already ridden, and ridden hard. "It's Redman and the sheriff, with some men from town." He glanced at Sarah. "They'll be looking for her."

When Sarah tried to break away, Samuel locked an arm around her throat. "You've ruined everything, bringing her here."

"I only did it 'cause you wanted her. I could've taken care of her back on the road. Hell, I could've taken care of her the night we torched her shed, but you said you didn't want her hurt none."

Carlson tightened his grip as Sarah clawed at his arm. Her vision grayed from lack of air. As if from a distance, she heard the voices, one mixing into the other.

"How long?"

"Ten minutes, no more . . . Kill her now."

"Not here, you idiot. . . . Hold them off. . . . In the hills."

Sarah's last thought before she lost consciousness was that Jake was coming, but too late.

"You listen to me." Barker stopped the men on the rise above the Carlson ranch. But it was Jake he was looking at. "I know you'd like to ride in there hell-bent, but you take a minute to think. If they've got her, we've got to go slow."

"They've got her." In his mind, the Carlson brothers were already dead.

"Then let's make sure we get her back in one piece. Will, I want you to break off, ease on over to the barn. Ed, I'd be obliged if you'd circle around the back. I don't want any shooting until it's necessary." With a nod, he spurred his horse.

Jim watched them coming and wiped the sweat off his brow. His men were all out on the range. Not that they'd have been any good, he thought. The only one who'd have backed them against the sheriff was Donley. And he was dead. Wetting his lips, he levered the rifle in the window.

He had to wait until they got close. That was what Sam had told him. Wait until they got close. Then he was to kill as many as he could. Starting with Redman.

Sweat dripped down into his eyes. His fingers twitched.

Sam had sent Donley to kill Redman, Jim remembered. But it was Donley who'd been buried. Now he was going to do it. He wet his lips when he caught Jake in the sight. He was going to do it right. But nerves had his finger jerking on the trigger.

Jake felt the bullet whiz past his cheek. Like lightning, he kicked one foot free of the stirrup to slide halfway down the side of his horse. Gun drawn, he rode toward the house while Barker shouted orders. He could hear the men scrambling for cover and returning fire, but his mind was on one thing and one thing alone.

Getting inside to Sarah.

Outside the doors, he leaped off. When he kicked them open, his second gun was drawn. The hall and the foyer were empty. He could hear the shouts of men and peppering gunfire. With a quick glance for any sign of her, he started up the stairs.

Jim Carlson's back was to him when he broke open the door.

"Where is she?" Jake didn't flinch when a bullet from outside plowed into the wall beside him.

From his crouched position, Jim turned slowly. "Sam's got her." With a grin, he swung his rifle up. For months he'd wanted another chance to kill Jake Redman. Now he took it.

He was still grinning as he fell forward. Jake slid his smoking guns back in their holsters. Moving quickly, he began to search the house.

Barker met him on the steps. "She ain't here. I found this on the floor." In his hand he held Sarah's miniature.

Jake's eyes flicked up to Barker's. They held there only seconds, but Barker knew he would never forget the look in them. Later he would tell his wife it was the look of a man whose soul had gotten loose.

Turning on his heel, Jake headed outside, with Barker close behind.

"Oh, God." For the first time since Jake had known him, Barker moved with speed. Pushing past Jake, he raced to where two of his men were carrying Will Metcalf.

"He isn't dead." Ed Cody laid Will down and held his head. "But we have to get him back to town, to the doc."

Barker crouched down as Will's eyes fluttered open. "You're going to be all right, son."

"Took me by surprise," Will managed, struggling not to gasp at the pain as Cody pressed a pad to the hole in his shoulder. "Was Sam Carlson, Sheriff. He had her—I saw he had her on the horse. Think they headed west."

"Good job, Will." Barker used his own bandanna to wipe the sweat off his deputy's brow. "One of you men hitch up a wagon, get some blankets. You get this boy to the doctor, Ed. Redman and I'll go after Carlson." But when he stood, all he saw of Jake was the dust his mustang kicked up as he galloped west.

Sarah came to slowly, nausea rising in her throat. Moaning, she choked it back and tried to lift a hand to her spinning head. Both wrists were bound tight to the saddle horn.

For a moment she thought she was still with Jim. Then she remembered.

The horse was climbing, picking its way up through dusty, dung-colored rock. She watched loose dirt and stones dislodged by the horse's hooves fall down a dizzying ravine. The man behind her was breathing hard. Fighting for calm, she tried to mark the trail they were taking and remember it. When she escaped—and she would—she didn't intend to wander helplessly through the rocks.

He stopped the horse near the edge of a canyon. She could see the thin silver line of a river far below. An eagle called as he swooped into the wide opening, then returned to a nest built in the high rock wall.

"Samuel, please—" She cried out when he pulled the rope from around her wrists and dragged her roughly to the ground. One look warned her that the calm, sane words she had meant to use would never reach him.

There was a bright, glazed light in his eyes. His face was pale and drenched with sweat. His hair was dark with it. She watched his eyes dart here and there, as if he expected something to leap out from behind a huddle of rock.

The man who had swept off his hat and kissed her fingers wasn't here with her now. If he had ever been part of Samuel Carlson, he had vanished. The man who stood over her was mad, and as savage as any beast that lived in the hills.

"What are you going to do?"

"He's coming." Still breathing rapidly, Carlson swiped a hand over his mouth. "I saw him behind us. When he comes for you, I'll be ready." He reached down to drag her to her feet. "I'm going to kill him, Sarah. Kill him like a dog." He pulled out his gun and rubbed the barrel against her cheek, gently, like a caress. "You're going to watch. I want you to watch me kill him. Then you'll understand. It's important that you understand. A man like that deserves to die by a gun. He's nothing, less than nothing. A crude gunslinger with Apache blood. He put his hands on you." A whimper escaped her as he dragged a hand through her hair. "I'm going to kill him for you, Sarah. Then we're going away, you and I."

"No." She wrenched free. The canyon was at her

back when she faced him. If she had stumbled another step she would have fallen back into nothing. There was fear. The taste of it was bitter in her throat. But it wasn't for herself. Jake would come, she knew, and someone would die. "I won't go anywhere with you. It's over, Samuel. You must see that. They know what you've done, and they'll hunt you down."

"A potbellied sheriff?" He laughed and, before she could evade him, closed his hand over her arm. "Not likely. This is a big country, Sarah. They won't find us."

"I won't go with you." The pain when he squeezed her arm nearly buckled her knees. "I'll get away."

"If I must, I'll keep you locked up, the way my mother was locked up. For your own good."

She heard the horse even as he did and screamed out a warning. "No, Jake, he'll kill you!" Then she screamed again, this time in pain, as Carlson bent her arm behind her back. Calmly he put the gun to her temple.

"It's her I'll kill, Redman. Come out slow and keep your hands where I can see them, or the first bullet goes in her brain." He twisted her arm ruthlessly because he wanted Jake to hear her cry out again. He wanted Jake to hear the pain. "Now, Redman, or I'll kill her and toss her body over the edge."

"No. Oh, no." Tears blurred her vision as she watched Jake step out into the open. "Please don't. It won't gain you anything to kill him. I'll go with you." She tried to turn her head to look into Carlson's eyes. "I'll go anywhere you want."

"Not gain anything?" Carlson laughed again, and it echoed off the rocks and air. "Satisfaction, my dear. I'll gain satisfaction."

"Are you hurt?" Jake asked quietly.

"No." She shook her head, praying she could will

him back behind the rock, back to safety. "No, he hasn't hurt me. He won't if you go back."

"But you're wrong, my dear, quite wrong." Carlson bent his head close to hers, amused by the quick fury in Jake's eyes when he brushed his lips over Sarah's hair. "I'll have to, you see, because you won't understand. Unless I kill him for you, you won't understand. Your gunbelt, Redman." Carlson drew back the hammer for emphasis and kept the gun tight against Sarah's temple. "Take it off, slowly, very slowly, and kick it aside."

"No!" She began to struggle, only to have him drag her arm farther up her back. "I'll kill you myself." She wept in rage and fear. "I swear it."

"When I'm done here, my dear, you'll do exactly what I say, when I say. In time you'll understand this was for the best. Drop the belt, Redman." Carlson smiled at him and jerked his head to indicate that he wanted the guns kicked away. "That's fine." He took the gun away from Sarah's temple to point it at Jake's heart. "You know, I've never killed a man before. It always seemed more civilized to hire someone— someone like yourself." His smile widened. "But I believe I'm going to enjoy it a great deal."

"You might." Jake watched his eyes. He could only hope Sarah had the sense to run when it was over. Barker couldn't be far behind. "Maybe you'll enjoy it more when I tell you I killed your brother."

The muscles in Carlson's cheek twitched. "You bastard."

Sarah screamed and threw her weight against his gun hand. She felt the explosion, as if the bullet had driven into her. Then she was on her knees. Life poured out of her when she saw Jake sprawled on the ground, blood seeping from his side.

"No. Oh, God, no."

Carlson threw back his head and laughed at the sky. "I was right. I enjoyed it. But he's not dead yet. Not quite yet." His lips stretched back from his teeth as he lifted the gun again.

She didn't think. There was no room for thought in a mind swamped with grief. She reached out and felt the smooth grip of Jake's gun in her hand. Kneeling in the dirt, she balanced it and aimed. "Samuel," she murmured, and waited for him to turn his head.

The gun jumped in her hand when she fired. The sound of the shot echoed on and on and on. He just stared at her. Afraid she'd missed, Sarah drew back the hammer and calmly prepared to fire again.

Then he stumbled. He stared at her as his hand reached up to press against the blood that blossomed on his shirtfront. Without a sound, he fell back. He groped once in the air, then tumbled off the edge and into the canyon.

Her hand went limp on the gun. Then the shudders began, racking shudders, as she crawled to Jake. He'd pushed himself up on one elbow, and he held his knife in his hand. She was weeping as she tore at her petticoats to pad the wound in his side.

"I thought he'd killed you. You looked—" There was so much blood, she thought frantically as she tore more cloth. "You need a doctor. I'll get you on the horse as soon as—" She broke off again as her voice began to hitch. "It was crazy, absolutely crazy, for you to come out in the open like that. I thought you had more sense."

"So did I." The pain was searing, centering in his side and flowing out in waves of heat. He wanted to touch her, just once more, before he died. "Sarah . . ."

"Don't talk." Tears clogged her throat. His blood seeped through the pad and onto her hands. "Just lie still. I'm going to take care of you. Damn you, I won't

let you die." He couldn't see her face. Tired of the effort, he closed his eyes. He thought, but couldn't be
sure, that he heard horses coming. "You're a hell of a
woman," he murmured, and passed out.

When he awoke, it was dark. There was a bitter
taste in his mouth and a hollow throbbing at the
base of his skull. The pain in his side was still there,
but dull now, and constant. He lay still and wondered
how long he'd been in hell.

He closed his eyes again, thinking it didn't matter
how long he'd been there, since he wouldn't be leaving.
Then he smelled her, smelled the soft scent that was
Sarah. Though it cost him dearly, he opened his eyes
again and tried to sit up.

"No, don't." She was there, murmuring to him,
pressing him gently back on a pillow, then laying a cool
cloth against his hot face.

"How long—" He could only manage two whispered words before the strength leaked out of him.

"Don't worry." Cradling his head with her arm, she
brought a cup to his lips. "Drink a little. Then you'll
sleep again. I'm right here with you," she continued
when he coughed and tried to turn his head away.

"Can't—" He tried to focus on her face, but saw
only a silhouette. It was Sarah, though. "Can't be in
hell," he murmured, then sank back into the darkness.

When he awoke again, it was daylight. And she was
there, leaning over him, smiling, murmuring something
he couldn't quite understand. But there were tears drying on her cheeks, cheeks that were too pale. She sat beside him, took his hand and held it against her lips. Even
as he struggled to speak, he lost consciousness again.

She thought it would drive her mad, the way he

drifted in and out of consciousness that first week, with the fever burning through him and the doctor giving her no hope. Hour after hour, day after day, she sat beside him, bathing his hot skin, soothing when the chills racked him, praying when he fell back into that deep, silent sleep.

What had he said that day when he'd awakened? Pacing to the window, the one Maggie had told her Jake had sometimes sat in, she drew the curtain aside to look down at the empty street. He'd said it couldn't be hell. But he'd been wrong, Sarah thought. It was hell, and she was mired in it, terrified each day that he would leave her.

So much blood. He'd lost so much blood. By the time Barker had ridden up she'd nearly managed to stop it, but the ride back to town had cost him more. She had stanched still more while the doctor had cut and probed into his side to remove the bullet. She hadn't known that watching the bullet come out of him would be as bad as watching it go in.

Then the fever had raced through him, vicious and merciless. In a week he'd been awake only a handful of minutes, often delirious, sometimes speaking in what Lucius had told her was Apache. If it didn't break soon, she knew, no matter how hard she prayed, no matter how hard she fought, it would take him.

Sarah moved back to the bed to sit beside him and watch over him in the pale light of dawn.

Time drifted, for her even as it did for him. She lost track of minutes, then hours, then days. When morning came she held his hand in hers and thought over the time they'd had together. His hands had been strong, she thought. Biting back a sob, she laid her forehead on his shoulder. And gentle, too, she remembered. When he'd touched her. When he'd taught her.

With him she'd found something lovely, something powerful. A sunrise. A fast river. A storm. She knew now that love, desire, passion and affection could be one emotion for one man. From that first frantic discovery in the hay to the soft, sweet loving by the stream, he'd given her more than most women had in a lifetime.

"But I'm greedy," she murmured to him. "I want more. Jake, don't leave me. Don't cheat me out of what we could have." She blinked back tears when she heard the door open behind her.

"How is he?"

"The same." Sarah rose and waited while Maggie set a tray on the bureau. She'd long ago stopped arguing about eating. It had taken her only a few days to realize that if she wanted the strength to stay with Jake she needed food.

"Don't worry none about this breakfast, because Anne Cody made it up for you."

Sarah dashed away the hated, weakening tears. "That was kind of her."

"She asked about our boy here, and wanted you to know that Alice is doing just fine."

"I'm glad." Without interest, she folded back the cloth so that steam rose fragrantly from the biscuits.

"Looks like Carlotta skipped town."

"It doesn't matter." With no more interest than she had in the biscuits, she looked at her own face in the mirror. Behind her reflection, she could see Jake lying motionless in the bed. "The damage is done."

"Child, you need sleep, and not what you get sitting up in that chair all night. You go on and use my room. I'll stay with him."

"I can't." Sarah ignored the biscuits and took the coffee. "Sometimes he calls for me, and I'm afraid if

I'm not here he might . . . slip away. That's foolish, I suppose, but I just can't leave him, Maggie."

"I know." Because she did, Maggie set a comforting hand on Sarah's shoulder. The noise at the door had her turning back. "What are you doing sneaking around here, young John Cody?"

Johnny slipped into the doorway and stood with his hat crushed in his hands. "Just wanted to see him, is all."

"A sickroom ain't no place for nasty little boys."

"It's all right." Sarah waved him in and summoned up a smile. "I'm sure Jake would be pleased that you'd taken the time to visit him."

"He ain't going to die, is he, Sarah?"

"No." She found the confidence she'd lost during the night. "No, he isn't going to die, Johnny."

"Ma says you're taking real good care of him." He reached out a hand, then balled it at his side again.

"It's all right, boy," Maggie said, softening. "You can pet him as long as he don't know it. I do it myself."

Gingerly Johnny stroked a hand along Jake's forehead. "He's pretty hot."

"Yes, but the fever's going to break soon." Sarah laid a hand on Johnny's shoulder. "Very soon."

"Will's better," he said, giving Sarah a hopeful smile. "He's got his arm in a sling and all, but he's getting around just fine and dandy. Won't even let Liza fuss no more."

"Before long Jake won't let me fuss, either."

Hours later she dozed, lulled by the afternoon sun. She slept lightly, her head nestled against the wing of the chair and her hands in her lap on top of her journal. She'd written everything she felt, hoped, despaired of on those pages. Someone called her name, and she lifted a hand as if to brush the voice away. She only wanted to sleep.

"Sarah."

Now her eyes flew open, and she bolted out of the chair. Jake was half sitting up in bed, his brows drawn together in annoyance or confusion. And his eyes, she noted, were focused, alert and direct on hers.

"What the hell's going on?" he asked her. Then he watched, astonished, as she collapsed on the side of the bed and wept.

It was three weeks before he had the strength to do more than stand on his own feet. He had time to think—perhaps too much time—but when he tried to do anything, he found himself weak as a baby.

It infuriated him, disgusted him. When he swore at Maggie twice in one morning, she told Sarah their patient was well on the road to recovery.

"He's a tough one, Jake is," Maggie went on as they climbed the steps to his room together. "Said he was damn sick and tired of having females poking him, pouring things into him and trying to give him baths."

"So much for gratitude," Sarah said with a laugh. Then she swayed and clutched the banister for support.

Maggie grabbed her arm. "Honey, are you all right?"

"Yes. Silly." Shrugging it off, Sarah waited for the dizziness to pass. "I'm just tired yet, I think." One look at Maggie's shrewd face had her giving up and sitting carefully on the riser.

"How far along are you?"

It surprised Sarah that the direct question didn't make her blush. Instead, she smiled. "About a month." She knew the exact moment when she had conceived

Jake's child, on the riverbank under the moon. "I had the obvious sign, of course. Then, for the last few days, I haven't been able to keep anything down in the morning."

"I know." Pleased as a partridge, Maggie cackled. "Honey, I knew you were breeding three days ago, when you turned green at the sight of Anne Cody's flapjacks. Ain't Jake just going to fall on his face?"

"I haven't told him," Sarah said quickly. "I don't want him to know until he's . . . until we've . . ." She propped her chin in her hands. "Not yet, Maggie."

"That's for you to decide."

"Yes, and you won't say anything . . . to anyone?"

"Not a peep."

Satisfied, Sarah rose and started up the stairs again. "The doctor said he'd be up and around in a couple of days. We haven't been able to talk about anything important since he's been healing." She knocked on the door to his room before pushing it open.

The bed was empty.

"What— Maggie!"

"He was there an hour ago. I don't know where—" But she was talking to air, as Sarah was flying down the stairs again.

"Sarah! Sarah!" His hand wrapped around a licorice whip, Johnny raced toward her. "I just saw Jake riding out of town. He sure looked a lot better."

"Which way?" She grabbed the surprised boy by the shoulders. "Which way did he go?"

"That way." He pointed. "I called after him, but I guess he didn't hear me."

"Damned hardheaded man," Maggie muttered from the doorway.

"So he thinks he can just ride off," Sarah said

between her teeth. "Well, Jake Redman is in for a surprise. I need a horse, Maggie. And a rifle."

He'd thought it through. He'd had nothing but time to think over the last weeks. She'd be mad, he figured. He almost smiled. Mad enough to spit, he imagined, but she'd get over it. In time she'd find someone who was right for her. Who was good for her.

Talking to her wouldn't have helped. He'd never known a more stubborn woman. So he'd saddled up and ridden out of Lone Bluff the way he'd ridden out of countless towns before. Only this time it hurt. Not just the pain from his still-healing wound, but an ache deeper, sharper, than anything that could be caused by a bullet.

He'd get over it, too, he told himself. He'd just been fooling himself, letting himself pretend that she could belong to him.

He'd never forget how she'd looked, kneeling in the dirt with his gun in her hand. His gun. And there had been horror in her eyes. He'd taught her to kill, and he wasn't sure he could live with that.

The way he figured it, she'd saved his life. The best he could do for her was return the favor and get out of hers.

She was rich now. Jake remembered how excited Lucius had been when he'd come to visit, talking on and on about the mine and how the gold was all but ready to fall into a man's hands. She could go back east, or she could stay and build that big house with the parlor she'd told him about.

And he would . . . he would go on drifting.

When he heard the rider coming, instinct had him wheeling his horse around and reaching for his gun. He swore, rubbing his hand on his thigh, as Sarah closed the distance between them.

"You bastard."

He acknowledged her with a nod. There was only one way to handle her now, one way to make certain she turned around and left. Before just looking at her made him want to crawl.

"Didn't know you could ride, Duchess. You come out all this way to tell me goodbye?"

"I have more than that to say." Her hands balled on the reins while she fought with her temper. "Not a word, Jake, to me, to anyone? Just saddle up and ride out?"

"That's right. When it's time to move on, you move."

"So you're telling me you have no reason to stay?"

"That's right." He knew the truth sometimes hurt, but he hadn't known a lie could. "You're a mighty pretty woman, Duchess. You'll be hard to top."

He saw the hurt glow in her eyes before her chin came up. "That's a compliment? Well, you're quite right, Jake. I'll be very hard to top. You'll never love another woman the way you love me. Or want one," she said, more quietly. "Or need one."

"Go on back, Sarah." He started to turn his horse but stopped short when she drew the rifle out of its holster and aimed it heart-high. "You want to point that someplace else?"

For an answer, she lowered it a few strategic inches, smiling when his brow lifted. "Ever hear the one about hell's fury, Jake?"

"I get the idea." He shifted slightly. "Duchess, if it's all the same to you, I'd rather you pointed it back at my chest."

"Get off your horse."

"Damn it, Sarah."

"I said off." She cocked the lever in two sharp movements. "Now."

He leaned forward in the saddle. "How do I know that's even loaded?"

"How do you know it's loaded?" She smiled, brought it up to her eye and fired. His hat flew off his head.

"Are you crazy?" Stunned, he dragged a hand through his hair. He could almost feel the heat. "You damn near killed me."

"I hit what I aim at. Isn't that what you said I should learn to do?" She cocked the rifle again. "Now get off that horse before I shoot something more vital off you."

Swearing, he slid down. "What the hell are you trying to prove with all this?"

"Just hold it right there." She dropped to the ground. Giddiness washed over her, and she had to lean one hand against her mount.

"Sarah—"

"I said hold it right there." She shook her head to clear it.

"Are you sick?"

"No." Steady again, she smiled. "I've never felt better in my life."

"Just crazy, then." He relaxed a little, but her pallor worried him. "Well, if you've a mind to kill me after spending the better part of a month keeping me alive, go ahead."

"You're damn right I kept you alive, and I didn't do it so you could leave me the minute you could stand up. I did it because I love you, because you're everything I want and everything I intend to have. Now you tell me, you stand there and tell me why you left."

"I already told you. It was time."

"You're a liar. Worse, you're a coward."

Her words had the effect she'd hoped for. The cool,

almost bored look in his eyes sizzled into heat. "Don't push me, Sarah."

"I haven't begun to push you. I'll start by telling you why you got on that horse and rode away. You left because you were afraid. Of me. No, not even of me, of yourself and what you feel for me." Her chin was up, a challenge in her eyes as she dared him to say it was untrue. "You loved me enough to stand unarmed in front of a madman, but not enough to face your own heart."

"You don't know what I feel."

"Don't I? If you believe that, you're a fool, as well as a liar." The fresh flash of fury in his eyes delighted her. "Don't you think I knew every time you touched me, every time you kissed me?" He was silent, and she drew a long breath. "Well, you can get on that horse and you can ride, you can run into the hills, to the next town. You can keep running until you're hundreds of miles away. Maybe you'll be fast enough, just fast enough to get away from me. But before you do you're going to tell me."

"Tell you what?"

"I want you to tell me you love me."

He studied her. Her eyes glowed with determination, and her cheeks were flushed with anger. Her hair, caught by the wind, was blowing back. He should have known then and there that he'd never had anywhere to run.

"A man'll say most anything when a woman's pointing a rifle at his belly."

"Then say it."

He bent to pick up his hat, slapping it against his thighs twice to loosen the dust. Idly he poked his finger through the hole in the crown.

"I love you, Sarah." He settled the hat on his head. "Now do you want to put that thing away?"

The temper went out of her eyes, and with it the glint of hope. Without a word, she turned to secure the rifle in the holder. "Well, I had to threaten it out of you, but at least I heard you say it once. Go ahead and ride off. I won't stop you. No one's holding a gun on you now."

She wouldn't cry. No, she swore to herself she wouldn't hold him with tears. Fighting them back, she tried to struggle back into the saddle. He touched her arm, lightly, not holding, when he wanted more than anything he'd ever wanted in his life to hold her.

"I love you, Sarah," he said again. "More than I should. A hell of a lot more than I can stand."

She closed her eyes, praying that what she did now would be right for both of them. Slowly she turned toward him, but she kept her hands at her sides. "If you ride away now, I'll come after you. No matter where you go, I'll be there. I'll make your life hell, I swear it."

He couldn't stop the smile any more than he could stop his hand from reaching up to touch her face. "And if I don't ride away?"

"I'll only make your life hell some of the time."

"I guess that's a better bargain." He lowered his head to kiss her gently. Then, with a groan, he crushed her hard against him. "I don't think I'd've gotten very far, even if you hadn't shot at me."

"No use taking chances. Lucky for you I was trying to shoot over your head."

He only sighed and drew her away. "You owe me a hat, Duchess." Still amazed, he drew it off to poke at the hole. "I guess I'd have to marry any woman who could handle a gun like that."

"Is that a proposal?"

He shrugged and stuck his hat back on his head. "Sounded like it."

She lifted a brow. "And it's the best you can do?"

"I haven't got any five-dollar words." Disgusted, he started back to his horse. Then he stopped and turned back. She was waiting, her arms folded, a half smile on her face. So he swore at her. "There's a preacher comes into town once every few weeks. He can marry us proper enough, with whatever kind of fuss you figure would satisfy you. I'll build you a house, between the mine and the town, with a parlor if that's what you want, and a wood floor, and a real bedroom."

To her it was the most eloquent of proposals. She held out her hands. "We'll need two."

"Two what?"

"Two bedrooms," she said when his hands closed over hers again.

"Listen, Duchess, I've heard they've got some odd ways of doing things back east, but I'm damned if my wife is going to sleep in another room."

"Oh, no." Her smile lit up her face. "I'm going to sleep in the same room, the same bed as you, every night for the rest of my life. But we'll need two bedrooms. At least we will by spring."

"I don't see why—" Then he did, so abruptly, so stunningly, that he could only stare at her. If she had taken the rifle back out and driven it butt-first into his gut he would have been less shaken. His fingers went slack on hers, then dropped away. "Are you sure?"

"Yes." She held her breath. "There's going to be a child. Our child."

He wasn't sure he could move, and was less sure he could speak. Slowly, carefully, he framed her face with his hands and kissed her. Then, when emotions swamped him, he simply rested his forehead against hers. "Two bedrooms," he murmured. "To start."

Content, she wrapped her arms around his waist. "Yes. To start."

Impulse

CHAPTER 1

She knew it was crazy. That was what she liked best about it. It was crazy, ridiculous, impractical and totally out of character. And she was having the time of her life. From the balcony of her hotel suite Rebecca could see the sweep of the beach, the glorious blue of the Ionian Sea, blushed now with streaks of rose from the setting sun.

Corfu. Even the name sounded mysterious, exciting, glamorous. And she was here, really here. Practical, steady-as-a-rock Rebecca Malone, who had never traveled more than five hundred miles from Philadelphia, was in Greece. Not just in Greece, she thought with a grin, but on the exotic island of Corfu, in one of the most exclusive resorts in Europe.

First-class, she thought as she leaned out to let the sweet breeze ruffle over her face. As long as it lasted, she was going first-class.

Her boss had thought she was suffering from temporary insanity. Edwin McDowell of McDowell, Jableki and Kline was never going to understand why a promising young CPA would resign from her position with one of the top accounting firms in Philadelphia. She'd made a good salary, she'd enjoyed excellent benefits and she'd even had a small window in her office.

Friends and associates had wondered if she'd suffered a breakdown. After all, it wasn't normal, and it certainly wasn't Rebecca's style to quit a solid, well-paying job without the promise of a better one.

But she'd given her two weeks' notice, cleared out her desk and had cheerfully walked out into the world of the unemployed.

When she'd sold her condo and then in one frantic week, auctioned off every possession she owned—every stick of furniture, every pot and pan and appliance—they'd been certain she'd gone over the edge.

Rebecca had never felt saner.

She owned nothing that didn't fit in a suitcase. She no longer had any tax-deferred investments or retirement plans. She'd cashed in her certificates of deposit, and the home entertainment center she'd thought she couldn't live without was now gracing someone else's home.

It had been more than six weeks since she'd even looked at a calculator.

For the first—and perhaps the only—time in her life, she was totally free. There were no responsibilities, no pressures, no hurried gulps of cold coffee. She hadn't packed an alarm clock. She no longer owned one. Crazy? No. Rebecca shook her head and laughed into the breeze. For as long as it lasted, she was going to grab life with both hands and see what it had to offer.

Aunt Jeannie's death had been her turning point. It had come so suddenly, so unexpectedly, leaving Rebecca without any family. Aunt Jeannie had worked hard for most of her sixty-five years, always punctual, always responsible. Her position as head librarian had been her whole life. She'd never missed a day, never failed to do her duty. Her bills had been paid on time. Her promises had always been kept.

More than once Rebecca had been told she took after her mother's older sister. She was twenty-four, but she was—had been—as solid and sturdy as her maiden aunt. Two months into retirement, two months after dear Aunt Jeannie began to make plans to travel, to enjoy the rewards she'd worked so hard to earn, she was gone.

After Rebecca's grief had come the anger, then the frustration, then slowly, the realization that she was traveling the same straight road. She worked, she slept, she fixed well-balanced meals that she ate alone. She had a small circle of friends who knew she could be counted on in a crisis. Rebecca would always find the best and most practical answer. Rebecca would never drop her own problems in your lap—because she didn't have any. Rebecca, bless her, was a port in any storm.

She hated it, and she'd begun to hate herself. She had to do something.

And she was doing it.

It wasn't running away as much as it was breaking free. All her life she'd done what was expected of her and tried to make as few waves as possible while doing it. All through school a crushing shyness had kept her more comfortable with her books than with other teenagers. In college a need to succeed and justify her aunt's faith had locked her tightly into her studies.

She had always been good with figures—logical, thorough, patient. It had been easy, perhaps too easy, to pour herself into that one area, because there, and really only there, had she felt confident.

Now she was going to discover Rebecca Malone. In the weeks or months of freedom she had, she wanted to learn everything there was to know about the woman within. Perhaps there wasn't a butterfly inside the cocoon she'd wrapped herself in so comfortably, but whatever she found—whoever she found—Rebecca hoped she would enjoy her, like her, perhaps even respect her.

When the money ran out, she'd get another job and go back to being plain, practical Rebecca. Until that time she was rich, rootless and ready for surprises.

She was also hungry.

Stephen saw her the moment she entered the restaurant. It wasn't that she was particularly striking. Beautiful women passed through the world every day and they usually warranted a glance. But there was something about the way this one walked, as if she were ready for anything, even looking forward to it. He stopped, and because business was slow at this hour he took a second, longer look.

She was tall for a woman, and more angular than slender. Her skin was pale, and that made him think she had only just arrived at the resort or was shy of the sun. The white sundress that left her shoulders and back bare accented the lack of color and gave dramatic contrast to her short cap of raven hair.

She paused, then seemed to take a deep breath. Stephen could almost hear her satisfied sigh. Then she smiled at the headwaiter, and followed him to her table, tossing her head back, so that her hair, which she wore arrow-straight, swung away from her chin.

A nice face, Stephen concluded. Bright, intelligent, eager. Especially the eyes. They were pale, an almost translucent gray. But there was nothing pale in their expression. She smiled at the waiter again, then laughed and looked around the restaurant. She looked as if she'd never been happier in her life.

She saw him. When Rebecca's gaze first skimmed over the man leaning against the bar, her automatic shyness kicked in and had her looking away. Attractive men had stared at her before—though it wasn't exactly a daily event. She'd never been able to handle it with the aplomb—or even cynicism—of most of her contemporaries. To cover her momentary embarrassment, she lifted her menu.

He hadn't meant to linger more than a few moments longer, but the impulse came suddenly. Stephen flicked a hand at the waiter and had him scurrying over, nodding quickly at Stephen's murmured request and hurrying off. When he returned it was to deliver a bottle of champagne to Rebecca's table.

"Compliments of Mr. Nickodemus."

"Oh." Rebecca followed the waiter's gaze over to the man by the bar. "Well, I—" She brought herself up short before she could stammer. A sophisticated woman wouldn't stutter over a gift of champagne, she reminded herself. She'd accept it graciously, with dignity. And maybe—if she wasn't a complete fool—she'd relax enough to flirt with the man who offered it.

Stephen watched the expressions pass across her face. Fascinating, he mused, and realized that the vague boredom he'd been feeling had vanished. When she lifted her head and smiled at him, he had no idea that her heart was pounding. He saw only a casual invitation, and he answered it.

He wasn't just attractive, Rebecca realized as he crossed to her table. He was gorgeous. Eye-popping, mouth-dropping gorgeous. She had an image of

Apollo and ancient Greek warriors. Thick blond hair streaked by the sun fell over the collar of his shirt. Smooth, bronzed skin was marred—and somehow enhanced—by a faint scar under his jawline. A strong jaw, she thought. A strong face, with the darkest, deepest blue eyes she'd ever seen.

"Good evening, I'm Stephen Nickodemus." His voice wasn't accented, it was rounded, rich. He might have come from anywhere. Perhaps it was that, more than anything else that intrigued her.

Lecturing herself on poise and image, she lifted her hand. "Hello. I'm Rebecca, Rebecca Malone." She felt a quick flutter when he brushed his lips over her knuckles. Feeling foolish, she drew her hand away and balled it in her lap. "Thank you for the champagne."

"It seemed to suit your mood." He studied her, wondering why he was getting such a mix of signals. "You are by yourself?"

"Yes." Perhaps it was a mistake to admit it, but if she was going to live life to the fullest she had to take some risks. The restaurant wasn't crowded, but they were hardly alone. Take the plunge, she told herself, and tried another smile. "The least I can do is offer you a glass."

Stephen took the seat across from her, brushing the waiter aside to pour the wine himself. "You are American?"

"It shows."

"No. Actually, I thought you were French until you spoke."

"Did you?" That pleased her. "I've just come from Paris." She had to force herself not to touch her hair. She'd had it cut, with trepidation and delight, in a French salon.

Stephen touched his glass to hers. Her eyes bubbled with life as cheerfully as the wine. "Business?"

"No, just pleasure." What a marvelous word, she thought. *Pleasure.* "It's a wonderful city."

"Yes. Do you go often?"

Rebecca smiled into her glass. "Not often enough. Do you?"

"From time to time."

She nearly sighed at that. Imagine anyone speaking of going to Paris "from time to time." "I nearly stayed longer, but I'd promised myself Greece."

So she was alone, restless and on the move. Perhaps that was why she had appealed to him, because he was, too. "Is Corfu your first stop?"

"Yes." She sipped at her drink. A part of her still believed it was all a dream. Greece, champagne, the man. "It's beautiful. Much more beautiful than I imagined it could be."

"It's your first trip, then?" He couldn't have said why that pleased him. "How long do you stay?"

"As long as I like." She grinned, savoring the feeling of freedom. "And you?"

He lifted his glass. "Longer, I think, than I had planned." When the waiter appeared at his side, Stephen handed over the menu, then spoke to him in soft, quick Greek. "If you don't object, I'd like to guide you through your first meal on the island."

The old Rebecca would have been too nervous to sit through a meal with a stranger. The new Rebecca took a second, deeper sip of champagne. "I'd love it. Thank you."

It was easy. Easy to sit, to laugh, and to sample new and exotic tastes. She forgot that he was a stranger, forgot that the world she was living in now was only temporary. They didn't speak of anything important— only of Paris, and the weather, and the wine. Still, she was sure it was the most interesting conversation of her life. He looked at her when he spoke to her, looked at her as though he were delighted to spend an hour talking of nothing. The last man she'd had dinner with had wanted her to give him a discount when she did his taxes.

Stephen wasn't asking her for anything more than her company for dinner. When he looked at her it seemed unlikely that he'd care if she knew how to fill out Schedule C.

When he suggested a walk along the beach, she agreed without a qualm. What better way to end an evening than a walk in the moonlight?

"I was looking out at this from my window just before dinner." Rebecca stepped out of her shoes, then dangled them from her fingers as she walked. "I didn't think it could look more beautiful than it did at sunset."

"The sea changes, like a woman, in the light." He paused to touch a flame to the end of a slim cigar. "So men are drawn to her."

"Are you? Drawn to the sea?"

"I've spent my time on her. I fished in these waters as a boy."

She'd learned at dinner that he'd grown up traveling the islands with his father. "It must have been exciting, moving from place to place, seeing new things almost every day."

He shrugged. He'd never been sure whether the restlessness had been born in him or had been a product of his upbringing. "It had its moments."

"I love to travel." Laughing, she tossed her shoes aside, then stepped into the surf. The champagne was making her head swim and the moonlight felt as soft as rain. "I adore it." She laughed again when the spray washed up to dampen her skirts. The Ionian Sea. She was standing in it. "On a night like this I think I'll never go home."

She looked so vibrant, so alive, standing in the surf with her white skirts billowing. "Where's home?"

She glanced over her shoulder. The flirtatious look was totally unplanned and completely devastating. "I haven't decided. I want to swim." On impulse, she dived into the surf.

Stephen's heart stopped when she disappeared. He'd already kicked off his shoes and started forward when she rose up again. For a second time, his heart stopped.

She was laughing, her face lifted to the moonlight. Water cascaded from her hair, from her skin. The drops that clung to her were the only jewels she wore. Beautiful? No, she wasn't beautiful. She was electric.

"It's wonderful. Cool and soft and wonderful."

With a shake of his head, he stepped in far enough to take her hand and pull her toward shore. She was a little mad, perhaps, but engagingly so. "Are you always so impulsive?"

"I'm working on it. Aren't you?" She combed her hand through her dripping hair. "Or do you always send champagne to strange women?"

"Either way I answer that could be trouble. Here." He shrugged out of his jacket and draped it over her shoulders. Unframed, washed clean, her face glowed in the moonlight. There was a graceful kind of strength in it, to the sweep of cheekbone, the slightly pointed chin. Delicate—except for the eyes. One look there showed power, a power that was still. "You're irresistible, Rebecca."

She stared at him, confused all over again, as he gathered the neck of the jacket close around her throat. "I'm wet," she managed.

"And beautiful." With his hands still on the jacket, he brought her toward him. "And fascinating."

That made her laugh again. "I don't think so, but thanks. I'm glad you sent me the champagne and guided me through my first meal." Her nerves began to jangle. His eyes stayed on hers, journeying only once to her mouth, which was still damp from the sea. Their bodies were close, close enough to brush. Rebecca began to shiver, and she knew it had nothing to do with wet clothes and the breeze.

"I should go in . . . change my dress."

There was something about her. The impulsiveness, the easy flirtatiousness, hid an unmistakable innocence that baffled and attracted him. Whatever it was, he wanted more.

"I'll see you again."

"Yes." She prayed for her heartbeat to slow. "It's not a very big island."

He smiled at that, slowly. She felt, with a mixture of relief and regret, the relaxation of his hands. "Tomorrow. I have business early. I'll be done by eleven, if that suits you. I'll show you Corfu."

"All right." Better judgment and nerves be damned. She wanted to go with him. "I'll meet you in the lobby." Carefully, because she suddenly wasn't sure she could manage it, she stepped back. Moonlight silhouetted him against the sea. "Good night, Stephen."

She forgot to be sophisticated and dashed toward the hotel.

He watched her go. She puzzled him, puzzled him as no woman had since he'd been a boy and too young to understand that a woman was not meant to be understood. And he wanted her. That wasn't new, but the desire had come with surprising speed and surprising force.

Rebecca Malone might have started out as an impulse, but she was now a mystery. One he intended to solve. With a little laugh, he bent to scoop up the shoes she'd forgotten. He hadn't felt quite so alive in months.

CHAPTER 2

Stephen wasn't the kind of man who rearranged his schedule to spend the day with a woman. Especially a woman he barely knew. He was a wealthy man, but he was also a busy man, driven by both pride and ambition to maintain a high level of involvement in all his projects. He shouldered responsibility well and had learned to enjoy the benefits of hard work and dedication.

His time on Corfu wasn't free—or rather hadn't been planned as free. Mixing business and pleasure wasn't his style. He pursued both, separately, with utter concentration. Yet he found himself juggling appointments, meetings, conference calls, in order to have the afternoon open for Rebecca.

He supposed any man would want to get to know a woman who flirted easily over a champagne flute one moment and dived fully dressed into the sea the next.

"I've postponed your meeting with Theoharis until five thirty this evening." Stephen's secretary scribbled on a notepad she had resting on her lap. "He will meet you for early cocktails in the suite. I've arranged for hors d'oeuvres and a bottle of ouzo."

"Always efficient, Elana."

She smiled and tucked a fall of dark hair behind her ear. "I try."

When Stephen rose to pace to the window, she folded her hands and waited. She had worked for him for five years, she admired his energy and his business acumen, and—fortunately for both of them—had long since gotten over an early crush. There was often speculation about their personal relationship, but though he could be friendly—even kind when it suited him— with Stephen, business was business.

"Contact Mithos in Athens. Have him fax that report by the end of the day. And I want to hear from Lereau by five, Paris time."

"Shall I call and give him a nudge?"

"If you think it's necessary." Restless, he dug his hands in his pockets. Where had this sudden discontent come from? he wondered. He was wealthy, successful, and free, as always, to move from place to place. As he stared out at the sea, he remembered the scent of Rebecca's skin. "Send flowers to Rebecca Malone's suite. Wildflowers, nothing formal. This afternoon."

Elana made a note, hoping she'd get a look at this Rebecca Malone before long. She had already heard through the grapevine that Stephen had had dinner with an American woman. "And the card?"

He wasn't a man for poetry. "Just my name."

"Anything else?"

"Yes." He turned and offered her a half smile. "Take some time off. Go to the beach."

Pad in hand, she rose. "I'll be sure to work it in. Enjoy your afternoon, Stephen."

He intended to. As she left him, Stephen glanced at his watch. It was fifteen minutes before eleven. There was work he could do to fill in the time, a quick call that could be made. Instead, he picked up Rebecca's shoes.

After three tries, Rebecca settled on an outfit. She didn't have an abundance of clothes, because she'd preferred to spend her funds on travel. But she had splurged here and there on her route through Europe. No tidy CPA suits, she thought as she tied a vivid fuchsia sash at the waist of her sapphire-colored cotton pants. No sensible shoes or pastel blouses. The last shock of color came from a primrose-hued blouse cut generously to layer over a skinny tank top in the same shade as the slacks.

The combination delighted her, if only because her firm had preferred quiet colors and clean lines.

She had no idea where she was going, and she didn't care.

It was a beautiful day, even though she'd awoken with a dull headache from the champagne, and the disorientation that went with it. A light, early breakfast on her terrace and a quick dip in the sea had cleared both away. She still had trouble believing that she could lounge through a morning as she pleased—and that she'd spent the evening with a man she'd just met.

Aunt Jeannie would have tut-tutted and reminded her of the dangers of being a woman alone. Some of her friends would have been shocked, others envious. But they would all have been astonished that steady Rebecca had strolled in the moonlight with a gorgeous man with a scar on his jawline and eyes like velvet.

If she hadn't had his jacket as proof, she might have thought she'd dreamed it. There had never been anything wrong with her imagination—just the application of it. Often she'd pictured herself in an enticing place with a gorgeous man, with moonlight and music. Imagined herself, she remembered. And then she'd turned on her calculator and gotten down to business.

But she hadn't dreamed this. She could still remember the giddy, half-terrified feeling that had swarmed through her when he'd gathered her close. When his mouth had been only an inch from hers and the sea and the champagne had roared in her head.

What if he had kissed her? What tastes would she have found? Rich, strong ones, she mused, almost able to savor them as she traced a fingertip over her lips. After just one evening she was absolutely certain there would be nothing lukewarm about Stephen Nickodemus. She wasn't nearly so certain about Rebecca.

She probably would have fumbled and blushed and stammered. With a shake of her head, she pulled a brush through her hair. Exciting men didn't tumble all over themselves to kiss neat, practical-minded women.

But he'd asked to see her again.

Rebecca wasn't certain whether she was disappointed or relieved that he hadn't pressed his advantage and kissed her. She'd been kissed before, held before, of course. But she had a feeling—a very definite feeling—that it wouldn't be the same with Stephen. He might make her want more, offer more, than she had with any other man.

Crossing bridges too soon, she decided as she checked the contents of her big straw bag. She wasn't going to have an affair with him, or with anyone. Even the new, improved Rebecca Malone wasn't the type for a casual affair. But maybe— She caught her lower lip between her teeth. If the time was right she might have a romance she'd remember long after she left Greece.

For now, she was ready, but it was much too early to go down. It would hardly make her look like a well-traveled woman of the world if she popped down to the lobby and paced for ten minutes. This was her fantasy, after all. She didn't want him to think she was inexperienced and overeager.

Only the knock on the door prevented her from changing her mind about her outfit one more time.

"Hello." Stephen studied her for a moment, unsmiling. He'd nearly been certain he'd exaggerated, but she was just as vibrant, just as exciting, in the morning as she had been in the moonlight. He held out her shoes. "I thought you might need these."

She laughed, remembering her impulsive dunk in the sea. "I didn't realize I'd left them on the beach. Come in a minute." With a neatness ingrained in her from childhood, she turned to take them to the bedroom closet. "I'm ready to go if you are."

Stephen lifted a brow. He preferred promptness, but he never expected it in anyone but a business associate. "I've got a Jeep waiting. Some of the roads are rough."

"Sounds great." Rebecca came out again, carrying her bag and a flat-brimmed straw hat. She handed Stephen his jacket, neatly folded. "I forgot to give this back to you last night." Should she offer to have it cleaned? she wondered when he only continued to look at her. Fiddling with the strap of her bag, she decided against it. "Does taking pictures bother you?"

"No, why?"

"Good, because I take lots of them. I can't seem to stop myself."

She wasn't kidding. As Stephen drove up into the

hills, she took shots of everything. Sheep, tomato plants, olive groves and straggly sage. He stopped so that she could walk out near the edge of a cliff and look down at a small village huddled near the sea.

She wouldn't be able to capture it on film; she wasn't clever enough. But she knew she'd never forget that light, so pure, so clear, or the contrast between the orange tiled roofs and the low white-washed walls and the deep, dangerous blue of the water that flung itself against the weathered rock that rose into harsh crags. A stork, legs tucked, glided over the water, where fishing boats bobbed.

There were nets drying on the beach and children playing. Flowers bloomed and tangled where the wind had planted them, more spectacular than any planned arrangement could ever be.

"It's beautiful." Her throat tightened with emotion, and with a longing she couldn't have defined. "So calm. You imagine women baking black bread and the men coming home smelling of fish and the sea. It looks as though it hasn't changed in a hundred years."

"Very little." He glanced down himself, surprised and more than a little pleased that she would be touched by something so simple. "We cling to antiquity."

"I haven't seen the Acropolis yet, but I don't think it could be any more spectacular than this." She lifted her face, delighted by the way the wind whipped at it. Here, high above the sea, she absorbed everything—the salty, rough-edged bite of the wind, the clarity of color and sound, and the man beside her. Letting her camera dangle from its strap, she turned to him. "I haven't thanked you for taking the time to show me all of this."

He took her hand, not to raise it to his lips, just to hold it. It was a link he hadn't known he wanted. "I'm enjoying seeing the familiar through someone else's eyes. Your eyes."

Suddenly the edge of the cliff seemed too close, the sun too hot. Could he do that just by touching her? With an effort, Rebecca smiled, keeping her voice light. "If you ever come to Philadelphia, I'll do the same for you."

It was odd. She'd looked almost frightened for a moment. Fragile and frightened. Stephen had always carefully avoided women who were easily bruised. "I'll consider that a promise."

They continued to drive, over roads that jarred and climbed and twisted. She saw her first of the *agrimi*, the wild goat of Greece, and the rocky pastures dotted with sturdy sheep. And everywhere, rich and defiant, was the intense color of flowers.

He didn't complain when she asked him to stop so that she could snap pictures of tiny blue star blossoms that pushed their way through cracks in the rock. He listened to her delight as she framed a thick, thorny stem topped with a ragged yellow flower. It made him realize, and regret, that it had been years since he'd taken the time to look closely at the small, vital things that grew around him.

He looked now at Rebecca standing in the sunlight, her hat fluttering around her face and her laugh dancing on the air.

Often the road clung to cliffs that plunged dizzily into the sea. Rebecca, who was too timid to fight rush-hour traffic, found it exhilarating.

She felt almost like another person. She *was* another person, she thought, laughing as she held on to her hat to keep the wind from snatching it away.

"I love it!" she shouted over the wind and the noise of the engine. "It's wild and old and incredible. Like no place I've ever been."

Still laughing, she lifted her camera and snapped his picture as he drove. He wore sunglasses with amber lenses and had a cigar clamped between his teeth. The wind blew through his hair and chased the smoke behind them. He stopped the Jeep, took the camera and snapped a picture of her in turn.

"Hungry?"

She dragged her tousled hair back from her face. "Starving."

He leaned over to open her door. A current passed through her, sharp and electric, strong enough to make him pause with his arm across her body and his face close to hers. It was there again, he thought as he waited and watched. The awareness, ripe and seductive. And the innocence, as alluring as it was contradictory. In a test—a test for both of them—he lifted a hand to stroke her cheek. It was as soft as her scent.

"Are you afraid of me, Rebecca?"

"No." That was true; she was nearly sure of it. "Should I be?"

He didn't smile. Through the amber lenses she saw that his eyes were very intense. "I'm not entirely sure." When he pulled away he heard her release an unsteady breath. He wasn't feeling completely steady himself. "We'll have to walk a little first."

Confused, her mind churning, she stepped out onto the dirt path. A woman on a simple date didn't tremble every time a man got close, Rebecca told herself as Stephen lifted the picnic basket out of the back. She was behaving like a teenager, not a grown woman.

Troubled by his own thoughts, Stephen stopped beside her. He hesitated, then held out a hand. It felt good, simply good, when she put hers in it.

They walked through an olive grove in a companionable silence while the sun streamed down on dusty leaves and rocky ground. There was no sound of the sea here, but when the wind was right she could hear the screech of a gull far away. The island was small, but here it seemed uninhabited.

"I haven't had a picnic in years." Rebecca spread the cloth. "And never in an olive grove." She glanced around, wanting to remember every leaf and pebble. "Are we trespassing?"

"No." Stephen took a bottle of white wine from the basket. Rebecca left him to it and started rummaging in search of food.

"Do you know the owner?"

"I'm the owner." He drew the cork with a gentle pop.

"Oh." She looked around again. It should have occurred to her that he would own something impressive, different, and exciting. "It sounds romantic. Owning an olive grove."

He lifted a brow. He owned a number of them, but he had never thought of them as romantic. They were simply profitable. He offered her a glass, then tapped it with his own. "To romance, then."

She swept down her lashes, battling shyness. To Stephen, the gesture was only provocative. "I hope you're hungry," she began, knowing she was talking too fast. "It all looks wonderful." She took a quick sip of wine to ease her dry throat, then set it aside to finish unpacking the basket.

There were sweet black olives as big as a man's thumb, and there was a huge slab of sharp cheese. There were cold lamb and hunks of bread, and fruit so fresh it could have been just plucked from the stem.

Gradually she began to relax again.

"You've told me very little about yourself." Stephen topped off her wine and watched her bite into a ripe red plum. "I know little more than that you come from Philadelphia and enjoy traveling."

What could she tell him? A man like him was bound to be bored with the life story of the painfully ordinary Rebecca Malone. Lies had never come easily to her, so she skirted between fact and fiction. "There's little more. I grew up in Philadelphia. I lost both of my parents when I was a teenager, and I lived with my aunt Jeannie. She was very dear, and she made the loss bearable."

"It's painful." He flicked his lighter at the end of a cigar, remembering not only the pain, but also the fury he had felt when his father had died and left him orphaned at sixteen. "It steals childhood."

"Yes." So he understood that. It made her feel close to him, close and comfortable. "Maybe that's why I like to travel. Every time you see a new place you can be a child again."

"So you don't look for roots?"

She glanced at him then. He was leaning back against the trunk of a tree, smoking lazily, watching carefully. "I don't know what I'm looking for."

"Is there a man?"

She moved her shoulders, determined not to be embarrassed. "No."

He took her hand, drawing her closer. "No one?"

"No, I . . ." She wasn't certain what she would have said, but could say nothing at all when he turned her palm upward and pressed his lips to its center. She felt the fire burst there, in her hand, then race everywhere.

"You're very responsive, Rebecca." He lowered her hand but kept it in his. He could feel the heat, but he wasn't sure whether it had sprung to her skin or to his own. "If there's no one, the men in your Philadelphia must be very slow."

"I've been too . . . busy."

His lips curved at that. There was a tremor in her voice, and there was passion in her eyes. "Busy?"

"Yes." Afraid she'd make a fool of herself, she drew her hand back. "This was wonderful." Trying to calm herself, she pushed a hand through her hair. "You know what I need?"

"No. Tell me."

"Another picture." She sprang to her feet and, steadier, grinned. "A memento of my first picnic in an olive grove. Let's see . . . you can stand right over there. The sun's good in front of that tree, and I should be able to frame in that section of the grove."

Amused, Stephen tapped out his cigar. "How much more film do you have?"

"This is the last roll—but I have scads back at the hotel." She flicked him a quick laughing glance. "I warned you."

"So you did." Competent hands, he thought as he watched her focus and adjust. He hadn't realized he could be as attracted to competence as he was to beauty. She mumbled to herself, tossing her head back so that her hair swung, then settled. His stomach tightened without warning.

Good God, he wanted her. She'd done nothing to make him burn and strain this way. He couldn't accuse her of taunting or teasing, and yet . . . he felt taunted. He felt teased. For the first time in his life he felt totally seduced by a woman who had done nothing more than give him a few smiles and a little companionship.

Even now she was chattering away as she secured her camera to the limb of a tree. Talking easily, as though they were just friends, as though she felt nothing more than a light, unimportant affection. But he'd seen it. Stephen felt his blood heat as he remembered the quick flash of arousal he'd seen on her face. He'd see it again. And more.

"I'm going to set the timer," Rebecca went on, blissfully unaware of Stephen's thoughts. "All you have to do is stand there. Once I get this damn thing set, I'm going to run over so it'll take one of both— There." She interrupted herself, crossed her fingers and ran to Stephen's side in a dash. "Unless I messed up, it'll snap all by itself in—"

The rest of the words slid down her throat as he crushed her against him and captured her mouth.

CHAPTER 3

Heat. Light. Speed. Rebecca felt them, felt each separate, distinct sensation. Urgency. Demand. Impatience. She tasted them, as clearly as wild honey, on his lips. Though she'd never experienced it, she had known exactly what it would be like to be with him, mouth to mouth and need to need.

In an instant the world had narrowed from what could be seen and understood to a pure, seamless blanket of emotion. It cloaked her, not softly, not in comfort, but tightly, hotly, irresistibly. Caught between fear and delight, she lifted a hand to his cheek.

God, she was sweet. Even as he dragged her closer, aroused by the simplicity of her acceptance, he was struck by—disarmed by—her sweetness. There had been a hesitation, almost too brief to be measured, before her lips had parted beneath his. Parted, invited, accepted.

There was a sigh, so soft it could barely be heard, as she stroked her hands up his back to his shoulders. Curious, simple, generous. A man could drown in such sweetness, fall prisoner to such pliancy. And be saved by it. Beneath the patterned shade of the olive tree, she gave him more than passion. She gave him hope.

Charmed, he murmured some careless Greek phrase lovers might exchange. The words meant nothing to her, but the sound of them on the still air, the feel of them stroking across her lips . . . seduction. Glorious seduction.

Pleasure burst in her blood, in her head, in her heart, thousands of tiny bubbles of it, until she was straining against him.

The quiet explosion rocked him. It tightened his chest, fuddled his mind. She fitted into his arms as if she'd been born for him. As if, somehow, they had known each other before, loved before, hungered before. Something seemed to erupt between them, something molten, powerful, dangerous. But it wasn't new. It was ancient, a whispering echo of ageless passions.

She began to tremble. How could this be so right, so familiar? It wasn't possible to feel safe and threatened at the same time. But she did. She clung to him while a dim, floating image danced through her head. She had kissed him before. Just like this. As her mind spun, she heard her own mindless murmurs answer his. As freely, as inescapably as the sun poured light, response flowed from her. She couldn't stop it. Frightened by her sudden loss of control, she struggled against him, against herself.

He slipped his hands up to her shoulders, but not to free her, to look at her. To look at how their coming together had changed her. It had changed him. Passion had made her eyes heavy, seductive. Fear had clouded them. Her lips were full, softened and parted by his. Her breath shivered through them. Under his hands he could feel the heat of her skin and the quick, involuntary trembling of her muscles.

No pretense here, he decided as he studied her. He was holding both innocence and delight in his hands.

"Stephen, I—"

"Again."

Then his face filled her vision and she was lost.

Differently. Should she have known that one man could hold one woman in so many different ways? That one man could kiss one woman with such stunning variety? There was gentleness now, as familiar and as novel as the urgency. His lips persuaded rather than demanded. They savored instead of devouring. Her surrender came as quietly, and as unmistakably, as her earlier passion. The trembling stopped; the fear vanished. With a complete trust that surprised them both, she leaned against him, giving.

More aroused by her serenity than by the storm that had come before, Stephen pulled back. He had to, or what had begun would finish without either of them saying a word. As he swore and pulled out a cigar, Rebecca placed a hand on the olive tree for support.

Moments, she thought. It had been only moments, and yet she felt as though years had passed, racing backward or forward, perhaps spinning in circles. In a place like this, with a man like this, what difference did it make what year it was? What century?

Half terrified, she lifted a hand to her lips. Despite her fear, they curved under her touch. She could still taste him. Still feel him. And nothing, nothing, would ever be quite the same again.

He stared out at the rough and dusty land he'd known as a boy, and beyond, to the stark, tumbling rocks where he and other wild things had climbed.

What was he doing with her? Furious with himself, he drew on the cigar. What was he feeling? It was new, and far from comfortable. And it was comfort he preferred, he reminded himself. Comfort and freedom. Bringing himself under control, he turned to her again, determined to treat what had happened as a man should—lightly.

She just stood there, with the sun and the shade falling over her. There was neither recrimination nor invitation in her eyes. She didn't flinch or step forward, but merely stood, watching him with the faintest of smiles, as if . . . As if, Stephen realized, she knew what questions he was asking himself—and the answers.

"It grows late."

She felt the ache and fought not to let it show on her face. "I guess you're right." She dragged a hand through her hair—it was the first sign of her agitation—then walked over to pick up her camera. "I should have a picture to remember all this by," she said, forcing brightness into her voice. Her breath caught when his fingers closed over her arm and whirled her around.

"Who are you?" he demanded. "What are you?"

"I don't know what you mean." The emotion burst out before she could stop it. "I don't know what you want."

With one jerk he had her tumbling against him. "You know what I want."

Her heart was in her throat, beating wildly. She found it strange that it was not fear but desire that she felt. She hadn't known she was capable of feeling a need that was so unreasonable, so reckless. It was almost purifying to experience it, and to see it mirrored in his eyes.

"It takes more than one afternoon." Didn't it? Her voice rose as she tried to convince herself. "It takes more than a picnic and a walk in the moonlight for me."

"One moment the temptress, the next the outraged innocent. Do you do it to intrigue me, Rebecca?" She

shook her head, and his fingers tightened. "It works,"
he murmured. "You've hardly been out of my mind
since I first saw you. I want to make love with you, here,
in the sun."

Color flooded her face, not because she was embarrassed, but because she could imagine it, perfectly. And
then what? Carefully she leveled her breathing. Whatever impulses she had followed, whatever bridges she
had burned, she still needed answers.

"No." It cost her to go against her own needs and
say it. "Not when I'm unsure and you're angry." She
took a deep breath and kept her eyes on him. "You're
hurting me, Stephen. I don't think you mean to."

Slowly he released her arm. He was angry, furious, but not at her refusal. The anger stemmed from
the need she pulled from him, a need that had come
too fast and too strong for him to channel. "We'll go
back."

Rebecca merely nodded, then knelt to gather the remains of the picnic.

He was a busy man, much too busy to brood about
a woman he barely knew and didn't understand at
all. That was what Stephen told himself. He had reports
to read, calls to make and paperwork—which he had
both a talent and a distaste for—to deal with. A couple
of simple kisses weren't enough to take a man's mind
off his work.

But there hadn't been anything simple about them.
Disgusted, Stephen pushed away from his desk and
wandered to the terrace doors. He'd left them open because the breeze, and the fragrances it brought, helped
him forget he was obligated to be inside.

For days he'd worked his way through his respon-

sibilities, trying to ignore the nagging itch at the back
of his mind—the itch that was Rebecca. There was no
reason for him to stay on Corfu. He could have handled
his business in Athens, or Crete, or in London, for that
matter. Still, he'd made no plans to leave, though he'd
also made no attempt to approach her.

She . . . concerned him, he decided. To be drawn to
an attractive woman was as natural as breathing. To
have the attraction cause discomfort, confusion, even
annoyance was anything but natural. A taste of her
hadn't been enough. Yet he hesitated.

She was . . . mysterious. Perhaps that was why he
couldn't push her from his mind. On the surface she
appeared to be an attractive, free-spirited woman who
grabbed life with both hands. Yet there were undercur-
rents. The hints of innocence, of shyness. The sweetness.
The complexity of her kept him wondering, thinking,
imagining.

Perhaps that was her trick. Women had them . . .
were entitled to them. It was a waste of time to begrudge
them their illusions and their feminine magic. More
than a waste of time, it was foolish, when a man could
enjoy the benefits. But there was more, and somehow
less, to Rebecca than innate feminine magic.

When he had kissed her, though it had been the first
time, it had been like coming back to a lover, to a love,
after a painful separation. When his lips had found
hers, something had filled him. A heat, an impatience,
a knowledge.

He knew her, knew more than her name and her
background and the color of her eyes. He knew all of
her. Yet he knew nothing.

Fantasies, he told himself. He didn't have time for
them. Leaning a hip against the railing, he lit a cigar
and watched the sea.

As always, it pulled at him, bringing back memories of a childhood that had been careless and too short. There were times, rare times, when he allowed himself to regret. Times when the sun was a white flash of heat and the water was blue and endless. His father had taught him a great deal. How to fish, how to see both beauty and excitement in new places, how to drink like a man.

Fifteen years, Stephen thought, a smile ghosting around his mouth. He still missed him, missed the companionship, the robust laughter. They had been friends, as well as parent and child, with a bond as easy, and as strong, as any Stephen had ever known. But his father had died as he would have wanted to—at sea and in his prime.

He would have taken one look at Rebecca, rolled his eyes, kissed his fingers and urged his son to enjoy. But Stephen wasn't the boy he had once been. He was more cautious, more aware of consequences. If a man dived into the sea, he should know the depth and the currents.

Then he saw her, coming from the sea. Water ran down her body, glistening in the strong sun, sparkling against skin that had warmed in the last few days to a dusky gold. As he looked, as he wanted, he felt his muscles clench, one by one, shoulders, stomach, thighs. Without his being aware, his fingers tightened, snapping the cigar in two. He hadn't known that desire could arouse a reaction so akin to anger.

She stopped, and though he knew she was unaware of him, she might easily have been posing. To taunt, to tease, to invite. As drops of water slid down her, she stretched, lifting her face skyward. Her skimpy suit rested low over her boyish hips, shifted enticingly over the subtle curve of her breasts. At that moment, she was totally absorbed in her own pleasure and as unselfconscious as any young animal standing in the sun. Nothing had ever been so alluring.

Then, slowly, seductively, she combed her fingers through her hair, smiling, as if she enjoyed the wet, silky feel of it. Watching her, he felt the air back up and clog in his lungs. He could have murdered her for it, for making him want so unreasonably what he did not yet understand.

She plucked a long, mannish T-shirt from a straw bag and, after tugging it on, strolled barefoot into the hotel.

He stood there, waiting for the need to pass. But it built, layered with an ache that infuriated him and a longing that baffled him.

He should ignore her. Instinct warned him that if he didn't his life would never be the same. She was nothing more than a distraction, a momentary impulse he should resist. He should turn away, go back to work. He had commitments, obligations, and no time to waste on fantasies. With an oath, he tossed the broken cigar over the rail.

There were times, he thought, when a man had to trust in fate and dive in.

CHAPTER 4

Rebecca had hardly shut the door behind her before she turned back to answer the knock. The sun and the water had left her pleasantly tired, but all thoughts of a lazy catnap vanished when she saw Stephen.

He looked wonderful. Cool, a little windblown, intense. For days she'd wondered about him, wondered and wished. She felt her pulse skip and her lips curve just at the sight of him. With an effort, she kept her voice breezy.

"Hello. I wasn't sure you were still on the island."

It wasn't really a lie, she told herself. An offhand inquiry had assured her that Mr. Nickodemus hadn't checked out, but she hadn't actually seen him.

"I saw you come up from the beach."

"Oh." Unconsciously she tugged at the hem of her cover-up. To Stephen the small gesture was one more contradictory signal. "I can't seem to get enough of the sun and the sea. Would you like to come in?"

By way of an answer he stepped through and shut the door behind him. It made a very quiet, a very final sound. Rebecca's carefully built poise began to crumble. "I never thanked you for the flowers." She made a gesture indicating the vase near the window, then brought her hands back together and linked them in front of her. "They're still beautiful. I . . . I thought I might run into you, in the dining room, on the beach, or . . ." Her words trailed off when he lifted a hand to her hair.

"I've been busy." He watched her eyes, eyes that were as clear as rainwater, blur at the slight touch. "Business."

It was ridiculous, she knew, but she wasn't at all sure she could speak. "If you have to work, I doubt you could pick a more beautiful place."

He stepped closer. She smelled of the water and the sun. "You're enjoying the resort, and the island."

Her hand was in his now, caught lightly. It took only that to make her knees weak. "Yes, very much."

"Perhaps you'd like to see it from a different perspective." Deliberately, wanting to test them both, he lifted her hand to his lips. He grazed her knuckles—it was barely a whisper of contact—and felt the jolt. She felt it, and he could see that she did, so it couldn't just be his imagination. "Spend the day with me tomorrow on my boat."

"What?"

He smiled, delighted with her response. "Will you come with me?"

Anywhere. Astonished, she stepped back. "I haven't any plans."

"Good." He closed the distance between them again. Her hands fluttered up in flustered defense, then settled again when he made no attempt to touch her. "Then I'll make them for you. I'll come for you in the morning. Nine?"

A boat. He'd said something about a boat. Rebecca

drew in a deep breath and tried to pull herself together. This wasn't like her—going off into daydreams, feeling weak-kneed, being flooded with waves of desire. And it felt wonderful.

"I'd like that." She gave him what she hoped was an easy woman-of-the-world smile.

"Until tomorrow, then." He started for the door, then turned, a hand on the knob. "Rebecca, don't forget your camera."

She waited until he'd closed the door before she spun in three quick circles.

When Stephen had said "boat," Rebecca had pictured a trim little cabin cruiser. Instead, she stepped onto the glossy mahogany deck of a streamlined hundred-foot yacht.

"You could live on this," Rebecca said, then wished she'd bitten her tongue. But he only laughed.

"I often do."

"Welcome aboard, sir," a white-uniformed man with a British accent said.

"Grady. This is my guest, Miss Malone."

"Ma'am." Grady's cool British reserve didn't flicker for an instant, but Rebecca felt herself being summed up.

"Cast off when you're ready." Stephen took Rebecca's arm. "Would you like a tour?"

"Yes." A yacht. She was on a yacht. It took all her willpower to keep her camera in the bag. "I'd love to see it all."

He took her below, through four elegantly appointed cabins. Her comment about living on board had been said impulsively, but she could see now that it could be done easily, even luxuriously.

Above there was a large glassed-in cabin in which

one could stretch out comfortably, out of the sun, and watch the sea, whatever the weather. She had known that there were people who lived like this. Part of her job had been to research and calculate so that those who did paid the government as little as possible. But to be there, to see it, to be surrounded by it, was entirely different from adding figures on paper.

There was a masculine feel to the cabin, to the entire boat—leather, wood, muted colors. There were shelves filled with books and a fully stocked bar, as well as a stereo system.

"All the comforts of home," Rebecca murmured, but she'd noted that there were doors and panels that could be secured in case of rough weather. What would it be like to ride out a storm at sea, to watch the rain lash the windows and feel the deck heave?

She gave a quick gasp when she felt the floor move. Stephen took her arm again to steady her.

"We're under way." Curious, he turned her to face him. "Are you afraid of boats?"

"No." She could hardly admit that the biggest one she'd been on before this had been a two-passenger canoe at summer camp. "It just startled me." Under way, she thought as she prayed that her system would settle. It was such an exciting, adventurous word. "Can we go out on deck? I'd like to watch."

It was exciting. She felt it the moment the wind hit her face and rushed through her hair. At the rail, she leaned out, delighted to see the island shrink and the sea spread. Because she couldn't resist and he didn't laugh at her, she took half a dozen pictures as the boat sped away from land.

"It's better than flying," she decided. "You feel a part of it. Look." With a laugh, she pointed. "The birds are chasing us."

Stephen didn't bother to glance at the gulls that wheeled and called above the boat's wake. He preferred to watch the delight and excitement bloom on her face. "Do you always enjoy so completely?"

"Yes." She tossed her hair away from her face, only to have the wind rush it back again. With another laugh, she stretched back from the railing, her face lifted to the sun. "Oh, yes."

Irresistible. With his hands at her waist, he spun her toward him. It was like holding a live wire. The shock rippled from her to him, then back again. "Everything?" His fingers spread over her back and, with the slightest pressure, moved her forward until their thighs met.

"I don't know." Instinctively she braced her hands on his shoulders. "I haven't tried everything." But she wanted to. Held close, with the sound of the water and the wind, she wanted to. Without giving a thought to self-preservation, she leaned toward him.

He swore, lightly, under his breath. Rebecca jolted back as if he had shouted at her. Stephen caught her hand as he nodded to the steward, who had just approached with drinks. "Thank you, Victor. Just leave everything." His voice was smooth enough, but Rebecca felt the tension in his hand as he led her to a chair.

He probably thought she was a fool, she decided. All but tumbling into his arms every time he touched her. He was obviously a man of the world—and a kind man, she added as she sipped her mimosa. Not all powerful men spoke kindly to those who worked for them. Her lips curved, a little wryly, as she sipped again. She knew that firsthand.

His body was in turmoil. Stephen couldn't remember, even in his youth, having had a woman affect him so irrationally. He knew how to persuade, how to seduce—and always with finesse. But whenever he was around this woman for more than five minutes he felt like a stallion being spurred and curbed at the same time.

And he was fascinated. Fascinated by the ease with which she went into his arms, by the trust he saw when he looked down into her eyes. As he had in the olive grove, he found himself believing he'd looked into those eyes, those rainwater-clear eyes, a hundred times before.

Still churning, he took out a cigar. The thought was fanciful, but his desire was very real. If there couldn't be finesse, perhaps there could be candor.

"I want you, Rebecca."

She felt her heart stop, then start up again with slow, dull throbs. Carefully she took another sip, then cleared her throat. "I know." It amazed her, flattered her, terrified her.

She seemed so cool. He envied her. "Will you come with me, to my cabin?"

She looked at him then. Her heart and her head were giving very different answers. It sounded so easy, so . . . natural. If there was a man she could give herself to, wholly, he was with her now. Complications, what complications there were, were her own.

But no matter how far she had run from Philadelphia and her own strict upbringing, there were still lines she couldn't cross.

"I can't."

"Can't?" He lit his cigar, astonished that they were discussing making love as though it were as casual a choice as what dinner entrée to choose. "Or won't?"

She drew a breath. Her palms were damp on the

glass, and she set it down. "Can't. I want to." Her eyes, huge and lake-pale, clung to his. "I very much want to, but . . ."

"But?"

"I know so little about you." She picked up her glass again because her empty hands tended to twist together. "Hardly more than your name, that you own an olive grove and like the sea. It's not enough."

"Then I'll tell you more."

She relaxed enough to smile. "I don't know what to ask."

He leaned back in his chair, the tension dissolving as quickly as it had built. She could do that to him with nothing more than a smile. He knew no one who could excite and solace with so little effort.

"Do you believe in fate, Rebecca? In something unexpected, even unlooked-for, often a small thing that completely and irrevocably changes one's life?"

She thought of her aunt's death and her own uncharacteristic decisions. "Yes. Yes, I do."

"Good." His gaze skimmed over her face, quickly, then more leisurely. "I'd nearly forgotten that I believe it, too. Then I saw you, sitting alone."

There were ways and ways to seduce, she was discovering. A look, a tone, could be every bit as devastating as a caress. She wanted him more in that moment than she had ever known she could want anything. To give herself time, and distance, she rose and walked to the rail.

Even her silence aroused him. She had said she knew too little about him. He knew even less of her. And he didn't care. It was dangerous, possibly even destructive, but he didn't care. As he watched her with the wind billowing her shirt and her hair he realized that he didn't give a damn about where she had come from, where she had been, what she had done.

When lightning strikes, it destroys, though it blazes with power. Rising, he went to her and stood, as she did, facing the sea.

"When I was young, very young," he began, "there was another moment that changed things. My father was a man for the water. He lived for it. Died for it." When he went on it was almost as if he were speaking to himself now, remembering. Rebecca turned her head to look at him. "I was ten or eleven. Everything was going well, the nets were full. My father and I were walking along the beach. He stopped, dipped his hand into the water, made a fist and opened it. 'You can't hold it,' he said to me. 'No matter how you try or how you love or how you sweat.' Then he dug into the sand. It was wet and clung together in his hand. 'But this,' he said, 'a man can hold.' We never spoke of it again. When my time came, I turned my back on the sea and held the land."

"It was right for you."

"Yes." He lifted a hand to catch at the ends of her hair. "It was right. Such big, quiet eyes you have, Rebecca," he murmured. "Have they seen enough, I wonder, to know what's right for you?"

"I guess I've been a little slow in starting to look." Her blood was pounding thickly. She would have stepped back, but he shifted so that she was trapped between him and the rail.

"You tremble when I touch you." He slid his hands up her arms, then down until their hands locked. "Have you any idea how exciting that is?"

Her chest tightened, diminishing her air even as the muscles in her legs went limp. "Stephen, I meant it when I said . . ." He brushed his lips gently over her temple.

"I can't. I need to . . ." He feathered a kiss along her jawline, softly. "To think."

He felt her fingers go lax in his. She was suddenly fragile, outrageously vulnerable, irresistibly tempting. "When I kissed you the first time I gave you no choice." His lips trailed over her face, light as a whisper, circling, teasing, avoiding her mouth. "You have one now."

He was hardly touching her. A breath, a whisper, a mere promise of a touch. The slow, subtle passage of his lips over her skin couldn't have been called a kiss, could never have been called a demand. She had only to push away to end the torment. And the glory.

A choice? Had he told her she had a choice? "No, I don't," she murmured as she turned to find his lips with hers.

No choice, no past, no future. Only now. She felt the present, with all its needs and hungers, well up inside her. The kiss was instantly hot, instantly desperate. His heart pounded fast and hard against hers, thunderous now, as he twisted a hand in her hair to pull her head back. To plunder. No one had ever taken her like this. No one had ever warned her that a touch of violence could be so exciting. Her gasp of surprise turned into a moan of pleasure as his tongue skimmed over hers.

He thought of lightning bolts again, thought of that flash of power and light. She was electric in his arms, sparking, sizzling. Her scent, as soft, as seductive, as a whisper, clouded his mind, even as the taste of her heightened his appetite.

She was all woman, she was every woman, and yet she was like no other. He could hear each quick catch of her breath above the roar of the motor. With her name on his lips, he pressed them to the vulnerable line of her throat, where the skin was heated from the sun and as delicate as water.

She might have slid bonelessly to the deck if his body hadn't pressed hers so firmly against the rail. In wonder, in panic, she felt his muscles turn to iron wherever they touched her. Never before had she felt so fragile, so at the mercy of her own desires. The sea was as calm as glass, but she felt herself tossed, tumbled, wrecked. With a sigh that was almost a sob, she wrapped her arms around him.

It was the defenselessness of the gesture that pulled him back from the edge. He must have been mad. For a moment he'd been close, much too close, to dragging her down to the deck without a thought to her wishes or to the consequences. With his eyes closed, he held her, feeling the erratic beat of her heart, hearing her shallow, shuddering breath.

Perhaps he was still mad, Stephen thought. Even as the ragged edges of desire eased, something deeper and far more dangerous bloomed.

He wanted her, in a way no man could safely want a woman. Forever.

Fate, he thought again as he stroked her hair. It seemed he was falling in love whether he wished it or not. A few hours with her and he felt more than he had ever imagined he could feel.

There had been a few times in his life when he had seen and desired on instinct alone. What he had seen and desired, he had taken. Just as he would take her. But when he took, he meant to keep.

Carefully he stepped back. "Maybe neither of us has a choice." He dipped his hands into his pockets. "And if I touch you again, here, now, I won't give you one."

Unable to pretend, knowing they were shaking, she pushed her hands through her hair. She didn't bother to disguise the tremor in her voice. She wouldn't have known how. "I won't want one." She saw his eyes darken quickly, dangerously, but she didn't know his hands were balled into fists, straining.

"You make it difficult for me."

A long, shuddering breath escaped her. No one had ever wanted her this way. Probably no one ever would again. "I'm sorry. I don't mean to."

"No." Deliberately he relaxed his hands. "I don't think you do. That's one of the things about you I find most intriguing. I will have you, Rebecca." He saw something flicker in her eyes. . . . Excitement? Panic? A combination of the two, perhaps. "Because I'm sure of it, because I know you're sure of it, I'll do my best to give you a little more time."

Her natural humor worked through the sliver of unease she felt. "I'm not sure whether I should thank you politely or run like hell."

He grinned, surprising himself, then flicked a finger down her cheek. "I wouldn't advise running, *matia mou*. I'd only catch you."

She was sure of that, too. One look at his face, even with the smile that softened it, and she knew. Kind, yes, but with a steely underlying ruthlessness. "Then I'll go with the thank-you."

"You're welcome." Patience, he realized, would have to be developed. And quickly. "Would you like to swim? There's a bay. We're nearly there."

The water might, just might, cool her off. "I'd love it."

CHAPTER 5

The water was cool and mirror-clear. Rebecca lowered herself into it with a sigh of pure pleasure. Back in Philadelphia she would have been at her desk, calculator clicking, the jacket of her neat business suit carefully smoothed over the back of her chair. Her figures would always add up, her forms would always be properly filed.

The dependable, efficient Miss Malone.

Instead, she was swimming in a crystal-clear bay, letting the water cool and the sun heat. Ledgers and accounts were worlds away. Here, as close as a handspan, was a man who was teaching her everything she would ever want to know about needs, desires, and the fragility of the heart.

He couldn't know it, she thought. She doubted she'd ever have the courage to tell him that he was the only one who had ever made her tremble and burn. A man as physically aware as he would only be uncomfortable knowing he held an inexperienced woman in his arms.

The water lapped around her with a sound as quiet as her own sigh. But he didn't know, because when she was in his arms she didn't feel awkward and inexperienced. She felt beautiful, desirable and reckless.

With a laugh, Rebecca dipped under the surface to let the water, and the freedom, surround her. Who would have believed it?

"Does it always take so little to make you laugh?"

Rebecca ran a hand over her slicked-back hair. Stephen was treading water beside her, smoothly, hardly making a ripple. His skin was dark gold, glistening-wet. His hair was streaked by the sun and dampened by the water, which was almost exactly the color of his eyes. She had to suppress an urge to just reach out and touch.

"A secluded inlet, a beautiful sky, an interesting man." With another sigh, she kicked her legs up so that she could float. "It doesn't seem like so little to me." She studied the vague outline of the mountains, far out of reach. "I promised myself that no matter where I went, what I did, I'd never take anything for granted again."

There was something in the way she said it, some hint of sadness, that pulled at him. The urge to comfort wasn't completely foreign in him, but he hadn't had much practice at it. "Was there a man who hurt you?"

Her lips curved at that, but he couldn't know that she was laughing at herself. Naturally, she'd dated. They had been polite, cautious evenings, usually with little interest on either side. She'd been dull, or at least she had never worked up the nerve to spread her wings. Once or twice, when she'd felt a tug, she'd been too shy, too much the efficient Rebecca Malone, to do anything about it.

With him, everything was different. Because she loved him. She didn't know how, she didn't know why, but she loved him as much as any woman could love any man.

"No. There's no one." She closed her eyes, trusting

the water to carry her. "When my parents died, it hurt. It hurt so badly that I suppose I pulled back from life. I thought it was important that I be a responsible adult, even though I wasn't nearly an adult yet."

Strange that she hadn't thought of it quite that way until she'd stopped being obsessively responsible. Stranger still was how easy it was to tell him what she'd never even acknowledged herself.

"My aunt Jeannie was kind and considerate and loving, but she'd forgotten what it was like to be a young girl. Suddenly I realized I'd missed being young, lazy, foolish, all the things everyone's entitled to be at least once. I decided to make up for it."

Her hair was spread out and drifting on the water. Her eyes were closed, and her face was sheened with water. Not beautiful, Stephen told himself. She was too angular for real beauty. But she was fascinating . . . in looks, in philosophy . . . more, in the open-armed way she embraced whatever crossed her path.

He found himself looking around the inlet as he hadn't bothered to look at anything in years. He could see the sun dancing on the surface, could see the ripples spreading and growing from the quiet motion of their bodies. Farther away was the narrow curving strip of white beach, deserted now, but for a few birds fluttering over the sand. It was quiet, almost unnaturally quiet, the only sound the soft, monotonous slap of water against sand. And he was relaxed, totally, mind and body. Perhaps he, too, had forgotten what it was like to be young and foolish.

On impulse he put a hand on her shoulder and pushed her under.

She came up sputtering, dragging wet hair out of her eyes. He grinned at her and calmly continued to tread water. "It was too easy."

She tilted her head, considering him and the distance between them. Challenge leaped into her eyes, sparked with amusement. "It won't be the next time."

His grin only widened. When he moved, he moved fast, streaking under and across the water like an eel. Rebecca had time for a quick squeal. Dragging in a deep breath, she kicked out. He caught her ankle, but she was ready. Unresisting, she let him pull her under. Then, instead of fighting her way back to the surface, she wrapped her arms around him and sent them both rolling in an underwater wrestling match. They were still tangled, her arms around him, her hands hooked over his shoulders, when they surfaced.

"We're even." She gasped for air and shook the water out of her eyes.

"How do you figure?"

"If we'd had a mat I'd have pinned you. Want to go for two out of three?"

"I might." He felt her legs tangle with his as she kicked out lazily. "But for now I prefer this."

He was going to kiss her again. She saw it in his eyes, felt it in the slight tensing of the arm that locked them torso to torso. She wasn't sure she was ready. More, she was afraid she was much too ready.

"Stephen?"

"Hmm?" His lips were a breath away from hers. Then he found himself underwater again, his arms empty. He should have been furious. He nearly was when he pushed to surface. She was shoulder-deep in the water, a few feet away. Her laughter rolled over him, young, delighted, unapologetic.

"It was too easy." She managed a startled "whoops" when he struck out after her. She might have made it—she had enough of a lead—but he swam as though he'd been born in the water. Still, she was agile, and

she almost managed to dodge him, but her laughter
betrayed her. She gulped in water, choked, then found
herself hauled up into his arms in thigh-deep water.

"I like to win." Deciding it was useless to struggle,
she pressed a hand to her heart and gasped for air. "It's
a personality flaw. Sometimes I cheat at canasta."

"Canasta?" The last thing he could picture the slim,
sexy bundle in his arms doing was spending a quiet evening playing cards.

"I can't help myself." Still breathless, she laid her
head on his shoulder. "No willpower."

"I find myself having the same problem." With a
careless toss, he sent her flying through the air. She hit
the water bottom first.

"I guess I deserved that." She struggled to her feet,
water raining off her. "I have to sit." Wading through
the water, she headed for the gentle slope of beach. She
lay, half in and half out of the water, not caring that
the sand would cling to her hair and skin. When he
dropped down beside her, she reached out a hand for
his. "I don't know when I've had a nicer day."

He looked down to where her fingers linked with
his. The gesture had been so easy, so natural. He wondered how it could both comfort and arouse. "It's
hardly over."

"It seems like it could last forever." She wanted it to
go on and on. Blue skies and easy laughter. Cool water
and endless hours. There had been a time, not so long
before, when the days had dragged into nights and the
nights into days. "Did you ever want to run away?"

With her hand still in his, he lay back to watch a
few scattered rags of clouds drift. How long had it been,
he wondered, since he'd really watched the sky? "To
where?"

"Anywhere. Away from the way things are, away

from what you're afraid they'll always be." She closed her eyes and could see herself brewing that first cup of coffee at exactly 7:15, opening the first file at precisely 9:01. "To drop out of sight," she murmured, "and pop up somewhere else, anywhere else, as someone completely different."

"You can't change who you are."

"Oh, but you can." Her tone suddenly urgent, she rose on her elbow. "Sometimes you have to."

He reached up to touch the ends of her hair. "What are you running from?"

"Everything. I'm a coward."

He looked into her eyes. They were so clear, so full of enthusiasm. "I don't think so."

"But you don't know me." A flicker of regret, then uncertainty, ran across her face. "I'm not sure I want you to."

"Don't I?" His fingers tightened on her hair, keeping her still. "There are people and circumstances that don't take months or years before they're understood. I look at you and something fits into place, Rebecca. I don't know why, but it is. I know you." He tugged her down for the lightest, the briefest, of kisses. "And I like what I see."

"Do you?" She smiled. "Really?"

"Do you imagine I spend the day with a woman only because I want to sleep with her?" She shrugged, and though her blush was very faint, he noticed it and was amused by it. How many women, he wondered, could kiss a man into oblivion, then blush? "Being with you, Rebecca, is a difficult pleasure."

She chuckled and began to draw circles in the wet sand. What would he say, what would he think, if he knew what she was? Or, more accurately, what she wasn't? It didn't matter, she told herself. She couldn't let it spoil what there was between them.

"I think that's the most wonderful compliment I've ever had."

"Where have you been?" he murmured.

When she moved restlessly, he held her still. "Don't. I'm not going to touch you. Not yet."

"That's not the problem." With her eyes closed, she tilted her chin up and let the sun beat down on her face. "The problem is, I want you to touch me, so much it frightens me." Taking her time, she sat up, gathering her courage. She wanted to be honest, and she hoped she wouldn't sound like a fool. "Stephen, I don't sleep around. I need you to understand, because this is all happening so quickly. But it's not casual."

He lifted a hand to her chin and turned her to face him. His eyes were as blue as the water, and, to her, as unfathomable. "No, it's not." He made the decision quickly, though he had been turning the idea over in his mind all day. "I have to go to Athens tomorrow. Come with me, Rebecca."

"Athens?" she managed, staring at him.

"Business. A day, two at the most. I'd like you with me." And he was afraid, more than he cared to admit, that when he returned she might be gone.

"I . . ." What should she say? What was right?

"You told me you'd planned to go." He'd push if necessary. Now that the idea had taken root, Stephen had no intention of going anywhere without her.

"Yes, but I wouldn't want to be in the way while you're working."

"You'll be in my way whether you're here or there."

Her head came up at that, and the look she gave him was both shy and stunning. He stifled the need to take her again, to roll until she was beneath him on the sand. He'd said he'd give her time. Perhaps what he'd really meant was that he needed time himself.

"You'll have your own suite. No strings, Rebecca. Just your company."

"A day or two," she murmured.

"It's a simple matter to have your room held for you here for your return."

Her return. Not his. If he left Corfu tomorrow she would probably never see him again. He was offering her another day, perhaps two. Never take anything for granted, she remembered. Never again.

Athens, she thought. It was true that she had planned to see it before she left Greece. But she would have gone alone. A few days before, that had been what she thought she wanted. The adventure of seeing new places, new people, on her own. Now the thought of going with him, of having him beside her when she first caught sight of the Acropolis, of having him want her with him, changed everything.

"I'd love to go with you." She rose quickly and dived into the water. She was in over her head.

CHAPTER 6

Athens was neither East nor West. It was spitted meat and spices roasting. It was tall buildings and modern shops. It was narrow, unpaved streets and clamorous bazaars. It had been the scene of revolution and brutality. It was ancient and civilized and passionate.

Rebecca quite simply fell in love at first sight.

She'd been seduced by Paris and charmed by London, but in Athens she lost her heart. She wanted to see everything at once, from sunrise to moonlight and the heat-drenched afternoon between.

All that first morning, while Stephen was immersed in business meetings, she wandered. The hotel he'd chosen was lovely, but she was drawn to the streets and the people. Somehow she didn't feel like a visitor here. She felt like someone who had returned home after a long, long journey. Athens was waiting for her, ready to welcome her back.

Incredible. All her life she had accepted the parameters set for her. Now she was touring Old Athens, with its clicking worry beads and its open-fronted shops, where she could buy cheap plaster copies of monuments or elegant antiques.

She passed tavernas, but she was too excited to be tempted by the rich smells of coffee and baking. She heard the clear notes of a flute as she looked up and saw the Acropolis.

There was only one approach. Though it was still early, other tourists were making their way toward the ruins in twos and in groups. Rebecca let her camera hang by its strap. Despite the chattering around her, she felt alone, but beautifully so.

She would never be able to explain what it felt like to stand in the morning sun and look at something that had been built for the gods—something that had endured war and weather and time. It had been a place of worship. Even now, after centuries had passed, Rebecca felt the spiritual pull. Perhaps the goddess Athena, with her gleaming helmet and spear, still visited there.

Rebecca had been disappointed that Stephen couldn't join her on her first morning in Athens. Now she was glad to be alone—to sit and absorb and imagine without having to explain her thoughts.

How could she, after having seen so much, go back to so little? Sighing, she wandered through the temples. It wasn't just the awe she felt here, or the excitement she had felt in London and Paris, that had changed her. It was Stephen and everything she'd felt, everything she'd wanted, since she'd met him.

Perhaps she would go back to Philadelphia, but she would never be the same person. Once you fell in love, completely, totally in love, nothing was ever the same.

She wished it could be simple, the way she imagined it was simple for so many other women. An attractive man, a physical tug. But with Stephen, as with

Athens, she'd lost her heart. However implausible it seemed, she had recognized the man, as well as the city, as being part of her, as being for her. Desire, when tangled up with love, could never be simple.

But how could you be sure you were in love when it had never happened to you before? If she were home, at least she would have a friend to talk to. With a little laugh, Rebecca walked out into the sunlight. How many times had she been on the receiving end of a long, scattered conversation from a friend who had fallen in love—or thought she had. The excitement, the unhappiness, the thrills. Sometimes she'd been envious, and sometimes she'd been grateful not to have the complication in her own life. But always, always, she'd offered calm, practical, even soothing advice.

Oddly enough, she didn't seem to be able to do the same for herself.

All she could think of was the way her heart pounded when he touched her, how excitement, panic and anticipation fluttered through her every time he looked at her. When she was with him, her feelings and fantasies seemed reasonable. When she was with him, she could believe in fate, in the matching of soul to soul.

It wasn't enough. At least that was what she would have told another woman. Attraction and passion weren't enough. Yet there was no explaining, even to herself, the sense of rightness she experienced whenever she was with him. If she were a fanciful person she would say it was as though she'd been waiting for him, waiting for the time and the place for him to come to her.

It sounded simple—if fate could be considered simple. Yet beneath all the pleasure and that sense of reunion was guilt. She couldn't shake it, and she knew she wouldn't be able to ignore it much longer. She wasn't the woman she had let him believe her to be. She wasn't the well-traveled at-loose-ends free spirit she pretended to be. No matter how many ties she'd cut, she was still Rebecca Malone. How would he feel about her once he knew how limited and dull her life had been?

How and when was she going to tell him?

A few more days, she promised herself as she began the walk back. It was selfish, perhaps it was even dangerous, but she wanted just a few more days.

It was midafternoon before she returned to the hotel. Ignoring the fact that she might be considered over-eager, she went straight to Stephen's suite. She couldn't wait to see him, to tell him everything she'd seen, to show him everything she'd bought. Her easy smile faded a bit when his secretary Elana opened the door.

"Miss Malone." Gracious and self-confident, Elana waved her in. "Please sit down. I'll let Stephen know you're here."

"I don't want to interrupt." Rebecca shifted her bags, feeling gauche and foolish.

"Not at all. Have you just come in?"

"Yes, I . . ." For the first time, Rebecca noticed that her skin was damp and her hair tousled. In contrast, Elana was cool and perfectly groomed. "I really should go."

"Please." Elana urged Rebecca to a chair. "Let me get you a drink." With a half smile, Elana began to pour a tall glass of iced juice. She had expected Stephen's mystery lady to be smooth, controlled and stunning. It pleased her a great deal to find Rebecca wide-eyed, a little unsure, and clearly a great deal in love.

"Did you enjoy your morning?"

"Yes, very much." She accepted the glass and tried to relax. Jealousy, she realized, feeling herself flush at the realization. She couldn't remember ever having experienced the sensation before. Who wouldn't be jealous? she asked herself as she watched Elana walk to the phone. The Greek woman was gorgeous, self-contained, and coolly efficient. Above all, she had a relationship with Stephen that Rebecca knew nothing about. How long has she known him? Rebecca wondered. And how well?

"Stephen's just finishing up some business," Elana said as she hung up the phone. With easy, economical moves, she poured herself a drink, then walked to the chair facing Rebecca. "What do you think of Athens?"

"I love it." Rebecca wished she'd taken the time to brush her hair and freshen her makeup. Lecturing herself, she sipped at her juice. "I'm not sure what I expected, but it's everything and more."

"Europeans see it as the East, Asians see it as the West." Elana crossed her legs and settled back. It surprised her to realize that she was prepared to like Rebecca Malone. "What Athens is is Greek—and, more particularly, Athenian." She paused, studying Rebecca over the rim of her glass. "People often view Stephen in much the same way, and what he is is Stephen."

"How long have you worked for him?"

"Five years."

"You must know him well."

"Better than some. He's a demanding and generous employer and an interesting man. Fortunately, I like to travel and I enjoy my work."

Rebecca rubbed at a spot of dust on her slacks. "It never occurred to me that farming required so much traveling. I never realized how much was involved in growing olives."

Elana's brows rose in obvious surprise, but she continued smoothly when Rebecca glanced back at her. "Whatever Stephen does, he does thoroughly." She smiled to herself, satisfied. She hadn't been certain until now whether the American woman was attracted to Stephen or to his position. "Has Stephen explained to you about the dinner party this evening?"

"He said something about a small party here at the hotel. A business dinner."

"Men take these things more lightly than women." Feeling friendlier, Elena offered her first genuine smile. "It will be small, but quite extravagant." She watched as Rebecca automatically lifted a hand to her hair. "If you need anything—a dress, a salon—the hotel can accommodate you."

Rebecca thought of the casual sportswear she'd tossed into her bag before the impulsive trip to Athens. "I need everything."

With a quick, understanding laugh, Elana rose. "I'll make some calls for you."

"Thank you, but I don't want to interfere with your work."

"Seeing that you're comfortable is part of my work." They both glanced over when the door opened. "Stephen. You see, she hasn't run away." Taking her glass and her pad, she left them alone.

"You were gone a long time." He hated the fact that he'd begun to watch the clock and worry. He'd imagined her hurt or abducted. He'd begun to wonder if she would disappear from his life as quickly as she'd appeared in it. Now she was here, her eyes alive with pleasure, her clothes rumpled and her hair windblown.

"I guess I got caught up exploring." She started to rise, but before she could gain her feet he was pulling her out of the chair, seeking, finding her mouth with his.

His desperation whipped through her. His hunger incited her own. Without thought, without hesitation, she clung to him, answering, accepting. Already seduced, she murmured something, an incoherent sound that caught in her throat.

Good God, he thought, it wasn't possible, it wasn't sane, to want like this. Throughout the morning while all the facts and figures and demands of business had been hammering at him, he'd thought of her, of holding her, of tasting her, of being with her. When she had stayed away for so long he'd begun to imagine, then to fear, what his life would be like without her.

It wasn't going to happen. He scraped his teeth over her bottom lip, and she gasped and opened for him. He wouldn't let it happen. Where she came from, where she intended to go, no longer mattered. She belonged to him now. And, though he'd only begun to deal with it, he belonged to her.

But he needed some sanity, some logic. Fighting himself, Stephen drew her away from him. Her eyes remained closed, and her lips remained parted. A soft, sultry sound escaped them as her lashes fluttered upward.

"I . . ." She took a deep breath and let it out slowly. "I should go sightseeing more often."

Gradually he realized how hard his fingers were pressing into her arms. As if he were afraid she would slip away. Cursing himself, he relaxed. "I would have preferred to go with you."

"I understand you're busy. I'd have bored you silly, poking into every shop and staring at every column."

"No." If there was one thing he was certain of, it was that she would never bore him. "I'd like to have seen your first impression of Athens."

"It was like coming home," she told him, then hurried on because it sounded foolish. "I couldn't get enough." Laughing at herself, she gestured toward her bags. "Obviously. It's so different from anywhere I've ever been. At the Acropolis I couldn't even take any pictures, because I knew they couldn't capture the feeling. Then I walked along the streets and saw old men with *kom—konbou—*" She fumbled over the Greek and finally made a helpless gesture.

"*Kombouloi*," he murmured. "Worry beads."

"Yes, and I imagined how they might sit in those shadowy doorways watching the tourists go by, day after day, year after year." She sat, pleased to share her impressions with him. "I saw a shop with all these costumes, lots of tinsel, and some really dreadful plaster copies of the monuments."

He grinned and sat beside her. "How many did you buy?"

"Three or four." She bent down to rattle through her bags. "I bought you a present."

"A plaster statue of Athena?"

She glanced up, eyes laughing. "Almost. Then I found this tiny antique shop in the old section. It was all dim and dusty and irresistible. The owner had a handful of English phrases, and I had my phrase book. After we'd confused each other completely, I bought this."

She drew out an S-shaped porcelain pipe decorated with paintings of the wild mountain goats of Greece. Attached to it was a long wooden stem, as smooth as glass, tipped by a tarnished brass mouthpiece.

"I remembered the goats we'd seen on Corfu," she

explained as Stephen examined it. "I thought you might like it, though I've never seen you smoke a pipe."

With a quiet laugh, he looked back at her, balancing the gift in both hands. "No, I don't—at least not of this nature."

"Well, it's more ornamental than functional, I suppose. The man couldn't tell me much about it—at least not that I could understand." She reached out to run a finger along the edge of the bowl. "I've never seen anything like it."

"I'm relieved to hear it." When she sent him a puzzled look, he leaned over to brush her lips with his. *"Matia mou*, this is a hashish pipe."

"A hashish pipe?" She stared, first in shock, then in fascination. "Really? I mean, did people actually use it?"

"Undoubtedly. Quite a number, I'd say, since it's at least a hundred and fifty years old."

"Imagine that." She pouted, imagining dark, smoky dens. "I guess it's not a very appropriate souvenir."

"On the contrary, whenever I see it I'll think of you."

She glanced up quickly, unsure, but the amusement in his eyes had her smiling again. "I should have bought you the plaster statue of Athena."

Taking her hands, he drew her to her feet. "I'm flattered that you bought me anything." She felt the subtle change as his fingers tightened on hers. "I want time with you, Rebecca. Hours of it. Days. There's too much I need to know." When she lowered her gaze, he caught her chin. "What are those secrets of yours?"

"Nothing that would interest you."

"You're wrong. Tomorrow I intend to find out all there is to know." He saw the quick flicker of unease in her eyes. Other men, he thought with an uncomfortable surge of jealousy. The hell with them. "No more evasions. I want you, all of you. Do you understand?"

"Yes, but—"

"Tomorrow." He cut her off, suddenly, completely, frustratingly Greek. "I have business that can't be avoided now. I'll come for you at seven."

"All right."

Tomorrow was years away, she told herself. She had time to decide what she would say, how she would say it. Before tomorrow came tonight. She would be everything she'd ever wanted to be, everything he wanted her to be.

"I'd better go." Before he could touch her again, she bent to gather her bags. "Stephen . . ." She paused at the door and turned to look at him as he stood in the middle of the room, comfortable with the wealth that surrounded him, confident with who and what he was. "You might be disappointed when you find out."

She left quickly, leaving him frowning after her.

CHAPTER 7

She was as nervous as a cat. Every time she looked in the mirror Rebecca wondered who the woman was staring back at her. It wasn't a stranger, but it was a very, very different Rebecca Malone.

Was it just the different hairstyle, poufed and frizzed and swept around her face? Could it be the dress, the glittery spill of aquamarine that left her arms and shoulders bare? No, it was more than that. More than makeup and clever stylists and glamorous clothes. It was in her eyes. How could she help but see it? How could anyone? The woman who looked back from the mirror was a woman in love.

What was she going to do about it? What could she do? she asked herself. She was still practical enough to accept that some things could never be changed. But was she bold enough, or strong enough, to take what she wanted and live with the consequences?

When she heard the knock on the door, Rebecca took a deep breath and picked up the useless compact-sized evening bag she'd bought just that afternoon. It was all happening so fast. When she'd come back from

Stephen's suite there had been a detailed message from
Elana listing appointments—for a massage, a facial,
hair-styling—along with the name of the manager of
the hotel's most exclusive boutique. She hadn't had
time to think, even for a minute, about her evening with
Stephen. Or about any tomorrows.

Perhaps that was best, she decided as she pulled
open the door. It was best not to think, not to analyze.
It was best to accept and to act.

She looked like a siren, some disciple of Circe, with
her windswept hair and a dress the color of seductive
seas. Had he told himself she wasn't beautiful? Had he
believed it? At that moment he was certain he'd never
seen, never would see, a more exciting woman.

"You're amazing, Rebecca." He took her hand and
drew her to him so that they stood in the doorway
together. On the threshold.

"Why? Because I'm on time?"

"Because you're never what I expect." He brought
her hand to his lips. "And always what I want."

Because she was speechless, she was glad when he
closed the door at her back and led her to the elevators.
He looked different from the man she had first met, the
one who dressed with such casual elegance. Tonight
there was a formality about him, and the sophistication
she had sensed earlier was abundantly apparent in the
ease with which he wore the black dinner jacket.

"The way you look," he told her, "it seems a shame
to waste the evening on a business dinner."

"I'm looking forward to meeting some of your
friends."

"Associates," he said with an odd smile. "When
you've been poor—and don't intend to be poor again—
you rarely make friends in business."

She frowned. This was a side of him, the business

side that she didn't know. Would he be ruthless? She looked at him, saw it, and accepted it. Yes, a man like Stephen would always be ruthless with what belonged to him. "But enemies?"

"The same rule, in business, applies to friends and enemies. My father taught me more than fishing, Rebecca. He also taught me that to succeed, to attain, you must learn not only how to trust, but how far."

"I've never been poor, but I imagine it's frightening."

"Strengthening." He took her hand again when the elevator doors opened. "We have different backgrounds, Rebecca, but, fortunately, we've come to the same place."

He had no idea *how* different. Trust. He had spoken of trust. She discovered she wanted to tell him, tell him everything. Tell him that she knew nothing of elegant parties and glamorous lifestyles. She was a fraud, and when he found out he might laugh at her and brush her aside. But she wanted him to know.

"Stephen, I want to—"

"Stephen. Once more you outdo us all in your choice of women."

"Dimitri."

Rebecca stopped, caught on the brink of confession. The man who faced her was classically handsome. His silver mane contrasted with bronzed skin lined by a half century of sun. He wore a mustache that swept majestically over gleaming teeth.

"It was kind of you to invite us here this evening, but it would be kinder still to introduce me to your lovely companion."

"Rebecca Malone, Dimitri Petropolis."

A diamond glittered on the hand he lifted to clasp Rebecca's. The hand itself was hard as rock. "A pleasure.

Athens is already abuzz with talk of the woman who arrived with Stephen."

Certain he was joking, she smiled. "Then Athens must be in desperate need of news."

His eyes widened for a moment, then creased at the corners when he laughed. "I have no doubt you will provide an abundance of it."

Stephen slipped a hand under Rebecca's elbow. The look he sent Dimitri was very quick and very clear. They had competed over land, but there would be no competition over Rebecca.

"If you'll excuse us a moment, Dimitri, I'd like to get Rebecca some champagne."

"Of course." Amused—and challenged—Dimitri brushed at his mustache as he watched them walk away.

Rebecca had no way of knowing that to Stephen a small dinner party meant a hundred people. She sipped her first glass of wine, hoping she wouldn't embarrass them both by being foolishly shy and tongue-tied. In the past, whenever she had found herself in a crowd, she had always looked for the nearest corner to fade into. Not tonight, she promised herself, straightening her shoulders.

There were dozens of names to remember, but she filed them away as easily as she had always filed numbers. In the hour before dinner, while the guests mixed and mingled, she found herself at ease. The stomach flutters and hot blushes she'd often experienced at parties and functions simply didn't happen.

Perhaps she was the new Rebecca Malone after all.

She heard business discussed here and there. Most of it seemed to be hotel and resort business—talk of remodeling and expansions, mergers and takeovers. She found it odd that so many of the guests were in that trade, rather than prosperous farmers or olive growers.

Stephen came up behind her and murmured in her ear, "You look pleased with yourself."

"I am." He couldn't know that she was pleased to find herself at ease and comfortable in a party of strangers. "So many interesting people."

"Interesting." He brushed a finger over her wispy bangs. "I thought you might find it dull."

"Not at all." She took a last sip of champagne, then set the glass aside. Instantly a waiter was at her side, offering another. Stephen watched her smile her thanks.

"So you enjoy parties?"

"Sometimes. I'm enjoying this one, and having a chance to meet your associates."

Stephen glanced over her shoulder, summing up the looks and quiet murmurs. "They'll be talking about you for weeks to come."

She only laughed, turning in a slow circle. Around her was the flash of jewels and the gleam of gold. The sleek and the prosperous, the rich and the successful. It pleased her that she'd found more to talk about than tax shelters.

"I can't imagine they have so little on their minds. This is such a gorgeous room."

She looked around the huge ballroom, with its cream-and-rose walls, its glittering chandeliers and its gleaming floors. There were alcoves for cozy love seats and tall, thriving ornamental trees in huge copper pots. The tables, arranged to give a sense of intimacy, were already set with ivory cloths and slender tapers.

"It's really a beautiful hotel," she continued. "Everything about it runs so smoothly." She smiled up at him. "I'm torn between the resort in Corfu and this."

"Thank you." When she gave him a blank look, he tipped up her chin with his finger. "They're mine."

"Your what?"

"My hotels," he said simply, then led her to a table.

She spoke all through dinner, though for the first fifteen minutes she had no idea what she said. There were eight at Stephen's table, including Dimitri, who had shifted name cards so that he could sit beside her. She toyed with her seafood appetizer, chatted and wondered if she could have made a bigger fool out of herself.

He wasn't simply prosperous. He wasn't simply well-off. There was enough accountant left in Rebecca to understand that when a man owned what Stephen owned he was far, far more than comfortable.

What would he think of her when he found out what she was? Trust? How could she ever expect him to trust her now? She swallowed without tasting and managed to smile. Would he think she was a gold digger, that she had set herself up to run into him?

No, that was ridiculous.

She forced herself to look over and saw that Stephen was watching her steadily. She picked up her fork with one hand and balled up the napkin in her lap with the other.

Why couldn't he be ordinary? she wondered. Someone vacationing, someone working at the resort? Why had she fallen in love with someone so far out of her reach?

"Have you left us?"

Rebecca jerked herself back to see Dimitri smiling at her. Flushing, she noticed that the next course had been served while she'd been daydreaming. "I'm sorry." With an effort she began to toy with the *salata Athenas*.

"A beautiful woman need never apologize for being lost in her own thoughts." He patted her hand, then let his fingers linger. He caught Stephen's dark look and smiled. If he didn't like the boy so much, he thought, he wouldn't get nearly so much pleasure from irritating him. "Tell me, how did you meet Stephen?"

"We met in Corfu." She thought of that first meal they had shared . . . quiet, relaxed, alone.

"Ah, soft nights and sunny days. You are vacationing?"

"Yes." Rebecca put more effort into her smile. If she stared into her salad she would only embarrass herself, and Stephen. "He was kind enough to show me some of the island."

"He knows it well, and many of the other islands of our country. There's something of the wanderer in him."

She had sensed that. Hadn't that been part of the attraction? Hadn't Rebecca just discovered the wanderer in herself? "Have you known him long?"

"We have a long-standing business relationship. Friendly rivals, you might say. When Stephen was hardly more than a boy he accumulated an impressive amount of land." He gestured expansively. "As you can see, he used it wisely. I believe he has two hotels in your country."

"Two? More?" Rebecca picked up her glass and took a long swallow of wine.

"So you see, I had wondered if you had met in America and were old friends."

"No." Rebecca nodded weakly as the waiter removed the salad and replaced it with moussaka. "We only just met a few days ago."

"As always, Stephen moves quickly and stylishly." Dimitri took her hand again, more than a little amused by the frown he saw deepening in Stephen's eyes. "Where is it in America you are from?"

"Philadelphia." Relax, she ordered herself. Relax and enjoy. "That's in the Northeast."

It infuriated Stephen to watch her flirting so easily, so effectively, with another man. She sat through course after course, barely eating, all the while gifting Dimitri with her shy smiles. Not once did she draw away when the older man touched her hand or leaned close. From where he sat, Stephen could catch a trace of her scent, soft, subtle, maddening. He could hear her quiet laugh when Dimitri murmured something in her ear.

Then she was standing with him, her hand caught in his, as he led her to the dance floor.

Stephen sat there, battling back a jealousy he despised, and watched them move together to music made for lovers. Under the lights her dress clung, then swayed, then shifted. Her face was close, too damn close, to Dimitri's. He knew what it was like to hold her like that, to breathe in the scent of her skin and her hair. He knew what it was to feel her body brush against his, to feel the life, the passion, bubbling. He knew what it was to see her eyes blur, her lips part, to hear that quiet sigh.

He had often put his stamp on land, but never on a woman. He didn't believe in it. But only a fool sat idly by and allowed another man to enjoy what was his. With a muttered oath, Stephen rose, strode out onto the dance floor and laid a hand on Dimitri's shoulder.

"Ah, well." The older man gave a regretful sigh and stepped aside. "Until later."

Before she could respond, Rebecca was caught against Stephen. With a sigh of her own, she relaxed and matched her steps to his. Maybe it was like a dream, she told herself as she closed her eyes and let the music

fill her head. But she was going to enjoy every moment
until it was time to wake up.

She seemed to melt against him. Her fingers moved
lightly through his hair as she rested her cheek against
his. Was this the way she'd danced with Dimitri? Stephen wondered, then cursed himself. He was being a
fool, but he couldn't seem to stop himself. Then again,
he'd had to fight for everything else in his life. Why
should his woman be any different?

He wanted to drag her off then and there, away from
everyone, and find some dark, quiet place to love her.

"You're enjoying yourself?"

"Yes." She wouldn't think about what he was, not
now. Soon enough the night would be over and tomorrow would have to be faced. While the music played and
he held her, she would only think of what he meant to
her. "Very much."

The dreamy tone of her voice almost undid him.
"Apparently Dimitri entertained you well."

"Mmm. He's a very nice man."

"You moved easily from his arms to mine."

Something in his tone pried through the pleasure
she felt. Carefully she drew back so that she could see
his face. "I don't think I know what you mean."

"I believe you do."

She was tempted to laugh, but there was no humor
in Stephen's eyes. Rebecca felt her stomach knot as it
always did when she was faced with a confrontation. "If
I do, then I'd have to think you ridiculous. Maybe we'd
better go back to the table."

"So you can be with him?" Even as the words came
out he realized the unfairness, even the foolishness, of
them.

She stiffened, retreating as far as she could from

anger. "I don't think this is the place for this kind of discussion."

"You're quite right." As furious with himself as he was with her, he pulled her from the dance floor.

CHAPTER 8

S top it." By the time he'd dragged her to the elevators, Rebecca had gotten over her first shock. "What's gotten into you?"

"I'm simply taking you to a more suitable place for our discussion." He pulled her into the elevator, then punched the button for their floor.

"You have guests," she began, but he sent her a look that made her feel like a fool. Falling back on dignity, she straightened her shoulders. "I prefer to be asked if I want to leave, not dragged around as though I were a pack mule."

Though her heart was pounding, she sailed past him when the doors opened, intending to breeze into her own rooms and slam the door in his face. In two steps he had her arm again. Rebecca found herself guided, none too gently, into Stephen's suite.

"I don't want to talk to you," she said, because she was certain her teeth would begin to chatter at any moment. She didn't argue well in the best of circumstances. Faced with Stephen's anger, she was certain she would lose.

He said nothing as he loosened his tie and the first two buttons of his shirt. He went to the bar and poured two brandies. He was being irrational and he knew it, but he seemed unable to control it. That was new, he decided. But there had been many new emotions in him since Rebecca.

Walking back to Rebecca, he set one snifter by her elbow. When he looked at her . . . he wanted to shout, to beg, to demand, to plead. As a result, his voice was clipped and hard.

"You came to Athens with me, not with Dimitri or any other man."

She didn't touch the snifter. She was certain her hands would shake so hard that it would slip out of her grip. "Is that a Greek custom?" It amazed her—and bolstered her confidence—to hear how calm her voice was. "Forbidding a woman to speak to another man?"

"Speak?" He could still see the way Dimitri had bent his head close to hers. Dimitri, who was smooth and practiced. Dimitri, whose background would very likely mirror Rebecca's. Old money, privileged childhoods, quiet society. "Do you allow every man who speaks to you to hold you, to touch you?"

She didn't blush. Instead, the color faded from her cheeks. She shook, not with fear but with fury. "What I do, and with whom I do it, is my business. Mine."

Very deliberately he lifted his snifter and drank. "No."

"If you think that because I came here with you, you have the right to dictate to me you're wrong. I'm my own person, Stephen." It struck her even as she said it that it was true. She was her own person. Each decision she made was her own. Filled with a new sense of power, she stepped forward. "No one owns me, not you, not anyone. I won't be ordered, I won't be forced, I won't be pressured." With a flick of her skirts, she turned. He had her again quickly, his hands on both of her arms, his face close.

"You won't go back to him."

"You couldn't stop me if that was what I wanted." She tossed her head back challengingly. "But I have no intention of going back downstairs to Dimitri, or anyone else." She jerked her arms free. "You idiot. Why should I want to be with him when I'm in love with you?"

She stopped, her eyes wide with shock, her lips parted in surprise. Overwhelmed by a combination of humiliation and fury, she spun around. Then she was struggling against him. "Leave me alone! Oh, God, just leave me alone!"

"Do you think I could let you go now?" He caught her hair in his hand, dragging it back until her eyes met his. In them she saw triumph and desire. "I feel as though I've waited all my life to hear you say those words." He rained kisses over her face until her struggles ceased. "You drive me mad," he murmured. "Being with you, being without you."

"Please." Colors, shapes, lights were whirling in her head. "I need to think."

"No. Ask me for anything else, but not more time." Gathering her close, he buried his face in her hair. "Do you think I make a fool of myself over every woman?"

"I don't know." She moaned when his lips trailed down her throat. Something wild and terrifying was happening inside her body. "I don't know you. You don't know me."

"Yes, I do." He pulled away just far enough to look down at her. "From the first moment I saw you, I knew you. Needed you. Wanted you."

It was true. She knew it, felt it, but she shook her head in denial. "It's not possible."

"I've loved you before, Rebecca, almost as much as I do now." He felt her go still. The color fled from her face again, but her eyes stayed steady on his.

"I don't want you to say what isn't real, what you're not sure of."

"Didn't you feel it, the first time I kissed you?" When he saw the acknowledgment in her eyes, his grip tightened. He could feel her heart thundering, racing to match the rhythm of his own. "Somehow you've come back to me, and I to you. No more questions," he said, before she could speak. "I need you tonight."

It was real. She felt the truth and the knowledge when his mouth found hers. If it was wrong to go blindly into need, then she would pay whatever price was asked. She could no longer deny him . . . or herself.

There was no gentleness in the embrace. It was as it had been the first time, lovers reunited, a hunger finally quenched. All heat and light. She gave more than she'd known she had. Her mouth was as avid as his, as seeking. Her murmurs were as desperate. Her hands didn't shake as they moved over him. They pressed, gripped, demanded. Greedy, she tugged the jacket from his shoulders.

Yes, he'd come back to her. If it was madness to believe it, then for tonight she'd be mad.

The taste of her, just the taste of her, was making his head swim and his blood boil. He nipped at her lip, then sucked until he heard her helpless whimper. He wanted her helpless. Something fierce and uncivilized inside him wanted her weak and pliant and defenseless. When she went limp in his arms he dived into her mouth and plundered. Her response tore at him, so sweet, so vulnerable, then suddenly so ardent.

Her hands, which had fluttered helplessly to her side, rose up again to pull at his shirt, to race under it to warmed flesh. She could only think of how right it felt to touch him, to press against him and wait for him to light new fires inside her.

With an oath, he swept her up into his arms and carried her to the bedroom.

The moon was waning and offered only the most delicate light. It fell in slants and shadows on the bed, dreamlike. But the vibrating of Rebecca's pulse told her this was no dream. There was the scent of jasmine from the sprigs in the vase beside the bed. It was a scent she would always remember, just as she would remember how dark and deep were the color of his eyes.

Needful, desperate, they tumbled onto the bed.

He wanted to take care with her. She seemed so small, so fragile. He wanted to show her how completely she filled his heart. But his body was on fire, and she was already moving like a whirlwind beneath him.

His mouth was everywhere, making her shudder and arch and ache. Desires she'd never known sprang to life inside her and took control. Delirious, she obeyed them, reveled in them, then searched for more.

They rolled across the bed in a passionate war that would have two victors, touching, taking, discovering. Impatient, he peeled the dress from her, moaning as he found her breasts with his hands, his lips, his teeth. Unreasoning desire catapulted through him when he felt her soar.

Her body felt like a furnace, impossibly hot, impossibly strong. Sensations rammed into her, stealing her breath. Mindless and moaning, she writhed under him, open for any demand he might make, pulsing for any new knowledge he might offer.

Finally, finally, she knew what it was to love, to be

loved, to be wanted beyond reason. Naked, she clung to him, awash in the power and the weakness, the glory and the terror.

He raced over her as if he already knew what would make her tremble, what would make her yearn. Never before had she been so aware, so in tune with another.

She made him feel like a god. He touched, and her skin vibrated under his hand. He tasted, and her flavor was like no other. She was moist, heated, and utterly willing. She seemed to explode beneath him, lost in pleasure, drugged by passion. No other woman had ever driven him so close to madness. Her head was thrown back, and one hand was flung out as her fingers dug into the sheets. Wanton, waiting, wild.

With her name on his lips, he drove into her. His breath caught. His mind spun. Her cry of pain and release echoed in his head, bringing him both triumph and guilt. His body went rigid as he fought to claw his way back. Then she seemed to close around him, body, heart, soul. As helpless as she, he crossed the line into madness and took her with him.

CHAPTER 9

Aftershocks of passion racked her. Stunned and confused, she lay in the shadowed light. Nothing had prepared her for this. No one had ever warned her that pleasure could be so huge or that need could be so jagged. If she had known . . . Rebecca closed her eyes and nearly laughed out loud. If she had known, she would have left everything behind years ago and searched the world for him.

Only him. She let out a quiet, calming sigh. Only him.

He was cursing himself, slowly, steadily, viciously. Innocent. Dear God. She'd been innocent, as fresh and untouched as spring, and he'd used her, hurt her, taken her.

Disgusted with himself, he sat up and reached for a cigar. He needed more than tobacco. He needed a drink, but he didn't trust his legs to carry him.

The flick of his lighter sounded like a gunshot. For an instant his face, hardened by anger and self-loathing, was illuminated.

"Why didn't you tell me?"

Still floating on an ocean of pleasure, she blinked her eyes open. "What?"

"Damn it, Rebecca, why didn't you tell me you hadn't been with a man before? That this—that I was your first?"

There was an edge of accusation in his voice. For the first time, she realized she was naked. Her cheeks grew hot as she fumbled for the sheet. One moment there was glory; the next, shame. "I didn't think of it."

"Didn't think of it?" His head whipped around. "Don't you think I had a right to know? Do you think this would have happened if I had known?"

She shook her head. It was true that she hadn't thought of it. It hadn't mattered. He was the first, the last, the only. But now it occurred to her that a man like him might not want to make love with an inexperienced woman. "I'm sorry." Her heart seemed to shrivel in her breast. "You said that you loved me, that you wanted me. The rest didn't seem to matter."

She'd cried out. He'd heard the shock and pain in her voice. And he hadn't been able to stop himself. Yes, he needed a drink. "It mattered," he tossed back as he rose and strode into the other room.

Alone, she let out a shuddering breath. Of course it mattered. Only a fool would have thought otherwise. He'd thought he was dealing with an experienced, emotionally mature woman who knew how to play the game. Words like *love* and *need* and *want* were interchangeable. Yes, he'd said he loved her, but to many love was physical and physical only.

She'd made a fool of herself and she'd infuriated him, and all because she'd begun a relationship built on illusions.

She'd knowingly taken the risk, Rebecca reminded

herself as she climbed out of bed. Now she'd pay the price.

He was calmer when he started back to the bedroom. Calmer, though anger still bubbled inside him. First he would show her how it should have been, how it could be. Then they had to talk, rationally, coherently.

"Rebecca . . ." But when he looked at the bed it was empty.

She was wrapped in a robe and was hurling clothing into her suitcase when she heard him knock. With a shake of her head, she rubbed the tears from her cheeks and continued her frenzied packing. She wouldn't answer. . . . She wouldn't answer and be humiliated again.

"Rebecca." The moment of calm he'd achieved had vanished. Swearing through gritted teeth, he pounded on the door. "Rebecca, this is ridiculous. Open this door."

Ignoring him, she swept bottles and tubes of toiletries off the bureau and into her bag. He'd go away, she told herself, hardly aware that she'd begun to sob. He'd go away and then she'd leave, take a cab to the airport and catch the first plane to anywhere.

The sound of splintering wood had her rushing into the parlor in time to see the door give way.

She'd thought she'd seen fury before, but she'd been wrong. She saw it now as she stared into Stephen's face. Speechless, she looked from him to the broken door and back again.

Elana, tying the belt of her robe, rushed down the hall. "Stephen, what's happened? Is there a—"

He turned on her, hurling one short sentence in clipped Greek at her. Her eyes widened and she backed away, sending Rebecca a look that combined sympathy and envy.

"Do you think you have only to walk away from me?" He pushed the door back until it scraped against the battered jamb.

"I want—" Rebecca lifted a hand to her throat as if to push the words out. "I want to be alone."

"The hell with what you want." He started toward her, only to stop dead when she cringed and turned away. He'd forgotten what it was like to hurt, truly hurt, until that moment. "I asked you once if you were afraid of me. Now I see that you are." Searching for control, he dipped his hands into the pockets of the slacks he'd thrown on. She looked defenseless, terrified, and tears still streaked her cheeks. "I won't hurt you again. Will you sit?" When she shook her head, he bit off an oath. "I will."

"I know you're angry with me," she began when he'd settled into a chair. "I'll apologize if it'll do any good, but I do want to be alone."

His eyes had narrowed and focused. "You'll apologize? For what?"

"For . . ." What did he expect her to say? Humiliated, she crossed her arms and hugged her elbows. "For what happened . . . for not . . . explaining," she finished lamely. "For whatever you like," she continued as the tears started again. "Just leave me alone."

"Sweet God." He rubbed a weary hand over his face. "I can think of nothing in my life I've handled as badly as this." He rose, but stopped again when she automatically retreated. "You don't want me to touch you." His voice had roughened. He had to swallow to clear his throat. "I won't, but I hope you'll listen."

"There's nothing more to say. I understand how you feel and why you feel it. I'd rather we just left it at that."

"I treated you inexcusably."

"I don't want an apology."

"Rebecca—"

"I don't." Her voice rose, stopping his words, stopping her tears. "It's my fault. It's been my fault all along. No, no, no!" she shouted when he took another step. "I don't want you to touch me. I couldn't bear it."

He sucked in his breath, then let it out slowly. "You twist the knife well."

But she was shaking her head and pacing the room now. "It didn't matter at first—at least I didn't think it would matter. I didn't know who you were or that I would fall in love with you. Now I've waited too long and ruined everything."

"What are you talking about?"

Perhaps it was best, best for both of them, to lay out the truth. "You said you knew me, but you don't, because I've done nothing but lie to you, right from the first moment."

Slowly, carefully, he lowered himself to the arm of a chair. "What have you lied to me about?"

"Everything." Her eyes were drenched with regret when she looked at him. "Then, tonight . . . First I found out that you own hotels. *Own* them."

"It was hardly a secret. Why should it matter?"

"It wouldn't." She dropped her hands to her sides. "If I was what I'd pretended to be. After we'd made love and you—I realized that by pretending I'd let you have feelings for someone who didn't even exist."

"You're standing in front of me, Rebecca. You exist."

"No. Not the way you think, not the way I've let you think."

He prepared himself for the worst. "What have you done? Were you running away from America?"

"No. Yes." She had to laugh at that. "Yes, I was running." She gathered what composure she had left and folded her hands. "I did come from Philadelphia, as I told you. I've lived there all my life. Lived there, went to school there, worked there." She found a tissue in the pocket of her robe. "I'm an accountant."

He stared at her, one brow lifting, as she blew her nose. "I beg your pardon?"

"I said, I'm an accountant." She hurled the words at him, then whirled away to face the window. Stephen started to rise, then thought better of it.

"I find it difficult to imagine you tallying ledgers, Rebecca. If you'd sit down, maybe we could talk this through."

"Damn it, I said I'm an accountant. A CPA specializing in corporate taxes. Up until a few weeks ago I worked for McDowell, Jableki and Kline in Philadelphia."

He spread his hands, taking it all in. "All right. What did you do? Embezzle?"

She tossed back her head and nearly exploded with laughter. If she said yes he'd probably be intrigued. But the time for intrigue was over. The time for the truth was now. "No. I've never done anything illegal in my life. I've never even had a parking ticket. I've never done anything at all out of the ordinary until a few weeks ago."

She began to pace again, too agitated to keep still. "I'd never traveled, never had a man send a bottle of champagne to my table, never walked along the beach in the moonlight, never had a lover."

He said nothing, not because he was angry or bored but because he was fascinated.

"I had a good job, my car was paid for, and had good, conservative investments that would have ensured me a comfortable retirement. In my circle of friends I'm known as the dependable one. If someone needs a sitter they know they can call Rebecca. If they need advice or someone to feed their fish while they're on vacation they don't have to worry. I was never late for work, never took five minutes extra for lunch."

"Commendable," he said, and earned a glare.

"Just the type of employee I imagine you'd like to hire."

He swallowed a chuckle. He'd been prepared for her to confess she had a husband, five husbands, a prison record. Instead she was telling him she was an accountant with an excellent work record. "I have no desire to hire you, Rebecca."

"Just as well." She turned away and started to prowl the room again. "You'd undoubtedly change your mind after I tell you the rest."

Stephen crossed his ankles and settled back. God, what a woman she was. "I'm anxious to hear it."

"My aunt died about three months ago, suddenly."

"I'm sorry." He would have gone to her then, but he could see she was far from ready. "I know how difficult it is to lose family."

"She was all I had left." Because she needed something to do, she pushed open the balcony doors. Warm, fragrant night air rushed in. "I couldn't believe she was gone. Just like that. No warning. Of course, I handled the funeral arrangements. No fuss, no frills. Just the way Aunt Jeannie would have wanted. She was a very economical woman, not only in finances but in dress, in speech, in manner. As long as I can remember, people compared me to her."

Stephen's brow lifted again as he studied the woman being buffeted by the breeze—the short red silk robe, the tousled hair.

"Soon after her death—I don't know if it was days or a week—something just snapped. I looked at myself, at my life, and I hated it." She dragged her hair back, only to have the wind catch it again. "I was a good employee, just like my aunt, a good credit risk, a dependable friend. Law abiding, conservative and boring. Suddenly I could see myself ten, twenty, thirty years down the road, with nothing more than I had at that moment. I couldn't stand it."

She turned around. The breeze caught at the hem of her robe and sent it dancing around her legs. "I quit my job, and I sold everything."

"Sold?"

"Everything I owned—car, apartment, furniture, books, absolutely everything. I turned all the cash into traveler's checks, even the small inheritance from my aunt. Thousands of dollars. I know it might not sound like a lot to you, but it was more than I'd ever imagined having at once."

"Wait." He held up a hand, wanting to be certain he understood everything. "You're telling me that you sold your possessions, *all* your possessions?"

She couldn't remember ever having felt more foolish, and she straightened her shoulders defensively. "Right down to my coffeepot."

"Amazing," he murmured.

"I bought new clothes, new luggage, and flew to London. First-class. I'd never been on a plane before in my life."

"You'd never flown, but took your first trip across the Atlantic."

She didn't hear the admiration in his voice, only the amusement. "I wanted to see something different. To *be* something different. I stayed at the Ritz and took pictures of the changing of the guard. I flew to Paris and had my hair cut." Self-consciously she lifted a hand to it.

Because he could see that she was overwrought, he

was careful not to smile. "You flew to Paris for a haircut."

"I'd heard some women discussing this stylist, and I— Never mind." It was no use trying to explain that she'd gone to the same hairdresser, to the same shops, for years. The same everything. "Right after Paris, I came here," she went on. "I met you. Things happened. I let them happen." Tears threatened. She could only pray he didn't see them. "You were exciting, and attracted to me. Or attracted to who you thought I was. I'd never had a romance. No one had ever looked at me the way you did."

Once more he chose his words carefully. "Are you saying that being with me was different? An adventure, like flying to a Paris salon?"

She would never be able to explain what being with him had meant to her. "Apologies and explanations really don't make any difference now. But I am sorry, Stephen. I'm sorry for everything."

He didn't see the tears, but he heard the regret in her voice. His eyes narrowed. His muscles tensed. "Are you apologizing for making love with me, Rebecca?"

"I'm apologizing for whatever you like. I'd make it up to you if I could, but I don't know how, unless I jump out the window."

He paused, as if he were considering it. "I don't think this requires anything quite that drastic. Perhaps if you'd sit down calmly?"

She shook her head and stayed where she was. "I can't handle any more of this tonight, Stephen. I'm sorry. You've every right to be angry."

He rose, the familiar impatience building. But she was so pale, looked so fragile, sounded so weary. He hadn't treated her gently before. At least he could do so now.

"All right. Tomorrow, then, after you've rested." He started to go to her, then checked himself. It would take time to show her that there were other ways to love. Time to convince her that love was more, much more than an adventure. "I want you to know that I regret what happened tonight. But that, too, will wait until tomorrow." Though he wanted to touch a hand to her cheek, he kept it fisted in his pocket. "Get some rest."

She had thought her heart was already broken. Now it shattered. Not trusting her voice, she nodded.

He left her alone. The door scraped against the splintered jamb as he secured it. She supposed there might have been a woman somewhere who'd made a bigger fool of herself. At the moment, it didn't seem to matter.

At least there was something she could do for both of them. Disappear.

CHAPTER 10

It was her own fault, she supposed. There were at least half a dozen promising accounting positions in the want ads. Not one of them interested her. Rebecca circled them moodily. How could she be interested in dental plans and profit sharing? All she could think about, all she'd been able to think about for two weeks, was Stephen.

What had he thought when he'd found her gone? Relief? Perhaps a vague annoyance at business left unfinished? Pen in hand, Rebecca stared out of the window of the garden apartment she'd rented. In her fantasies she imagined him searching furiously for her, determined to find her, whatever the cost. Reality, she thought with a sigh, wasn't quite so romantic. He would have been relieved. Perhaps she wasn't sophisticated, but at least she'd stepped out of his life with no fuss.

Now it was time to get her own life in order.

First things first. She had an apartment, and the little square of lawn outside the glass doors was going to make her happy. That in itself was a challenge. Her old condo had been centrally located on the fifth floor of a fully maintained modern building.

This charming and older development was a good thirty miles from downtown, but she could hear the birds in the morning. She would be able to look out at old oaks and sweeping maples and flowers she would plant herself. Perhaps it wasn't as big a change as a flight to Paris, but for Rebecca it was a statement.

She'd bought some furniture. *Some* was the operative word. Thus far she'd picked out a bed, one antique table and a single chair.

Not logical, Rebecca thought with a faint smile. No proper and economical living room suite, no tidy curtains. Even the single set of towels she'd bought was frivolous. And exactly what she'd wanted. She would do what she'd secretly wanted to do for years—buy a piece here, a piece there. Not because it was a good buy or durable, but because she wanted it.

She wondered how many people would really understand the satisfaction of making decisions not because they were sensible but because they were desirable. She'd done it with her home, her wardrobe. Even with her hair, she thought, running a hand through it. Outward changes had led to inner changes. Or vice versa. Either way, she would never again be the woman she'd been before.

Or perhaps she would be the woman she'd always been but had refused to acknowledge.

Then why was she circling ads in the classifieds? Rebecca asked herself. Why was she sitting here on a beautiful morning planning a future she had no interest in? Perhaps it was true that she would never have the one thing, the one person, she really wanted. There would be no more picnics or walks in the moonlight or frantic nights in bed. Still, she had the memories, she had the moments, she had the dreams. There would be no regrets where Stephen was concerned. Not now, and not ever. And if she was now more the woman she had been with him, it had taken more than a change in hairstyle.

She was stronger. She was surer. She was freer. And she'd done it herself.

She could think of nothing she wanted less than to go back into someone else's firm, tallying figures, calculating profit and loss. So she wouldn't. Rebecca sank into the chair as the thought struck home.

She wouldn't. She wouldn't go job hunting, carrying her résumé, rinsing sweaty palms in the restroom, putting her career and life in someone else's hands again. She'd open her own firm. A small one, certainly. Personalized. Exclusive, she decided, savoring the word. Why not? She had the skill, the experience, and—finally—she had the courage.

It wouldn't be easy. In fact, it would be risky. The money she had left would have to go toward renting office space, equipment, a phone system, advertising. With a bubbling laugh, she sprang up and searched for a legal pad and a pencil. She had to make lists—not only of things to do but of people to call. She had enough contacts from her McDowell, Jableki and Kline days. Maybe, just maybe, she could persuade some of her former clients to give her a try.

"Just a minute," she called out when she heard the knock on the door. She scribbled a reminder to look for file cabinets as she went to answer. She'd much rather have some good solid oak file cabinets than a living room sofa.

She knew better than to open the door without checking the security peephole, but she was much too involved with her plans to think about such things.

When she opened the door, she found herself face-to-face with Stephen.

Even if she could have spoken, he wasn't in the mood to let her. "What in the hell do you think you're doing?" he demanded as he slammed the door behind him. "Do you deliberately try to drive me mad, or does it come naturally to you?"

"I—I don't—" But he was already yanking her against him. Whatever words she might have spoken dissolved into a moan against his lips. Her pad fell to the floor with a slap. Even as her arms came up around him he was thrusting her away.

"What kind of game are you playing, Rebecca?" When she just shook her head, he dug his hands into his pockets and paced the wide, nearly empty room. He was unshaven, disheveled and absolutely gorgeous. "It's taken me two weeks and a great deal of trouble to find you. I believe we'd agreed to talk again. I was surprised to discover you'd not only left Athens, but Europe." He swung back and pinned her with a look. "Why?"

Still reeling from his entrance, she struggled not to babble. "I thought it best that I leave."

"You thought?" He took a step toward her, his fury so palatable that she braced herself. "You thought it best," he repeated. "For whom?"

"For you. For both of us." She caught herself fiddling with the lapels of her robe and dropped her hands. "I knew you were angry with me for lying to you and that you regretted what had happened between us. I felt it would be better for both of us if I—"

"Ran away?"

Her chin came up fractionally. "Went away."

"You said you loved me."

She swallowed. "I know."

"Was that another lie?"

"Please don't." She turned away, but there was no-where to go. "Stephen, I never expected to see you again. I'm trying to make some sense out of my life, to do things in a way that's not only right but makes me happy. In Greece, I guess, I did what made me happy, but I didn't think about what was right. The time with you was . . ."

"Was what?"

Dragging both hands through her hair, she turned to him again. It was as if the two weeks had never been. She was facing him again, trying to explain what she feared she could never explain. "It was the best thing that ever happened to me, the most important, the most unforgettable, the most precious. I'll always be grate-ful for those few days."

"Grateful." He wasn't sure whether to laugh or mur-der her. Stepping forward, he surprised them both by slipping his hands lightly around her throat. "For what? For my giving you your first fling? A fast, anonymous romance with no consequences?"

"No." She lifted a hand to his wrist but made no at-tempt to struggle. "Did you come all this way to make me feel more guilty?"

"I came all this way because I finish what I begin. We'd far from finished, Rebecca."

"All right." Be calm, she told herself. When a man was this close to the edge, a woman's best defense was serenity. "If you'll let me go, we'll talk. Would you like some coffee?"

His fingers tightened reflexively, then slowly re-laxed. "You've bought a new pot."

"Yes." Was that humor in his eyes? she wondered. "There's only one chair. Why don't you use it while I go into the kitchen?"

He took her arm. "I don't want coffee, or a chair, or a pleasant conversation."

It seemed serenity wouldn't work. "All right, Stephen. What do you want?"

"You. I'd thought I'd made that fairly obvious." When she frowned, he glanced around the apartment. "Now tell me, Rebecca, is this what you want? A handful of rooms to be alone in?"

"I want to make the best of the rest of my life. I've already apologized for deceiving you. I realize that—"

"Deceiving me." He held up a finger to stop her. "I've wanted to clear that point up myself. How did you deceive me?"

"By letting you think that I was something I'm not."

"You're not a beautiful, interesting woman? A passionate woman?" He lifted a brow as he studied her. "Rebecca, I have too much pride to ever believe you could deceive me that completely."

He was confusing her—deliberately, she was sure. "I told you what I'd done."

"What you'd done," he agreed. "And how you'd done it." He brought his hand to her throat again, this time in a caress. His anger hadn't made her knees weak. She felt them tremble now at his tenderness. "Selling your possessions and flying to Paris for a new hairstyle. Quitting your job and grabbing life with both hands. You fascinate me." Her eyes stayed open wide when he brushed his lips over hers. "I think the time is nearly over when you'll be so easily flattered. It's almost a pity." He drew her closer, slowly, while his mouth touched hers. Relief coursed through him as he felt her melt and give. "Do you think it was your background that attracted me?"

"You were angry," she managed.

"Yes, angry at the idea that I had been part of your

experiment. Furious," he added before he deepened the kiss. "Furious that I had been of only passing interest." She was heating in his arms, just as he remembered, just as he needed, softening, strengthening. "Shall I tell you how angry? Shall I tell you that for two weeks I couldn't work, couldn't think, couldn't function, because you were everywhere I looked and nowhere to be found?"

"I had to go." She was already tugging at his shirt to find the flesh beneath. To touch him again, just for a moment. To be touched by him. "When you said you regretted making love . . ." Her own words brought her back. Quickly she dropped her hands and stepped away.

He stared at her for a moment, then abruptly swore and began to pace. "I've never thought myself this big a fool. I hurt you that night in a much different way than I'd believed. Then I handled it with less finesse than I might the most unimportant business transaction." He paused, sighing. For the first time she saw clearly how incredibly weary he was.

"You're tired. Please, sit down. Let me fix you something."

He took a moment to press his fingers to his eyes. Again he wanted to laugh—while he strangled her. She was exactly what he needed, what he understood. Yet at the same time she baffled him.

"You weaken me, Rebecca, and bring out the fool I'd forgotten I could be. I'm surprised you allowed me to set foot into your home. You should have—" As quickly as the anger had come, it faded. As quickly as the tension had formed, it eased. Everything he'd needed to see was in her eyes. Carefully now, he drew a deep breath. A man wasn't always handed so many chances at happiness.

"Rebecca, I never regretted making love with you."

He stopped her from turning with the lightest of touches on her shoulder. "I regretted only the way it happened. Too much need and too little care. I regret, I'll always regret that for your first time there was fire but no warmth." He took her hands in his and brought them to his lips.

"It was beautiful."

"In its way." His fingers tightened on hers. Still so innocent, he thought. Still so generous. "It was not kind or patient or tender, as love should be the first time."

She felt hope rise in her heart again. "None of that mattered."

"It mattered, more than I can ever tell you. After, when you told me everything, it only mattered more. If I had done what my instincts told me to do that night you would never have left me. But I thought you needed time before you could bear to have me touch you again." Slowly, gently, he drew the tip of her finger into his mouth and watched her eyes cloud over. "Let me show you what I should have shown you then." With her hands locked in his, he looked into her eyes. "Do you want me?"

It was time for the truth. "Yes."

He lifted her into his arms and heard her breath catch. "Do you trust me?"

"Yes."

When he smiled, her heart turned over. "Rebecca, I must ask you one more thing."

"What is it?"

"Do you have a bed?"

She felt her cheeks heat even as she laughed. "In there."

She was trembling. It reminded him how careful he had to be, how precious this moment was to both of them. The sun washed over the bed, over them, as he lay beside her. And kissed her—only kissed her, softly, deeply, thoroughly, until her arms slipped from around him to fall bonelessly to her sides. She trembled still as he murmured to her, as his lips brushed over her cheeks, her throat.

He had shown her the desperation love could cause, the sharp-edged pleasure, the speed and the fury. Now he showed her that love could mean serenity and sweetness.

And she showed him.

He had thought to teach her, not to learn, to reassure her but not to be comforted. But he learned, and he was comforted. The need was there, as strong as it had been the first time. But strength was tempered with patience. As he slipped his hands down her robe to part it, to slide it away from her skin, he felt no need to hurry. He could delight in the way the sun slanted across her body, in the way her flesh warmed to his touch.

Her breath was as unsteady as her hands as she undressed him. But not from nerves. She understood that now. She felt strong and capable and certain. Anticipation made her tremble. Pleasure made her shudder. She gave a sigh that purred out of her lips as she arched against his seeking hands. Then he nipped lightly at her breast and she bounded from serenity to passion in one breathless leap.

Still he moved slowly, guiding her into a kind of heated torment she'd never experienced. Desire boiled in her, and his name sprang to her lips and her body coiled like a spring. Chaining down his own need, he set hers free and watched as she flew over the first peak.

"Only for me," he murmured as she went limp in his arms. "Only for me, Rebecca." With his own passions strapped, he slipped into her, determined to watch her build again. "Tell me you love me. Look at me and tell me."

She opened her eyes. She could barely breathe. Somehow the strength was pouring back into her, but so fast, so powerfully. Sensation rolled over sensation, impossibly. She moved with him, pressed center to center, heart to heart, but all she could see were his eyes, so dark, so blue, so intense. Perhaps she was drowning in them.

"I love you, Stephen."

Then she was falling, fathoms deep, into his eyes, into the sea. With her arms locked around him, she dragged him under with her.

He pulled her against him so that he could stroke her hair and wait for his pulse to level. She'd been innocent. But the surprise, the one he'd been dealing with for weeks, was that until Rebecca he'd been just as innocent. He'd known passion, but he'd never known intimacy, not the kind that reached the heart as fully as the body. And yet . . .

"We've been here before," he murmured. "Do you feel it, too?"

She linked her fingers with his. "I never believed in things like that until you. When I'm with you it's like remembering." She lifted her head to look at him. "I can't explain it."

"I love you, Rebecca, only more knowing who you are, why you are."

She touched a hand to his cheek. "I don't want you to say anything you don't really feel."

"How can a woman be so intelligent and still so stupid?" With a shake of his head, Stephen rolled on top of her. "A man doesn't travel thousands of miles for this, however delightful it may be. I love you, and though it annoyed me for quite some time I'm accustomed to it now."

"Annoyed you."

"Infuriated." He kissed her to cut off whatever retort she might make. "I'd seen myself remaining free for years to come. Then I met a woman who sold her coffeepot so she could take pictures of goats."

"I certainly have no intention of interfering with your plans."

"You already have." He smiled, holding her still when she tried to struggle away. "Marriage blocks off certain freedoms and opens others."

"Marriage?" She stopped struggling but turned her head to avoid another kiss.

"Soon." He nuzzled her neck. "Immediately."

"I never said I'd marry you."

"No, but you will." With his fingertips only, he began to arouse her. "I'm a very persuasive man."

"I need to think." But she was trembling again. "Stephen, marriage is very serious."

"Deadly. And I should warn you that I've already decided to murder any man you look at for more than twenty seconds."

"Really?" She turned her head back, prepared to be angry. But he was smiling. No one else had ever smiled at her in quite that way. "Really?"

"I can't let you go, Rebecca. Can't and won't. Come back with me. Marry me. Have children with me."

"Stephen—"

He laid a finger to her lips. "I know what I'm asking you. You've already started a new life, made new plans. We've had only days together, but I can make you happy. I can promise to love you for a lifetime, or however many lifetimes we have. You once dived into the sea on impulse. Dive with me now, Rebecca. I swear you won't regret it."

Gently she pressed her lips to his fingertip, then drew his hand away. "All my life I've wondered what I might find if I had the courage to look. I found you, Stephen." With a laugh she threw her arms around him. "When do you want to leave?"